FATES OF VEILORE BOOK TWO

FATE OF KINGS

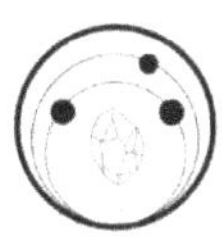

IRELAND LYDON

AN IMPRINT OF VEILORE PRESS

This book is a work of fiction. Names, characters, businesses, organizations, places, events and incidents either are the product of the author's imagination or are used fictitiously. Any resemblance to actual persons, living or dead, events, or locales is entirely coincidental.

Book and Cover design by Veilore Press

ISBN: 9798990265141 (Paperback)

ISBN: 9798990265134 (Hardback)

First Printing Edition 2025

I will not say: do not weep; for not all tears are an evil.

J. R. R. Tolkien

Veil of Fate and Fire

Beneath the sky's unyielding gaze,
where whispered oaths in shadow blaze,
hearts entwine in war's embrace,
bound by love, by loss, by fate.

A prince of ruin, a warrior's claim,
where fire meets wrath, where sorrow flames.
One reaches forth, one turns away—
the trial of hearts too proud to break.

A vow in gold, a name entwined,
a blade of honor, hearts confined.
She stands beside, though fate denies,
a crownless knight with loyal eyes.

A love eclipsed, a silken snare,
woven soft in moonlit air.
She calls his name where dreams dissolve,
his touch—a ghost she can't absolve.

Three threads that weave, then pull apart,
desire, devotion, a fractured heart.
Yet in the dusk where shadows sigh,
love still lingers—though denied.

JORN
MONSELT
PORT OF NORD
BRAC
HILVAER
JORN CITY
DENO
EIR
FOREST OF DERN
DERN
FOREST OF AAVIN
AUGUSTA
AAVIN
R'HUN
THOURNS
FIELD OF THOURNS
ALNWICK
WESTERN GAP
SANCIA
LEJAL
FELOUR
SIGN
MVORS
DIVNA

Treacherous Seas
ENTHEAS
TAUF
THELGH
LEDENJOUR
PORT OF GHELFIN
TAASTRA
TAUDREN
CITY OF CORAD
CORAÐ
EHLMOR
EHLMOR ISLES
NIHTAR ISLA
VELIORE

FATE OF KINGS

Fate of Kings is a fantasy romance novel that ultimately has a happy ending. However, all of the books within the series include elements that may not be suitable for all readers. Such as death, murder, blood, mentions of suicide and suicidal notions, rape, SA and descriptions of past SA, magical hallucinogenics, captivity, and sexual acts are all mentioned within the series. Readers who are sensitive to such elements please take note.

Fate of Kings

BEFORE

Signe, Realm of Corad.

T*hen what shall you do?"*

Elsa thought over again the words of the elf from Entheas. Sir Lahrs had stayed for a fortnight in the great city of Signe, waiting for her answer, but her head ached with the possibilities that would emerge from her being a companion to the princess. She would be alone, Sir Lahrs had made it clear that there was no need for another to attend the youngest daughter of King Sabian.

Her head lowered at the remembrance of Queen Natalia, to which the realm grieved the death of their beloved queen. Elsa had never met her in court, she had not been presented there to be eligible for courtship. Now, she would never go there, unless it was as the companion of Princess Brendolyn.

"I have not seen you look so serious in months. What has captured your thoughts, dearest little sister? Not the nearing departure of your odious tutors."

Elsa turned from the window, where she had been standing as she watched the carriage take away the elf that could change the path of her life. Sir Lahrs was long gone, and Elsa now stood looking out over the empty cobbled courtyard. Behind her, stood her eldest brother, Eugene, with his thick arms crossed over his broad chest. A glint in his stoney eyes and his dark hair swooped back away from his face.

Eugene waited patiently for her answer.

"It is not that…Eugene, I am not sure I can leave."

There was a serious look that crossed Eugene's chiseled features, his jaw set in a hard line as he crossed the small space of the sitting room to stand beside his sister at the window. Elsa felt her chest tighten, gulping back a wave of emotion that threatened to take over.

"You have not decided then if you shall go with Sir Lahrs when he returns after my wedding in the spring? He assured me it would be a promising situation." Eugene softened, keeping his tone even.

"It would be an honor to be a companion to the princess, it is just that…"

Eugene's stoney eyes flicked to the door as if someone would barge right in at that moment. But there was no one coming today. The knights had all gone to train in Nihtar for the quarter moon. It was calm and quiet in Signe without the ruckus of men in the training yard. Eugene returned his eyes to Elsa, and she felt his concern like needle pricks in her fingertips.

"He is not here, Elsa. He cannot claim you."

There was power in his words, but the flicker of doubt had already begun to settle into Elsa's heart. Eugene was the closest to Elsa, practically the one who raised her, to teach her how to fight, to use magick. It pained Elsa to keep a part of her truth from her dearest brother. Eugene knew about the brand, but he only knew in part the truth of how deeply the magick bonded her to the knight. She dared not even speak his name in fear of him.

"Does father know?" Elsa asked in a hushed voice. "About the brand?"

Eugene sighed. "No. He does not know, or we would not be having this conversation, Elsa. You know the laws of our people. That our father would be forced to uphold the old magick and give you over to Alaric."

Elsa trembled.

"So there is no choice but to accept Sir Lahrs' offer." A lump was firmly lodged in Elsa's throat, her chin trembling as tears welled in her eyes.

"There is always a choice. You can go to Divna, and take the Silent Oath, you have already been taught the languages of the three realms. He cannot touch you there under the laws of the sisterhood."

Elsa wiped her running nose on the sleeve of her tunic.

"Elsa," Eugene took hold of each of Elsa's arms, looking into her eyes, "please take to heart the guidance of your closest and dearest brother. I would wish for you to remain here and take charge of Fathers household when I am gone. Or find a great ship to sail away on and discover beyond the great seas, but that path was taken from you by someone you were meant to trust. Your path is destined to do greater than what Signe can give you."

Embracing his middle, Elsa clung to her brother desperately, gritting her teeth against the burst of sharp intense pain that erupted within her through the brand upon her ribs—it was agony. Elsa wept into her brothers' tunic. A mixture of a broken heart and the pain of the magick that burned through her.

"You will write to me, won't you, when I am in Alnwick?"

Eugene chuckled, touching the top of her head to smooth the wild hairs that had fallen from her braid. "Every day, if you'd like."

Elsa pulled away, becoming more serious. "You shall have a new wife, and you shall live in Entheas. You cannot write every day."

"I shall write every day until you are perfectly settled in Alnwick. How else shall I discover what princesses get up to when they are not dancing with courtiers at parties and balls?" He was jesting, making Elsa laugh.

"Sir Lahrs told me Princess Brendolyn is not like that, but perhaps it is because she is faie." Elsa frowned. "Perhaps she is very lonely."

"An honest consideration. Who else would be perfect to keep a lonely girl company than my fiery sister who can teach her more than needlepoint and silks?"

Elsa smiled, taking a glance out through the window. Beyond the courtyard, over the wall of the estate, she saw the sun beginning to set. The night was drawing closer, creeping up Elsa's spine, and unsettling her. Her smile fell.

"Nightmares again?"

She quickly glanced at Eugene, a blush heating her cheeks.

"This one was a vision, I am certain of it, Eugene." Elsa wrung her fingers together nervously. "I was standing in a field of lavender, nothing but lavender...then I could hear it calling to me, like a whisper."

Eugene furrowed his brow, crossing his arms as he listened, ready to decipher the visions that so often plagued her. He held the gift, as only a few of the elven lineage possessed. Eugene was good at deciphering the visions he had, he was the one who taught Elsa her magick.

"It was my destiny…my freedom. Like I was meant to be somewhere else…meant to be with *someone* else." She felt foolish. "The magick has become stronger these last few months. Perhaps it is silly to believe them when they are not so clear."

"There is always truth in the sight." Eugene nodded. "What else did you see?"

She took a deep breath. "I saw my future in a pair of eyes that glistened like emeralds. He will lead me to my destiny."

CHAPTER 1

Denorn, Realm of Jorn. 2001.

As the ship's prow sliced through the misty dawn, Denorn's harbor emerged from the haze—a maze of bustling docks and sway of small seafaring vessels. Pavan stood at the rail, his gaze fixed on the lively, salt-stung city below, as he pulled his Vohlgrum pelt tighter around his neck to stave off the chill of the morning sea breeze. The harbor was alive with activity; white sails from galleons, sloops, and fishing boats were neatly furled, their crews already scaling rigging and unloading cargo. Pavan watched with a growing sense of unease as men scampered about the merchant vessel that had brought them from the southern shores of Entheas.

The tang of salt clung to his lips. He shielded his eyes from the glaring sun that had risen above them, trying to pierce through the vibrant chaos of the harbor to get a clearer view of the city. Returning to this place made his pulse quicken with a mix of anxiety and anticipation.

When the ship finally docked and the gangplank was lowered with a resonant thud, Pavan disembarked alongside the other travelers. The sensation of solid ground beneath his feet was both comforting and disorienting after days at sea. As he stepped onto the boardwalk, the ground beneath him swayed slightly, a reminder of how precarious land could feel after so much time adrift.

He glanced back at the ship, a smile creeping onto his face as Svein, the colossal half-giant, lumbered down the gangplank. Svein's broad grin and the weight of his sack—packed with the remnants of his belongings—gave Pavan a tinge of sadness, remembering the loss of the home in Ledenjour. Thoughts to the skeletal shops and homes they left behind. After months of hard winter in the mountain, what remained of the old mining town was in ruins.

"Hah! Just in time for day tide. Let's find a drink, eh?" Svein's voice boomed with a cheerful roughness as he adjusted the sack over his shoulder.

Spending the winter in Ledenjour had forged a bond between them. Svein, with his hearty laughter and unexpected talent for singing, had become a source of unexpected warmth. Pavan recalled the nights by the fire, where Svein's deep baritone had filled their small camp with stories and songs, despite Thad's refusal to join in.

Pavan nodded, his eyes scanning the bustling boardwalk. "A real bed sounds wonderful. But where's Thad?"

Anxiety tightened in his chest as he scanned the crowd for the faie. The bustling harbor seemed to swallow him in its chaos. Svein's heavy hand clapped reassuringly on Pavan's shoulder, its warmth cutting through his worry.

"Don't fret, lad. Our little friend will turn up soon enough."

Pavan shook off the giant's hand, his worry etched in the furrow of his brow. "I can't help but worry when he's not right by my side."

They stood at the edge of the boardwalk, each second stretching into an eternity. Pavan's fingers drummed impatiently against his thighs, his magick flickering restlessly beneath his skin. He couldn't shake the feeling that something was off, that something was holding Thad back. Worry flickering in Pavan, causing every shift of lifted barrel and blow of the whistle to rake beneath his skin.

Finally, Thad appeared at the end of the gangplank, stepping into view with a radiant smile that tugged at Pavan's heart. He hurried forward, his relief palpable, but Thad's strong hand halted him before he stepped too close, a touch to the socket of his shoulder which made Pavan frown.

"I am your servant," Thad said, offering a respectful nod as he took the heavy sack from Pavan's shoulder and adjusted it onto his own. The reality of their new surroundings, the eyes of strangers, reminded him of Thad's advice on decorum in the customary cultures they were venturing into. This was not Entheas, and roles would need to be observed.

Pavan's jaw tightened. "That is beyond my capabilities. You expect me to order you about, to belittle you in a place such as this?"

"I expect you to do as you are told." Thad smirked.

Thad's gaze swept across the bustling streets of Denorn, where opulence and squalor intertwined in a vibrant tapestry. Pavan, his eyes narrowed in discontent, observed the wealthy elite draped in shimmering silks and adorned with metals that caught the sun's gleam. Their sharply dressed servants trailed behind, their attire a stark contrast to Thad's. The faie had chosen to don a dark, quilted jacket over a wool tunic and old breeches—an uncharacteristic choice for someone of his usual elegance.

"Come, my lord, the inn is this way," Thad declared, his voice ringing out with a forced cheerfulness that seemed almost theatrical. The announcement drew curious glances from the townspeople and merchants peddling their wares. Pavan felt the weight of their stares, the scrutiny almost palpable as they made their way through the crowded streets of Denorn.

Pavan followed, his discomfort evident. The street, vibrant with activity, was a labyrinth of sights and sounds. The city square loomed ahead, its canvas tents and noisy merchants evoking a painful familiarity. The pungent mix of bread, fish, livestock, and sweat wafted through the air, twisting Pavan's gut with anxiety. He instinctively took a step back, the growing panic almost overwhelming him. A large, steady hand—Svein's—gripped his shoulder, grounding him in the present. Svein's sharp eyes scanned the crowd, ever vigilant for any signs of danger.

Thad's orange eyes flashed with concern as he noticed Pavan's distress. "Do not linger," he instructed softly, his voice barely above a whisper.

Pavan's jaw tightened, but he said nothing. Instead, he pressed forward with Thad and Svein, navigating through the increasingly crowded streets. The city's morning bustle was a sensory overload, with shopkeepers shouting their bargains and street vendors calling out their wares. The vibrant displays of textiles and the alluring scents from bakeries and grilled meat carts clashed with Pavan's growing unease.

They reached the inn, a modest structure overshadowed by the grandeur of its surroundings. As they entered, a thin man with a sharply pointed nose approached, his rapid-fire dialect making it hard for Pavan to follow. But Thad, with practiced ease, took control of the conversation. His voice, rich with enchantment, wove a spell of persuasion.

"You must forgive my lord's fatigue. We seek only your finest room. Your establishment is renowned in his court, and only the best will suffice," Thad said, his tone almost musical.

The innkeeper's eyes widened as Thad presented a heavy velvet pouch filled with gold. The man's fingers trembled slightly as he took the pouch, weighing it with a mixture of awe and greed as the glint of gold was enough to sway him.

"Of course, my lord," the innkeeper said with a bow, though a hint of worry crept into his voice. "We only have modest suites, and none that would fit your...impressive companion."

Pavan followed the innkeeper's gaze to Svein, who towered behind him. Svein's bulk almost brushed the doorframe, and his eyes sparkled with amusement.

"A good chair and decent food will be more than sufficient," Svein rumbled, his deep voice causing the innkeeper to bow even lower.

"Excellent, excellent," the innkeeper stammered, handing over a large brass key attached to a chain that jingled with promise. "Up the stairs, your room awaits."

With a final, hurried bow, the innkeeper retreated, disappearing into the shadows of the inn. Svein, eager to escape the formality, ducked through a thick curtain into the lively heart of the inn. The room beyond was a cacophony of sounds and smells. Thick wax candles melted into ornate chandeliers, casting a warm, flickering light over a room filled with a jumble of tables—some set upon barrels, others propped on metal sheets. The air was heavy with the scents of ale and dust.

Pavan watched as Svein made his way to the bar, settling in with a cask of ale. The patrons—some lounging in tattered wingback chairs by a crackling hearth, others clustered at the bar—gave the half-giant curious glances, but their interest soon turned back to their own conversations.

Thad, holding the jingling keys, glanced nervously at Pavan, whose frown deepened. "I'm tired," Pavan admitted, his voice carrying the weight of exhaustion.

Recognizing that further planning could wait, Thad led Pavan up the creaking stairs to the quieter upper corridor. The dim hallway, lined with doors, contrasted sharply with the lively scene below. At the end of the corridor, they found their room—a surprisingly spacious retreat with two large windows offering a view of the city. A large bed dominated one side of the room, and a dressing screen separated a lavish copper bathtub from the rest of the space.

Pavan's attention was drawn less to the room's elegance than to the need for respite. He shrugged off the Vohlgrum pelt, letting it fall to the floor in a heap. Without a word, he pulled Thad into a tight embrace, their bodies pressing together as the door shut behind them. The room's calm contrasted sharply with Pavan's inner turmoil, creating a sanctuary where the outside world's chaos was temporarily shut out.

"These long days have been agony," Pavan sighed, seeking every curve of Thad's sides, his hips. Each caress made Pavan draw closer. Now bringing his hands up to gently touch the curve of the faie's neck, feeling the pulse of heartbeat beneath his touch.

"You should rest. We were so long upon the ship you had to keep your magick contained," Thad began, earnestly wishing for his command.

Pavan shook his head, leaning forward to kiss the faie heartily on the lips, before breaking free to smile. "I cannot sleep, when you awaken me fully *mo ghrá*."

Thad sighed, accepting the second kiss, deeper than the first, and clutching Pavan with eager tenderness. But it did not last, Thad pulled back and Pavan frowned.

"I am serious, you need rest, Pavan. This place has much to unsettle your magick." Thad began to walk about the room, going to the bed to turn down the blankets.

"I am in control. I wish to have you."

Thad looked up, as Pavan neared him.

"You have had me. We shared in our mind space before we left the shores of Ledenjour. Surely you must be satisfied?"

Thad began to undo each of the hooks of Pavan's jacket, tossing the garment aside, reaching up to grab hold of Pavan's tunic, but Pavan held his hand. So close, Pavan could smell the woodsy scent, with the faint citrus tang of magick that basked the faie. Thad was beautiful.

"I could never be satisfied enough. Our time in the shared mind space is limited, it was a long winter. Our connection never lasts for long."

"Any longer and your magick would be too much for me."

"I shall control myself."

Pavan earned a hard punch in his chest.

"This is a serious matter," Thad warned, but there was a playful hint at the edge of the impish man's lips. His side smile quirked, flashing white teeth.

"I am the most serious of men, Thad."

Pavan wanted another kiss. Eager to taste the burning desire coil in the pit of his stomach. He leant down but Thad put a hand over his mouth, keeping their lips from touching. Pavan growled, pulling Thad closer, but still Thad resisted. Pavan nipped at Thad's long fingers, making him wince. Pavan chuckled, taking his chance to take another kiss, but Thad's face turned away. Growling again, Pavan nipped at the exposed neck, his teeth sinking into tender flesh, causing the faie to gasp.

"Impish brat," Pavan scolded him, tightening his hold around Thad's waist. Thad sighed but said nothing. Pavan nipped again, softer, teeth grazing the curve of Thad's jaw.

Satisfaction eased Pavan now trailing his lips closer to the faie's exposed throat. When the scent was heightened, magick coiled in his blood, clawing to the surface. Pavan hummed, grasping at Thad's waist, guiding them back.

Thad gripped Pavan's hair. "Pavan, you need sleep."

Pavan felt the bed behind his legs, smirking against Thad's skin, he tipped them back. Leaning over Thad, who was laid out beneath him. Pavan caressed his soft cheek, looking into Thad's magnificent orange eyes.

"I need *you*," he growled, kissing Thad's pulse point and drawing out a breathy moan from the man beneath him.

Magick danced dangerously close to the surface at each press of Pavan's lips against the soft skin of the faie's neck. Pavan wanted more, eagerly yanking at the layers of Thad's doublet tunic, seeking the smooth skin beneath.

"Pavan, your magick," Thad breathed, his hands raking through Pavan's hair.

"I am in control."

Pavan leaned up to kneel between Thad's thighs, unlacing the faded jacket to grasp at the front of the tunic, the thin material ripped easily apart, exposing the faie's chest. Thad frowned, indignant.

"This was my favorite shirt," he protested.

"I shall buy you dozens of shirts." Pavan smiled, leaning more firmly over him. "Enter my mind, Thad. Share another moment with me, we can handle the connection."

Thad began to speak again, but his words faltered when Pavan kissed his jaw, trailing down to the line of his collar, then to the newly exposed freckled skin of his chest. Pavan could taste the salt, humming in satisfaction, tasting the newly invigorated scent of citrus. Magick burning through his skin.

"Pavan." Thad shifted, grasping at Pavan's arms.

Pavan blinked, trying to bring himself up from the depths of magick that consumed him, but he wanted it. His hands sought the skin beneath him, holding with unbearable strengths into the flesh beneath is touch. Warm and supple, Pavan could easily penetrate the skin, his nails began to scrape at the throat. Eagerly drinking in the scent that warmed through him, tangling in the web of his own magick.

Crack!

Pavan's eyes shot open, shock electrifying his senses. He staggered backward, clutching at his nose, which had been twisted and bloodied. The scent of iron mingled with the acrid tang of raw magick, pressing in on him. With a snarl of frustration, he willed his nose back into place, the sharp pain a mere fraction of the torment gnawing at his heart. His gaze dropped to Thad, who lay exposed beneath him, his fair skin marred with bruised teeth marks.

A wave of panic surged through Pavan, and he attempted to rise, but Thad's grip was like iron. With a powerful yank, Thad pulled Pavan back down. Pavan struggled initially, his efforts futile against Thad's unyielding strength. Realization hit him like a cold wave—Thad was stronger, and resistance was pointless.

"Sleep, Pavan." Thad's voice was a soft, firm command, filled with an unshakable calm. "I am here. You must rest."

The intensity of Thad's grip, combined with the soothing cadence of his voice, began to drown out the chaos within Pavan. Reluctantly, he surrendered, letting his body relax into the hold that anchored him. The turmoil of the moment began to blur as exhaustion, tinged with the lingering effects of magick, began to seep into his bones.

CHAPTER

2

His legs burned but he pressed on through the pain as he ran. In his nightmare he was surrounded by trees that shifted in the breeze, their opalescent hue shimmering against the sun that peaked through the leaves above him, each the color of garnets. The blood trees. Pavan slowed, breathing heavy against the pounding in his chest. Heart racing, he gasped, looking around the silent forest. Nothing moved, nothing breathed.

Pavan blinked, red oozed from the trees, his feet sunk deep in red. Raising his hands, Pavan gasped, blood coated his fingertips. He could taste the coppery tang as the smell of blood permeated his senses.

Lowering them again to look. Every garnet tree was cut, leaving only stumps of charred wood behind. Ash falling from the sky, fluttering down like the first snowfall. Pavan breathed out, his breath visible in vapors before his lips.

A whispering voice echoed.

It was calling him.

Pavan stepped away, his foot slipping on muddy ground causing Pavan to fall. Falling down into the darkness, he landed against the rough stones beneath.

Groaning, Pavan pushed himself to stand, breathing in the stagnant air. He was alone. Bitterly left in the cold and darkness. Calling out, but he had no voice. Stepping into the dark. There was nothing.

"*Isaac!*" a voice hissed, bringing with it fiery pain behind Pavan's eyes.

He winced, gripping his head. But the voice was there, soothing in his memories, caressing the darkest parts of his past.

Isaac.

Awaking with a start, Pavan looked around him desperately, but Thad was not beside him. Groaning, he slowly sat up, weighted and heavy. Magick was settled back again, but Pavan was irritable, glaring about the room. Nighttime had descended upon them, lamps had been lit, basking the room in a warm flickering glow.

Pavan sighed, rubbing his face.

The door opened with a creek, and Pavan jumped, launching his frame to the nearby wall, hiding himself behind the tall wardrobe. His heart raced wildly, even when he saw Thad enter.

"Pavan?" Thad looked around, to find Pavan where he was hiding.

He looked warily at the door, hearing the loud drift of laughter and voices coming from the inn's tavern below. At once, Thad shut the door, concerned. Pavan could taste the bitterness in the air as he pressed himself further back against the wall.

"You have been asleep for many hours. Would you like to eat?" Thad asked as he stopped with his feet just touching Pavan's.

"No." Pavan shook his head.

Thad sighed, reaching out to take hold of Pavan's hand. "You must eat something. Come with me, Svein has a table waiting downstairs."

"I can't." Pavan's voice shook, conveying too much of his emotion.

"You were dreaming again?" Thad asked, furrowing his eyebrows.

Pavan gulped, as the cold damp of the dream fell away, letting him regain the thoughts of clarity he desperately wanted.

"You were right," he muttered, caressing the soft hand that was on his own. "It was too soon to test my magick. I am exhausted."

"Let us begin with a drink. Then tomorrow, you can seek those answers you desire." Thad pulled Pavan by the hand, kissing his knuckles roughly.

He shook. "It is useless to seek such advice here."

"Useless would be to not seek answers, Pavan. There is one that can give them. Meilyr has given you where to look, all you must do is seek her out."

He remembered the words scrawled upon the parchment, within one of the letters sent to Ledenjour not long before they were to sail.

Seek the Chapel of Light, enter and she will be waiting.

"Cryptic. I am to meet with a woman I have never met, in a place I don't know where to find, all in search of the answer to a question I have never asked."

Thad pulled at his hand, that impish smile curled the edges of his lips.

Unable to resist the quiet demand, Pavan followed. Walking after the faie, emerging below to the tavern where he saw Svein laughing and drinking. They joined the half giant at the table, Pavan said nothing, but did not shrink away.

Jovial tunes played for the room by a man in a white hat and checkered coat of patchwork who played a lute, accompanied by a tall willowy faun who plucked at a harp and a small woman who beat upon a three patched drum.

"Your wine, my lord," Thad whispered, his lips brushing Pavan's ear.

Shivering, Pavan took a slow drink, knowing it was water and not wine. Smiling at the faie who now joined them at the table, sitting close by but so far away, listening as those that sang the jaunty tale of the fisherman. Pavan did not know the words, but he tapped his foot along, laughing as the drunken Svein stumbled on clomping feet as he tried to dance. Catching Thad's eyes, there was a spark in them, a delight that Thad felt listening to the music.

As Pavan stepped out of the door to their modest room within the inn, Thad's voice followed him, laden with concern. "Be careful out there," Thad warned, his hand reaching out to grasp Pavan's arm with a firm but fleeting hold.

Pavan glanced back, a small smile tugging at his lips. "Am I not always careful?"

Thad's eyes flashed with frustration. "You're a fool who courts danger for sport," he snapped.

"Then come with me," Pavan suggested, a hint of challenge in his tone.

Thad looked away, his expression troubled. "There are matters I must attend to."

With a sigh, Pavan took Thad's hand, their fingers lingering in a moment of silent connection. "I will return."

Pulling Thad closer, Pavan kissed him, their bodies pressing together as magick sparked between them. The warmth from their touch infused Pavan with a sudden, calming heat. He reluctantly drew away, his heart pounding.

"You better return," Thad said, his voice a low murmur.

Pavan nodded, but uncertainty gnawed at him. He had no knowledge of these streets beyond a basic familiarity and struggled with the language. He ventured out, heading away from the bustling market they had traversed earlier. Following a tall cobbled wall, Pavan's eyes wandered to a stone building with slender panes of colored glass. A bell tower chimed, sending a flurry of birds into the sky.

He trailed the wall until he reached a gate, peering into the well-kept grounds beyond. Marble planters and honeysuckle hedges framed a narrow path leading to a grand structure. The bell chimed again, its sound resonating with a certain solemnity.

"Favor find you," a soft voice startled him. Pavan turned to see a tall, slender woman with piercing gray eyes. Her braids, adorned with a veil and pearl hairpin, framed her face with an air of quiet authority.

"Forgive me, I heard the bell. Am I permitted to enter?" Pavan asked, glancing back at the imposing building.

"This is a sanctuary for the lost, a place where one might find themselves again. Are you lost, fair one?" The woman's voice was gentle, her gaze unwavering as she stepped through the gate.

"No, I am not lost, but I seek answers," Pavan admitted, feeling a pang of embarrassment.

The woman's smile grew warm. "Here, those who seek answers hidden from their own sight may find them. Come, it is cooler inside."

Pavan followed her through the threshold. The bustling noise of the street faded into a soothing hum. Lavender filled the air, easing his senses.

"I am seeking someone..." Pavan began, but the woman placed a finger to her lips, signaling silence.

She led him through a vast chamber that reminded him of grand chapels he had seen in Paris and Venice, though more understated. The space was lined with benches occupied by a few subdued figures. A large stained-glass window at the head of the hall depicted a radiant woman encircled by flames, her golden light casting a serene glow.

Pavan's breath quickened as he took in the scene. The woman's soft cough drew him from his reverie, and she guided him to a side door and down a narrow corridor into a comfortable room. Shelves lined with books filled one wall, and a long table with ornately carved chairs stood in the center.

"This is a place of sanctuary," the woman said, her voice melodious. "Our doors are open to those seeking their own path to Ehnarea's light."

"Is this a church?" Pavan asked cautiously.

"It is a place where answers may be revealed to those who seek them," she replied with a song-like quality. "You may call me Arienne."

Pavan struggled to meet her gaze, his cheeks burning with a mix of shame and confusion

"You feel unworthy, Pavan?" Arienne's voice was a soothing balm, but it only heightened his discomfort. She knew his name when he had not given it.

"I know I am unworthy," he scoffed.

Arienne took his hands in hers, her grip firm and her eyes penetrating. As she studied him, her dark eyes shifted to a pale hue.

"So much sadness resides within you," she murmured. "Tell me, what do you wish to find?"

Pavan hesitated before speaking, "Who I am..."

A compassionate smile spread across her face, her hands warming in his grasp. Despite his instinct to flee, Pavan found himself unable to pull away.

"You seek refuge from an ancient magick," Arienne said softly. "But you fear the danger within your blood too much. You are not your father." Her magick gently flowed over his palms, seeking to connect.

Pavan yanked his hands away, the mention of his father stirring a deep turmoil within him. A haunting voice echoed in his mind: *Isaac.* He felt his heartbeat quicken, his magick swirling around him in a frantic pulse.

"My father was…he is…" Pavan began, but the words caught in his throat. The presence of magick around him intensified, threatening to break free.

"Pavan." Arienne's voice seemed distant as the noise in his mind grew louder.

"I must go."

Arienne's grip on his wrist tightened painfully, preventing him from leaving easily. She lifted his wrist, revealing a tattered ribbon visible beneath his tunic cuff.

"Ah, you have been touched by Ehnarea's Light. Perhaps in time, you will meet your destiny once more." Her smile was delicate, almost serene.

"I have no destiny here."

"Return in two days," Arienne urged. "I shall provide the answers you seek. Until then, may Ehnarea's Light guide you and bring you peace."

Pavan, heart racing, hurried from the room, afraid Arienne might stop him again. He burst back into the bustling street, his magick crackling around him. He navigated through the throngs of people, seeking distraction in the vibrant life of the city.

He soon found himself on a corner where a man beat a handmade drum rhythmically, while a woman with fiery hair danced gracefully beside him. The colorful fabric of her skirts fluttered as she twirled. Pavan watched, mesmerized by the dance, his attention drawn to the unexpected beauty of the moment.

But his fascination was shattered as a pair of guards from Denorn stormed over, shoving the drummer to the ground and shouting at the woman. Pavan's gut twisted with anger as he watched the scene unfold.

"Stop this," Pavan shouted, stepping forward and grabbing the arm of one guard.

"Mind your own business," the guard growled, his face reddening with rage. He tried to shove Pavan aside, but Pavan stood firm.

"They have done nothing wrong," Pavan insisted, releasing the guard's arm.

"They're trespassing and can't pay their dues. They need to leave," the guard sneered, his accent thick and disdainful.

Pavan reached into his tunic, pulling out a pouch of coins. He tossed it to the guard, who fumbled with it before it clattered to the ground.

"Here is their tithe," Pavan said. "Now, it would be better if you cleared out."

The guard's face twisted with fury as he eyed the pouch. "They're filth from Eir. Keep your charity."

Pavan bent to retrieve the pouch, but a looming figure appeared beside him. The guard's red face loomed over him, his stance menacing.

"Are you a faie sympathizer?" the guard spat, his tone threatening.

Pavan stood tall, unflinching. "Your Lord of Denorn benefits from the labor of all, faie or otherwise. Without them, your stalls and shops wouldn't thrive."

The guard's face reddened further, his rage palpable. Pavan could hear the murmurs of the crowd, their whispers mixing with the growing laughter at the scene.

"You need a lesson in respect," the guard snarled.

Pavan smirked. "Good day, sir."

Turning, he offered a hand to the drummer and dancer. But the guard, his patience exhausted, grabbed Pavan roughly by the tunic and yanked him back. A punch landed squarely on Pavan's cheek, pain flaring through him by the bronze laden fist. He stumbled, blood seeping from his lip, but he remained unbothered, even as the flare of magick bubbled beneath the surface of his skin.

"Now, you'll feel my wrath, in the name of Lord Bannon," the guard sneered.

Pavan spat blood onto the ground. "Your lord is a fool," he hissed, stepping back.

As the guard lunged again, Pavan evaded, the crowd's laughter growing louder. Pavan danced around the guard's wild swings, the man's clumsy movements becoming more erratic. The laughter of the crowd grew louder, the guard's frustration mounting with every missed blow. Unnoticed, Pavan slipped through the crowd and vanished down the street, his magick still crackling at his fingertips. He hurried back to the inn, the sense of urgency driving him as his footfalls felt a thousand times heavier.

Thad awaited him, anger flickering in his orange eyes. "Where have you been?"

"I found the chapel. I'll return in a few days," Pavan said, walking to the window and scanning the street below, but seeing no trace of the guard. He had not been followed.

"Perhaps I should accompany you next time."

Pavan avoided Thad's gaze, his mind preoccupied with the events of the day. "I can manage on my own. I am not a child."

"We've discussed this," Thad said sharply.

Pavan snapped. "We didn't discuss anything. You commanded me to stay hidden, and I obeyed."

"It's best to be cautious."

Pavan scoffed, gripping the windowsill tightly, his frustration palpable.

"Is this about our first day here?" Thad's voice softened. "You didn't harm me."

Pavan shut his eyes, struggling to calm the turmoil within him. "It's not that," he said quietly, still scanning the street below for any sign of pursuit.

Thad's presence grew closer, the warmth of his body brushing against Pavan's. "Pavan, look at me."

Pavan reluctantly turned his head, meeting Thad's gaze. The faie's face went pale as he took in the bruise forming on Pavan's nose.

"What happened?" Thad asked, his hand gently touching the bruise.

Pavan winced, the magick within him already working to heal the damage. "I had an altercation on the way back from the chapel."

"The square?" Thad asked, his concern evident.

"Yes," Pavan replied. "The guard was harassing a musician and his dancer for being from Eir. He spat at me and called me a faie sympathizer."

"Eir is full of thieves and blackhearts," Thad said dismissively.

"They were just playing music," Pavan shot back. "The guard struck them down. I couldn't just stand by."

"What did you do?" Thad's voice was edged with worry.

Pavan recalled the scene with a mix of satisfaction and anger. "I made him look a fool. The crowd laughed him off, and I slipped away."

Thad's face turned even whiter. "Did you strike him?"

"I didn't need to. He was so inept, he couldn't even see me slipping away," Pavan said with a wry smile.

"Stay inside," Thad said urgently, heading for the door. "I need to see someone. Don't leave this inn."

As thunder rumbled outside and dark clouds gathered, Pavan felt a mix of relief and apprehension. He watched Thad leave, the door closing behind him with a soft click. Pavan sank into a chair, the events of the day weighing heavily on him. The magick within him still simmered, and the voice that echoed in his mind was a constant reminder of the turmoil he faced.

CHAPTER 3

T had took to the streets in the rain, his boots pounding upon the cobbled stones as he pulled up his collar to the chilled breeze of the sea wind. He trembled, stepping through the large iron worked gate, to climb the polished steps of the whitewashed front of the wealthiest of the city. Not a part of those that were guarded by men in bronze, but the businessmen and merchants that kept their pockets lined with Jorn silver.

He pound his fist hard, masking the thundering pounding of his heart. There is a bellow from within and a raspy voice, then the door was yanked open. Standing before Thad was a hunched man, with thin wiry grey hair and thick rimmed spectacles, holding in his hand the letter that was delivered to him that morning.

"Is your master Lord Hoban?" Thad asked, the man squinted his eyes.

"Faie? No dealings with faie." The man sniffed, readying to shut the door, but Thad pressed his boot against it, stopping the wood with a loud thunk.

"I need to speak to Lord Hoban," Thad hissed, his voice edged with magick.

The man at the door was puzzled, looking Thad over with his squinting eyes behind the thick spectacles, before stepping aside.

"Thank you." Thad advanced, entering the dimly lit room, removing his long jacket, that dripped unfavorably from the leather onto the stone floor.

"There," the man wheezed, pointing a finger behind Thad.

It was apparent there was resistance, but Thad gracefully applied himself to hang the wet jacket upon the many hooks that hung on the wall before following the man deeper into the house.

"This way," the man gestured, shuffling down the darkened corridor, towards the belly of the house.

Entering into a parlor, Thad was told to wait while the man inquired to his master. It was there that Thad remained. Rain outside darkened the room within, casting shadows against the shelves, and the chairs. His eyes scanned the dusty knick-knacks that lined the shelves. Trinkets of travel and a line of old leather books without names, lined the shelves.

"So, you are a faie." A deep voice made Thad start, turning suddenly as a large man entered. His large frame easing into one of the chairs set beside an unlit fire.

"Lord Hoban…" Thad bowed, his cheeks growing red.

"Damned Ferick, never lights these damned fires. Ferick!" Hoban shouted, his voice filling the space.

Thad shivered but quickly shifted forward. Muttering under his breath, he waved a hand over the hearth, a thick fire roared into place. At once, Thad retreated, but there was a grunt of surprise, and a hand grasped Thad's arm. He trembled. Glancing at last into the face he knew, a face he had not seen in so many years.

"Thaddeus."

"Lord Hoban," Thad's voice was soft, his eyes lowered, unable to meet the lumbering man's gaze. He was released, allowing him to sit in the chair opposite of Hoban.

"Are you an apparition?" the large man rasped, his face now gone quite pale.

Thad shook his head. "I am real."

A long moment of silence, but finally Hoban smiled, leaning forward, getting a better look at Thad where he sat.

"You're supposed to be dead."

Thad smirked. "Is that what Gaur told you?"

Hoban growled, making an unamused face as he righted himself. "Orin Gaur, the blackheart, he was a piss poor man who deserved the axe."

Thad winced, pushing back his conflicting emotions for the man who was once his master. He turned his attention to the letter in his hand, unfolding the parchment.

"Your address was given to me by the archives."

Hoban whistled. "Little Thaddeus, not so little anymore. I see you were fed and well kept. What lord holds your reins now, I would like to recommend myself to him."

Thad scowled at the man, who eyed him with pale blue eyes that glowered at him. It had been a long time, but Thad could still remember everything about this man. He knew all about his preferences, his weaknesses for wine and pleasures, knew how dangerous he truly was.

"I am a free man, Hoban," Thad said, pointedly.

Hard eyes met his own wild ones as Hoban leaned back in his chair, folding his large hands over his thick middle. "What is your business with me, Little Thad?"

"Orin was a great businessman, he kept ledgers with all of the names of the men he had dealings with. There was one man who he never named, but I know this man to be of importance." Thad felt his mouth going dry, hesitating as he saw the darkness in Hoban's sharp gaze.

"What great interest you have, after all these years, Little Thad?"

Thad felt the danger, the sharpness in Hoban's gaze. Thad knew the business that Hoban dealt in, not only as the owner of many blacksmiths in Denorn, but also as a skilled weaponist, a carver. Memories crackled into the edges of Thad's reserve, his heartbeat quickened, his skin began to crawl, remembering all of the caresses those hands touched over his skin.

"Orin Gaur was many things, Sir Hoban, but he valued his profession. He would not have thrown it away on a whim."

Hoban smiled, a cruel wicked smile. "He only ever valued one thing, Thaddeus."

"He valued money."

The great bulk of a man leaned forward, a wry smile parting his lips, eyeing Thad with a gaze that made his skin crawl.

"How many of his pigeons did he give up in order to keep you to himself? All those other boys he cursed and cast aside, but not you. No one could ever get close enough to you, Little Thad."

Thad gulped, clutching the parchment hard in his fist.

"Who did he answer to, Hoban? All I need is his name." Thad kept his nerves, pushing back the coarse anger and bitter resentment.

"Come sit on my lap, and I can whisper it in your ear," Hoban leered, resting a large hand on his knee.

Thad gulped, his eyes flickering over the hand, the knee. A sickening feeling flickered with the past.

"I am a free man, Hoban. I do not give myself to any man," Thad stated flatly, his voice remarkably calm.

Hoban leaned forward, his smile growing wider.

"Come now, Little Thad, humor an old friend."

Thad stiffened, the man's voice crawling hard under Thad's skin, speaking as he once did many years ago. Thad stepped forward, breaking the distance between them to lean into Hoban's space. Thad drew a dagger from his belt and pressed it flush against the large man's throat. The blade glinted from the fire that roared to life, Thad's magick making the room hotter.

"I am not your *friend*, Hoban. I am a free man," Thad hissed. Beneath him the large man shifted, but Thad pressed the blade closer to the skin, and red began to seep from beneath the sharpened edge.

"You would be a fool to kill me. He will find you, and then perhaps you would have wished to sit on my knee when he is done with you."

Tears burned angrily from Thad, his magick coiling and grasping, he could taste it on his tongue. "Tell me his name."

Hoban growled. "I will not."

Thad removed his dagger, replacing it with his own hand, his thumb pressed against the pressure point. Digging in deep until Hoban gurgled, grasping at the hand, choking for breath. Lord Hoban thrashed, kicking his legs, but Thad was immoveable, pressing his knee deep into the larger man's thigh.

"His name, and I will let you live." Thad gritted his teeth, drawing closer to the man's face as veins began to bulge on the large purpling face.

Hoban garbled, trying to speak but Thad tightened his grasp.

"Sorry, I couldn't hear you," Thad nearly shouted.

Hoban thrashed, his pulse now growing weaker beneath Thad's grasp.

At last, Thad released the large man to a drooling gasping mess. Thad straightened as he watched the color returning to the lord's protruding features. A bruise beginning to swell on the thick neck beside the slender line cut into the skin below the collar. A thick garble of a laugh echoed from Hoban's lips.

"You still have the touch of your master in you, Little Thad. Only his ruthlessness could ebb its vines into your gentle ways."

"Give me his name," Thad said, his voice flowing with magick.

"Lord Simeon Bannon," Hoban sneered, then a cruel smile befell the man's mouth. Eyes wild. "There is a name you did not expect, Little Thad. Does this please you? Does your curiosity give the answers you seek? Revenge for a master, revenge for the wrongs done to you, to know it was sanctioned by the king himself?"

Thad grimaced, clenching the dagger hard in his grasp.

"Pity that you were taken so soon. You did not see the horror in Orin, when it was Bannon himself who spoke the oath against him. It was rewarding enough, seeing the man bleed out in the square. Pity," Hoban leered, roaming the length of Thad's frame, while a hand grasped the bulge forming in his trousers. Reaching out to touch Thad's hip. "I have missed the comforts of your faie cunt."

Grasping the hand that caressed him, Thad yanked the meaty flesh back until he heard it snap. Ignoring how Hoban screamed in agony, Thad bent the large man's arm, returning the blade to the tenderest part of Hoban's throat.

Deep magick tore from him as his faie voice slithered from his lips. "Forget my face, Hoban. No longer desire my flesh, nor another's again. Keep your days in solitude, forget your own comforts, your own desires. When your days are drawing to a close, at the last moment when your heart begins to stop, you will remember me. You will remember every child you ruined, every wrong you have ever made. In your final breath, beg for your freedom, like I did. Beg with your tears as you feel every moment you raped me, that you raped Yarin, Gavyn, Gahl. Only then, may you die."

Thad stepped back, pocketing his dagger, glaring down at the slumped form of Hoban. Vacant pools of blue looked up at him, drool shimmered in the corner of the large man's mouth.

Seated at the small desk near the window, Pavan heard the rain, looking up from his red leather book, the one he had kept from the horse master in Ledenjour. Drinking his warm mead, Pavan let the words of Shakespeare dull his mind, taking him away from himself if only for a moment. But lightning struck, illuminating the little corner where he read in the small little parlor of the inn and Pavan was brought back to himself. Returning to the pain behind his eyes and the long wearisome nights.

Thad had not yet returned from his errand. After discussing with Thad about what had happened in the square, Pavan was watching closely out of the little window where he sat, watching for the storm of guards. Worry tightening in his gut that Thad was discovered and hauled off to a dungeon somewhere.

At last, the door to the inn opened, Pavan sat upright, watching two merchants who entered. He sighed, but spotted a figure slumped ascending the staircase beyond. At once, Pavan rushed up, hurrying to the stairs, detained only for a moment by the slow-moving men to move from the doorway.

Water trailed up and up, leading to their door. Thad must have been walking in the rain for some time.

"Thad." Pavan entered, but the room was chilly, silent.

He looked around, placing his book aside, cautiously shutting the door behind him. It was not a dream, Pavan knew that the faie had returned, but there was no movement within.

A sound drew Pavan's eyes down, looking around the dressing screen hesitantly. A pile of wet garments lay dripping over the seat of a stool, muddy boots cast aside without care and Thad was sitting in the copper basin. Pavan slowly approached.

Thad was crying.

"Thad..." Pavan whispered, maneuvering to crouch around the copper bathtub, looking down at Thad who wept openly. He wore only his linen trousers, his damp skin painted with the many freckles Pavan had so often seen, now stood out against the paleness of his skin.

Pavan touched the bent knee, feeling the cold skin beneath his palm. "Will you tell me what is wrong...Can I help you?"

Thad shook his head; more tears fell fast.

Pavan shuddered, witnessing the rare emotion Thad never expressed. Thad was always so bottled up, so reserved, but there was something wrong. Pavan felt the shiver of magick, the grief and despair that rolled from the faie. Pavan could not even guess as to what it could mean, or what the cause.

"You are cold," Pavan said at last. Calming his own racing heart, reaching to take Thad's cold hand but Thad would not look at him. Pavan sighed. "May I warm you?"

It was a long moment, before Thad slowly gave a nod, struggling to shift himself up, trying to stand. Pavan immediately stood, leaning to scoop Thad up in his arms but Thad gasped, wincing.

Pavan frowned.

"Are you hurt?" Pavan asked softly, walking around the dressing screen, taking the room in a few strides to place Thad gently on the bed. Thad wept into the bend of Pavan's neck but said nothing.

Pavan retrieved his pelt from the place it hung, eagerly placing it over Thad's shivering body. He looked frail, dejected. Trembling as he curled on himself, turning away from Pavan. Quickly Pavan removed his boots, climbing onto the bed, wrapping his arms around Thad. The faie flinched but remained silent.

Wrapping his body as snug against the faie, Pavan let his magick warm him. It became natural after so many long nights in Ledenjour winter. Now, it was second nature, but there was a stiffness to Thad, a resistance when Pavan touched him.

"Let me in, Thad...let me help you, as you have done so many times for me." Pavan spoke words he so often heard himself, kissing the curve of Thad's temple, breathing in the scent of citrus. "Let me in."

Thad trembled as Pavan placed his hand upon the temple of the faie. There was no resistance as Pavan closed his eyes, letting the wave of the magick crash over him. Gasping into the depths of his mind, seeking the threshold he knew so well.

Pavan found the corridor of doors, drawing nearer to the door.

"Thad, you must let me enter," he whispered, meeting resistance when he tried. Behind the oaken door, there was a flickering light.

Pavan saw another doorway open, letting the light through.

"A memory," Pavan sighed, feeling the emotion thick in his throat. A vibrancy of magick drawing him in closer.

He entered the room beyond the waiting door, feeling the sweltering heat at once, as he walked amongst the unfamiliar furniture that shimmered in the cast of the memory. It danced with light coming in through the painted glass window or swirling colors. Pavan searched the room, knowing Thad to be near.

"Thad," Pavan whispered.

"I can't." There was a voice, making Pavan turn suddenly.

"You must, Thaddeus, Lord Hoban is not going to leave until he has seen you." A thin man, with neatly styled brown hair stood in the doorway, glowering into the room. The man wore a deep burgundy vest over a billowing black tunic, with eyes that shimmered in the light.

Sobs echoed in the room. Pavan searched again for the source, following the man that entered the room as he found what he wanted hidden within a wardrobe that sat upon the furthest wall.

The man sighed, crouching down. *"Why are you so petulant?"*

A shuddering sob. *"He is so unkind to me."*

Pavan walked closer, to stand behind the man that crouched before the wardrobe. Looking in at the faie who clutched to himself within the hanging of silks and cotton garments. Thad was young, perhaps barely sixteen, with soft youthful skin and long copper hair that touched his collar. He was dressed in his under linens, clutching his knees to his chest, tears streaming down his face.

"It would not be so if you let him take you, but instead you fight him, Little Pigeon." A soft cooing voice, laced with malice dripped from the man's tongue.

"Please," Thad begged. *"He is too big. It hurts."*

Pavan felt sick, as he watched the scene unfold. His magick flaring with rage as the man coerced a child to such horrific acts, unfeeling to let the pleas go unnoticed.

"You shall take him, he has paid handsomely."

A knock came at the door. Standing there was a guard in bronze. *"Lord Gaur, there is a lord here to see you."*

"Thank you, Leuthere. Please take Thaddeus to Lord Hoban's room and see to it he stays there. I shall not be disturbed in my meetings with the high council." The man stood, and Pavan watched as he strode out without a second glance back at the wardrobe.

Pavan was helpless, watching as the guard reached in, grabbing a fistful of Thad's hair to yank him out, kicking and screaming. Dragging Thad as he sobbed and cried into the corridor. Pavan rushed to follow, but the room shifted, the memory changed into a newer memory. He stood in a darkened sitting room, looking down at a large fat man sitting in a winged armchair, glaring up at a stone-faced Thad who held a dagger to the man's throat.

"I am not your friend, *Hoban. I am a free man,"* Thad hissed, pressing the blade closer to the man's throat. Putting his weight into the action.

"You would be a fool to kill me. He will find you, and then perhaps you would have wished to sit on my knee when he is done with you."

Pavan felt the pain that Thad felt, tears sprang to his eyes. *"Tell me his name."*

Lord Hoban growled. *"I will not."*

Thad removed his dagger, replacing it with his own hand, his thumb pressed against the pressure point, digging in deep until Hoban gurgled, choking for breath. Lord Hoban thrashed, kicking his legs, but Thad was immoveable.

"His name, and I will let you live." Thad pressed until the man's face was purple.

Pavan squeezed his eyes shut, clenching down hard as he pulled himself back. Gasping out of the memory with a cold sweat, clinging hard to the body before him, he wrapped his arms closer about Thad's middle, coming out of the magick haze of their shared mind., each breath sharp and painful.

Blinking away the tears, Pavan kissed Thad's temple, then he kissed his neck, breathing in his scent. "Thad."

"Hold me, Pavan," Thad finally spoke. "Hold me until the memory of that man vanishes. I remember his breath, every caress."

Without hesitation, Pavan did as he was asked, wrapping his arms around Thad to hold him close to his chest, resting his hand over the flat of the faie's sternum, feeling the quick heartbeat beneath. They stayed like that, for what felt like an eternity, while Pavan listened to Thad breath while he settled, falling asleep in his arms. Matching his breath, Pavan soon found his eyelids growing heavy, clinging to the faie.

Tiredness ached in his bones, the use of his magick clouding him with fatigue. Pavan leaned up slowly to ease himself from beneath the slumbering frame—Thad looked serene in the arms of sleep. Pavan touched the curve of the chiseled jaw, noting every freckle that painted the pale cheek. He could still feel the inkling of pain beneath the surface. It would be easy to enter Thad's mind again, to take all of the memories that burdened him.

Pavan drew close, his lips grazing the curve of Thad's chin.

Magick shivered and Pavan pulled back with regret as the sharp bitterness left a tang on his tongue. Leaving Thad to sleep upon the bed, Pavan withdrew to the hearth, slouching in one of the high backed chairs. His body was alive with the change of magick, as he felt it move languidly within. Pavan closed his eyes, breathing slower.

Behind him, the door opened, receiving the heavy footfalls of Svein as he entered. Pavan peered over his shoulder, watching the large man ease himself into the chair beside him, nearest to the dying fire. Pavan watched in amazement as the material of the chair stretched and strained under the weight but did not break.

"Inn keeps' gone ter bed…" Svein grumbled, stretching his legs out to seek out the warmth of the fire. "That one sleepin' now?"

"Yes." Pavan nodded, looking briefly at the bundle of fur, before turning to look at Svein.

Receiving a low grunt of approval, Svein relaxed back in his chair and Pavan was glad to have them all at peace within the little room. Night blackened the sky beyond their window, the low burning fire casting shadows over the walls.

"Perhaps tomorrow we should remove ourselves from here." Pavan began, leaning back, glancing over at the half giant beside him.

"What's the rush? There are plenty of delights here to entertain us," Svein grunted.

"I have a feeling," Pavan sighed, rubbing his palm over his face.

Chuckling, the half giant stretched. "You and your feelings. I am certain we would be halfway across the realms. Does Thad agree with your plans?"

"I have not spoken of it…this development is new. There is a darkness looming over this place, one I do not favor to think of."

Before Svein could respond, there was a knock at the door. Pavan started, the half giant tensed, gripping Pavan's arm before he could stand, shaking his head. The knock came again, and Pavan stood, his heart hammering in his chest.

"Wait," Svein hissed.

Pavan turned, looking at the bed. Thad was sitting, awakened by the knocking, the faie was standing in a flourish, drawing his arms through an outer tunic, and Pavan saw the flash of a blade. Svein stood, shifting himself between Pavan and the door.

Thad opened the door.

"Forgive me," said a voice from the other side. A man's voice, young by the sound of it, and Pavan heard the accent with his Common. "I was looking for your master."

Thad held the dagger out of sight, watching the man at the door. Pavan looked around Svein's bulk, attempting to see who it was.

"My master is not well, come back in the morning."

Thad went to swiftly shut the door, but a boot thudded hard against it. Again, the voice of the man was lower, urgent.

"Please, I saw him in the square." Something flickered within Pavan.

Pavan stepped out, getting a better view of the stranger at the door, his eyes widening to see the dark-haired drummer with his boot in the doorway, his face dirtied, and his eyes wild. Pavan gripped Thad's arm.

"I know you." Pavan nodded.

"Please," the man was urgent, his eyes glancing down the darkened hall, "you must come away tonight. There are guards searching every inn. They are looking for you."

CHAPTER

4

Signe, Realm of Corad.

Sir Eero tugged at his tunic. Adorned with the latest fashions of Corad, he was not used to the silk that was wrapped around his collar. He walked the great hall of the grand estate of Duke Laronn, on invitation from the duke's eldest son.

"Eero!" Eugene's voice boomed over the music. "You made it! Have you danced with anyone yet?"

"I don't know anyone here. It is difficult to ask a lady to dance when no introduction has been made."

"And no introduction has ever been made on a dance floor?" Eugene shook him by the shoulder, still smiling. Then, what reason would he have to frown now that he was married to Tatiana, a relation of Duchess Kristjana of Tauf. They had courted for three summers, awaiting the approval of their prospective families.

"Why not my sister?" Eugene gestured to a girl with red hair who was dancing with a dark haired elf. A young girl, Eero was almost certain she was hardly old enough to be dancing with anyone but her father or brothers.

"Don't tell me that was your scheme this whole time?"

"What scheme?"

"Make me come all this way, just to introduce me to your sister. Don't you think she's a bit young?" Eero could see the length of auburn hair lying flat about her shoulders. She barely filled out her gown. He frowned.

"There's no scheme, Eero. I invited you because you're my friend, not because you and my sister would be an excellent pair. You said you had not been introduced to anyone, I merely offered to make an introduction. What you do with it is up to you." Eugene smiled at his own cleverness.

Eero rolled his eyes.

"Your honor to my livelihood would be taken more eagerly should I have been in search of a lady to take as my wife. But currently my duty is to the Prince of Jorn. And your sister is too young to be married, even by Signe standards."

"Ah, but that is the beauty of a match between you and Elsa, which I am not suggesting of course. You see, her dowry includes a title and land for her. So she may marry anyone she likes without worry of rank or title. You cannot tell me it is not a little tempting, the idea of giving up your service to the prince to be a lord of Signe?"

Eugene was clearly drunk and needed to return to his wife. If he had been sober the insinuations would have been more subtle.

"It's not. I would never marry anyone just for a title."

"I know. That's precisely why I want you to dance with her." Eugene let out a sigh, leaning closer. "Please Eero. It is not my place to ask but I think my sister is in danger. I believe you are the one who is going to save her."

Eero turned back toward the girl. She smiled to cover a wince when the lord she was dancing with rested his hand on her waist. "You've had one of your dreams?"

The sight was unreliable. Magick of that nature in the dwindling elven ancestry was difficult to digest, Eero had only met with two elves that held the sight. Lady Kristjana was the only one that remained alive.

It was so difficult to see the difference between truth and wishes but Eero had never known Eugene to be wrong, not when it came to visions of his family. Eero remembered how Eugene's first vision was of his mother's death. How it would lead to his father's madness. It was why he had insisted on creating inheritances for each of his siblings.

"It was different than the others but I saw you and her together. I saw you taking care of her."

"You know you are not meant to tell people about their futures. Or try to bring them about yourself. It changes their destiny. Just like with your mother."

"I did not change my mother's destiny. She still died." Though, the baby she was meant to lose had lived. A daughter. The same little girl Eero watched so intently now. Eugene schooled his features. "I would not even consider introducing you if it weren't for my dream, you are far too old for her, but I know that you are good."

Eero groaned inwardly as the words prickled at his empathy. "I will ask her to dance but that is all. I have no intention of rushing fate."

"That is all I ask."

As the current dance ended Eero made his way across the room toward the girl, preparing to ask her to dance. But the girl with auburn hair was gone in the mass of strange looks and fancy dress. Sir Eero would have to wait for the dance.

Magick from the brand burned through Elsa whenever her dance partner touched her.

She thought it was just the activity and the snug fit of her gown and kept pushing the pain out of her mind. Her partner, Sir Fridrick, was an excellent dancer and kept up a lively conversation that made Elsa laugh. Though, she expected little else from a gentleman Eugene had most intentionally introduced her to. A gentleman he expected to be a fine match for Elsa, if she took a liking to him. He was an elf, the second son of a lord in Entheas. Elsa liked the point of his ears beneath his dark hair and the way they seemed to redden when he was about to make a joke. Flirting with him came quite naturally. It was all jokes and quiet observations, light and golden. So different from the dark undertones that painted every conversation with Alaric. Dark tones she now understood to be a violent, all consuming, desire.

Her gaze darted to Alaric as the song came to an end. The golden and white tunic he wore gave him a lordly quality. He had risen quickly through the ranks of her father's knights as he proved himself as a fighter. Enough to warrant an invitation to Eugene's wedding feast. She wished it didn't. He was always near now, watching her.

She forced her eyes back to Sir Fridrick as the music came to an end, smiling at the handsome young lord, unable to make her attachment. Sir Lahrs was waiting for her answer by the end of the week. With Alaric so close, she no longer needed any more time to decide to be the princesses companion in Alnwick.

"Thank you for such a pleasant dance, but our dance has come to an end."

Sir Fridrick took her hand, dark eyes locked on hers. "The pleasure has truly been mine, I hope it is a pleasure you will allow me to have again very soon, Lady Elsa." He kissed her hand and the pinch in her ribs turned to a burn.

She swallowed her grimace, blushing at the attention. "I would like that."

Elsa turned away from Sir Fridrick, taking deep breaths as she made her way toward her seat. She would not let the pain or Alaric's watchful eye ruin Eugene's wedding feast for her. Not when it was meant to be a happy occasion.

Before she reached her seat, another gentleman approached her. "Lady Elsa, might I have the honor of your next."

"Oh, I would be—"

Alaric's hand clamped hard around her elbow before she could finish.

"Unfortunately, Lady Elsa will not be able to join you on the dance floor as she is needed in the kitchens. Urgently."

"Yes, most unfortunate. Perhaps later this evening, my lady."

"I—"

"Perhaps," Alaric answered for her. "If you'll excuse us." He turned, half dragging Elsa away from the dance floor, but not toward the kitchens, instead steering them down a dark corridor, shoving her into the darkened room.

So far from the feast Elsa could no longer hear the music. Nor would anyone hear the conversation that passed between her and Alaric. It was dark, save for the light of the moon that shimmered through the window.

Elsa glared up at the knight. "Alaric, what are you doing?"

"What am I doing?" He towered over her, bracing his arms around her so she was trapped against the wall. "What are you doing flitting and flirting across the dance floor like a painted whore. Like you are not spoken for?"

"I'm not spoken for, Alaric. I don't care what you did to me. And I wasn't flirting. I was dancing with my brother's guests. Now let me go." She tried to push him away.

Alaric slammed her back, pinning Elsa to the wall. "You are spoken for because I have claimed you. You are my wife and we are in love."

"This isn't love and I don't want any part of it. Now release me or I'll scream and you won't be able to hide what you've done."

He leaned so close, she could feel the heat of his body through the layers of clothing between them. His breath was hot on her ear as he pressed his mouth against it, growling, "Do it." His hand pressed to the brand before sliding over the watery fabric to fondle her breast, tugging at the silk neckline. She could hear the expensive fabric starting to tear. "Go on then. Scream. Ruin your brother's night."

"I will." Elsa trembled.

"You won't, because you and I both know there are only two ways that will end. Your father will have to give in to the law when he realizes we are bound. Or…" He caressed her through the fabric, his lips hot against the bend of her neck. "One of your brothers will challenge me to a duel for your honor. I wonder which one I will have the pleasure of killing. Will it be Eugene? Will he abandon his lovely new wife just to die for you? Or will it be one of the others? Erek, or Edgar perhaps? It doesn't matter which. Either way, you will be my wife by nightfall. So go on. *Scream.*"

Her voice failed her.

"That's what I thought." Alaric glared into her eyes. "You are mine and you are not to dance with another man."

"I can't do that. I cannot refuse a dance if it is not already spoken for. It would be an insult to my father's allies. I promise you I am not flirting with any of them, but I am the lady of this house for one more night and this is my duty to Signe. Please, you have to understand that." Elsa hated herself for begging. If they were lucky enough to survive, she would still be ruined and sent away. And she had to get out of this room, away from his touch.

He tucked a finger against her chin, bringing her eyes to meet his, almost gently. "I do understand that, my love. And I am willing to be generous with you, but first, you must prove you know who you belong to. I will not allow any man to lay claim on what is mine."

"What do you want me to do?"

He brushed his thumb over her lips. "Show me your loyalty. Kneel."

She did not move.

"Go on, Elsa. Prove to me you are a loyal wife and I will be generous with you."

Generous. Generous if she let him take her. Alaric did not care if she danced with someone else. He only cared about having her whenever he desired. About controlling her.

She shoved his hand away. "No."

Alaric's eyes burned with anger at her refusal. "What did you say to me?"

"No! If you want me then you have to take me and live with the knowledge that you forced me. That I don't want you and I don't love you!"

"Fine." Alaric's grip tightened. She started to scramble away, but Alaric was too strong. "If that is what you want, that is what I will give you. It makes no difference to me." He spun her around so her back was pressed to his chest, dragging her away from the doors, to the desk at the center of the room. "But know that I will not be gentle with you." He pushed her down on the desk, twisting her arm behind her back until she cried out in pain. "Your bruises can serve as a reminder that your body is mine and I will do with it as I please."

She waited a moment before fixing her gown. Surprised there were no tears, only rumpled fabric that could easily be dismissed as sitting too long to crease the silk. Finding some cool water and a handkerchief to dab on her face. The gilded mirror above the mantle showed that, while Alaric had been rough with her and her hair had come undone, hanging loose around her shoulders, she did not look as if she had been torn apart. Only as if she had become sidetracked and lost in some sort of game. Her appearance shocked her. She did not feel like the girl staring back at her. She was not that girl anymore. Surely such a change would show in her reflection.

Moving hurt, but she forced herself to straighten, walking back out to the ball.

"Elsa!" Her brother Erek's voice echoed over the music almost the minute she stepped back into the golden light. "Eugene has another lord to introduce to you..." Erek's voice trailed off, looking at her. "Are you all right?"

"I'm fine. I'll...I'll find Eugene and apologize for any delay."

Erek stepped in front of her. "He can wait. Elsa, where have you been?"

Her throat went dry. Could Erek see what had happened to her? If he found out, Alaric would surely kill him in a duel for her. "Nowhere. Just leave it Erek, please."

He followed her, never one to listen to his younger sister. "Wait, Elsa. Tell me what happened. Did one of the lords try to hurt you? I saw Alaric watching you earlier."

"Erek, please leave it. I promise you I'm...I'm fine." She stumbled over the lie and Erek heard it. Erek knew.

"Elsa..."

"Not here, at least. Please. I can't—This is Eugene's day, I cannot ruin it for him. I shall be leaving for Alnwick with Sir Lahrs."

Erek stiffly wrapped his arms around her before she started to cry as if he was afraid to actually touch her. "I think I want some hot chocolate, this feast bores me. Come down to the kitchens with me and we'll see if the cook will make us some."

"What about the lord Eugene wants to introduce to me?"

"He'll get over it."

Elsa walked with Erek in the gardens. She was leaving for Alnwick and she wished to have one last look at her home, never knowing when she would see it again. A sigh passed her lips, and she took in a breath of fresh air. A hint of citrus clung to the air, the orange grove would soon be in season.

"Are you sure you don't want me to accompany you? Stay with you until you are settled in Alnwick?" Erek was the youngest of her brothers, and the one Elsa was closest to, besides Eugene. She looked into his bright blue eyes, his dark hair swooped down over his eye and she resisted the urge to push it back.

Elsa smiled. "I don't think you are quite what the king is looking for in a lady companion for the princess."

"What makes you so certain? I host excellent tea parties."

"That is certainly true. Though you do invite a surprising number of pirates to them."

"It makes things more interesting."

Elsa let out a laugh.

Erek frowned deeper. "I could go with you, you know. To keep you safe from Alaric."

"There is no place safer than the king's household, Erek. You know this."

"You won't be with the king's household."

"No, but I will be with his daughter. And I shall be travelling with Sir Lahrs, that means a great deal to Eugene. He has told me many great things about the knight."

"Eugene is not always right about everything. He can get the sight confused with a wish sometimes."

Elsa reached out, snaking her fingers with his, squeezing Erek's hand. "You're thinking of Evangeline, aren't you?"

Erek didn't answer. He couldn't. Not when a gaping hole opened in his chest at the mention of his one-time fiancé's name. There was great pain written on his face.

"You really loved her, didn't you?"

"Loved would imply that those feelings are in the past." He hung his head. "And they are anything but past."

"Then why don't you go to her? Find her and marry her. You shouldn't let Alaric's misdeed keep you from the person you love."

"It's not that simple, Els."

Her dark eyes burned, her voice turning sharp. "It should be. You're a fourth son. Who cares who you marry or if her virtue is intact? She wasn't untrue to you. You shouldn't be punished because she fell into a cruel man's clutches. Neither should she."

Elsa felt a sharp pain in her chest. Elsa was no longer just speaking about Evangeline but about herself, about all the things she believed she could never have because of Alaric's cruelty. She knew what it was like to be tricked by the man with quick words and a sharp tongue.

Erek squeezed her hand again. "It shouldn't matter but I don't even know where she is. If she is in Tauf or with the Silent Sisters or…" He swallowed the lump forming in his throat. "If she is already married to another. Even if I did, who's to say she would even speak to me. She trusted me to deal with Alaric and instead of protecting her I let Father break off our engagement. I didn't even have the courage to tell her myself."

"Those aren't insurmountable problems, Erek." Her fingers brushed over her ribs for half a breath before pulling him down to eye level so she could kiss his forehead. "This is a fate you can change. All you have to do is find her."

Erek wrapped his sister up in a tight hug. Holding her to his chest so she didn't see the tears that welled in his eyes. "You can change your fate too, Els. Eugene saw it. Saw that being the princess' companion will lead you to your true love. Someone who will break your curse."

She shook her head. "In that, I believe Eugene mistook a wish for the sight. I have no intention of ever being fooled by love again."

He tightened his grip, hoping what Eugene saw was true. That tying Elsa's fate to Princess Brendolyn would lead her to what she needed, to a love that was real. Hoping he could press as much love and protection as he could into her skin, not wanting this to be goodbye. Not wanting this to be the last time they saw each other.

"Miss Laronn!" a voice called up from the carriage. "We must set off if we are to reach Alnwick."

"I am coming." She started to pull away.

Erek caught her by the hand. "Elsa, if you ever have need of me. Of anything at all…"

"I won't." She smiled. "*Hesitate*, I mean. I'll send word if I ever need you. I'll write to you in Tauf. I shall send it care of Lady Evangeline, to her hopeless husband." Her smile faltered. "Don't worry about me, Erek. I will be fine. I will be happy with the princess and if I am not, I will write to you. But you deserve to be happy too. You and Evangeline. Please promise me you will find her."

"I'll try."

"No, you have to promise."

"Fine. I promise."

"Lady Elsa!"

"I must go." She hugged him one last time. "Write to me."

"I will, the moment I reach Tauf."

Her smile became real and genuine. Then she was hurrying toward the carriage where an older couple waited. Disappearing.

CHAPTER

5

Denorn, Realm of Jorn.

It was the stench of magick that greeted Simeon as he strode across the small room. A hot, coppery tang of mixed scents, one as sweet as honeysuckles, the other deep and woodsy. These were smells that made him sneer. Glancing to the small bed, noticing the rumpled bedding.

They were here. Simeon knew they had gone in haste.

"Tell me about them," he demanded, glancing to the inn keep who stood at the door, the man's frame hunched, hands worrying together in front of him.

"They are not of this realm, my lord. They gave me plenty of gold and kept to themselves," the man stammered.

Simeon could taste the fear seeping from every pore. He sniffed, his gaze flickering to the guard who accompanied them.

"You told me he was of great magick."

The inn keeper coughed. "Faie, they were. I remember them clear as day."

Simeon glared at the guard.

"You allowed a faie to slip through your grasp, what a pity." He kept his voice low, letting his words sink deep into the guards nerves, watching the man flare with unease.

"My lord, let me find him, let me bring him to you."

Maneuvering around the furnishings, Simeon approached the guard, and the air rippled. This man was foolish, with his sun burnt skin, the dry yellow hair slippery with oil. Simeon was not pleased with the foolish actions of a man who wore his insignia.

He took hold of the guard, flexing his fingers against the thick neck, leaning forward to breathe in the stench of his fear. It was easy to penetrate his mind, each of his guards had upon training been broken down for this purpose. Each man under his banner were his eyes should he need it. This was one of those times.

Sifting through the man's mind, Simeon slid against the morning as the man struggled to admit his wrongs, a smile formed on his lips, remembering the trembles of fear. Sliding further back, Simeon sought after the memories of that morning, seeking the one they searched for in the many faces of the guards mind.

Sliding back through the laughter, the humiliation, until he found what he was after.

"They are filth, bred of Eir that shall be swept from the great Lord of Denorn's streets. Keep your pity coins." Simeon saw the pouch of coins tossed down, the coins shimmering in the sun.

Leaning down before him, was the stranger. Tall and dark, but his face obscured by hair. Simeon moved as the guard did, stepping closer to intimidate the man. Waiting for the face, he looked up, and Simeon sniffed. Memories flowed together, the man's face blending with so many he had seen before. Drawing a hideous disfigured face, his voice spoke, but Simeon could not hear but for the screech of wails.

Simeon drew out of the guards mind with a snap.

"My lord," the guard rasped.

Looking into dark eyes, Simeon saw the pupils of the man so wide, it obscured the color of his irises. The whites went red with blood and the taste of death lingered over him.

"You have displeased me," Simeon hissed, his thumb pressing deeper into the guard's neck., his nail just above the thick vein that pulsed under his hand.

"Please...my...lord..." the guard tried to plead, choking on each attempt at breath.

One swipe and the sharp edge of Simeon's nail split the tender skin causing blood began to pour from the guards throat. He watched, delighting in the panic, the thick fingers that grasped at his gaping wound, attempting to stop the flow of blood.

Simeon smiled as blood peppered the air with a delectable aroma. He watched the man slump, collapsing at his feet. Vacant eyes glossy, void of life, the guard died in a heap. Blood pooling out in droves across the wooden floor.

"Clean this up." Simeon turned to the inn keep, waving his hand over the stunned man's pale expression.

At once, the innkeeper recoiled, his eyes widened.

"My lord," he wheezed.

Simeon smiled at the dutiful bow presented to him. Watching the innkeeper mechanically set to work preparing to dispatch the guards body. He stopped at the door, turning to look at the innkeeper who began to unfasten the buckles of the dead guards breastplate, being careful not to step upon the thick pooling of blood.

"Have his clothes returned to my estate. Your efforts will be heavily compensated." Simeon tasted the sharp magick on his tongue. "You shall speak of this to no one or the fate of your children, and your children's children shall be your undoing."

Leaving the innkeeper, he departed, returning to the night air, as a gilded carriage rolled up alongside. Simeon hastened inside when the door was opened. Looking up to the man waiting within. Leuthere smiled.

"You have discovered them, my lord?"

Simeon leaned back, taking one last look upon the inn as the carriage rolled away.

"There is something different about this one, Leuthere," he told him coldly. "Have your men stationed at every road that leaves the city. Check every cart and wagon, there shall be a heavy tax should the merchants leave before this magick is found."

He slid his eyes to the man who delighted in this course of action. Leuthere would follow his word without hesitation, he would kill for him should the need arise. There was no mystery to how the man first became his prized killer. Simeon did not find it difficult to buy the man to his cause after the death of his old master, Orin Gaur. It was the businessman Simeon had to thank for shaping the ruthless heart of Leuthere who had been one of Orin's firsts. A young boy taken from a shipwreck off the coast of Taastra. There was something in him, ready to please that unlocked the brutality within Leuthere. One Simeon appraised when they first met many years ago.

"At once, my lord."

Pavan glared at the man who stood watching him, learning his name to be Harmond. They stood in the threshold of the chapel—Arienne's place of worship. It felt wrong to hide here, to come slinking in through the side doors, to the kitchens now cold from unuse for the night.

"Explain yourself," Thad hissed. Drawing aside his cloak to expose the undress of remaining in his under breeches. "How did you find us?"

"After the guard had gone, I knew there was going to be trouble. I stole away with my companion to this place, I knew we would be safe." He was timid, keeping a distance from them all.

Thad scoffed.

"I know how it sounds, but I believe it was best." Harmond unlatched his jacket, tossing back his hood to reveal the same head of dark wavy hair.

"You sully this place with ill deeds." Thad was angry.

Pavan felt the faie seething from where he stood in the shadow of the kitchens. A chill ran through him—Pavan was cold. Walking to the large barren hearth, Pavan muttered the incantation, watching the hearth roar to life with fire.

"This man is a friend," Pavan reminded Thad with a stern glance.

Thad's lip slid back, revealing his teeth. "That is not a promise of discretion, Pavan. You cannot trust a man of Eir to not turn us in should the need arise."

"I take it you have not had pleasant dealings with us before."

"Thad, there is no other option but to trust him. This man has honored a duty to help. Does it matter what the past of his people have done to take away from the friendship given to us now?" Pavan asked. Seeing Thad clearly in the flicker of light, the warmth on his back was nothing compared to the warmth when he saw those orange eyes lift to his.

"I am indebted to him, for saving the life of myself and of the Lady Vahliene." Harmond bowed, a fist raised over his chest.

"You are a servant of Hugo Jax, then?" Thad's frown remained on his lips.

Harmond looked taken aback. "You know of Hugo Jax?"

"I am well acquainted with many of the high lords and bannerman under this realm. There are countless names I have been acquainted with for many years, Hugo Jax was given his title by the people, after the death of their late Lord Zhaldec." Thad spoke with contempt. Pavan saw the strain in the faie's reserve as he spoke of his past life. Tasting the sour tang of guilt and bitterness in the air.

Harmond nodded slowly.

"He was, as you have said, but we are not thieves, nor are we murderers and thugs." The man paused, catching Pavan's eyes. He drew a breath of confidence. "We are destitute. A poor city that once thrived in abundance."

"Why has your city fallen?" Pavan asked.

Harmond glanced quickly at Thad but returned to look at Pavan as he spoke again. "We have been taxed so heavily, when we have come to Denorn to earn coins. Now, we have stretched out warehouses and soon we shall have nothing left to feed our people."

"What is your main source of income?" Pavan asked.

Here, there was a shift, and he saw the man blush. Harmond looked away, unable to look him in the eyes.

"Answer him!" Thad demanded.

Harmond flinched, looking up sharply. Pavan saw the twist of shame, as the man lingered over the words that sat on the tip of his tongue.

"We once had the largest theatre in Jorn. Many would travel far and wide all over the realm to see our greatest shows. Trained fire breathers, illusionists that awed the room, shapeshifters, actors—" He stopped, watching Pavan blankly.

Pavan felt the darkening in his chest, the room flickered in cold and deepening the room in magick. He checked himself, his look now turned to Thad, seeing the faie was equally affected.

"What happened to this great theatre?" Svein asked, his voice breaking the tension of silence in the room.

"It was destroyed, years ago...after a siege upon our town took many of the people..." Harmond grew silent again.

Pavan felt ice in his blood. "Your people...were they faie?"

Harmond's eyebrows rose. "Yes, we were once a great city of faie, but since the attack, there are not many left with faie in their blood...and what remains is more than three generations back. Hugo Jax was said to be the last of the faie blood. That is why the people wanted him on their seat. And Vahliene...she is one of the last remnants."

Pavan nodded. "She would have been arrested today."

"She would have been killed," Thad hissed. They both looked at him. Harmond was horror stricken, Pavan gave Thad a look of caution but the faie ignored him. "If she has enough of magick within her blood, if they were to discover her...they would have her killed."

Harmond licked his lips. He was pale.

"She...she has no magick." Harmond shook his head, clearly distressed. "Her hair...and perhaps her eyes, but...no. She holds no magick."

"Faie are forbidden in these lands, you know this." Thad was direct. "*Magick* is forbidden in these lands."

"Yes." Harmond nodded.

"You see that I am faie?" Thad held the man's gaze, there was fear flickering in the man's chest. "That we...are faie?"

"Yes." It was barely audible and Harmond looked terrified under the orange gaze of Thad. Those dark eyes then flickered to Pavan.

"He is faie?" Harmond asked. "His magick is less pronounced, but there is something more..."

Thad stepped between them, not letting Harmond step closer. At once the man stumbled back, his boot hitting the step making him fall back with a yelp.

"He is faie, because I said he is faie...now, I must ask your silence in this matter. We do not want unwanted eyes to see, or whisper of unwanted matters to reach abroad. Do I make myself understood?"

He did not need his faie voice, Pavan knew, but Thad had a way of intimidation, he had seen it before in the training yard, in the matters of trade. Thad was solid in his ideas, with everything he held a firmness of unwavering tact.

Behind them, the inner door leading out from the kitchens to the rest of the great chapel opened. Standing in the doorway, looking down at them was the great Lady Arienne herself. Dressed in long silken robes, her hair lay down her back, covered loosely with a veil pinned behind her ears to cover it.

"Welcome, wary travelers. Come, here shall be rest against the untamed night."

47

CHAPTER

6

"Forgive this untimely intrusion," Pavan began, as they entered the little office. It was the same as it had been before, but the thick curtains were drawn over the large windows, and a low burning fire kept the space warm.

Arienne held up a hand.

"I am aware of your danger." She addressed the others as they came into the room. Harmond was the last and shut the door behind him, sealing them into the quiet. "Thank you, Harmond, for seeking them out as I requested."

"Of course." Harmond bowed.

She smiled, casting her eyes to Thad, who stood nearest to the hearth. Her thin, long fingers touching his arms. Pavan saw the faie shrink back, but he did not say anything. Even as she unclasped his cloak, letting it fall to the floor.

With a delicate wave, a silken robe was draped from her hand. Her magick tasted of lilacs and honey, Pavan admired her as she dressed Thad in the robe. The shimmering fabric clinging to Thad's frame, the length gently touching the stone beneath his feet.

Thad blushed, unable to meet the warm gaze. Arienne caressed his cheek, her smile delighted, encapsulating them both.

"Do not be uneasy, son of Safir, you are welcome here."

He stepped back, frowning, but bowed quickly. Hurrying away from her to sit at the far end of the room.

"Arienne," Harmond insisted, stepping forward when Thad was at a safer distance away. Emboldened now to address the great lady of light. She looked at him with a smile.

"Do not burden your heart, Harmond. Lady Vahliene was escorted to her father in safety." Arienne anticipated the man's unease, and once it was softened, she offered a hand to the desk which now held trays of food and a set of goblets for drink. She poured it herself, each glass filled with deep colored wine.

Svein drank gladly, muttering his thanks around mouthfuls of food. Harmond was equally at peace, sitting beside Svein. They began to talk in hushed tones. Thad was at the other side of Svein, but he did not eat or drink. Laying his head down to rest upon the arm that lay over the edge of the table. Pavan wanted to go to him, wanted to embrace the faie, but there was a sharpness to Arienne, those wise grey eyes locked upon him, motioning him along with her as she walked.

He followed her into a small doorway, leading into a little anteroom draped in velvet. Housing a trickle of water in a small fountain. His eyes scanned the farthest wall, taking in a slim bed draped with silk curtains that hung delicately over four posts.

Arienne approached him, raising a hand to touch the hair that fell over his temple. Her finger was cold to the touch and Pavan could not take his eyes away from her—she was beautiful. He could feel the magick flutter between them causing him to sigh.

"Rest your weary heart, Pavan," she spoke, her words flooding him with warmth and he leaned further into her touch.

"Who am I, Arienne?"

"You know who you are, child. Do not let your past define your destiny, Pavan..." She sounded other worldly, her skin shimmering in the low light and her magick dancing around them.

Pavan swallowed the lump in his throat.

"I cannot control that part of me, the one thirsting for blood," he whispered, his chin trembling.

She nodded, smoothing her hand along his cheek, resting at the joint of his neck and shoulder.

"In time, it shall be so, by Ehnarea's light..." Arienne took Pavan by the hand, leading him further into the room, until they came to a recess in the wall lined with shelves that housed various objects. Pavan could feel the magick of each. They called to him, as he looked closer. But there was one that made him recoil.

A dark metal, shimmering like an oil slick. Made of thin metal bent and woven together in an intricate way. It reminded Pavan of the Celtic knots, patterned in such a way that one could not see where one began and the other ended.

Arienne took up this small circle, only three fingers in width, presenting it to Pavan. Securing it to the inner portion of his tunic, the little item made him feel a chill. His body dampened in heightened magick.

"It is an enchanted relic, one made by my sister's hand. I believe you are acquainted with her son, he bestowed this artifact to me. Along with this…" She turned back to the shelf, retrieving a wrapping of fine leather, the size of a small shoebox and extending the bundle to Pavan.

It was heavy, so he took it to the bed to unwrap it—A book. He turned over the cover to reveal the inner pages yellowed with age. The pages were lined with fine ink, in a hand-written script of elven dialect, along with runes and shapes written on the margins.

"My nephew knew you would find me, he guided your soul to my doorstep."

Pavan looked up. "Meilyr?"

Arienne nodded, smiling. "He speaks well of you, and your companions. He speaks of the little one…your faie friend, with regard as his own son."

Pavan began to rewrap the book and her slender hand rested on his own. He trembled.

"Meilyr is kind to give these to me."

"It will keep you hidden as it had kept Meilyr unseen from the eyes of those who would seek him out. Where he is now, there is no need for such relics…"

Pavan glanced up. "Who is it that seeks me?"

She smiled but Pavan knew she would not tell him. He accepted the gifts, thanking her again before walking with her from the room to rejoin the others.

As he sat beside Thad, the faie watched him closely, looking him over with a questioning glance, before Pavan brought forward the book. Then, shifting aside the front of his tunic, he let Thad see the little relic pinned to his inner tunic.

Thad's eyes went wide.

"That is Meilyr's charm, how did you get that?" he asked under his breath, glancing at the woman who was across the room.

Pavan leaned closer, taking Thad by the hand. He desperately wanted to kiss him but refrained for fear of being watched—Harmond was so near to them. Instead, he smiled warmly, lacing their fingers together.

"Arienne is kin to Meilyr. He sent these trinkets to her to give to me. It shall keep me hidden from unwanted eyes," Pavan whispered, tracing the lines on the back of Thad's hand.

Thad sighed. "Leave it to him to think of such things…Here, you should eat."

Encouraged by this fact, Thad reached forward, unlacing their hands to bring food onto a plate; Fruits, cheeses, dried meats, all fresh and inviting. Thad reached to fill a cup with wine.

"Are you his servant?" Harmond voiced, from his seat at the other side of Svein.

Thad placed the cup before Pavan, returning to his seat and eyeing the man with a cold glare. "I am no one's servant," he hissed bitterly.

Harmond slowed his chewing, looking from Pavan to Thad. Beside him, the half giant hid behind his goblet, leaning back further in his chair to sit out of the way.

"Forgive my forwardness…I do not mean any disrespect, but you have a duty to this man?"

Pavan felt the ripple in Thad's manner. Quickly gripping his wrist, staying the hand that clenched into a fist at the faie's side hastening to respond to Harmon's inquiries.

"He is my companion, Harmond. Duty and honor have their dual respect as I am bound to him as he is to me. I request there is no more inquiry upon the matter."

Harmond flushed, giving a stern nod.

Svein coughed, his cup hitting the table loudly. His bulky frame shifted on the chair, the wood groaning under his massive frame.

"Shall we remain hidden behind these walls all night, or shall we find ourselves in search of another dwelling?" he asked.

"Eir. We can return to Eir," Harmond stated.

"That is the first place they shall look, don't be a fool," Thad responded flatly, not looking up from his plate.

Arienne emerged before them. "At sunrise, my caravan of honey casks is scheduled to be delivered to the king…the guards cannot detain them. On the morrow, you shall be with them, but you shall not take the king's road."

"Honey? You think the guards of Denorn would let even a cart roll through these gates?" Thad demanded.

The woman smiled, sweetly.

"Take heart, Thaddeus. For Ehnarea blesses us all…now rest…your journey is not yet over." Arienne turned, her bare feet soundless as she gracefully took leave of the offices.

Pavan wondered if she had any intention of returning to them before the sun came up but he was tired, wary. Perhaps it was better that they slept. He stood, looking down at Thad.

"I wish to sleep," he told him. Quickly looking up to Harmond and Svein, addressing the half giant next. "Remain close at hand should I need you."

Turning from the table, Pavan felt the faie close behind, thankful that Thad was quick to join him. Pavan held firmly to the leather book wrapped in leathers, but it would have to wait. He had time to read through the pages.

Now, he needed rest. Pavan wanted comfort.

Shutting the door to the bedchamber, Pavan was confident it was meant for them. Seeing steam rising from a wash basin he took the liberty to wash his face and neck, easing away the worry from his aching bones. Two hands grasped his tunic, turning him slightly as Thad began to unlace the sides. Pavan smirked, but said nothing, allowing the faie to remove his outer garments. Standing in dark gray linen trousers and a thin shirt, Pavan felt the chill of the room.

Thad stood inches from him and Pavan could smell the sweetness of his magick, the warmth of his breath, as the faie reached up to pull free the little leather strap holding Pavan's hair at bay. Dark tresses tumbled down, tickling his cheek and neck.

"My lord is ready for bed." Thad's voice sent a shiver along Pavan's spine.

Catching the faie's wrist before he turned away Pavan brought them closer. Leaning in to place a gentle kiss upon supple lips, hearing the delicate sigh fall free.

"Not without a kiss good night…" Pavan began to feel the fluttering of desire, his blood hot beneath the surface as magick danced under his fingertips.

Thad pushed him back. "You have had your kiss. Now, to bed."

Pavan went back willingly, being guided towards the bed, holding on to the faie's wrist, it was impossible for either of them to let go. He wanted to remain in this darkened room, to stay hidden away in this bedchamber forever.

"Stay with me," he begged.

Thad pushed Pavan back to sit at the edge of the bed. Slotting himself to stand between his knees, Thad raked back the mess of dark hair from Pavan's face bringing himself down to place a kiss upon Pavan's temple.

"Am I to sleep out there…with that man? Not a chance."

Pavan pulled back, looking up at bright orange eyes. "He is not so bad. Thad…what do you truly have against him?"

Sighing heavily, Thad stood straight but Pavan would not allow him to back away. Pavan brought him close to his body, lying them back so they were side by side.

"It's not him…it's just…" Thad was flushed, licking his lips and avoiding Pavan's gaze.

"Thad…" Pavan raised up slightly, gazing down. "Was it him…that man who owned you?"

"Orin Gaur," Thad breathed, a tear slipping from the corner of his eye. "He was born in Eir…he was faie. He was the reason Eir has fallen. Orin used his influence to ruin the place of his birth…"

Pavan frowned. "Why would he ruin them?"

"He was ashamed of being faie. After leaving Eir as a child to live with his father in Denorn he was brought up to be humiliated by who his mother was. His father was human…his father had been manipulated by her faie voice." Thad wiped at the tears that stained his cheek. "I shouldn't be so affected by the man who used me for so long…but I have been influenced in so many things."

Pavan took Thad's hand. "Are you ashamed, Thad?"

"I am ashamed of who I had become under his influence. I am ashamed of the lies he made me believe…no, I am not ashamed of being faie, but what he used me to accomplish because of it."

"You are strong," Pavan stated firmly, touching the curve of Thad's jaw as fresh tears fell free from orange eyes.

"I am ashamed I cannot be more after all these years. I have tried to run from the past, to be free of his influence, but now I shall be faced with the very place that shall break me."

Pavan gripped Thad's hands, quieting the shaking he found there. Looking directly into those fierce orange eyes, both shimmering with tears.

"You are not Orin Gaur, Thaddeus Brousevier. You are not that twisted man who sought only his own selfish greed, who held dark magick over you. Do not compare your life to his, your wrongs done under the guidance of a blackheart." Pavan pressed his forehead to Thad's and grasping at the faie's waist, bringing them closer together.

"Pavan." Thad was breathless. His tears quieted.

"You are beautiful. Fierce in honor, Thad." Pavan tilted the faie's chin up, kissing a wet cheek. "Don't doubt my heart. Don't forget the heart I freely give to you. Forget about our broken pasts, the wretched blackhearts made out to drag us beneath the dirt...Be here, with me. Be here, where only love lives."

Now Thad trembled. "Don't say it...you *cannot* say it."

Pavan knew, he knew it was dangerous, but he needed Thad to know. He leaned close, his lips brushing close to the faie's.

"I won't say it but know that I would give you everything, Thad. Know that you are so special to me. So dear to my heart." Pavan pressed in, kissing Thad with eager lips. His hands roaming down the length of him, grasping to his hips in desperation.

Thad welcomed the deepened kiss, roaming his hands upward to tangle his fingers in the length of Pavan's hair.

Desire coiled its grip, latching on and Pavan tensed.

Yanking back suddenly and stumbling away from the bed. It was hot in the room, his vision spotting with lightheadedness. Breathing slowly, trying to focus his breath. Pavan was there, by the sea. Each breath taking him there. Calming the heat rising within him to the cool waves that crashed at his feet and the voice lulled him.

He searched for her, in his visions, looking for the dark-haired apparition that steadied his racing heart. Blinking against the bright burning sun, Pavan saw her further up the beach, nearly waist deep in the waves. He stepped forward, but she was further now, the waves crashing in around them, pulling him deeper. Pulling him under the cold rushing sea foam.

Pavan gasped, returning to his body. Trembling against the visions as his blood eased. He blinked, straightening himself to face Thad who was seated upon the bed watching him.

"Come to bed." Thad reached out a hand.

Pavan stepped the distance, taking the hand offered. Relaxing himself against the bedclothes—the pillows smelled of lavender. His eyelids grew heavy as he wrapped his arm around Thad's middle, letting himself fall into a dreamless slumber.

CHAPTER

7

Each shift of the wagon moved the large barreled casks that housed honey ale made by the honey farmers of the chapel of light. Three wagons full of these casks set out in the morning hours, Pavan huddled beneath his Vohlgrum pelt, sitting between the seat and the casks, hidden out of sight beneath a canopy hung overhead.

Across from him, Thad sat with his limbs bent down so they touched Pavan's outstretched legs. They remained silent, listening to the wheels upon the cobbled street, hearing the clops of horses hooves, canting against the slow whistle of Svein.

Nearing the edge of town, where the road led to the gates to the west, the wagon began to slow. Above him, Pavan heard Svein, his voice coming in through the canvas.

"Guards, at the gate, they have stopped the first two wagons..." Pavan heard the half giant say.

Anticipation thrummed through him as they began to shift forward, rolling onward towards the gate. Pavan held himself taught, slowing his breath as he pressed his hand against the knotted metal charm pinned to his inner tunic.

He was protected, no one could sense him.

But the men at the gate, guards whose armor clanked with every step, were required to inspect the wagon's goods.

"These are devout wares, sir, from Lady Arienne herself as a gift to the king," Harmond said, his tone affirming.

"No exceptions. There are trickster folk about."

"Trickster? You mean those blackhearts of Eir they have been whispering about?" Svein spoke, his tone mocking.

"No exceptions."

Pavan tensed, concentrating. Listening to the steps of the guard, the one who made his way to the back of the wagon. Listening closely, calming his nerves Pavan steadied his thoughts on the man. It would need to be quick, one look was all he needed for this to work.

Drawing back the canvas flap, the guard's face peered in. His eyes scanned the casks with an inquisitive quirk of the brow. Pavan felt his heart flutter, looking into those eyes. Melding through with magick, Pavan reached into those watchful eyes. Magick pounding through Pavan's head, it began to burn, but he held himself steady as the guard looked directly at them. Unchanged, unnoticed. He could not see them. Only seeing the casks of honey ale, where he and Thad sat waiting.

Blinking hard, the guard drew back, rubbing at his eyes. Grumbling about the dust in his eyes. Walking back around the side to call to the others at the gate.

They were free to go.

Pavan finally let out a breath, looking at Thad. A smirk played on the faie's lips. Not letting their words break the spell of silence Pavan reached out where Thad met him in the middle. Electricity vibrated the air, raising the hairs on Pavan's arm. Magick dance from his fingertips to Thad's, a faint glow shimmering. Fire flickered from Thad's fingers.

Separating, as the wagon jostled them, breaking the spell Pavan smiled, tucking himself down into the embrace of his Vohlgrum pelt. Lulling as the wagon slowly made its way from the great city of Denorn.

After a time, Pavan pulled out the book from within the bag he held secure under his arm. Removing the wrappings, tucking it back into the bag, sliding it against the red leather of his little book of Shakespeare. To those words he would return, but for now Pavan was eager to read the book meant for his own eyes. As a guide given to him by Meilyr Pavan would spend however long it took to read this book front to back, back to front.

Memorizing lines came easy to Pavan, back home in London he never forgot any of them. Now, he could utilize this talent in other ways. In useful ways of remembering every spell, incantation, ward, and illusion.

It was a book of all of this, along with memos written by the author, and in the margins Pavan could make out the scribbles of others in their time, but some were written in languages Pavan did not understand—that would be another object of his study. It would be simple, Pavan already spoke fluent French because of his mother, and Arabic from his grandfather. Italian was easy to read, and he knew quite a lot of Portuguese and German. Pavan was confident in the languages of Jorn and Corad, and even the written language of the elves would prove easy for him to master.

He was roused from his reading by the shouts that reached him. Not the shouts of distress, but the shouts of welcome. He heard children laughing, glancing out from a space of the canvas to see the small scampering feet chasing after the wagon as it continued on. They had reached the village of Eir.

Glancing quickly at Thad, who was intrigued by the sounds, he was glancing out from the space between the canvas just as Pavan was. Pavan returned his eyes to the world beyond the wagon, sneaking a small glimpse through the split in the canvas.

Rolling to a stop, the sounds of voices full of excitement came to them. Shouts of the name Harmond brought a pang of pride to Pavan, hearing the overwhelming joy as the village welcomed their lost man. Pavan pushed aside the barreled casks, eager to emerge into the village beyond.

He emerged, stepping down from the back of the wagon, looking out at the dozens of surprised faces that greeted him. Many pairs of widened eyes taking him in, Pavan tried to ignore their racing hearts. Turning back to Thad, the faie tense as he stepped out of the wagon.

"Pavan, Thad," Harmond called, drawing their attention to the front of the wagon. Standing beside Svein, he motioned they follow. Heading to the large building they had arrived in front of in the street.

Noticing how close the buildings sat together; some three stories high, others built like stepping blocks. Beneath them, the street was smoothed with stone, but Pavan could see the edges worn, the cracks, and the broken places where missing stones left holes in the ground. Plants in planter boxes hung from balustrades above their heads, dripping with green and vibrant flowers. Narrow passages between the buildings led further into the city.

Before them, they approached a large stone structure with doors painted a deep green. Nearing the door, it opened and rushing from the depths within was the same girl from the square. Her vibrant hair the shade of fire as she rushed out to greet them, wrapping her arms around Harmond in a fond embrace.

"Vahliene." The voice was deep and they all looked to the door.

Pavan saw the man who stepped out to greet them—Hugo Jax was a tall man with dark hair, and eyes the color of sea glass. Those eyes scanned over them, taking in the group that stood on his doorstep. Uneasiness shifted his gaze from Svein and Thad, to Pavan.

"Come inside, we have much to talk about."

It was cool within the large stone building, to the home of Hugo Jax. Entering into the foyer, two stories high, with a large chandelier overhead, their footsteps echoed in the space with Pavan following after the rest of them.

"Please, follow Harmond upstairs to the guest wing. We shall meet at the dinner bell." Hugo faced them, nodding them all welcome and motioning with his hand to an arched doorway, where a stairway led up to the second level.

"This way." Harmond escorted them.

At first look, the magnificence of this beachside villa was basked in the richness of marble, fine silks, and blossomed flowers in the alcoves of every hallway. But the silks were faded, tattered at the edges, the stone was cracked and chipped.

Pavan saw all this as they walked along the upper landing, following Harmond as the man led them through to an open space on the other side of wooden doors.

"There is a lot of Coradian influence," the man began, walking to the large window to open the thin silk chiffon drapes, bringing in more natural light, a soft breeze, and a view of the sea beyond the line of the city below.

"Was it once belonging to the southern realm?" Svein asked, his head touching the lower ridge of the chandelier above them.

Harmond sighed. "It was under the rule of the king of old, all of the coastal cities took influence from the Corad Capital. Now, this wing shall be of your use. This is the sitting room, there is a larger bedchamber through there...and two more at the other side."

"Thank you." Pavan could see the hesitation as Harmond looked uneasy.

"Do not feel you need to change your dress, Hugo is not a man that keeps to the social standards of class. Come as you are, there shall be a hot meal prepared." Harmond bowed before hurrying from the room.

Pavan unlatched his cloak, draping it over the nearest chair and letting his body fall into the seat. All of his muscles ached, his mind throbbing.

"I could sleep here forever," he grumbled as he closed his eyes.

"There shall be time for that, Pavan, but first we must talk," Thad encouraged. Pavan could feel the faie kneel close to him.

He groaned. "Talk, I cannot talk. I am tired."

"Pavan." Thad gripped his hand, sending chills through him. "How are we to approach them? We are from across the sea, it is possible they could not approve. But we must not tell them what you are, Pavan."

"Am I to hide who I am, Thad?" Pavan finally looked up, those orange eyes watching him.

"For now, Pavan…for now, until we know we can trust these people. Do you trust me?" Thad asked, keeping his voice low.

Pavan reached up, touching Thad's cheek.

"I always trust you."

The faie smiled, lighting up the features of his face. Affection overflowing, Pavan leant forward, wanting to kiss him. He stopped, drawing back slightly. His heart thumping hard in his chest.

"It is best to maintain the illusion of respectability amongst them while we remain under Lord Hugo Jax. It will be torture, to keep my hands off you. It is for the best, is it not?" Pavan smirked.

Thad frowned, displeased. "Of course."

"Now, I wish to sleep…Have we talked enough for your worries, Thad?" Pavan asked, leaning back to lull against the chair. His eyelids had grown so heavy, he was truly so tired. He had used so much magick in such a short amount of time, Pavan could feel it in his bones.

"For now." Thad sounded far off. His fingers slipped away from Pavan's grasp.

It was too late, Pavan could not keep himself from falling. His breathing slowed as the lapse of his dreams overtook him. It must have been the sea air from the window, the distant sounds of the ocean calling to him that Pavan found himself standing in the sand.

Dreaming. He was dreaming of the sea. So blue, the cold foam washed up over his feet, rising to his ankles. Then he began to hear it, like the whisper of the breeze, a voice lofting towards him.

It was beautiful, enchanting. Calling to him.

Pavan searched the waves, but it was not there. Her voice was not from the sea. Slowly, Pavan turned, drawn closer to it still. Pavan called out to it, but the singing did not stop. It was clear against the wind. Standing upon the embankment, nestled within the long grass stood a girl. His heart began to race and he took a step forward. It was the one who came to him before, the one who wrapped the ribbon around his wrist.

He reached for the ribbon, but his skin was smooth beneath the fold of the tunic he wore. Panic settled as he searched for her again but she was gone, the dark-haired girl disappeared. Magick fluxed, Pavan began to drag, his feet sinking deeper into the sand. He stepped out, trying to reach the place she had once stood.

Each step sinking him beneath the sand, each step burning his muscles to reach the embankment. Crawling his way through the brush, felt like an eternity. Pavan swayed, uneasy, pulling away from the sea to stand upon the rocks looking out over a vast field.

Lavender, as far as the eye could see.

Pavan...

Dinner was set in the back of the villa alongside a wall of open doorways leading out to a vast garden. Candles had been lit, illuminating the room in a soft glow. The height of the heavy beams made of deep stained wood. A welcoming dining space set out for a private affair.

Hugo Jax sat at the head of the table, beside him to his left, his wife smiling. And at the man's right sat his youngest daughter, Juliette. Pavan was seated by the eldest daughter, Vahliene, who was sitting beside her sister. Harmond was seated across from Pavan, with Svein at his side. Thad was so far from Pavan, at the left side of Svein and at the end of the table.

They locked eyes, if only for the briefest of moments and warmth spread over Thad's cheeks causing Pavan to smirk.

"How is your meal, sir?" Vahliene asked, drawing Pavan's attention to her.

"It is very flavorful," he acknowledged, looking down to his plate of veal with roasted vegetables and cream.

Vahliene laughed. "Had you not had a flavor in your great city? Denorn is known for its variety of meals."

"Our cook at the inn was tolerable, but I cannot admit to having tasted many meals at any other establishments."

"Inn, you stayed at the inn?" Juliette chimed in, her young and youthful vigor catching Pavan off guard. She must be about thirteen years old.

"Yes, the inn. It was comfortable and dry."

"How long have you been in our realm?" Hugo Jax asked, drawing into this conversation by the lack of any other.

Pavan felt his eyes flicker to Thad, but he was honest with his host.

"We come from Ledenjour, across the water in Entheas. We have been in Denorn for a few weeks."

Harmond laughed. "A few weeks and you already begin to draw the attention of Denorn's guards."

"Harmond, for shame," tsked the woman beside him. Juliana was a beautiful woman with long, dusty rose hair and the bluest eyes Pavan had ever seen. Pavan could see where Vahliene and Juliette got their attributes. Each with brightly hued hair and vibrant blue eyes, both as pretty as their mother.

"Forgive me, my lady. But I have hardly ever seen such a man stand against them in the way Pavan did. He did not provoke them, he stood his ground."

Svein raised a glass. "Here, here."

Pavan felt heat rise to his ears. "It was nothing."

Vahliene chuckled, her own food forgotten, the slim fingers touching his hand with the softest touch. Pavan felt his skin grow hot, unable to look away from her.

"Nothing, sir? For it was your doing that saved me. I am not ignorant of the danger being apprehended in Denorn would put me in, and had it not been for you I certainly would have been put to the trials." Her voice was silky, a purr in Pavan's ear.

"Then it was my pleasure, returning you safely to your fathers table." Pavan forced a pleasant smile.

He pulled his hand away, reaching for his glass to fill it with more water. His mouth suddenly dry, he needed to quench the unwavering thirst.

"Very well said. I commend you, Pavan, for your bravery." Hugo likewise took up his glass, raising it for Pavan's honor, before taking a drink of the amber liquid.

"I must thank you, Lord Hugo, for allowing me and my companions harborage in your city. It must be a great hindrance to you, at this time." Pavan knew his words struck a nerve, he felt the sudden chill that struck through Hugo Jax as he spoke them. But the man needed to be measured, to be sure they would not be unwelcomed here.

Hugo held his temperament easy. "Nonsense. Any friend of my daughters is a friend to me."

"How long shall we be welcome?"

All the eyes of the table turned to Thad, who was watching them, his food untouched.

"Thaddeus, I presume?" Hugo inquired, glancing at Harmond for confirmation. "You are welcome in Eir, as long as your hearts are at ease."

Thad was straight faced, unmoving.

"I am faie." His tone was unchanged, but Pavan heard the thumping of his heart. "Does that bother you?"

Hugo smiled, returning to the consumption of his meal. "Not at all, my grandmother was part faie...my wife, is also faie."

Thad nodded. "Do you know who I am?"

There was a long silence, Hugo Jax held on to Thad's gaze for longer than was necessary. Finally, the man placed his fork and knife aside.

"I know of you, Thaddeus. I knew of your master, Orin Gaur. But what business he held in Denorn, his station of the old world, is not of my concern. What matters is the future...our future."

Like a dive into ice water, Pavan felt the air rip from his lungs. His eyes locked hard on the lord of this city, the man who held his gaze so pointedly upon Thad, Pavan felt the rise of magick within him clawing at his throat to be free.

"I wish you to be welcome here, Thaddeus. I wish us to become friends, you and I..." Hugo Jax went on.

"Friends?" There was an icy undertone to Thad's bite.

Hugo smiled. "You were known to be a great businessman as Lord Gaur's right-hand man."

"You believe that I can be that man for you?" Thad was sharp.

It was undeniable to Pavan how uncomfortable Thad was, he could sense it in the way the faie held himself, the tone of his voice, but Pavan could not bring himself to speak. His magick fluxed, dancing beneath the surface.

"I have business ventures that could use the eyes of one of value, that can determine if it is well worth committing myself to," Hugo replied.

"I am no longer a businessman, my lord. I am not of that mind anymore," Thad replied, his features complacent.

"Pavan...he is as equal to any businessman," Svein cut through, breaking the stare between the men at opposite ends of the table.

"Svein, that is an overstatement." Pavan shook his head.

But the half giant laughed. "He has modesty, my lord. Pavan is the best of us all. He has led our village through battle, against the rogues of the sea. I have witnessed him take down a Vohlgrum, with his bare hands. He is stronger than most and as strong willed as any lord."

"Svein," Thad hissed under his breath.

"Vohlgrum? Rogues?" Juliana gasped, her eyes wide with wonder.

"Well, you do have modesty. Your pelt, the one you wore, that is a Vohlgrum pelt, is it not?" Hugo asked, his attention so interested in Pavan, they all watched him closely.

"Yes, it is so." Pavan could only nod.

"Ha!" Hugo slammed an open palm down upon the table, beaming with wild excitement.

"Papa," Vahliene smiled, "you frighten our guests, they are not accustomed to such exclamations." Turning away from her father, Vahliene addressed Pavan directly. "You fought off rogues? You must be strong with magick."

Pavan forced a smile. "I have no magick."

"But your eyes are the brightest green. Your grandparents must have been faie..." Vahliene slid her hand onto his once more, looking into his eyes.

"Yes, my grandparents." Pavan felt flush under her inquiring eyes, her skin was soft, but the magick that fluttered beneath the skin was soft and yielding, she did not guard herself, but seemed to willingly flare with it.

"Vahliene," her mother said her name, breaking the contact.

She turned away from Pavan, to speak in a low hushed way across the table with her mother, as they all commenced with their meal. Pavan couldn't think, his skin felt wrong, itching where she touched him.

CHAPTER

8

Alnwick, Realm of Corad.

As Elsa's carriage rumbled through the grand gates of Alnwick, she was struck by the sheer scale of the estate that unfolded before her. The sprawling grounds stretched endlessly, dotted with manicured gardens, cascading fountains, and ancient oak trees that seemed to whisper secrets of centuries past. The estate was a testament to opulence, its stone walls adorned with intricate carvings and its towers rising majestically into the sky. Elsa had always considered her home in Signe impressive, but Alnwick dwarfed it with its grandeur.

As she disembarked, Lahrs greeted her with a warm but apologetic smile. His tunic, a deep blue with gold trim, reminded Elsa of the blue pools in Signe. "Lady Elsa, welcome to Alnwick. I must apologize for Princess Brendolyn's absence. She seems to have taken refuge somewhere since breakfast, and despite my best efforts, I cannot locate her at the moment."

Elsa offered a sympathetic smile, though her curiosity was piqued. "A wayward princess, it seems I am not the only one destined to run away from my tutors. But I am eager to meet her, whenever the chance arises."

Lahrs smiled, genuinely pleased. "Allow me to escort you, perhaps we shall meet with her in the corridors." He gestured towards the impressive entrance hall, where high ceilings and towering columns spoke of both elegance and history. The floors were a polished marble that gleamed under the light of ornate chandeliers.

As they moved through the grand corridors and into the lavish dining hall, Elsa marveled at the meticulous details—each room seemed to outshine the previous one. They passed through a gallery of portraits, each painting capturing the dignified faces of past inhabitants of Alnwick. Lahrs was knowledgeable as he gave an account detailing the history and significance of each area, but Elsa's attention was often drawn to the grandeur surrounding her.

When they reached the library, Elsa's pace slowed. The room was a magnificent expanse of dark mahogany shelves stretching from floor to ceiling, packed with books bound in leather and gold leaf. A large, arched window let in soft, diffuse light, casting a warm glow over the rows of volumes. The scent of aged paper and polished wood filled the air, and Elsa felt a deep sense of tranquility wash over her.

"I'll leave you to explore," Lahrs said, noticing her fascination. "Please, take your time. I must attend to lunch preparations."

Elsa nodded, her eyes never leaving the library's depths as Lahrs departed. She walked slowly through the aisles, her fingers trailing over the spines of ancient tomes. She was drawn to the upper levels of the library, where a wrought iron staircase spiraled upwards. The view from the loft provided a panoramic perspective of the room, and she was struck by the immense collection of books—each shelf brimming with knowledge and history.

As she wandered the upper level, her attention was caught by a faint, melodious sound drifting through the quiet room. Intrigued, she followed the sound until she reached a small, secluded loft area. There, she heard the singing more clearly, a sweet, haunting melody that seemed to float through the air.

Carefully, Elsa climbed a narrow staircase leading to an even higher platform. The song grew louder, accompanied by the occasional soft thump. Peering over the railing of the loft, Elsa's eyes widened in surprise. There, hanging from a sturdy beam, was Princess Brendolyn—upside down, her legs wrapped around the beam and her head hanging below. She was completely absorbed in her singing, her voice carrying a whimsical tune.

Elsa's initial shock quickly gave way to amusement. She couldn't help but laugh softly at the sight. Princess Brendolyn, oblivious to her presence, continued her impromptu performance, her hair cascading like a waterfall.

As Elsa watched, the princess finally noticed her and stopped abruptly, her cheeks flushing with embarrassment. She scrambled to right herself, her graceful movements betraying her initial surprise.

"Princess Brendolyn, I presume?" Elsa said, stepping forward with a warm smile. "I must say, this is quite the unique introduction."

Brendolyn, still slightly disheveled but now smiling sheepishly, descended gracefully from the beam and brushed herself off. "I didn't realize we had company. I hope I didn't startle you."

"Not at all," Elsa replied, her gaze softening. "It's a pleasure to meet you, even under such...unusual circumstances."

Brendolyn laughed, a sound that was as melodious as her singing. "I suppose I've been hiding from responsibilities, and perhaps from myself as well. I hope you'll forgive my unconventional welcome."

Elsa's eyes sparkled with understanding. "I think it's rather charming. But tell me, what was the song you were singing?"

"Oh, just a little something to pass the time," Brendolyn said with a shrug, though her eyes twinkled with a hint of mischief. "Are you Lady Elsa?"

"Yes. I was expected to arrive today. Did Lahrs not tell you?"

Brendolyn rolled her eyes. "He is odious. I have been looking at maps all week and he bores me so I've been hiding. I did not realize today was the day of your arrival."

Elsa laughed. "I have only ever heard Lahrs to be intelligent and interesting. At least that is what Eugene has always said."

"Lahrs is the smartest man I know. But he can be exceedingly dull when he makes me study. Which is often."

"My tutors were never dull. I found my lessons on needlepoint very relaxing."

Brendolyn sighed. "Needlepoint is useless. I never learned."

"Did you have a governess?"

"No."

Elsa was shocked, her eyes expressing it. "No governess? But surely you were taught an instrument? Or how to mend a bonnet, or stockings?"

"I never learned because Lahrs had not taught me." Brendolyn shrugged. "But he had taught me to ride horseback, archery, and to dance, and to hold a sword..."

"You are not at all what I imagined a princess to be."

Brendolyn smiled. Standing before Elsa at nearly the same height. The princess, not dressed in shoes, was slightly shorter. Brendolyn took hold of Elsa's hand. A jolt of magick tingled against Elsa's palm, looking into the large yellow eyes.

"You are not what I imagined a companion to be." There was a brightness to her voice, lofty with magick. Elsa suddenly felt a strong sense of something towards the young innocent face looking back at her. "Shall we be friends?"

Elsa smiled, taking hold of Brendolyn's other hand. "We shall always be together, until the end of our days and Ehnarea takes us to the Veil."

She knew the feeling now, the sudden surge that overpowered her. It was not magick, nor the unwavering beauty of the yellow faie eyes, but the overwhelming power to protect Brendolyn's innocence from everyone around her. Elsa's chest ached, as the mark upon her ribs began to burn, reminding her of the brand.

Elsa reluctantly let go.

"Brendolyn!" Lahrs's voice reverberated through the hushed expanse of the library, bouncing off the tall shelves and ornate ceilings.

The princess's head jerked up in surprise, and she giggled, her face lighting up with mischief. She grabbed Elsa's hand in a firm yet playful clasp, her grip warm and reassuring. Without waiting for a response, she pulled Elsa further along the loft, her laughter ringing like chimes in the vast, quiet space. They hurried down the spiral staircase, the ironwork railing casting intricate shadows on the stone steps beneath their feet.

As they descended, Elsa glanced over her shoulder to see Lahrs at the far end of the library. His posture was a mix of frustration and exasperation, arms crossed and brow furrowed. When their eyes met, Brendolyn's smirk widened, her laughter echoing off the high, arched ceilings. In response, Lahrs's expression softened, though he remained a silent sentinel of authority.

With a sudden shift, Brendolyn tugged Elsa toward a narrow, dimly lit staircase hidden behind a tapestry. The steps led them deeper into the bowels of the estate. Sunlight filtered in through narrow slits in the high windows, casting narrow beams across the cold stone walls, where their hurried footsteps echoed with each descent.

"Will he be angry?" Elsa asked, her breath coming in quick, shallow bursts. Her cheeks flushed from the brisk pace.

Brendolyn's eyes sparkled with a mix of defiance and excitement. "He's a dear friend but far too serious. We can't spend the whole day buried in scrolls and lectures. I refuse to be cooped up indoors!"

They emerged into a lower alcove, where the grandeur of the estate gave way to a more serene, yet equally impressive, inner courtyard. The corridor stretched long and wide, its polished marble gleaming with a soft radiance. A fountain bubbled in the center, its waters reflecting a tranquil melody. Brendolyn led the way with determined strides, weaving through the garden entrance that Lahrs had shown Elsa earlier.

"The gardens are our sanctuary," Brendolyn said, her voice carrying an infectious joy. "It's where we can escape the rigidity of the estate and truly breathe."

Elsa felt a flutter of anxiety as they raced past the corridors, her gaze scanning for any sign of interference—maids or guards who might halt their escape. She saw a few figures in aprons and glimpsed the gleam of swords, but none made any move to stop them. Instead, their faces held a mixture of amusement and resignation. With a shake of their heads, they allowed the princess and her guest to pass unhindered.

Brendolyn's freedom within the estate was palpable, a stark contrast to the constraints Elsa was accustomed to. The walls of Alnwick, while imposing, also held an allure of independence that Elsa began to understand. In the solitude of this northern home, the princess had created her own realm of escapism, where laughter and spontaneity were rare treasures.

As they neared the outer doors, Elsa glanced back and saw Lahrs's familiar figure on an upper balcony, his expression now softened into a tolerant smile. He raised a hand in a casual wave, his gesture a silent acknowledgment of Brendolyn's rebellious streak.

"Come on, Elsa!" Brendolyn urged, pulling her into the open air.

The sudden warmth of the sun bathed Elsa's face, and she stepped onto the soft, verdant grass of the gardens. The sensation of the ground beneath her toes was an unexpected pleasure. Her shoes, ill-suited for the lush terrain, slipped with each step, but she allowed them to fall, reveling in the cool touch of the stone pathways.

The gardens stretched out like a living tapestry, each turn revealing vibrant beds of flowers and winding paths. Brendolyn led the way with an exuberance that matched the garden's colors. Elsa followed closely, the contrast between the freedom of the gardens and the weight of her responsibilities was stark. Yet, as she walked beside Brendolyn, Elsa felt a sense of liberation and kinship that transcended her obligations.

CHAPTER

9

Eir, Realm of Jorn.

Pavan meandered through the lush gardens behind Hugo Jax's villa, where the sprawling estate met the edge of a cliff. The gardens were a tapestry of color, a row of flowering shrubs and carefully manicured hedges, all set against the backdrop of the sea. Below, the water sparkled under the midday sun, a seamless expanse of clear blue that mirrored the sky. In the tranquility of his solitude, Pavan pulled from his jacket the letters he carried with him always. Each one bent and wrinkled from constant reading.

A sudden voice broke his thoughts. "Pavan."

Startled, Pavan turned to find Vahliene standing beside him. Her vibrant blue eyes, the color of the sea on a stormy day, held his gaze with an intensity that made his heart skip. Her warm smile seemed to light up the garden around them. Concealing the letters from sight, at his side.

"You are well, Vahliene?" he asked, trying to keep his voice even.

She smiled, catching sight of his fidgeting hands. "I have interrupted an intimate moment. Forgive the intrusion."

He pocketed the letters, silencing the pounding of his heart.

Vahliene spoke again. "You have news?"

"Old letters." Pavan turned, so they could walk the length of the garden together. His eyes scanned the greenery for a chaperone, or an attendant but discovered quickly that she walked alone.

"From a lover, perhaps," she ventured to ask. Her blush could have been mistaken for the brightness of the sun, it had grown hot in the early hours. "They looked quite old, I presume she is far away?"

"They are not from a lover," Pavan corrected her. "They are from my brother, who lives in Entheas...he lives in Tauf with his new wife." A sense of sadness overtook him, clinging to the memories of London and shaking them off quickly when he noticed Vahliene watching him intently.

"You disapprove of this union?"

Pavan tried to smile. "I have hardly been without him, but I am happy with his choice of bride. Farren is a strong warrior who is skilled in many things. I have recent news that they are expecting their first child in the autumn months."

"But you are saddened."

Pavan glanced over the view of the ocean, his heart beating wildly. "It has always been Malcom's dream to have a family. He talked about settling down, having children...he is able to have the life he wanted..."

Vahliene took his hand and he felt his magick coiling beneath the surface, dancing at the touch she so readily gave him. "Do you want a family of your own?"

Unyielding was the harsh reality that plagued Pavan, remembering the pie maker, Sophie, feeling her body in his hands all those months ago. Pavan drew his hand away from Vahliene delicately, and pulled a rose from the nearest bush, giving it to her in an easy transition. Vahliene took it, smelling the delicate flower, a hint of a smile played at her lips.

"I cannot."

Extending her hand again, Vahliene was determined. "Come, let me show you the village."

"It is unwise to leave the villa..." Pavan took a cautious step back.

Tucking the flower behind her ear, Vahliene laughed, grasping hold of Pavan's arm, guiding them out of the gardens and onto the lane that led down in a slanted curve through the nestled buildings that flanked the road.

"You are perfectly safe in my company."

The heart of the village was nestled at the foot of the estate; three charming stone buildings framed the cobblestone street, their windows glowing with the inviting light of the afternoon. The village bustled with activity—children played in the streets, vendors called out their wares, and the aroma of freshly baked bread drifted through the air.

"You have not told me where you grew up, or where you were born." She kept her conversation light, as they walked.

"Entheas."

Vahliene gave him a look. "That is where you came from, but I wish to know where you were born, Pavan. You do not speak as any traveler we have known before. We have frequented Denorn and have known many sailors who travel the world."

"Far away from here."

Vahliene slowed, looking at Pavan more seriously. "Across the Treacherous Seas? I have heard stories of the magick kin that come down from the realm beyond the oceans."

"I am not from there, but a great distance from here. I lived with Malcom, and my uncle." Pavan found it easy to talk to her, but the more he spoke, the more his heart ached.

"Your mother and father?" Vahliene spoke quite hushed.

"Dead. As well as another brother." Pavan's magick darkened, it began to fester at the core, what little hope in belief his mother and brother had survived that night long ago began to dwindle into a deepening wound in his heart.

"No more melancholy. Let us get something to eat, there are many sweets shops that sell the most divine cakes. I know a place that makes the most heavenly pies—"

Pavan's face paled. "No. Not pies," he stammered, a sudden flush of heat rising to his cheeks. "Anything but pie, Vahliene."

Vahliene's expression shifted from amusement to concern as she observed his agitation. She placed a gentle hand on his, and Pavan felt a tremor run through him. His heart raced as he reached for the small, magical amulet hidden beneath his tunic, its enchantment providing a calming effect that pulsed softly against his skin.

"Are you unwell, Pavan?" Vahliene's voice was soft and full of worry. "You look quite pale. Perhaps we should go back? I should not have spoken so forward before."

The heat of her gaze and her touch made Pavan's throat feel dry and constricted. He longed to retreat from the overwhelming sensations, but then he caught the distant sound of music drifting down the lane—a lilting melody beckoning with the promise of respite.

"Let us not return just yet," Pavan managed to say, forcing a smile despite the turmoil within. "I hear music. Perhaps a dance?"

Vahliene's eyes lit up with interest. "I would love to dance."

Thad stood at the large, arched window of the villa's upper chamber, his gaze fixed intently on the bustling street below. The city beyond was alive with color and movement; carts laden with fresh produce trundled by their wheels creaking rhythmically, and merchants called out their wares with spirited enthusiasm. Thad's eyes darted between the passing figures, searching for any sign of Pavan—a tall, dark silhouette amidst the vibrant chaos—or Vahliene, whose fiery red hair was a beacon against the backdrop of the town.

Every time a cart rolled past or a pedestrian strolled by Thad's heart skipped a beat. The pangs of jealousy he felt when he had first seen Pavan and Vahliene together in the gardens still stung sharply. The sight of Pavan and Vahliene, radiant and full of life, had struck a chord deep within him. They had looked strikingly well-matched, the elegance of the noble lady contrasting vividly with the brooding allure of Pavan's broad figure.

Thad's mind replayed the scene from earlier: Vahliene had taken Pavan's arm with an easy grace, her laughter ringing out like music as they strolled down the garden path. Their departure had seemed almost theatrical, the sunlight catching the glint of Vahliene's hair and the confident stride of Pavan as they made their way towards the village square. They had moved with a perfect harmony that Thad found both captivating and infuriating.

The window frame, carved from dark mahogany, felt cool against his fingertips as he gripped it tightly. Thad's jealousy was a bitter undercurrent to his anxiety. He was keenly aware of Vahliene's allure, her charm that had enchanted so many. Her youth and vivacity were a stark contrast to the dark, somber aura of Pavan, making their companionship all the more perplexing.

With each passing minute, the city below seemed to blur into a kaleidoscope of movement and color. The distant sound of music, which had once seemed inviting, now felt like a distant reminder of the disconnect Thad felt—a reminder that he was not part of that vibrant dance of life, but a spectator waiting in the shadows.

"No sign of them yet, sir?" Hugo Jax, was not a silent man, who entered the room with such noise it irritated Thad greatly.

Glancing towards him only briefly as the man entered, before looking back towards the street below. Hoping for Pavan's swift return through the gate and back into the sanctuary of his arms.

"I was admiring your town, my lord." Thad spoke louder than he ought, masking the irritation in his voice.

A chuckle. "You are very dutiful to your companion, but he is safe with Vahliene. The village knows her well, no harm shall come to them."

"I have no doubt," he stated absently.

Thad saw the calm in the streets below. From what he knew of Eir told to him by countless others, he expected the slums, destitution of spirits, hungry peasants that paced the streets. Thad was ashamed to think of what he imagined the life of their lord, the life Hugo Jax was to live as a man of the people.

Now, seeing them content, seeing them happy, even in their lack of trade with the outside world, Thad was shaken by the resolution. He marveled at the happiness, even of the servants who tended to the rooms.

"Your friend is born of magick, like yourself?"

Thad felt the hairs on his neck raise. "He is faie."

Hugo chuckled and Thad turned to see the man standing at an identical window, looking out over the street below. He was tall, and stately. Dressed in fine garments, but Thad also saw the wariness, he saw the fading in the silks, the lackluster of shine in the metal brads and buckles that adorned the great Lord of Eir.

"Amazing to know there is a place where our people can thrive," Hugo stated, his pleasure in the prospect written on his face.

Thad hesitated. "There was only us in Ledenjour that were faie. In Tauf, perhaps...in the great elven city perhaps, but not elsewhere."

Hugo looked on, keeping his gaze out of the window.

"Then we are a dwindling people. As all the wise women have feared." There was a melancholy that hung in the air and Thad could only listen. "Augusta had fallen, which began the great decline. Such a great city is now reduced to industry. No magick to spark the great flames of the temples, no longer do the trees sing."

Shame burned in Thad, keeping his gaze hard out the window. Lost in the landscape of the old stone, the crumbling architecture beneath the thriving population above. He remembered the great war. He remembered listening to the lords boast of their success. Thad believed in the goodness of the destruction that befell them all, to not have to endure the alternative.

Gladly accepting the death of his own kind, of all the faie, reduced to nothing to save them from the fate far worse. He had seen so many young faie in Denorn vibrant and full of life, return from the tower of Hilvaer changed. Vacant of magick, obedient to their master. Thad was sickened by what he witnessed. He was ashamed by what he had helped to accomplish.

Hugo Jax spoke on. "Now, we must rebuild. They cannot silence our song, not forever. Not all of us have lost the gift of our voices, Thaddeus. Soon we shall continue the tradition, soon the streets shall be alive once more."

"Your town drains more profit than your import," Thad stated. It was a fact. He had seen the ledgers the night before. He has seen the last four months have declined the town even further.

Hugo coughed, drawing away from the window to his sideboard, pouring himself a drink. "Yes, it is true."

Thad scoffed. "You have done nothing to prevent it. You let your people continue their lives as if nothing has changed. They eat, dance, celebrate but not a word against you, they speak your praise at their abundance. Will they still speak your honor when they are starving?"

Hugo drank, the silence pounding in Thad's ears.

"You speak of this contract, and I have read it through." Thad sighed heavily. Gaining interest from the man, Thad felt the roll of anger in his belly.

"It is a great plan to align with Dern. They are our brothers in the fall of Augusta." Hugo was speaking calmly.

"Your contract has a fault..." Thad stated.

Hugo frowned, a rare sight.

Thad went on, "You intend to marry your eldest daughter to Lord Arvel."

A long pause. "It is spoken of as an excellent match. Lord Arvel is rich and holds sanction in Jorn as a high lord. With the alliance, we shall prosper, our trades shall be open."

Thad held his anger, swallowing it down.

"Lord Arvel is sixty-five, Hugo. Vahliene is nineteen." He held the lord's unwavering gaze, trying to be respectful. "She would not be loved by him. Her bloom shall be beaten from her."

Hugo paled. "He is a respectable man—"

"Lord Arvel is as tall as he is fat. Eating three portions of chicken every evening along with Taastra port wine. When he is cross, and that is very often, Arvel likes to inflict pain upon his horses when riding. When he isn't out riding on his hunt in the forest of Dern, he is with his whores. Shall I tell you how he likes to beat them, my lord?" Thad felt his face grow flush as he watched the color leave Hugo Jax, only to be replaced by a harrowing paleness.

"He has promised to rebuild."

Thad's lip twitched around his fury. "I was seventeen, the first time Lord Arvel visited Orin Gaur. He was there on business in Denorn, one of his ships transporting his horses from Corad was set to arrive. But the seller only gave him three, he was promised four. Arvel is not a patient man. He does not take lightly to being disappointed."

Hugo looked green.

"You know who I am, Hugo. You know my master. To keep his client satisfied, Lord Arvel returned every week, and every week I was flogged. Every week I was raped by that man for his displeasure. I have scars upon my back from his belt. I hold the ruin of his hands upon my body and my mind. I have read your contract with him...I have read the words he puts down on paper to give you hope, to give you reprieve." Thad hardened, his aching chest toughening his exterior. "He is a liar, Hugo. He will use your city for his drug dens, his horse races...and if you defy him, if you *displease* him? Arvel shall ruin her, Hugo. Would you be willing to sacrifice her innocence, for a handful of gold from the king?"

Hugo was horrified, pale, his drink forgotten. He stumbled back, collapsing onto a chair. "What else is there?" he muttered, a man utterly lost.

Thad was not heartless. He felt for Hugo, knowing what hopelessness he felt. He was a man trapped, like a mouse backed into a corner surrounded by hungry cats. Thad sighed, his thoughts resolute. Knowing there was a third option. A reasonable option.

Taking from his pocket the few gems he carried there, the few he held on his person, identical to the ones they kept safely in their room amongst their belongings. Thad placed the gems upon the small table set in the distance between them.

Hugo watched him, attentively, his eyes growing wide as he saw the glint of the stones, knowing their worth. Gems, once harvested in Ledenjour for centuries and sold for great sums in Jorn for little portions of what they now carried. Hugo had never seen such size.

"You know what they are?" Thad asked.

Hugo rubbed at his mouth, his eyes glinting with tears. "They are shielk glass, worth more than Entheas gold...but they say the last of the veins in Entheas were washed away."

"Ledenjour was the last of the great mining cities of this stone...Do you know of its worth?" Thad asked, seeing Hugo reach out to touch one, he shook his head. "This one is enough to withdraw your contract from Arvel."

Hugo's eyes flickered to Thad warily. "I never signed it."

Thad frowned. "Do you believe he would let it end there? This shall be traded for the gold you need to settle that debt, Hugo. And this one..." Thad moved the second gem to Hugo's other hand. "This one shall be enough to rebuild."

Pavan sank into the warmth of the small basin, the steaming water enveloping him in a soothing embrace. He sighed contentedly, lifting his hands and watching the water cascade from his open palms, each droplet catching the soft light of the flickering candles that lined the edge of the tub. The day's events replayed in his mind—the vibrant street of the town, the mesmerizing dance with Vahliene, and the magick that seemed to hum in sync with her every movement.

Returning to the villa after their walk had been a stark transition. The lively rhythm of the town faded as they entered the grand, imposing walls of the estate. Pavan had left Vahliene to retire to his room, seeking solitude to process the day. When he arrived, he found Thad waiting for him, his face clouded with an unsettling gloom.

It didn't take long for Thad to reveal the cause of his distress. "Hugo's retracting the contract with Dern," Thad said, his voice heavy with frustration. "We're not leaving. At least, not yet. Hugo's decided to keep us here for another year. I'll be helping him with his business, and we'll be involved in opening the trade routes with Corad."

The news hit Pavan like a cold wave. The sense of being trapped in a situation he could not control was stifling. The prospect of staying longer in this place, with its opulent façade hiding the political machinations beneath, was daunting.

Just then, a sharp knock at the door jolted Pavan from his thoughts. He straightened in the water, a splash echoing through the chamber as he turned to see who had arrived. The door creaked open, and Vahliene stepped into the bathing chamber.

Her entrance was almost ethereal. Her fiery red hair flowed loosely down her back, catching the light in a cascade of brilliant hues. She wore a simple cotton gown that clung to her curves with an understated elegance, a stark contrast to the opulence of the villa's surroundings. The gown, though plain, accentuated her grace and beauty, making her presence seem both intimate and startling.

Pavan's eyes widened, his heart racing at the unexpected sight. The warm glow from the candles danced across her skin, adding a softness to her already captivating appearance. He quickly looked away, trying to regain his composure, but the intrusion left him feeling exposed and unsettled.

"Pavan," Vahliene's voice was a gentle murmur, her tone soft and unassuming. "I didn't mean to startle you. I thought you might want some company, or perhaps a moment to talk."

Pavan sank deeper into the warmth of the basin, letting the water soothe his weary muscles. The steam rose in thick, fragrant clouds, filling the room with a heavy, oppressive heat. As he relaxed, his eyes remained fixed on Vahliene, who stood by the edge of the bath, her gaze roaming over his exposed chest with an intensity that made him uneasy. Her eyes lingering on the scar that was what remained of his brush with the longsword in Ledenjour, and the swipe of the great beast's claws that poisoned him.

"You should be in your chambers, Vahliene," Pavan said, his voice tinged with frustration. "The villa is quiet, and here you are, wasting your flattery on me."

Vahliene brushed a curl of her fiery red hair from her neck, her skin glistening with perspiration. The heat from the bath had intensified the room's sultry atmosphere. She met his gaze with a defiant sparkle in her sapphire eyes. "You don't know what I want," she replied softly.

Pavan shook his head. "You've come to seduce me, haven't you? To take from me what you desire before you're given away to a man unworthy of your honor."

Her eyes locked onto his, shimmering with a mix of sadness and determination. "I am to marry Lord Arvel of Dern," she said after a pause.

"Lord Arvel," Pavan repeated, his tone measured. "He will dictate every choice you make once you're married. This moment—this choice—is supposed to be yours."

Vahliene scoffed, her expression wavering as she struggled to maintain her composure. "I am resigned to this fate. A man who demands and never gives, a life dictated by my father's wishes. But tonight—tonight is mine."

"No," Pavan said firmly, rising from the basin. The hot water cascaded down his body as he stepped out, grabbing a cotton towel to wrap around his waist. The room's heat and the closeness of their proximity intensified his senses. His magick heightened as he approached Vahliene, her once-confident demeanor now diminished to a posture of defeat. Gently, he lifted her chin with his fingers, compelling her to meet his gaze.

Tears glistened in her eyes, and Pavan reached up to brush them away with tender care. "I cannot be your lover, Vahliene."

"Are you denying me?" Her voice was a soft whisper, laden with hurt. "Today, in the gardens, you wished for a family...you desire to be loved."

"That time for me is gone, Vahliene. I cannot hope for a wife to birth my children, nor the comfort of the devoted heart of someone dearest to me...I am doomed to a lonely life."

She reached out, touching his cheek to bring him close, her skin was soft, alluring in the low candlelight. Magick danced in a shimmer of tantalizing seduction, coiling towards him with a dangerous desire. Pavan wanted to run, wanted to pry himself from her touch in fear of hurting her, like he had hurt Sophie.

"Love cannot be forgotten by those who seek the comfort of their soul."

"You seek my love, when your heart sings for the lonely man that has captured you completely." He spoke gently, despite the crashing waves of torment in his blood with the pulse of her magick beneath his touch.

"Harmond has told you a falsehood."

"Harmond has said nothing to me," Pavan said, their bodies so close now it was difficult to pull away. Pavan's eyes flickered to the bare contrast of Vahliene's pale neck, to the rise and fall of her breast as she breathed faster. "I can feel your love for him, Vahliene...in the very pulse of your blood, there is no denying your love."

Drawing closer, Pavan could practically taste the magick pulsing through Vahliene's veins, it thrummed with urgency, pounding like a drum. She was vulnerable, weakened by any defense against him. Pavan wanted to take her magick, it would be easy to convince her to give it up to him. His thoughts became cold, shuddering at the thought.

Her face flushed. "It would ruin everything."

"You are not going to marry Lord Arvel," Pavan whispered and the thrill within her body soared. Her bright blue eyes searched him with wonder. "We have given your father respite, to break the contract. There is no union between Eir and Dern...You are free to love whom you desire, Vahliene."

"It is your doing?" Her voice trembled.

"I have done nothing." Pavan shrugged, capturing a stray tear that fell from Vahliene's eyes. "Do not be afraid to love Harmond."

She leaned up, kissing the curve of Pavan's cheek. "You are a good man, Pavan."

"Good night, Vahliene," he said, his voice steady despite the tumult inside him.

Without waiting for her response, Pavan quickly retreated from the chamber, his skin prickling with the residue of their encounter. He hurried down the corridor to the room he shared with Thad, struggling to contain the unsettling desire that still thrummed within him.

As he entered the room, the door clicked shut behind him with a loud finality. Thad, lounging comfortably on a small settee in a silken robe over his under trousers, looked up from his book with a warm smile.

"I almost thought you had drowned," Thad said with a chuckle, his eyes twinkling with curiosity.

Pavan hurried to kneel before Thad, slotting himself between Thad's legs, kissing the faie with passionate desperation. Pavan's hair dripped along the contours of his back, giving him the chills. Thad's skin was warm and Pavan followed the line of the faie's bare chest, grasping his narrow hips. Beneath him, Thad groaned.

"Cursed magick," Pavan growled, nipping at Thad's lip. "Can I not have you, Thad...can I not take you as mine..." Pavan mumbled, his lips trailing along the line of Thad's jaw, tasting the salty skin of the faie's throat.

"Pavan, is everything alright?" Thad gasped, his hands raking through dark hair.

"They all have magick. They all have a touch of magick in their blood. She most of all...I want to drain her life force, Thad." Pavan paused his kissing, desperately clinging to him and feeling the thump-thump of each heartbeat between them.

Thad tensed, but did not react, his hands gripping tighter into Pavan's hair, scraping his nails hard against his scalp, causing Pavan to groan.

"And you...*sweetest*, Thad," Pavan cooed, nuzzling into the dip of Thad's chin. "Sweetest magick of them all, but so strong to resist me. I could break you, couldn't I? I could drain your life in a moment."

"Pavan, enough," Thad hissed.

But Pavan's chest ached. "All these people trust me to keep them safe. Hugo trusted me in his home. He is a shepherd watching the wolf walk amongst his flock wearing sheep's skin. How long before I spill blood..."

Thad yanked hard on Pavan's hair. "Enough, Pavan. Don't talk like that."

Pavan hissed, yanking Thad by the hips, coming face to face with the faie, and those orange eyes wild. His body smelled of fear, trembling beneath him.

"I am a monster, Thad. If I cannot control that part of me, the world will burn in devastation," he rasped. "You can feel it, the danger I pose to those around me. You know the risks of being here. I sense your fear, you know it to be true."

Thad gulped, touching Pavan's cheek. "You have learned to control it."

"Not enough." Pavan bent low, his lips trailing over Thad's soft skin. "With the change of the seasons I grow in my strength, I have control but my need for more is all consuming. On these shores it is heightened by the presence of such pain and sorrow..."

Thad's jawline was smooth, as Pavan grazed his teeth over the curve of pale skin. His hands trailing from hips to chest, to throat. Then down again, his desire coiling in the pit of him, desperate to meld into the open mind before him.

"Pavan," Thad sighed, pulling Pavan in closer.

"If I fall too far, you must promise to stop me, whatever it takes," Pavan pleaded. "Your dagger was given to you by Meilyr. Promise me, it shall be your truest ally. Promise me, I can rely upon your hand."

Thad's eyes grew wide. "It would kill you."

"No." Pavan shook his head, smiling at the heightened smell of fear. "It wouldn't kill me. I would never ask you to do such a thing."

Desire mixed with the lustrous magick that clouded his mind and breathing in the scent of fear and want, Pavan grasped at the narrow hips of the faie. It was the nearest Pavan had ever come to losing himself, his desire so delightfully wound within his body, wishing to take hold. A groan fell from Thad's lips, as Pavan pressed himself further into the faie until he felt the rigid length pressed against him.

"Thad..." Pavan whispered, kissing the pulse point of the faie's neck.

Thad reached up to touch Pavan's cheek and a remarkable warmth spread over his skin at the touch. A smile played at the faie's lips as he leaned up to kiss him, languid, passionate and desperate, each breath melding them closer. Like diving into an icy pool, Pavan's mind fell backward, dragging Thad with him, stepping over the threshold of his own mind, into a room of calm. Pavan stood in the confines of the room as it shifted with magick. Pavan turned, seeing him standing in an aura of magick.

Thad's skin shimmered, his eyes bright like a blazing furnace.

There was no sharp pain of magick. Every touch was a dance of pleasure, sensations flowing in and out with ease and tranquility. Pavan thought of the sea, it was almost similar, but this was also something else, something deeper and richer. Pavan wrapped his arms around Thad's middle, bringing them closer.

"It won't last long," Thad gasped, clinging to Pavan for support.

They stumbled back, a bed plush beneath them, catching them as they fell. Pavan chuckled, leaning over Thad, their bodies flush. Leaning down to kiss the line of Thad's shimmering jaw.

"We are still entangled, perhaps someone shall walk in on us." Pavan pressed himself along the solid frame of Thad.

Shaking his head, Thad gripped hard into Pavan's hark hair. "Do not waste time...take me. Before it fades."

Pavan bent forward, kissing the faie's welcoming mouth and taking hold of the faie's wrists, pinning his hands above him. Pavan smirked as Thad wrapped his legs about his middle, attempting to flip them, but Pavan laughed as he leaned up to gaze into the fiery orange eyes beneath him.

"Try all you can, Thad, but your strength is not enough here." Pavan held firm, as he began to shift his hips, earning a pleased moan.

Eagerly taking every moment he could, Pavan pulled free what cloth he could find, exposing the expanse of freckled skin. Magick fizzled under his touch as each pass of his fingertips sent electric shockwaves up his spine, feeling the pleasure they both shared. As so many cold nights in Ledenjour had been spent this way, Pavan knew every inch of the body that lay before him. Pavan knew where to touch and bite to elicit the most sensation. It was easy to bring them closer, until they no longer knew where Pavan began or Thad ended. Becoming a tangled body of limbs that danced, gracefully moving together.

It ended at their peak, Pavan crashing back into his body gasping for breath. His arms trembling, the magick roaring to life within his body so suddenly he grimaced, pushing back Thad who trembled, and panting to catch his breath.

Pavan stood, stumbling away.

"Pavan, you must sit down," Thad advised, his breath coming in short, but Pavan shook his head.

"That was dangerous, Thad," Pavan hissed as his skin crawled with residual magick. Tumbling back, he sat on one of the sitting chairs nearby. They had not separated slowly, it was rushed and Pavan felt it in the very core of his being, as if parts of his soul had been ripped from him.

"God," Pavan groaned, his body shivering, desperate to hold on to the pleasure that rolled through him. Remembering the feeling of Thad's body, his smell, his voice.

"Pavan." Thad's voice felt far away.

He pulled back at the tender touch upon his arm. Recoiling from Thad's tenderness and unable to explain the sense of shame or disgust.

"It was your doing," he gulped, closing his eyes to the agony that began to settle. "Your magick bled into mine when we crossed. I can taste it...I can feel your agony. Your shame." Tears spilled from Pavan's eyes.

"Forgive me." Thad was soft as he knelt before Pavan, holding his hand.

The aftermath of their intense union left Pavan languishing in a haze of shame and lingering pleasure. His head lolled back, the once exhilarating connection now tainted by a sickening mix of regret and raw sensation. "I see them all, Thad," he murmured, his voice cracking. "I feel every one of them touching you." The realization was a festering wound, a putrid sensation that churned in his stomach.

Thad's expression shifted to one of stark, icy detachment. The warmth in his eyes faded, leaving only a stony resolve. He drew back, his face a mask of concern and sadness.

Pavan tilted his head back, struggling to cast off the remnants of their entwined magick. His skin prickled as the residual energy pulsed and shimmered beneath his pores. He focused on dispelling the magick that had intertwined with Thad's, drawing on the distant call of the sea for solace. The waves' rhythmic crash and the plaintive cry of seagulls reached him through the haze, a melody of calm amidst his inner turmoil.

Her voice, ethereal and soothing, began to sing softly in the recesses of his mind. It was a lullaby from the depths of his memory, the comforting song of the sea calling him to rest. Pavan allowed the oceanic calm to envelop him, the sound of the waves blending with her voice, guiding him into a state of tranquil sleep.

CHAPTER

10

Sunlight streamed through the tall windows, casting intricate patterns across the polished wooden floor. Thad moved swiftly through the grand house, the muted thud of his footsteps resonating through the hallway. Each step carried an urgent rhythm as he ascended the grand staircase, its banister cool beneath his touch. His mind raced, driven by the letter he had received—a missive sealed with an emblem he knew all too well.

The urgency quickened his pace as he neared the second-floor landing. He reached the door to the study, where he presumed the master of the house would be engrossed in his reading. Thad's hand tightened around the door handle, his breath catching in his throat.

With a sudden burst of motion, he pushed open the door, only to be met with an unexpected and disconcerting sight. His eyes widened in shock, his breath coming in short gasps as he took in the scene before him—Hugo's daughter and her betrothed were entangled in a passionate embrace, their muffled sounds of intimacy filling the room.

Thad's instinct was to retreat so he spun on his heel, trying to close the door shut quietly to preserve the sanctity of the moment. The sound of the door closing was accompanied by the sharp intake of breath from within, and a gasp echoed through the corridor.

"Forgive me," Thad smirked, attempting not to chuckle, unable to forget the looks upon Harmond and Vahliene as they scrambled away from each other.

"Wait," came the soft voice of Vahliene when Thad began to retreat.

He reluctantly turned back. Her cheeks were flush, her hair wild about her as she quickly hastened to right her gown. Thad tapped the letter in his hand.

"Please, you mustn't utter a word of this to my father."

"Does your father know you frequent the company of the chamberlain?" Thad stole a glance at the door over her head. "In your fathers private offices?"

Vahliene colored deeply, desperately grabbing Thad's arm.

"Please, Thaddeus. My father cannot know of this or he shall not approve of us being married," she whispered and Thad could feel the magick flutter around them.

"You have known Harmond for many years."

"Yes. And I have you to thank for allowing me the blessing of being his." Vahliene leaned close, placing a kiss upon Thad's cheek. Her warm lips made Thad's skin tingle.

"I have only set what is right...it was wrong of your father to sign a contract with Lord Arvel."

Vahliene's expression softened into a veil of melancholy. "I would have married him, to keep my father's position secure."

Thad's face lost all color, his smile collapsing into a somber frown. He withdrew from Vahliene, the delicate girl's curiosity evident in her stunning blue eyes. Her gaze, framed by cascades of dark copper hair, seemed to pierce through the veneer of Thad's composure.

"Lord Arvel would have altered your very essence, Vahliene," Thad said quietly, his voice heavy with concern. "He is a man known for his harsh ways. You deserve far more than a fate of cold obedience."

The pity in Vahliene's eyes deepened as she reached out, her fingers brushing a stray lock of Thad's hair from his forehead. There was something enchanting about her—something pure and untouched that spoke of ancient magick and untold beauty. Thad understood why songs were sung of her, why her name was wrapped in tales of wonder. It was as though the first blossoms of spring had emerged from the frost, their freshness undeniable.

"Is there not one you would sacrifice for, Thaddeus?" Vahliene's voice was gentle, but it carried a weight of unspoken longing.

Thad's heart raced, his thoughts churning as he turned his gaze away. His fingers drummed restlessly against the letter clutched in his hand, a stark reminder of his duty to find Hugo Jax and deliver the urgent message. "I've overstayed my welcome," he murmured, glancing at the door Vahliene had recently exited. "I must seek out your father."

As Thad began to leave, he heard Vahliene's hurried footsteps behind him. "Have I offended you, sir?" she asked, her voice tinged with concern.

His face flushed with a sudden heat and he dared not turn around. "You are mistaken. I am not offended."

"Is Pavan your lover?" The question was direct, cutting through the tension.

Thad faltered on the staircase, his heart pounding as he struggled to find his voice. "He has trouble sleeping," he managed, his throat tightening. "I assist him as a healer."

Vahliene's eyes glinted with curiosity. "My maid speaks of your habits—how you kneel before him, how his skin glows with ancient runes. She has heard you whispering in the elven tongue."

Thad's mouth felt dry. "Pavan is my lord. I serve him as my duty demands."

Vahliene smirked, a hint of mischief in her eyes. "Is that a rehearsed line, Thaddeus? It seems you have practiced it well to deflect those who might question you."

"That is no lie," Thad insisted. "I will serve him faithfully until my last breath."

Her smile widened. "There is your spirit, little faie. Speak of him from your heart, and your bond will strengthen."

"We are not bonded," Thad said, shaking his head firmly.

"Not in the old ways," Vahliene conceded, "but I can sense when closeness exists. Is he your destined match?"

Thad's voice trembled. "We are neither destined nor fated. Go to your love, Vahliene. Celebrate with Harmond as you prepare for your union," he urged.

Vahliene took Thad's hand, her gaze caught between uncertainty and hope.

Thad held her hand gently, his touch conveying a mixture of sorrow and resignation. "I lost my chance at happiness," he said softly. "But you have been granted what I could never have. Carry your love into your union, Vahliene. Live in the light for those who cannot."

He watched as she walked away, her form slipping back into the room where Harmond awaited. Thad remained on the step, an empty void opening within him. Memories of a past filled with dreams of a different future danced on the edge of his mind—a future once bright with promise, now overshadowed by loss and betrayal. The boy who had toiled in Monselt's salt beds, who had once aspired to take his place beside a girl with rose-hued eyes, was now just a shadow of what might have been.

The anger towards the usurper surged within him, his teeth grinding against the weight of past injustices. Hot tears of rage and frustration traced down Thad's cheeks. He wiped them away with a fierce determination, locking away those memories and steeling his heart against the painful reminders of what had been stolen from him.

Pavan stepped out into the warm night. Taking in the dazzling lights that hung high above from the thick twine from balustrade to balustrade. Flowers perfumed the air, with a hint of lavender on the breeze. He smiled, stepping out to join the other villagers as they made their way towards the center square. It would be there that Vahliene and Harmond waited for the guests to join in the celebrations of their union.

Keeping to the outer edges of the center, Pavan watched the scene unfold, taking in the beauty of laughter and joy. The people of Eir were content, celebrating the union of one so beloved by many. Vahliene was beautiful in her long gown spun in gold—a tradition of the elves that was brought to the realms and shared with the villages of faie centuries ago.

He smiled, when the young woman glanced his way, her fiery hair ornamented with a crown of flowers. Beads of glass dangled in the fall of her long hair, catching the lights to make it glisten like stars.

She broke away from her husband to walk towards him and Pavan felt the flutter of nerves, unsettled by the evening.

"Pavan." She opened her arms to him, embracing Pavan with such warmth it took his breath away.

"*Favor find you,*" he spoke in the traditional elven manner.

"You improve on your languages." She smiled, taking both of his hands in hers, they were soft, adorned with gold rings and the scent of lavender. It tickled Pavan's nose. He wanted to pull away, unsettled by the warmth.

"Only a little…" Pavan glanced at Harmond from across the way, seeing the joy as the man spoke with those closest to him. "You should rejoin your celebrations."

"You are so determined to be melancholy."

"I am not melancholy." Pavan smiled, attempting to pull away, but Vahliene would not have any of it, taking his arm in hers.

"Would you take a wife, now that my people shall thrive under the care of your companion. They already talk of rebuilding the theatre in your honor."

Pavan frowned. "I shall not have a wife, Vahliene."

"A husband, perhaps." She stopped so they stood near the outer edges of the celebrations, beneath a large trellis of vines. Away from the music it was calmer here, they could speak without raising their voices.

Pavan's face was hot. "It is illegal."

"In Jorn, there are rules." Vahliene nodded. "But in Eir, we do not uphold the common prejudices as they do in the great city. Here, you are free to be whom you wish…to love whom you wish. Whether elven, human, faie…or Ehlfern."

Pavan stumbled on what to say, but Vahliene soothed a hand over his jacket.

"Do not be afraid, none shall understand your true magick, Pavan." Vahliene touched his cheek. "You most certainly should not be afraid to love Thaddeus openly while you remain in Eir. Here, there are many who do not hide from that which Ehnarea blesses."

"Vahliene." Pavan shook his head.

"Think about it." Vahliene kissed his cheek, smiling warmly. "In time, you will understand the risk is worth the reward."

Turning from him, Pavan watched her walk back through the crowd, returning to Harmond's side in a wave of laughter and merriment.

"Will you be joining in the merriment?" Svein's voice cut through the sounds of the crowd and Pavan turned to look at the half giant.

"It is possible, I have not celebrated like this since our time in Ledenjour." Pavan smirked, watching the great half giant take a large drink of ale from the cup in his hand.

Svein barked a laugh. "Very true!"

Pavan saw the glint in the large man's eyes. Taking in the particularly clean garments, brushed hair and oiled beard. It suited the man to look so fine, standing amongst those that were fair and small. Pavan laughed to himself when three ladies with matching flower crowns came to stand with them, touching Svein's arm and laughing at his jokes.

"Don't wait forever, Pavan. Enjoy the night." Svein cheered, raising his glass as he let the three beautiful women lead him away, equally thrilled at their conquest.

Pavan stood at the outer edge long enough to watch him dance with each of them. But sorrow began to twist its way in Pavan's chest. His smile and enjoyment dampened as the night progressed. Looking back up the road at the building they had called their home for so many weeks. A light remained on in the upper rooms, in the corner of the house where Hugo Jax offices were housed. Thad had a conference with Hugo all morning, and they were not yet finished with the remaining documents needed for the rest of the season. Loneliness clouded him with sadness.

"Would you like to dance, Pavan?" He turned at the soft gentle voice of Juliette, Vahliene's young sister. She was dressed in white, with her long hair draped behind her like a veil. She wore a crown of small white flowers, indicating her innocence and youth.

"Perhaps one of Harmond's cousins would be a better partner."

She sighed, casting her eyes in the direction of the young men who crowded the ale cart, laughing and enjoying their pack of boisterous boys. Pavan saw the one he knew Juliette fancied, a boy of sixteen with short curled golden hair and pale light grey eyes.

"He is a fool," she said at last.

Pavan took Juliette by the hand, looping it with his arm, guiding her in a small walk around the square. Ducking under the arches of flowers that bloomed, perfuming their path. They remained quiet for a time, until Pavan broke the silence.

"Give him another year, Juliette, when his thoughts of battles and ships have faded into a softer calm of poetry and dancing. He admires your beauty, but he will not value your gentle nature if he is rushed to courtship."

Juliette slowed her steps, looking desperately up at Pavan with doelike eyes.

"It is terrible to wait," she whispered.

Pavan touched her hand, nestled in the curve of his arm, her skin was soft. She was delicate, her pulse fluttering with faint magick. Looking down at the young girl so desperate to grow up, searching for the love of the boy who barely glanced at her more than to think she was beautiful.

"But you will not need to wait for a dance," he reassured her.

Stepping forward towards the swirling color of dancers, Juliette beamed with radiance, giggling happily as Pavan took hold of her waist. Guiding her in the steps, following the crowd. It was liberating, to be able to move again. Pavan always enjoyed dancing, it was after all the first of his passions from a young age. Entering into ballet, along with the theatre. But it was because of Penelope that he truly practiced, exceeding the boys of his age to enter the older classes in order to dance with her.

"You look sad." Juliette shifted his thoughts.

"I am very happy." Pavan smiled, looking down at his worried partner, but the young girl stopped, reaching up to touch his cheek.

"You are crying."

Pavan wiped his tears away on his sleeve, his body flushed, shaking away the tremendous weight of sadness and returning himself to be content and happy. "It is nothing, Juliette. Let us keep dancing."

"I think there is someone who wants to dance with you." She pointed behind him.

Following her outstretched hand, Pavan saw at the edge of the square—Thad. Dressed in a silk tunic, covered by a moss green doublet embroidered with leaves. His hair was freshly brushed, radiantly beautiful and Pavan's heart beat faster.

"Go to him, Pavan." Juliette pushed on his arm.

They met in the center, Thad weaving his way through the dancing couples, as Pavan did the same. Standing near beneath the bright twinkling lights, Pavan was breathless. All these weeks they had kept apart in public, for fear of the talk amongst them. Thad was wary of whispers, he did not like the watchful eyes of those he did not know of trust. Pavan looked into the bright orange eyes.

"I was kept on business," Thad said, his cheeks flushed under Pavan's gaze.

"You're here now, *mo ghrá*." Pavan raised his hand, caressing Thad's cheek.

Feeling the hesitation in Thad, but the faie did not pull away. Leaning forward, Pavan wrapped his other arm about Thad's middle, bringing their chests flush. A rapid thump of heartbeat sounded between them. Pavan waited, breathing in Thad's scent as he watched for disapproval, by now Thad would have pulled back, or refused the touch. But Thad brought a hand up, to the fall of Pavan's dark hair.

"Tell me to stop." Pavan smirked.

Thad grasped the hair at the base of Pavan's neck. "Just kiss me."

Pavan kissed him hard. Savoring the taste on his tongue, longing for more. Bringing them closer, holding onto Thad tighter.

Pavan stumbled back, falling into the darkened room where the hearth lay cold, untouched for hours. His chest heaved as he tried to steady his breath, his eyes locked on the figure standing in the doorway. With a loud slam, the door shut, cutting off the faint sounds of revelry drifting from below. He had forgotten all about the celebrations when Thad grabbed his hand after the kiss they shared. Without hesitation, he had followed, climbing the steps into the vacant corridors where their rooms waited. Now, silence wrapped around the chamber, cold and unyielding.

Suddenly, fire roared to life in the hearth, an explosion of orange light that cast flickering shadows across the walls adorned with heavy tapestries. Thad stood before the flames, his hand slowly falling away as the brilliant inferno danced in his eyes. His silhouette loomed large, the shadow seeming to move with a will of its own.

"They talk about us," Thad murmured, his voice low, almost a whisper. "Have you heard the whispers?"

Pavan stepped closer, drawn by the heat of both flame and desire radiating from the faie. His hand hesitated before brushing against the silk of Thad's shirt. "We've never cared about their thoughts, Thad. Let them whisper."

Thad scoffed, the sound carrying a trace of bitterness. "I don't care what they think of me..."

Seizing the moment, Pavan let his hand rest firmly against the curve of Thad's tunic, feeling the strength beneath the fabric, his heart fluttering in rhythm with the faint pulse of magick under his touch. Leaning in, his breath warm against Thad's ear, he whispered, "But you care what they think of me."

His lips grazed Thad's skin, sending a shiver through the space between them as his fingers traced over the silk-clad chest, pulling their bodies closer together. "It doesn't matter to me, how they whisper about my magick, or how I choose to spend my days in your company. As long as I have you, Thad, the rest of it is nothing."

Thad tilted his head back, his copper hair brushing against the line of Pavan's jaw. In a single fluid motion, he reached behind Pavan's head, his hand tangling in the dark waves of his hair. He grasped the nape of Pavan's neck, drawing their faces mere inches apart, their breaths mingling as their lips hovered tantalizingly close.

"I am not fond of those who speak ill of what is mine," Thad whispered, his fair lashes brushing softly against the freckled curve of his cheeks. In the firelight, Pavan caught the faint shimmer of gold beneath Thad's skin—a glimmer of magick coursing through his veins, alive and pulsing.

Pavan smirked, his fingers drifting lower, skimming over the smooth silk until they paused at the edge of Thad's trousers. His voice dropped, a growl laced with the heat of desire as he leaned closer, his breath brushing against Thad's skin.

"*Mine,*" he murmured, the single word dripping with possession. Pavan felt the quickened rhythm of Thad's heartbeat beneath his touch, the tension between them crackling like fire in the still air.

"Take me," Thad whispered, his breath mingling with Pavan's, their lips brushing together in a tantalizing graze.

Pavan tensed, his voice low and strained with both desire and restraint. "Not here," he warned, the weight of his magick pressing heavily on his words. "It's too dangerous...I could siphon your soul."

Thad's smirk deepened, a glimmer of mischief flickering in his orange eyes. Without hesitation, he reached out, his fingers tracing a feather-light path along the curve of Pavan's throat. The touch was delicate yet deliberate, a whisper of sensation that sent heat coursing through Pavan's veins.

"Promises," Thad murmured, his tone a silken tease, daring and unafraid. His lips hovered close, the word dripping with both challenge and invitation, leaving Pavan caught in the intoxicating pull of temptation and fear.

Thad moved with deliberate grace, his steps slow and purposeful as he pushed Pavan back, the unexpected shove sending Pavan falling onto the settee that was placed nearest to the fire. Pavan gasped, grasping the back of the settee for balance. With a flick of his wrist,

Thad summoned new magick, the air between them crackling with power. Glowing runes formed shimmering chains that wound around Pavan's wrists and pulled his arms back. The bonds hummed with energy, the ancient symbols glowing faintly against his skin.

Pavan's breath hitched at the restraint. The magick pulsed, warm and unyielding, sending shivers down his spine. He strained against the chains, testing the strength of the magick Thad used, but they held firm, their grip immovable. His pulse quickened, a heady mixture of frustration and arousal igniting within him as he met Thad's smirking gaze.

"Your magick has gotten better," Pavan purred. "These are stronger than the chains you used on me in Ledenjour."

"I am confident in them holding." Thad grinned, his voice dripping with amusement and desire as he leaned into the space between Pavan's parted knees. "I could leave you chained forever. Would you like that?"

Pavan's lips parted to respond, but the words died in his throat as Thad's hands moved to his own shirt. Slowly, agonizingly, Thad began to undo each tie that kept the silk garment closed. Each motion revealed more of his freckled skin shimmering under the flickering light. Pavan's breath came faster, his eyes locked on the tantalizing sight.

"Stop struggling," Thad murmured, his tone soft yet commanding. He straddled Pavan, settling himself atop him with casual dominance. Pavan's muscles tensed beneath the weight, his body alive with need, but the chains denied him the satisfaction of touching Thad.

"It costs more magick to hold me, when not accompanied by another set of chains. I could easily break through." Pavan tugged at the glowing bonds again, his magick sparking faintly in protest.

Thad laughed softly, leaning down to press a feather-light kiss to Pavan's lips.

"Open your mind to me," Thad whispered against his mouth. "Think back on all the nights in Ledenjour we spent just like this, safeguarded beneath the blanket of snow. It is just like that, Pavan." His fingers traced patterns on Pavan's chest, skimming over his tunic before brushing against bare skin. The gentle touch sent heat coursing through Pavan's veins, his heartbeat hammering beneath Thad's palm.

Pavan closed his eyes, letting the tension ebb just slightly, surrendering to the sensation and the promise in Thad's voice. He felt the chain's pulse, not as a prison, but as an anchor—binding him in a way that was both thrilling and terrifying. It was easy to allow their minds to meld, as Thad reached up to touch the pulsing curve of his temple. Resting his head on the flat of his sweaty brow, encouraging the union of their minds. It was not rushed, as it had been when they first arrived in Jorn.

"This is how it should have been," Thad sighed. "Not rushed but savored with the protections of these chains."

"Do not regret what is past, Thad…"

They moved in tandem, breath for breath, heartbeats aligning in the hush of the room. Pavan reached the threshold at last—the doorway that existed between them, the passage through their minds.

Stepping through, he was met with the flush of heat, the air thick with longing. Here, no shadows lurked to pull them apart, no unseen forces clawed at their bond. In this shared space, Pavan moved freely, drawn toward Thad, who stood amid the heady scent of rosewater, his fingers curled into the slick fabric of Thad's shirt, holding him close.

"We don't have much time," Thad murmured, resting his head against Pavan's shoulder, his lashes fluttering shut.

Pavan pressed a kiss to his temple before drawing them both down into the bed. His mouth traced the curve of Thad's exposed neck, following the rise and fall of his breath, tasting the warmth of freckled skin. Even within the muted echoes of the mind space, the passion between them was intoxicating. His fingers dug into the flesh of Thad's hip as he trailed kisses upward, capturing his mouth in a heated kiss.

Thad groaned, fingers working at the laces of Pavan's trousers. In a swift motion, he flipped them, straddling Pavan's waist with a knowing smile, his lips flushed red. His nails raked down Pavan's chest, leaving behind shimmering trails of magick. Pavan hissed as identical marks bloomed over Thad's own skin, glistening across his freckled torso.

"Thad," Pavan growled, the name slipping between clenched teeth.

He surged up, claiming Thad's mouth again, hands gripping his hips with fervor. The need between them burned hotter, driving Pavan forward until he pressed Thad into the bed beneath him. He caught Thad's slender wrists, pinning them above his head, holding him captive beneath his weight. Thad didn't struggle—he only moaned, pleased.

"I can feel the magick slipping," Pavan admitted, his breath ragged as he kissed along Thad's throat.

One hand slid from Thad's wrists to cup his jaw, thumb pressing firmly into the curve of his neck.

"Then you'd better fuck me, Pavan," Thad hissed, wrapping his legs around his waist. "I grow impatient."

Lost in the urgency of their passion, Pavan entered Thad in a fervent rush, his lips trailing desperate kisses and sharp bites along Thad's neck. Their bodies moved in a steady rhythm, each thrust feeding the fire between them, their bond tightening as they felt what the other felt. Fingers interlaced, Pavan pressed his forehead to Thad's, magick burning where unseen chains bound him. The sensation clawed at his senses, the bond shifting, fraying at the edges, threatening to unravel.

"Not yet," Thad gasped, his grip tightening. His freckled skin glistened with sweat, his eyes dark and glassy with pleasure. He let his head fall back as Pavan drove into him harder.

A low growl rumbled in Pavan's throat as he tumbled over the edge, heat flooding through him. The world blurred. Then—an abrupt, searing ache. He was yanked back into his own body, his breath ragged, his limbs heavy. Above him, Thad slumped forward, chest rising and falling against his. His arms draped over Pavan's shoulders, copper hair falling into his flushed face.

"Pavan…" Thad licked his lips, pushing damp strands from his eyes. "Are you alright?"

Pavan's stomach churned, his body tight with the recoil of magick. He clenched his teeth, pain lancing through his jaw. The fire's glow was too bright, the air too thick. He squeezed his eyes shut, willing the nausea away.

Beside him, Thad's hands moved in slow, soothing strokes along his arms, helping him ease out of the magick's hold.

"It will pass soon," Pavan muttered, swallowing hard.

Thad pressed a kiss to his temple. "I'll get you something to eat."

It was true—hunger gnawed at him, raw and insatiable. He gave a small nod, uncertain if Thad saw it, then let himself sink into the quiet, allowing the magick to settle after the shared mind-space.

Thad rose from the settee, the warmth of his body leaving Pavan's side as he moved toward the hearth. The soft rustle of fabric followed as he adjusted his shirt, his bare feet silent against the stone floor. Pavan remained still, eyes half-lidded, feeling the ebb and flow of lingering magick coiling deep in his bones. The connection between them had been potent—so much so that his body still ached with the phantom sensations of their shared pleasure.

He exhaled slowly, flexing his fingers as the weight of the moment settled over him. Even in the aftermath, he could feel Thad, his presence humming in the back of his mind like a whisper, a tether that refused to fade.

A few moments passed before Thad returned, sitting beside with a plate in hand. The scent of roasted meat and spiced bread filled the space between them, awakening the gnawing hunger in Pavan's stomach. A small feast from what remained of the festivities.

"Eat," Thad murmured, offering him a piece of bread.

Pavan took it, chewing slowly, letting the warmth of it ground him. The food soothed the ache, though the emptiness inside him was more than just hunger. He glanced at Thad, who watched him closely, his freckled face still flushed, his copper hair mussed from their time together.

"You're magick is quieting," Thad noted, tilting his head.

Pavan swallowed, unsure of what to say. Words felt heavy, tangled in the exhaustion that clung to him. Instead, he reached out, his fingers brushing over the back of Thad's hand. A silent acknowledgement when the words he desperately wished to say was forbidden. Sleep was sneaking up on him.

Thad's expression softened. "It shall be right again, Pavan. We shall find a home here in Eir, one that will bring fortitude to these people."

"I trust you." Pavan kissed Thad's hand.

They sat like that for a while, the fire crackling in the hearth, the remnants of magick still thrumming faintly between them.

CHAPTER

II

Alnwick, Realm of Corad.

Sitting at her writing desk, overlooking the gardens, Brendolyn gazed at the acres of intricately placed flowers. The gardener who Lahrs had hired shortly after their arrival had executed a marvelous display of the vibrant colors that now blossomed and brought more life to the little home they had made in the country.

Brendolyn sighed, that was months ago, the winter had come and spring was now in full force. She would be able to take longer walks soon, no longer would she be confined to the inner gardens. She and her companion would be able to explore the grounds beyond the gate, they would take the paths into the woods.

"Another letter has arrived." The sound of her companion brought Brendolyn out of her thoughts.

Turning to look at Elsa, her auburn hair pulled back into a loosened braid. They were glad to not be dressed and preened as they would in the city, here they could be at ease in their dress.

"Lahrs is to return from Entheas soon." Brendolyn smiled, reading the words her knight wrote. But soon she frowned, her eyes scanning the next page. "He has been detained by a matter of urgency in Taastra. It seems there have been some issues with the trade ports in Denorn."

Elsa sat next to her, upon the little settee. "Trouble?"

"He doesn't say. Only that there is detaining the ships from leaving port." Brendolyn glanced through the letter again, searching for a better explanation.

"Here," Elsa extended a second letter, "maybe he explains it better in this one."

Brendolyn took the second letter, but her heart fluttered. It wasn't from Lahrs. It was posted from Jorn, but it was not Lahrs' seal, a flourish of an elven tree branch. This was new, this was significant. It was a wolf head, pressed into the deep red wax.

She gasped. "The royal insignia."

Ripping into the letter, Brendolyn scanned the length of the two pages of fine hand, written by the prince. He had promised to write, but Brendolyn had long ago given up on receiving such a letter. Her chest felt tight, she felt like laughing, crying. Every word upon the page bringing a smile to her lips.

"It is from your prince?" Elsa asked.

Brendolyn blushed, giggling. "He is not my prince, Elsa."

Leaning over her, Elsa read aloud some of the lines that were written just for her.

"*I cannot walk the warm gardens under the blooms of the flowers or smell their sweet perfumes without a thought of you.*" His words spoken aloud made her blush.

"He is the very definition of your prince, Bren." Elsa smiled.

Brendolyn tossed the letter onto her writing desk, burying her face in her hands, every inch of her hot. Brendolyn caught a glance at Elsa, who was smiling at her.

"It can't be...Elsa, do you believe he is in love with me?" Brendolyn asked, her voice faint.

"If he isn't in love with you, then he is the biggest idiot in all the realms." Elsa took up the letter, her finger trailing along the fine words.

Brendolyn could see her friend sink, she could feel her sudden shift. A sadness befalling her companion.

"Elsa," Brendolyn took the letter, placing her hands on her friends, "you told me once, of a knight who broke your heart."

"I once called him fine. He was tall, like your prince, he was charming...he told me he loved me, but it was a lie." She looked away, hiding her teary eyes.

"He did not deserve you," Brendolyn said plainly. "You are goodness and strong, he was a coward and a joke."

Elsa laughed, despite her tears, looking up to the princess. "You sound like my eldest brother, Eugene. He said as much."

"Well, he must be the smartest man, because he is right. I am right, too..." Brendolyn took hold of Elsa's hand. "One day you shall fall in love and leave me to rot in a nunnery, but you will write to me every day and tell me of your trials when your husband vexes you, when your children have begged you too much for sweets. But then I shall hear the sweetness and love you write of your family."

Elsa chuckled. "Perhaps you shall be the one writing to me at the nunnery. Your prince is very charming."

"He shall not marry me, Elsa. He is to be king one day. My path is not to be queen." Brendolyn became pensive, looking down at the forgotten letter. "He cannot marry me, he is intended for my sister."

Elsa slipped her hand away using her hands to speak in the language of the Silent Sisters.

"Then we shall both run away to Divna, together."

Brendolyn laughed, eyes gleaming as she stood to follow Elsa, together they laughed and ran through the castle. Forgetting the letter, forgetting the would be love. Hand in hand, they bound into the gardens. Bare feet trotting on the soft cool stone, as they had always done, finding their paths led to the outer hedges.

Freely, Brendolyn's hair fell about her. Reaching below her elbow, her dark tresses catching on the breeze. It was easy to forget when she was with Elsa. It was the easiest thing in the world to laugh and play with Elsa by her side. While Lahrs was away, it was no longer melancholy, no longer lonely to reside so far from the home beside the sea within the great castle of Corad.

Stepping out into the sunshine, Brendolyn waited for the carriage, Lahrs was expected home and she missed him. Elsa was within, talking with the cooks to be sure they prepared his favorite meal. It had been far too long, he stayed away longer this time.

At last, the carriage was seen driving up the lane towards the front gate.

Brendolyn's heart beat madly in her chest. Stepping down the steps, onto the gravel path, unable to contain her excitement.

Stopping at the gatehouse, she watched the familiar blonde elf emerge. Her smile broadened, picking up her skirts to hurry the distance nearly fifty feet away. She quickened her steps to see the elf turn her way, smiling broadly.

"I missed you," she exclaimed, wrapping her arms around his neck, embracing the familiar scent and fatherly embrace.

"What a welcome!" He beamed, spinning her in a circle.

Setting her down, Lahrs looked pleased. Brendolyn saw the sun had touched his fair skin, leaving a tan to contrast his silvery white hair. But those stormy grey eyes remained ever the same. Weathered from the days at sea, perhaps stuck aboard the ship while in port to await the signal to pass. Brendolyn loved to hear his stories, she knew that this would not be any different. She missed him desperately when he went away.

Brendolyn looped her arm with his, leading them towards the estate. She was ready to hear everything, but knew he was tired from the long hours of travel.

"Did you bring me any gifts?" she began.

"I have been gone for three months, and the princess has demanded of her gifts," Lahrs mocked, playfully, a knowing glint of amusement peaking at his lips.

She giggled, hitting his arm.

"You know I missed you dearly, Lahrs. But I know you, and your dedication to give me the world. Come now, there must be something in those trunks. You do not travel so laden with so many when you go across the sea." Brendolyn smiled.

Lahrs chuckled, patting her hand. "You are clever, Bren. But perhaps we shall talk while we take tea together in the cool comfort of the library."

To this, Brendolyn brightened.

"Elsa has been in the kitchens giving directions for your favorite meal tonight."

They walked into the front doors, the coolness of the foyer welcoming them from the warm sun, taking a moment to adjust before walking through the castle corridors, entering into the library. Servants had already been there, ready to welcome their master home. A tray of tea things waiting for them upon the round table nearest to the large windows overlooking the gardens.

"Come, sit," Brendolyn encouraged, smiling up at him. "I must tell you about my lessons that I have kept up while you have been in your duties to Entheas."

"You are very good."

"Well, at first it was so dull, Lady Madeline kept us in the upper library for far too long, I could hardly sit for one lesson of history, but after much persuasion she brought us down into the gardens where I could sit under the pergola. There we fared much better and I can recite to you the lines of kings as well as the first acts of *Hamlet* in Common..."

Lahrs sat, watching her. A curious look, one she had not seen since her queen mother died. Brendolyn's heart sank, straightening, an unease settling into her mind.

"Is everything alright?" she asked, observing his disquiet.

After an unordinary amount of time in silence, Lahrs shifted in his chair, gazing with curiosity and apprehension.

"There was an edict, in Denorn. They search for a faie who has upset the kings guard. He is whispered to be dangerous." Lahrs looked tired, he looked older than his thirty-four years. "I am afraid that travel with Jorn has been put on hold, until this unfortunate endeavor is resolved. All ships between the realms are to remain deferred."

Brendolyn sat down hard upon the chair. Staring blankly at the teacup before her. This was not the first news of such events, but she feared it would not be the last.

"There are whispers of riots, as one of the king's guards was found hanging in the square. He was stripped of his clothes and his throat was slit." Lahrs looked fatigued.

"And they believe this faie is the cause?"

Lahrs hesitated, knowing it would upset her. He had grown used to speaking more freely with Brendolyn, as she grew older, these affairs began to emerge between the realms. But when it included faie, or elves, there was a caution in Lahr's narrative that always gave her anxiety.

"He was without a soul, Brendolyn. There are only a few with the power to do so much to one person." He shook his head resignedly. "As a result, there shall be little travel amongst the realms. The usual roads are to be heavily taxed and guarded. There shall be vessels of the king's fleet patrolling the borders to ensure there is no passage into their territory."

"Would that include the post?" She felt her voice waver.

Lahrs was quiet, the great clock on the far wall ticking loudly. Until, at last the elf gave a heavy sigh.

"Sabian shall still send you letters; a messenger shall ride the distance between Alnwick and Corad City. It has not affected the trade and commerce in our realm. Rhun has sent a safeguard to the king that the borders are protected with magick, should there be any neglect on the western realm. They do not want another catastrophic event to unfold upon their soil."

"That is good."

Lahrs looked skeptical. "Are you executing a letter of particular importance?"

Brendolyn tried to laugh it away, the discouraged heartache that plagued her. "It is not that, I had hoped…that is, I cannot be certain it is…it is nothing, Lahrs."

"Prince Barrow has written, I presume?" he inquired and there was a hint of distance in him that was not something Brendolyn was used to with the elf, when he was usually so willing to give her anything she desired.

Brendolyn nodded. "I received a letter the week before last."

"I see." He nodded, leaning forward to resume the pouring of the tea. He needn't say anything, Brendolyn knew he disapproved; she saw the line of his frowning mouth, felt the flutterings of his heart where he sat across from her.

"He doesn't love me," she blurted, as soon as the words fell from her lips, she blushed. Catching his look, she saw Lahrs frown.

"Bren–"

"He can't love me, Lahrs. We know he is going to marry Lisetta. After my prince brother is at a safe age, they shall continue with the treaty to solidify our realms. They will be married, and I will remain here, with you, and Elsa." She spoke, swallowing around the lump forming in her throat.

Lahrs sighed heavily. "He has an attachment to you, Bren."

"We flirted in Jorn, but it was nonsense." Brendolyn felt as though her heart was about to burst. "He writes only to satisfy a promise he made to a foolish girl."

Angry tears burned in Brendolyn's eyes, threatening escape.

"I did not return to upset you, Bren," Lahrs went on, aware of her distress. "But it is my duty to advise you against such an attachment. In time, when you are of age, King Sabian shall send for suitors."

"I don't want suitors." She laughed, a bitter harsh thing that fell from her trembling lip and her tears fell freely from her eyes.

"When you are of age, Brendolyn. They will come."

"Who would want me, a faie bastard born of the king?" she hissed, her emotions bubbling in her throat. She saw the hurt in Lahrs eyes.

"There are lords that would accept your hand."

"Elven born, or faie, Lahrs? Or would they be the men that whisper of our people with contempt?" She no longer had the stomach for tea. "I know how they speak of us. Even in Corad we cannot run from the hate that spreads like dragon fire. Perhaps you have tried to shield me from it, but I am not blinded to the truth."

"Perhaps there are those from Entheas..."

"An arranged marriage, then."

"You will meet with someone you can connect to, Brendolyn."

"As I have never met with another soul but yourself, or Elsa, and the servants hired under your hand, that is very unlikely. I do not attend parties, I rarely leave this castle but to take walks to the Chapel of Light within the village. The only time I ever felt—"

She froze, her heart breaking, thinking of the green eyes that come to her still in her dreams. Tears rushing hot, cascading down her cheeks at the thought of him now. Sold to the realm that would kill him, that would break him of his magick. He must have been faie, there is no other explanation for him being sold.

"There is no one, Lahrs," she breathed. "Hope for my future is doomed. From my birth I was destined to be alone."

Lahrs grasped her hand, his worry fluttering the room with magick. She felt it shifting around her, his warm hand holding hers so tenderly.

"Bren, forgive me, I didn't mean to upset you." He was soft, his hand rubbed hers, but the ache deepened.

Brendolyn fell further into herself. Her tears fell freely, even as Lahrs wrapped his arms around her, bringing her up into his arms, embracing her in his warmth. Still, the sadness plagued her, pushing her down.

"I am so alone."

Lahrs kissed the top of her head, wiping away her tears. "You shall never be alone, Bren. As long as I have breath in my lungs, you shall never be alone. I promise."

She dabbed at her eyes, quieting her mind. Drawing back in only a little to look at the elf with more care. He spoke so calmly, but she could feel his sorrow. A taste of longing hung on her tongue that gave her unease.

"Tell me about your first love," she asked, her throat tightened as her tears subsided.

Lahrs was quiet for a long time. Tea things forgotten. In the quiet of the room, she could hear the birds flitting out of the window in the gardens below. A rush of a heartbeat as fast as the flutter of their wings.

"I am engaged to Duchess Kristjana," he began to speak, but stopped. A remnant of a tear fell from the corner of his eye, he brushed it aside without thought.

Brendolyn knew he was in love before her time, she remembered hearing stories of the girl from his youth. Silly stories of their courtship, but Brendolyn knew it didn't last. Lahrs never spoke of it now, but perhaps in the moment it could give Brendolyn hope.

"Tell me about the girl with the lilies...you used to tell me stories about her. You must have loved her so much to sail across the great sea to bring her the flower that she loved." Taking his hand in hers, Brendolyn brought his fingers up to kiss them.

"They were just stories, Bren..." Lahrs shook his head. His heart was beating faster, Brendolyn knew he was lying.

"You were forbidden to love her?" She knew it must have been the truth, he was barely sworn to knighthood when he became her guardian. "She was above your station."

Lahrs pulled his hand away. "Do not use your magick."

Brendolyn blinked, her fingertips began to tingle, looking down at her hands as the brightness of her faie magick began to fade back, returning her to her thoughts. Brendolyn had begun to use her magick upon him without realizing, and guilt rattled through her.

"Forgive me," she whispered.

"I do not speak of her, because to do so brings me pain, Brendolyn," he finally said, drawing her to look up. "You are right. She was above my station, and I loved her anyway. But she could not remain here in this world, not even after I begged her not to leave me. Nothing I could do would save her from the Veil."

A hurt filled her, tugging at her chest that dragged her down, her throat tightened as she watched the elf that she loved dearly begin to fade into grief. It was a rare thing, to feel Lahrs' sadness, but when it was felt, it burned in her like dragonfire.

"There are no lilies in Corad," Brendolyn whispered.

Lahrs smiled, through his pain he smiled. "Not anymore. Not since she left this realm for the next. It was as if she never existed. Without the gladiolus lily...I am alone."

Taking his hand, Brendolyn kissed it again, bringing his palm to her cheek.

"You are not alone, Lahrs. We have each other."

Denorn, Realm of Jorn.

Simeon Bannon stormed into his office, the dim room greeted him with silence and shadows. He flicked on the light with a sharp twist of his wrist, and a jolt of pain raced up his arm, making him wince. He looked down at his hand, where the skin stretched tight over his bones, ripples of arcane energy shimmering beneath the surface.

With a growl of frustration, Simeon marched across the room and seized a tome from the cluttered shelf. His anger exploded as he hurled the book to the floor. It landed with a thud, pages flaring out like wounded wings. In a violent fit, he ripped the remaining volumes from their perches, sending a cascade of books and loose pages across the floor.

Behind him, the door clicked softly, a subtle sound in the tempest of his rage. Simeon didn't bother to look back. He pressed his palms against the bookshelf, the magick flowing through him igniting his touch. The shelf groaned and shifted, revealing a hidden door concealed within the wall. Simeon gritted his teeth, enduring the searing pain as the door materialized.

"Follow me," he grumbled, casting a fleeting glance at Leuthere, who waited at the barred entrance.

Simeon pushed through the newly revealed door and stepped into a narrow passage that wound through his cluttered office. The path led him to an inner chamber, where the space opened up into a grand, circular room.

The chamber was an architectural marvel of ancient stone, its walls crowned with high, arched windows of stained glass. Sunlight streamed through, casting a mesmerizing dance of colors across the floor and walls, as if the very essence of the room was alive with swirling enchantment.

"Stand there." Simeon stood at the center of the circular room as light danced around him, looking over at the man who entered after him.

He watched the guard stand in place, the look of the man was like stone, but Simeon felt the flutter of his heart. He could feel the fear slipping in through the cracks.

"Here, my lord," Leuthere spoke, taking hold of the dagger at his belt. Extending the object, Simeon took it gladly.

Simeon held out his other hand, looking across the center circle at Leuthere. Fear fragranced the air, churning in his stomach. But Leuthere placed his hand in the open palm, obediently exposing the flesh of his palm.

"By your blood," Simeon sneered, watching the blade slice through the man's thin flesh.

Leuthere hissed but remained unmoved. Blinking up at Simeon with dutiful eyes, unwavering from his place, waiting as Simeon uttered beneath his breath. Beginning to feel the stirrings of magick flickering underneath.

"By your blood," Leuthere grit out, squeezing his fingers into a fist as blood trickled down over the palm of Simeon.

Each trickle of blood, invigorated through him, Simeon felt the flutter in his chest, a whisper in his ear. Taking the dagger, the blade sliced through his own palm. Whispering the words, the well-known spell.

Simeon…

His body shuddered, hearing the voice. Feeling the warmth of the blood trickle down his fingers.

"My lord." Leuthere's voice was distant.

"Leave me," Simeon hissed, turning away from the man.

Barely listening to the sounds of the retreating footsteps his mind opened to the voice. All around him, the room felt hot. His senses alive with the scent of blood. Magick pulsing as the blood seeped into his core.

"I feel your presence," Simeon gasped as he pulled, holding on to the connection he held, drawing from the blood.

Simeon...your magick is...strained.

He felt the chill wash over him, hearing the voice in his mind. His knees trembled under the force of it, collapsing on one knee, panting for breath. Searching the light of the dancing colors, watching as magick shifted languidly before his eyes.

"Your magick is mine...my blood, is your blood." Simeon reached out, desperate to touch the magick. His hand dripped blood, trickling further up his skin.

Limit your use, the time is almost here, Simeon. I feel the one near. He is almost in your grasp.

Simeon felt the pangs of regret, the sharp sting of guilt in his gut, thinking of the magick he felt before, the one in that room. It was new, young, yielding.

"There is one that has slipped through my fingers. One who I have felt. Please, give me your blessing and I shall seek him out."

Cold sharpened as a dagger to his heart, Simeon gasped, clutching to his chest. Collapsing down to one hand as magick twisted and coiled hard around his heart.

Patience, Simeon. Close is the hour to our glory. Do what you must to secure the throne and my power shall be yours to control.

Simeon grit his teeth. "As you command, it shall be done."

In a rush of agony, the voice was gone, ripping through him and burning his skin. Crying out in anguish and gripping tightly to his arm, his wounds began closing shut.

"My lord!" Behind him, Leuthere rushed forward from the darkness of the corridor, helping Simeon to his feet.

"I must return, Leuthere," Simeon hissed, cradling his aching arm close to his chest. "I must return to the king..."

"At once, my lord."

Leuthere helped Simeon through the darkened corridor, out into the ruined mess of his offices, walking over toppled bindings of scattered pages, blood dripping a path as they walked to the door. As the knight reached the handle, Simeon gripped his arm.

"Keep your men at their stations here, have them report on any movement. We must find the magick user."

Leuthere nodded sternly. "It shall be done, my lord."

CHAPTER

12

Signe, Realm of Corad. 2004.

Three summers come and go, emerging the small village of Alnwick into a new season. Taking a carriage ride into the city of Signe, Elsa accompanied her friend and their guardian, Lahrs, to the home of her family. They would stay in town, while Brendolyn was fitted for a new wardrobe.

"I detest being fitted. Poked, and pinned, they shall make me a little pin cushion," Brendolyn complained, as they neared the familiar roads leading to the beautiful sea town.

Elsa chuckled, admiring the view from their gilded carriage. How different it was to return in such fashion, after leaving without notice or regard in her father's chaise. Listening to the argument of necessary finery for Brendolyn to acquire as a grown young lady.

"You are nearly eighteen now, Bren. Your last fitting was eight years ago," Lahrs reminded his ward.

Brendolyn sighed, rolling her eyes. "Why can you not send for Lisetta's old gowns, as before?"

Lahrs sighed. "She is significantly taller, Bren, and has more prominent features that would make it impractical. Getting fitted is the best approach, King Sabian has already granted the extension of your yearly budget to accommodate for a new wardrobe."

Elsa could see the look of disgust as Brendolyn crossed her arms. "An extension on my budget for dresses. I could feed the village for a year with the sum one of my gowns shall cost."

Lahrs sighed, a heavier, resigned sound. One he gave when he was growing more exhausted with Brendolyn's stubbornness. Elsa could see the lines crease over his forehead, he tried to keep his calm façade intact, but Elsa knew he would cave soon.

"You shall be fitted, Bren. That is the end of it."

He surprised even Elsa. Staying firm under the pressure.

"Fine, but I will not enter Madame Fiore under the expectation I shall dress as one of her fashion plates. I choose my fabrics, I choose my colors." Brendolyn glared across the carriage at Lahrs expectantly.

"Agreed," the elf extended a hand.

Elsa held up the stained glass, watching it catch the light.

While Brendolyn was fitted for a new gown, she had snuck out of the apartment in town where they stayed in one of the royal houses. Brendolyn urged Elsa to escape and buy them some sweet buns from the bakery, even giving Elsa her personal purse. Madame Fiore had brought an entourage of ladies, with baskets and baskets of fabric swatches. They had been at it for hours, matching boots, hats, and reticules. Brendolyn was forbidden to consume more than the barest of meals and Madame Fiore was insistent on nothing to bloat the frame, her dresses were to fit a lady without.

Elsa chuckled, remembering Brendolyn's faces when the great dress maker turned her back. Now, the little glass shimmered in the light. It would be a lovely addition to the collection of trinkets that hung in the makeshift fort waiting for them back in Alnwick. Elsa knew it was silly, to hold on to such childlike notions of forts and bobbles, but it was the place Brendolyn and herself could escape to, to speak of the past and to dream about their future.

Elsa liked this particular shop for oddities and trinkets. Pocket watches, glass, and rings all lined the counter, nestled in velvet boxes, displayed for her to examine. It was a quick stop before Elsa stopped to deliver a letter. Eugene would be stationed home soon, she wanted to deliver the letter in hopes he would visit her in Alnwick.

"It's a lovely shade of blue," a man's voice sounded behind her, almost making her drop the glass. "Though I think it will be difficult to cut into shape."

Elsa set the glass aside, turning to look at the man blocking the door to the shop. He was a knight by his bearing, wearing a charming smile. He was older and studied her with clear gray eyes. The familiar appraisal left a shiver on her skin.

"I don't need to cut it." She turned back to the shopkeeper. "I'll take this one, will you wrap it for me?"

"Of course, my lady, two gold." He started to wrap the pane in paper as Elsa shuffled through her basket of sweet buns for the little purse Brendolyn had given her for her use.

"Allow me." The man leaned over Elsa, dropping two gold pieces on the counter.

Elsa glared. "Thank you but I can settle my accounts myself."

She snatched up her basket, turning to leave, hurrying from the little shop to step out into the warm sunshine. Signe was alive with townsfolk out for their evening errands. She scoffed, hearing the knight follow behind her.

"Will you at least permit me to carry your basket?"

"I do not require a knight to help me nor do I desire a knight's company. Perhaps you should try your luck with one of the other girls in town. I am busy."

"Is it specifically because I'm a knight that you don't want my company?" He cocked his head at her, a laughing, teasing smile in his eyes.

"I do not desire the company of any man who uses a charming smile as a weapon or believes he has a right to my company without even asking my name. Now, if you'll excuse me."

"I should have expected Eugene's sister to have a sharp wit."

Elsa froze before turning back to the man.

He had broad shoulders and strong arms. Sizing him up even briefly she knew he could overpower her if he wanted but he stayed a respectful distance away, watching her with curiosity.

"I recognize you from the family portrait he used to carry. Though you were much younger then. I'll admit, I was surprised to see you out and about, especially without the princess." He shrugged as he spoke. "As it happens, I'm on my way to Alnwick myself. Now, may I carry your basket?"

Elsa's grip on the basket tightened. He was friends with her brother? No. This was a trick of some sort. Knights never came to Alnwick and Eugene would have written to her if he was sending someone. He must have simply recognized her as Bren's companion and was looking to weasel his way into the king's good graces.

"No. You must have me mistaken for someone else."

Elsa turned away, ignoring as he called after her. She did not want to listen to him, or any other man. Hurrying back to the apartments, slipping in with the other ladies as they began to carry baskets of fabric swatches. Hurrying up the steps to the upper floors she could hear Madame Fiore shouting in Felourian. Lahrs trailing after her, in an attempt to calm her shouts.

Finding Brendolyn in the dressing room, wearing only her undergarments, hiding behind the dressing screen. Upon seeing Elsa approach, Brendolyn grabbed her friend by the arm, yanking her into hiding.

"Madame is enraged," she whispered.

Elsa chuckled. "What did you do?"

"I refused to wear her embroidered bodices. She even wanted me to wear a pannier cage. Imagine, stuffed into that box, I couldn't sit or run anywhere." Brendolyn rolled her eyes, digging into the basket Elsa held and taking a large bite of a sweet bun.

"I am sure they are the height of fashion." Elsa held her laughter. They hunched down when they heard Madame Fiore barging through the room in a fit of rage.

Brendolyn giggled. "Height of fashion, meaning gilded cages. I can wear stays, I can manage layers of petticoats, but panniers to make my gown the size of a house? Impossible."

"Maybe she will leave, after Lahrs has calmed her down."

Brendolyn took another sweet bun, sighing heavily. Her black hair falling about her shoulders, frizzy from hands touching it and attempting to pin it out of place.

"I saw a knight in town," Elsa admitted for she could not get the strange man out of her mind.

Brendolyn paused mid chew, locking eyes with Elsa for a long torturous moment. They heard the slamming of doors and shouts of Madame Fiore in the distance.

"It was not Alaric?" Brendolyn whispered harshly.

Elsa trembled but shook her head. "It was another knight...he claimed to be a friend of Eugene...Oh blessed light, I forgot to post my letter!"

Reaching into the basket, Elsa searched for the letter, but it was not there. Digging further below the sweet buns for the wrapped stained glass, but there was nothing but crumbs beneath the neatly wrapped buns.

"Elsa?" Brendolyn asked.

"It's gone, my letter." Elsa felt her chest tighten. It was impossible, it was there before she set out to the shops. She remembered placing it in the bottom of the basket at the bakery. Now, it was gone.

"Perhaps you already posted it?" Brendolyn suggested.

Elsa shook her head, it was all a flurry of emotion. She was so distressed by the knight, but why had he stopped her? Why must he have singled her out over every other shop, over every other lady in town?

"I must have." She shrugged it off, taking a sweet bun for herself.

"Bren!" Lahrs voice echoed from below, reaching them with such fierceness, and Brendolyn hid herself further down.

They locked eyes and Elsa smiled before laughing together.

"Come on, I don't think I can sit through another of Lahrs' lectures if we do not make haste." Elsa took Brendolyn by the hand. They would go down together.

Harbor of Signe, Realm of Corad.

Returning to the inn, just at the edge of the harbor, Sir Eero held the letter in hand. He felt a little regret, taking it from young Lady Elsa's basket, but he could tell she was flustered. Seeing Eugene's name written upon the letter, he knew he could deliver it himself. Sir Eero sighed, pulling the wrapped package from his pocket; he never intended to take it, but in his hastened grab for the letter, the stained glass was accidentally taken.

"Eero!" Ahead of him, he spotted the man in question. Approaching Eugene Laronn with a smile, taking his old friend by the hand, admiring the firm grip and welcoming smile.

"Eugene, good to see you." Eero smiled warmly.

Eugene clapped Eero upon the arm, their hands pressed together firmly. "I thought I imagined it when I heard my men tell me Prince Barrow was at the Boars Burrow."

"We shall only stay one night, I am afraid."

Eugene smiled, walking beside Eero down the lane, towards the inn in question.

"Nonsense, come to the estate, my father would be more than pleased to house the Prince of Jorn." Eugene was a delight; vibrant and much different than the young lady he had just left.

"Forgive me, Eugene, our arrival and departure should remain as less observed as possible. No one should know we travel. Even with the lift on the trades ban, it is not easy to make it through the patrolling ships in Denorn Harbor. But you were just the man I wished to see." Eero extended the letter. "I had the pleasure of bumping into your sister."

A shadow seemed to cross over Eugene, looking around them, before taking the post and looking from the seal to Eero.

"She is here?"

Eero nodded, noting the concern in his old friend. "She stays with the princess, I believe in the upper streets, near the crest."

Eugene pocketed the letter, smiling as he usually did, clapping Eero upon the arm. "Thank you, I shall read her letter after dinner. We can share a meal together, Eero. Catch up on old times. I have not seen you since my wedding."

"Of course," Eero agreed.

Walking the remainder of the lane, they arrived at the Boars Burrow, entering into the dining room, where they found Prince Barrow already sitting amongst Eugene's men.

All sailors who wore the moss green tunics after the Coradian flag. Upon their approach, Barrow stood, opening his arms in exclamation, and a drink in hand spilled onto the floor.

Sir Eero sighed heavily.

"Eero! Valiant man returns to my table, welcome, welcome!" Barrow was nearly shouting. Sir Eero took hold of the mug, easing his prince to sit back down.

"Marvelous," Barrow laughed, returning to the tales of their travels with the men around the table.

He would have wished the prince quiet on these matters, but there was no silencing the man. He was older now, his own man, on their tours of the realm. They were meant to be in Jorn. Visiting one of the great families, but Barrow had surprised Eero with a change of plan. A scheme of Barrow to come to Corad and seek his beautiful princess. Now, they were here, and Eero felt danger lurking over his shoulder like a great shade.

"In Alnwick, my beauty is waiting for me."

Eero stiffened, glaring at Barrow. Catching the eye of Eugene, who was tense, his friend glanced at the young blonde knight at the end of the table, who perked up with great interest as the prince boasted of Brendolyn's beauty. Eero recognized the knight as one of the men he had seen in Signe nearly four years ago at Eugene's wedding.

"Princess Brendolyn and her companions are in Alnwick?"

Eugene silenced him at once. "There is nothing for you there, Alaric."

The man glared back at his commander. Which Eero thought was rather foolish considering Eugene's size and strength. Though, now that he studied him, Eero thought Alaric might be a match for him—he was not quite so large but well-muscled.

"Of course, my lord. I only meant it as a surprise that the princess is not in Corad with her family. Excuse me, I need a pint." Alaric rose from the table, walking across the crowded room to the bar.

"Mine is empty as well," Barrow announced, rising to follow.

Eero sighed.

"He's drunk," Eugene grunted.

"I'm afraid so. That will make the morning difficult. I suppose I ought to go look after him." Eero smiled, half laughing with his old friend. "I'd hate to lose my head over losing the prince."

Eero made his way over to the bar where Barrow and Alaric drank side by side. Barrow was pleased with himself while the other man had a dark countenance about him. A resolve burning inside of him, Eero pressed himself into their little group, placing his hand over the hilt of his sword as precaution.

"Do you visit the princess often, Your Highness?" Alaric asked as Eero approached.

"As often as I can. I would never leave her side if it were possible." Barrow laughed while taking another drink.

"And is the lady Elsa Laronn still one of her companions?"

"Laronn? Eugene's sister? I doubt that," Eero stated.

As Barrow half shouted, "They are inseparable, the pair of them."

Alaric looked over Eero with a renewed interest. "I imagine she would be. Elsa loves her brothers but they are a bit protective. I think they might have locked her away to keep her from leaving Signe if given the choice. I suppose you spend a great deal of time with her, while the prince is occupied with his princess."

Barrow got up from the counter, disappearing through the men.

"I see her when we visit, yes," Eero lied. He had never spoken to her before today.

Alaric produced a letter from his pocket. "When you see her, will you deliver this?"

"What is it?"

"Just a letter. Elsa is an old friend of mine. We're quite close actually. I had been writing to her in Corad." He glared at Eugene again. "But it seems I was misinformed about the princess's location."

"Elsa has never mentioned a close friend before." Certainly not one who was a knight. He hesitated to take the letter.

"I doubt she would. Eugene does not approve of our friendship." The way the word dripped from Alaric's tongue told Eero it had been more than friendship. At least on Alaric's side. A sickening feeling settled in Eero, remembering how Elsa reacted, when he mentioned he was a friend of her brothers.

Idiot. He was the biggest idiot, for not realizing it sooner.

"He thinks I'm beneath them because I'm only a knight." A smile widened on Alaric's face. "He would think you are beneath them too."

"I am not a common knight, but a Knight of the Royal Guard. First, I held the knighthood for service to King Broderick but ascended into my title by his son when he was Lord of Brac. My allegiance and honor are bound to the princes of Jorn until my dying breath. Perhaps you are misinformed on who I am, Sir Alaric." Eero felt the grate of annoyance twinge in the back of his jaw.

Here, the blond scoffed.

"But you are not born of noble blood. That is where our lines differ, Sir Eero. My father's house was amongst the nobility, whilst yours were the footholds beneath the feet of your lords."

Eero could almost laugh. "I believe King Sabian abolished the heraldry of bannerman in Corad, to unite the realm under one rule. Your noble blood is no different than those who are...*beneath you.*"

"No matter. Will you deliver my letter, Sir Eero?"

Eero hesitated but took the offered parchment. Seeing out of the corner of his eye Barrow staggered off again, towards the stairs.

"It was...*interesting* meeting you, Sir Alaric."

There was a sick jealous tint to Eero's thoughts as he half carried his prince up the stairs to his room, putting the drunk love-sick prince to bed before he could babble anymore about Princess Brendolyn's beauty and charm and keeping a closed fist tightly over the parchment. When he stepped back into the corridor, Eugene was waiting for him, a hulking, brooding presence.

"May I speak with you for a moment, in private?"

Eero agreed, following him into the small room.

"That man you spoke to, the one asking after Princess Brendolyn and my sister."

"Alaric, yes. He was quite charming."

Eugene's jaw tensed, darkening the room. "He's a brute. I don't know what he told you, but he cannot be allowed anywhere near my sister. Now that he knows she's not in the palace surrounded by guards, she'll be in danger from him again."

Anger flushed against Eero's skin. "What kind of danger?"

"When my sister was younger, Alaric set his sights on her. He was always a charming friend to us. My brothers and I didn't think to worry about how close they were. Until they got older and it seemed he was so often alone with her finding excuses to take her away from the manor." Eugene shook his head, despairingly. "I sent a letter to Sir Lahrs before my marriage took place."

Eero was hot with anger now. "Why keep him in your service, then?"

"It's better to keep him where I can watch him than let him out in the world. Especially since I cannot protect Elsa from so far away."

"Why tell me all of this?"

"You travel to Alnwick." Eugene's fists curled and uncurled with frustration. "You can protect her where I cannot. I'm asking you as an old friend, someone I can trust completely."

Eero straightened, pride swelling in his chest. "Of course."

Sir Eero sat in the stables, early before the sun began to rise.

He listened to the soft sounds of the horses. It soothed him to be surrounded by that which he was familiar with. Closing his eyes briefly to listen to the short clops of hooves on the ground. Magick radiated from the great beasts that spoke in their hushed tones to each other. Swishing of a tail and quick bounce of a head. Impatient creatures, ready to be home again, to be spoiled by their oats and salt licks.

A sweet scent of lavender wafted over his senses. A flicker of memories coming to him, as if often did in times of quiet solitude. Before the war, before his injury to the side of his head that stole his memories of his childhood. He could vaguely see the figure of a garden, of the whisperings of magick as the bees spoke to each other while the great hound lounged at his feet.

It ended as quickly as it emerged, jolting up to straighten when a horse whined.

Eero rolled the letter in his hand, it was why he sat in the stables waiting. His gut twisted at the familiarity of words spoken within. Written with such words that made Eero question there being any truth of heart in the knight that wrote them.

A heavy step drew Eero's gaze up. Seeing the hooded figure approach, cloak drawn over his head, and a bag draped over his shoulder. Eero stood to full height, standing in Alaric's way.

"Sir Eero!" Alaric started, jumping slightly.

"Going somewhere?" Eero asked coolly, the letter flicked in his fingers.

Alaric scoffed. "I do not answer to you."

Sit Alaric made to shift around Eero, but Eero blocked the path, looking directly into the younger man's eyes. There was hostility, but Eero would not back down.

"Let me be very clear," Eero began, his tone calm, as he reached forward to tuck the letter he held into the front of Sir Alaric's jacket. "You will not give attention to Lady Elsa."

Alaric sneered. "Are you her lover?"

Eero felt his chest burn with anger, stepping closer to the knight, their eyes level. "I am her guardian. I am her knight, sworn to protect her."

The flicker in the knight changed from annoyance to uncertainty and Eero delighted in the flicker of fear. This boy needed to be put in his place. Eugene was hesitant to do what needed to be done to right the problem but Eero knew exactly how to handle men of this sort.

Alaric shifted, trying to lower his gaze. Trembling as sweat began to build on his brow.

"I was returning home," Alaric stammered, his fear radiating in his voice.

"Perhaps that is wisest...but perhaps you should remain here, at your station. Deserters get branded as traitors, do they not?"

All the color drained from the young knight's face, his eyes flickering in true fear. Alaric bowed, stepping back to retreat, but Eero quickly gripped the knight's arm. Leaning close to be so near the other man's face, he could see the shift in Alaric's pupils.

"If I hear one whisper of you stepping out of your brigade, I will find you, Alaric. If a word reaches my ear that you have written to her...that you have seen her..." Eero glanced down, sneering, then looked up again to the knight's eyes. "Then I shall have you castrated, for the blackheart you are."

CHAPTER

13

Returning home, Brendolyn was glad to be done with Madame Fiore and her oppressors of dress makers. Brendolyn returned to her world of simple gowns, the finery of her new wardrobe would arrive within the next few months after being worked upon by skilled hands. She would have to wear them, eventually.

Plucking at the frayed edges of her gown, her bodice stretched over her middle with effort, the ties straining at the seams. Her petticoat hems torn and patched, worn down with years of use. In truth, Brendolyn adored her patchworked gowns that clung to her curves. It would be difficult to see them put away, unloved. Brendolyn held fond memories of every tear, every adventure. Sewn together by her own hand, or the skilled stitch of Lahrs' own hand.

"Perhaps your father intends to bring you back to Corad City," Elsa thought out loud. They both sat in the shade of the large tree, having climbed up into the large oaken branches, hiding away from Lahrs and their morning instruction. Lahrs homecoming from Entheas had meant a swift return into their routine of lessons, no longer could they sit inattentive in the gardens while Lady Madeline read from her lesson book.

Brendolyn felt a knot in her throat. "It's possible. Santino is at a safe age, he is talking his nanny's ear off. Lisetta has sent me a portrait, perhaps it was time I returned."

Elsa reached for Brendolyn's hand.

Horses could be heard from their hiding place in a large tree off the courtyard that was wrapped by the entrance of the large estate. As both Brendolyn and Elsa watched the men on horses riding up to be greeted at the front doors of the large estate, Brendolyn was pleasantly surprised to recognize a head of golden locks dismounting from his horse. Prince Barrow.

"He's here, he never wrote to say he was coming. He's here!" Brendolyn gasped.

The descent from the tree was easy work, having done it a hundred times over. Brendolyn was smiling wide, grasping her dearest friend's hand, hurrying them along the gravel path, eager to see her beloved again. Her stomach twisted into knots.

"Oh, he is handsome," Elsa whispered, near enough to the doors while the servants attended to Barrow's horse.

They hurried faster, Brendolyn felt her face grow warm.

"Barrow!"

The Prince of Jorn turned, a smile brightened his already lovely features. Before he could say a word, Brendolyn wrapped her arms around his neck, embracing him. Kissing his cheek, familiarity and warmth between them. Barrow continued smiling as she finally let him go, admiring the gleaming the prince's eyes and blushing.

Lahrs approached, coughing and breaking the moment.

Brendolyn remembered herself, righting her stance and curtsying to Barrow, inviting him in. Barrow followed Lahrs inside, behind them Brendolyn and Elsa follow arm in arm, whispering to themselves fiercely.

"Brendolyn, lead our guests into the east library, I shall ring for tea." Lahrs smiled, but Brendolyn saw the look of trepidation he gave the prince. Barrow was not expected, but Lahrs was far too polite to refuse the prince a warm welcome.

"This way." She stood as she ought, remembering her training, motioning them through the front doors.

Elsa walked beside her, equally matched in grace and elegance. They led the way down the passages, until they reached the large doors that were propped open, stepping into the east library with satisfaction.

"It is delightful to see you again, Sir Eero." Brendolyn smiled, dipping in a slight curtsy when the knight entered after the prince.

"The delight is mine; this part of the realm is very fine this time of year." Eero nodded, he was dressed in dark blue, his doublet embroidered with silver leaves.

"How is my stallion? Taking care of his spirited nature, I hope?" Brendolyn saw a twinkle in the knight's eye at the mention of this particular horse. Brendolyn had ridden the stallion four times while in Jorn, an unmanageable creature who was impossible to tame.

"Wild as ever." Eero smiled.

"You are a horse master?" Elsa chimed in and Brendolyn smiled at her friend, knowing now that Elsa was not fond of horses, but knew the family she left were great horsemen.

"Yes, that I am." Eero nodded, he did not look surprised when Elsa took his arm gleefully.

"Tell me more about this stallion." Elsa steered the knight to the further end of the room, towards the two large windows, leaving the prince and princess to stand together. Brendolyn smiled to herself, turning to look up at Barrow.

He looked at her in amazement.

"How can you be even more beautiful than the last time I saw you?" Barrow marveled.

Brendolyn blushed. "Have I, really? To me I see no great difference but look at you. You've grown taller."

Barrow tucked a bit of hair behind her ear, standing so close to her she could smell his cologne—a perfume made of the blooms of the Duvaulian tree.

She smiled, his blue eyes a welcomed sight.

She ran her fingers along his jawline, then her thumb traced an invisible line from below his nose to his chin, grazing over his lips. Barrow's eyes glanced around, before leaning in to place a small kiss on Brendolyn's cheek, so near her lips it made Brendolyn breathless.

"We mustn't," he whispered, glancing quickly towards the door.

"Shall I receive a lecture from Sir Lahrs should he discover us?" Barrow asked, smiling, taking hold of Brendolyn's hand.

"To you he would be civil, and not think twice of, but me...I shall never hear the end of that lesson. But we are in close company." Brendolyn was affectionate, glancing towards the part of the room where Elsa stood talking with Sir Eero. "Let us speak as we desire, but our lips shall remain pure."

"As you wish." Barrow brought her hand up, pressing the warmth of his mouth to the curve of her knuckles. "Then let me kiss your maiden hand and be satisfied."

Eero smiled down at Lady Elsa, they stood not far from the devoted lovers, who smiled and whispered to each other. Giving them space, he addressed her companion.

"You are fond of horses?"

She went pale, her eyes quickly looking away. "No."

Eero nodded. "I see. You are upset."

Her hazel eyes narrowed slightly, but she remained graceful in her addresses. "I have nothing to say to you. Don't pretend I don't remember our meeting in Signe."

"Very true."

She scowled up at him, clearly holding back a fiery temper. Eero reached into his pocket and extended the wrapped glass to Elsa. She glared at him, but took the little package, tucking it away in her pocket hidden beneath the layers of skirt.

"I won't forgive you," she stated flatly.

"Of course."

After a long pause, she turned on him. "You stole my letter."

Eero smiled. "I *delivered* your letter. Eugene sends his regards, he shall write to you promptly."

"A thief and a king's guard, you are full of surprises, Sir Eero."

He chuckled. "I am a trained knight, but there is much I know, Lady Elsa. You come from a well-known family in Corad, one of the largest. Laronn is a Dukedom that has been the ideal of horsemanship throughout the realms."

"Well, shall you tell me more about my home, or shall we speak of things that won't bore me? I see no point in flattery, Sir Eero, I only give my friend her own freedom of speaking with the man she loves." Elsa spoke, her unapologetic tone and honesty catching Eero off guard, but he delighted in her ferocity.

"As you wish, my lady." Eero smiled.

There was a roll of silence between them, they stood side by side, tolerably dutiful to the two others who spoke in hushed tones, whispering to each other.

"How long are you in Corad?" Elsa broke the silence first.

"We are unofficially here. He is on tour of the Realm of Jorn, but Prince Barrow was wanting to get away from that for a day or two. Since the trade routes have been opened again, he seized the opportunity."

His words made Elsa lift a brow. "He is disobeying his terms of court, how very faie of him."

Eero chuckled, louder than he would have liked, Elsa grasped his arm and pulled him away, quickly glancing over their shoulders to see if they were heard, but Barrow was in deep conversation, sitting so near to Brendolyn, their hands together.

"You must not cause them alarm," Elsa spoke, glaring at Eero sternly.

Eero reached around her, grabbing a book off the shelf.

"Shall I read to you?" he enquired, flipping open the book. The pages fell open, but it was elvish that stared back at him.

Looking through the pages, he frowned, returning the book to its original place, extracting a second, only to discover a similar pattern. All of the books were written in another language, one he was not familiar with.

"This library has books from Entheas. Lahrs has them imported whenever he travels abroad. There are Common and other better-known languages in the west library," Elsa informed him.

Eero sighed. "He reads far too much for one man."

Elsa chuckled in agreement.

Barrow's brief respite had stretched from two days into a full week, and then another. By the second week, he and Brendolyn roamed the sun-drenched groves, reveling in the serenity of the warm, fragrant air. They wandered arm in arm, crossing a delicate bridge that spanned a gurgling stream, the gentle murmur of water beneath their feet.

The silence between them was long and companionable until Brendolyn broke it with a soft, almost mischievous smile. "I received a letter from your sister."

Barrow's brows knitted in surprise. "Fiona?"

She chuckled, a sound like tinkling bells, as they continued along the winding path leading to the western gardens. In the distance, the playful spray of fountains shimmered under the sunlight.

"Yes," Brendolyn said, her eyes twinkling. "She sent her well-wishes for my name day. She seems eager to become quite familiar with me, having heard so much about our time together." She observed the blush creeping across the prince's cheeks with a knowing smirk.

"I see," Barrow replied, nodding thoughtfully.

Brendolyn paused by a nearby fountain, her fingers skimming the surface of the cascading water. The droplets caught the sunlight, creating a glittering veil. "She's remarkably well-read. I look forward to our correspondence."

Barrow sighed, a note of melancholy in his voice. "She has had a lonely childhood. My father wishes she would stay in Brecs, the home he shared with my mother before his coronation. I visit her twice a year, but it's hardly enough."

Brendolyn turned her gaze back towards the entrance of the gardens, where Elsa and Eero were still absent. "It must be difficult for her, being so far from her family," she said softly.

Barrow's eyes softened. "Yes, it is. But I'm grateful she has you to write to. It's a small comfort."

A flicker of curiosity crossed Brendolyn's face. "Do you have many visitors in Jorn?"

"Courtiers, mostly," Barrow replied, his attention homing in on her with an intensity that made her cheeks flush. "Many from the old families still frequent the court."

Brendolyn's gaze fell, her curiosity shifting. "And many ladies?"

Barrow's lips curved into a teasing smile as he leaned closer, making her breath catch. His hands gently traced the intricate pleats of her silk gown, his touch sending shivers up her spine. His fingers roamed upward to the bow pinned at the center of her bodice, deftly tugging it loose. She felt a flush of heat spread across her face and a tightening ache between her thighs.

"Every day," he whispered, his breath warm against her ear. "But none compare to the wild little girl who frequents my dreams."

"For shame, Barrow," Brendolyn murmured, her voice trembling. "I am no longer a little girl."

"Indeed," he said, his blue eyes alight with a fiery glint. He grazed his fingers gently along the line of her collarbone. "May I kiss you?"

A radiant blush spread across her cheeks as she whispered, "Yes."

Leaning in, Barrow cupped her cheek, his touch tender as he pressed his lips to hers. The kiss was a gentle exploration, savoring the sweetness of her mouth. He pulled back slightly, his eyes taking in her flushed face.

"You are beautiful," he breathed, his voice filled with awe.

Brendolyn's fingers tangled in his golden hair, a smile lighting her eyes. "Kiss me more," she urged.

Barrow obliged, pressing his body flush against hers. Their lips met again, the kiss deepening as he pulled her closer. His hands roamed the many layers of her gown, seeking the curves beneath the fabric.

As he kissed down her jawline to the delicate curve of her neck, Brendolyn gasped, her hands gripping his hair. His lips grazed the edge of her bodice, igniting a breathless passion within her.

Pulling back momentarily, Barrow met her gaze, his eyes dark with emotion. "I love you," he whispered.

Her heart fluttered at his confession, but a pang of regret lingered. She touched his cheek, her eyes reflecting a mix of joy and sadness. Before she could respond, Elsa and Eero appeared, their entrance breaking the intimate moment.

Reluctantly, Brendolyn drew back as Barrow's gaze shifted away, his lips red and swollen from their kiss. She couldn't help but laugh softly.

"What's the joke?" Sir Eero asked, eyeing both of them with a mix of curiosity and amusement as he walked alongside Elsa.

"Nothing," Barrow said, shaking his head and smoothing his disheveled hair.

Elsa linked her arm with Brendolyn's, guiding her away along a winding path. "Do not kiss him so openly, Brendolyn," Elsa warned, glancing back at the prince and knight who were now engaged in a quiet conversation.

Brendolyn touched her lips absentmindedly. "He said he loved me," she whispered to Elsa, her voice tinged with both wonder and regret. "And I laughed at our foolishness."

Elsa's expression softened as she squeezed Brendolyn's hand reassuringly. "He shall endure," she said, her tone gentle.

CHAPTER

14

Seated at his writing desk, at a later hour than he usually does, to write a letter addressed to Kristjana, the duchess of Tauf, and his betrothed. It was their twelfth year of engagement and Lahrs desperately longed to be near her, as only she understood the depths of his heart, but the duties both of their lives followed did not allow them to meet more than twice a year.

This year was different, Lahrs was bound to Corad under the order of King Sabian, while the trade routes and eastern seaports remained on close watch since the attacks of the Scalanis pirates. There had not been an attack in months, but King Sabian had grown paranoid since returning to Corad.

Lahrs set aside his pen, closing the inkwell, while he waited for the wax to melt in the little brass pot held over the little lamp. Tiredness plagued him, rubbing his sore neck. There was the soft sound of the door click, glancing up to see the prince emerge into the dimly lit room causing Lahrs to frown.

"You wished to speak with me?" Lahrs did not stop his duty of folding the parchment, looping the ribbon of his house securely into the fold.

Prince Barrow was nervous, stumbling over his words. "Your travels in Entheas recently...I heard there were bandits, they burned a village and attacked."

"They have been dealt with." Lahrs smiled politely as he pressed his seal into the dark blue wax that he tipped onto the parchment, sealing the contents inside.

"Marvelous news."

"Tell me what it is you really wish to speak with me about."

Barrow's mouth falls open and a blush so deep christened the fair cheeks of the prince. "I only wish to ask about the affairs of Enth—"

"There are not many things in the realms that I am not aware of, Prince Barrow."

Lahrs watched the shade of the prince shift, his cheeks splotched, unable to hide his true feelings. He went on, "I know how much you think you are in love with her."

"Sir Lahrs, I can assure you that my intentions are pure."

"I am well aware of the intentions you seek with my duty, Barrow, and I cannot see her hurt in any way."

"I love her, Sir Lahrs."

Lahrs forced a smile. "You are no longer a boy, Barrow. I will not treat you as one. Where do you see your life with Brendolyn beyond the solitude and comfort of these walls? Out there in the world where your duty to your father and your realms shall meet you one day. You know what I speak of, do you not?"

There is a long pause. "It is not written into action—"

Lahrs cut him off. "That is a child's mentality, Barrow. You cannot wishfully will away a given treaty between two realms, between two royal houses. Your father went against the will of his kingdom and your grandfather went to war because of it...thousands of lives lost for the sake of your way of love. Do you want this for your people?"

The prince looked at Lahrs with widened eyes, his face pale.

"I cannot risk losing her."

"If you love her, Barrow, you will end it now. Save her from a painful heartbreak."

Barrow let tears fall from his eyes. Bouncing on his heels to still his emotions, but he was close to breaking. "I cannot..."

Lahrs sighed, leaning back in his chair, looking over the emotional wrecked prince before him. "Have you met a faie, Barrow?

Barrow shook his head, words too hard to form.

Lahrs nodded. "In a faie's lifetime, they fall in love once. They fall in love with only one other soul, one other that will fill the depth of them the moment they lay eyes upon them. If their love is taken too early, if they fall in love too soon, before the soul finds their destined match...they are much like elves in a way, some never find their other soul. Some find it but then that love is not returned. That love can never be shared again."

Barrow locked eyes with the elf, he gulped. "Why are you telling me this?"

Lahrs stood, now eye level with the prince. His chest became heavy with the protection, he could see the pain that would come from the young love blossoming between them that he knew could never last. It was impossible for them to be together.

"If you love her, if you have her, but do not keep her...you kill her chance of happiness the rest of her days. She will walk the rest of her life in torment and agony, the joys of her past will wither away from her, foods will never sate her appetite. She will fall into despair and fade away into nothing. She will die of a broken heart."

Tears rolled down the princes' cheeks. "I understand."

Barrow wished he could end it, to tell Brendolyn this could never be between them like they wanted, he wanted her to know he can't change the treaty, that they could never be together. But when he looked at her, when she smiled at him, when she kissed him. He didn't want to lose her. He wanted it to be like this forever.

"There is a festival in the village of Alnwick," Eero was saying to Barrow, as the prince buttoned the front of his plain blue tunic.

"Another? There seems to be a new festival every week."

Eero laughed. "Corad is known for the celebration of many joyous occasions. I am unsure of the nature of this one, but as with many there is dancing, and food, and a very likely chance of a more private meeting with a certain lady."

Barrow smirked at Eero in the reflection of the mirror.

"Very well. You've convinced me."

They were walking in the gardens, when Brendolyn happened upon them. Holding a finger to her lips to silence them she took Barrow's hand in hers.

They three walked into the stables.

Elsa was waiting near the doors. "There you are, I thought you would never get here."

"Come on. We cannot delay, the festival has already begun."

"Will Lahrs not come looking for you?" Barrow whispered, as he leaned into Brendolyn.

Brendolyn smirked. "That's part of the thrill."

She mounted the horse, looking down at the prince who stood beside her.

The village of Alnwick was adorned with lanterns, and flowers, hanging from twine. It was breathtaking, walking beneath the canopy on the main road. As they neared the square, they were greeted by the smells of cooked meat, and the enchanting music from musicians who played on every street corner.

Brendolyn walked beside Elsa, as the prince walked a few paces behind, beside Sir Eero. Admiring them as they thrived in the crowd. Gone unnoticed.

"Look at the dancing!" Brendolyn exclaimed, as they neared a group of sixteen couples who danced in a circle, their hands tied together with a silk ribbon.

"Come on," Barrow whispered, his hand placed at the small of her back, guiding her to the dancing. "I know how much you love to dance."

She was thrilled, weaving between the crowd as they came upon the dancing. A woman approached them with flowers and ribbon tied into her hair. She welcomed them, bowing, before tying a ribbon around Brendolyn's right hand, and Barrow's left.

"Favor find you," the woman acknowledged, motioning them to the dance.

Brendolyn's heart fluttered, as Barrow stood close to her. His hand, tied to hers, as he held her fingers. They followed the dance, giggling and fumbling as they did not know the steps.

Standing off, Sir Eero stood watch, with Lady Elsa beside him. They both watched the couples dance, his eyes keeping a watchful eye over the prince and princess.

"Love is gross." Lady Elsa frowned.

"You are not fond of the current festivities?" Eero mused, a hint of a smile finding his lips.

Lady Elsa looked up at him.

"I am happy for Brendolyn to be in love. But forgive my dislike of love in general."

"You need not apologize for knowing your own mind. But you are very young. Perhaps you shall find love one day."

Elsa quirked an eyebrow. "I am young, happily situated, and in no need of a man to order me about."

Eero laughed. "A spirited woman. There is no wonder why Bren chose you as a companion."

"Do you find yourself charming all of the lady's maids of Barrow's lovers, or have you become desperate in your old age?" Elsa was smirking, her eyes now watching the dance before them.

"Barrow has had no other lovers," Eero said flatly. "You think I'm old?"

Elsa smiled playfully. "You are nearly twice my age and lop around complaining of aches and pains—which is a sign of age, sir. How long were you a horse master before you became a knight?"

"I was a soldier."

He glanced down at the lady, who had suddenly become very quiet. "I became a knight after serving my king in the great war."

She looked up at him with a hint of a smile upon her lips. "You *are* old. Not surprising."

Eero chuckled, catching a look at the dancers. "Now, I certainly recognize your spirit, Lady Elsa. Eugene was equally spirited, when I knew him long ago."

Elsa frowned. "My brother is acquainted with so many knights. I cannot keep them all named. But I cannot remember him ever being a friend of a knight of Jorn."

"I knew him during the war. I was once a knight of Rhun. When the battle was over, I was misplaced in Jorn. Many of my memories are hazy, but I remember your family. Eugene was there in the training yard with all the other boys our age. We were all too young to fight in a war."

"Yes, Rhun was once a great city of this realm, before the war. You fought in the great battle?"

Eero began seriously. "I was."

"You told me you saw Eugene, in Signe. You gave him my letter." She looked desperate, searching.

"He was in Signe as our ship came into the harbor. He was with a small collective of knights. We stayed at the same inn, where he inquired after our affairs in Corad. When I mentioned Alnwick, I do remember a certain knight in his party who questioned after a young lady...Eugene was quite fervent with his knight that there was nothing in Alnwick but trouble."

"I don't recall being acquainted with any certain knight of Corad. My brothers are my only acquaintances."

Eero smirked. "You know Sir Lahrs."

"He is an elf of Entheas, sir. Do not patronize my knowledge," Elsa badgered him, keeping her head tall.

"I see." Eero straightened, glancing over the growing number of dancers, trying to keep his eyes on the prince and princess.

"You are quite certain this knight did not inquire more?" Elsa asked him then, her voice low.

Eero could see the concern in her hazel eyes.

"Sir Alaric shall never step foot in Alnwick, Lady Elsa. If he does not heed my first warning, then my sword shall convince him a final time."

Elsa sighed heavily. "Eugene told you."

"Eugene knew my destination, Lady Elsa. He cautioned me of Sir Alaric's true nature. He did not need to give me details, I have met his kind formerly. Before I left, I gave the knight some advice. He was very keen on following orders." He saw the slightly green hue as the lady turned.

"Oh," she breathed, unable to meet his gaze.

"If he does bother you here while I am not, write at once, Lady Elsa."

The same lady approached them, her smile bright, offering them a ribbon to dance.

"Oh, I don't dance." Elsa waved her off, flustered.

The woman beamed at them, then looked up at Eero. "Just one dance is all you need to receive the blessing of Ehnarea."

"I already have all the blessings I need," Eero said politely.

Beaming again, the lady looked to Elsa.

"Not me...we aren't a couple," Elsa stated. "We are here for our friends."

A look of recognition came over the lady. She looked over the couples already dancing, seeing the dark-haired maiden and the golden-haired man who embraced her.

"They are so in love, it was divine providence that they be united under Ehnarea's eyes tonight, above all others." She spoke, giving a passing couple a ribbon to join in with the dance.

Eero shifted, uncomfortably. "United? As in…" He saw them—they were surrounded by couples, lovers who danced, who walked together. He looked down at Elsa.

She was equally as shocked.

"Festival of Fertility, the Goddess Ehnarea blesses those upon this night as they dance with the lover's twine."

"They are getting married?" Elsa spoke first.

The lady bowed her head.

"You are certain it is a binding marriage?" Eero felt his stomach knot, casting a glimpse at the dancers, who had dwindled down to only a small few.

"Oh yes, they dance the lover's union, and then under Ehnarea, they become one."

"Excuse us," Elsa cut in, grabbing Eero by the arm and hurrying off. They weaved through the crowd looking over the heads of the crowd for the familiar prince and princess.

"I do not see them," Eero stated, looking down at Lady Elsa and her worried look.

Barrow led Brendolyn down the path that wound away from the dancers. It was a low trimmed hedge that looped around and around in a circular sphere, lights danced above them on thin strings, flower petals fell from above. Barrow smiled down at Brendolyn and they looked down at the joining of their hands. He slowly untied the ribbon, letting it fall at their feet.

"You are beautiful." Barrow smiled, stopping so he could caress the curve of her jaw.

She blushed.

He leaned into her, feeling the warmth of her body pressed to his. A sigh escaped him, his arm wrapped around her, pressing his hand to the small of her back.

Brendolyn reached up, her hand delving deep into the fall of his golden hair and gazing into his blue eyes. He was delighted as she leaned up onto the tips of her toes, kissing the corner of his mouth.

He kissed her fully as he had never done before—hungrily. Savoring the feel of her soft lips, the curve of her breast against his chest. Barrow pulled back, gasping.

"We should stop," he muttered, touching the curve of her reddened lips.

Brendolyn smiled, entwining her fingers with his, hurrying further and further into the maze of hedges, until they appeared out into the cool night air. It was quiet in the darkened edge of the wood. Barrow stopped, pulling Brendolyn back.

She was smiling as she reached up again to kiss his mouth.

"There is no better time, Barrow. We are alone," she whispered, her hand trailing the length of his neck.

"I could ruin you," he sighed, his stomach flopping and his body growing hot as Brendolyn pressed against him, her hands pulling at the front of his tunic.

Brendolyn yanked his tunic open, exposing the front of his chest.

"Perhaps I wish to be ruined, if no other man shall touch me." She sighed, kissing his neck. "You are all I want. You are the only one I shall ever want."

Barrow felt his soul set on fire, groaning as her teeth grazed his jaw and holding on to the curve of her waist.

"Not here, in the woods…" He shook his head.

He longed to touch her, to feel her under his hands, but the chill of the forest danced over the heat upon his neck. Brendolyn smiled, her lips pressed against his ear causing Barrow to shiver.

She pulled back, unlacing the front of her gown.

"Bren…Bren, what are you doing?" He was excited, but horrified, as he reached for her hands to stop her, but the princess stepped back continuing to unlace her bodice.

"I want you, Barrow." She smiled as she evaded his grasp and she tossed her bodice aside, standing before Barrow in her chemise, her corset, and her petticoat. He tried to hold her hand, as she reached for the ties of her skirts, but she kissed him.

Her arms were warm as she embraced him. She pressed him back and he stumbled over the uneven ground, colliding with the solid trunk of a tree. Brendolyn laughed, her lips hot on his neck as her hands trailed the length of his chest. She was deliberate, as her mouth kissed his pulse point, just below his ear. Barrow gasped when her hand shifted between them, palming him through his breeches.

"Bren," Barrow groaned.

"I don't want to wait another moment," Brendolyn whispered, kissing his mouth again.

Barrow felt like he was falling, his body hot and tense as he kissed her. Her body was hot against his as she rubbed him through the thin layer of wool between them. He wanted her, above anything else, his hands grasping her, holding her hips, her waist. Daring to trail his hands to grasp the curve of her backside through the layers of her skirts.

It was almost too much, Barrow quickly stilled her hand, breathing in heavily as he looked down upon her illuminated under the glow of the moon.

"We should wait…" he breathed, trying to calm the fires within him and bringing her hands up to kiss her fingers. "I want you but I want our joining to be gentle, not rushed. Not in the woods."

Brendolyn smiled.

"Always the romantic…very well." She nodded, reluctantly pulling back.

CHAPTER

15

B rendolyn felt hot, sitting at her vanity.

They had returned to the main square, flustered. Brendolyn had righted her bodice but her cheeks were flushed. Brendolyn felt a rush of heat flood her cheeks when Sir Eero looked over her, taking Barrow quickly aside, as Elsa walked with her to the horses that would take them home.

Now, she sat, dressed in her nightgown. Her mind trying to take in what Elsa had just informed her as Elsa helped her brush the length of her long onyx hair.

"We cannot be married." She shook her head.

"It was the Festival of Fertility, Brendolyn..." Elsa let the brush trail down the length of her curls.

Brendolyn felt a knot in her gut. "I had not realized. All the festivals blend together..." The brush slowed, Brendolyn looked through the reflection at Elsa, who was watching her closely.

"You are alright?" Elsa began. "Did...did something happen in the woods?" she asked, speaking around the subject carefully.

"No. Barrow did not touch me."

"That's good to hear...it would be a shame if I needed to murder him." Elsa smiled. Brendolyn chuckled.

"Now, shall I braid your hair, or would you like to do it yourself?" Elsa asked, replacing her brush upon the vanity.

"I can...you may retire if you wish to. I am exhausted." Brendolyn forced herself to yawn, standing to retrieve her robe. Draping it around her as she found her favorite book at her bedside.

Elsa smiled. "Stay out of trouble."

Brendolyn peaked over the edge of her book, looking up at Elsa. "I shall be asleep, Elsa. I can hardly get into much trouble while dreaming."

Sitting beside her, Elsa took her friend's hand.

"I know you well enough, Bren...if Barrow is to sneak into your rooms when everyone else has gone to bed..."

Brendolyn pressed Elsa's hand. "I am aware of love making, Elsa."

Her friend colored, pulling back.

"It's not that, Brendolyn. You have never been with a man. It shall be your first time, there are things that could happen...you can bleed. It could be painful—"

Brendolyn sat up next to Elsa, the flutter of her friend's heart and nerves causing her to panic and Brendolyn took Elsa by the hand.

"Elsa," she began softly, lacing their fingers together. "I know what Alaric did to you...he forced you and it was wrong, but—" She paused, working around her thoughts to speak without causing more distress in her dearest friend. "I trust Barrow, completely."

Elsa lowered her gaze, unable to meet her eye.

"Just promise me you will be careful?"

Brendolyn squeezed her friend's hand, kissing it fondly.

"If it happens, I wish it to be with him, Elsa. I will go to him tonight, when everyone has gone to bed."

Elsa frowned. "If Lahrs would find out."

She chuckled. "He would never imagine I would, Elsa. Besides, he was in his office writing his letters. You know it takes him hours. And his chambers are on the other side of the castle."

"I can't persuade you against this, I know your mind's made up...but I beg you to consider your heart, Bren. You're falling for him, I can see it in how you behave."

Brendolyn sighed heavily. Elsa was right, her resolve to not fall in love with Barrow was crumbling. Whenever she was around him, everything else seemed to fade away, when he was near her, there was nothing else.

"He makes me feel seen, he makes me less lonely."

Elsa kissed Brendolyn's hand.

"You are never alone, Bren. You have me, you have even Lahrs..." She paused, looking Brendolyn over with a wary look.

"Have you given up on him, your fated match?"

Sorrowful, Brendolyn shook her head. "He doesn't exist, Elsa. He never did...he was only in my imagination."

Barrow was readying for bed, when a knock comes gently to his door. Confused, Barrow looked to the mantle above the low burning fireplace. It was late in the hour, and he had not rung for tea.

Walking out the door, as a second knock came, a little louder, he opened it slightly, and his breath stilled as Brendolyn looked up at him with a mischievous smile.

"What are you doing?" Barrow whispered, as she pushed herself into his room.

"I have come to see my *husband*."

Barrow looked her over, dressed in a frilly robe, her dark hair wild about her, reaching the length of her back to her lower back. His cheeks colored, gulping as he stepped aside. He was shocked when Eero told him after returning to the estate of the ceremony of the Festival of Fertility. He was embarrassed. But looking down at Brendolyn now, took away any previous doubt.

"Forgive me, I had not realized before about the festival. I just know how much you love to dance." His voice faltered, as she placed a hand to his lips, silencing him.

"Don't be…" She let her eyes drift over him, tracing her fingertips along his jaw, then letting her thumb touch the curve of his lip leaning in to kiss him tenderly.

"Are you certain?" he asked, his hands tentatively reaching the curve of her hips. She was bare beneath and his body felt alive.

"I have never been more certain of anything."

His breath stilled, his heart hammering in his chest as he leaned in to press a kiss to the curve of her jaw. Lingering along the line of her neck, his hands grasping so tight to her, anchoring through the height of his lust. Barrow groaned, as Brendolyn grasped his hair. Barrow scooped her up, walking them to the bed within his chamber, placing her down gently and crawling to lay beside her.

She trembled as he pressed a kiss to her throat, breathing her in as he trailed a hand along the curve of her waist. He squeezed her breast, through the thin fabric of her robe, earning a breathy gasp.

Brendolyn tangled her fingers through his hair.

"Shall I stop?" Barrow asked but Brendolyn shook her head.

Kissing her, Barrow let his hand trail further down, squeezing her hip under a sure handed grasp. Swallowing her moan in a heated kiss, Barrow paused, letting his fingertips dance along the material of Brendolyn's thigh, slowly moving it up, and up until her leg lay bare. Barrow sighed, her skin raising in gooseflesh as he trailed his nails along her hip.

"Don't stop," Brendolyn spoke against his lips. Her own hands danced along the line of his open tunic, trailing along the smooth flesh of his chest.

Barrow did not stop, letting his hand fall between her thighs, watching her now with open eyes as he felt her. Ready, willing. His heart thrashed in his chest. Touching her gently, she kissed him, hard. Gripping the front of his tunic as she crashed her mouth to his. Feeling her pliant over his fingers as he slipped in and out slowly.

Eager, Brendolyn went to the laces on his breeches, unlacing them with quick fingers. Barrow sighed, then gasped when Brendolyn took him in hand. He was delirious. Drunk on her kiss, the heat around his fingers. She was beautiful.

"Tell me how far," Barrow whispered, lining himself with her heat. He trembled, grasping Brendolyn's thigh as he pressed forward and Brendolyn held tight to his shoulders.

She kissed him, desperately, looking up at him when he was finally seated within her, his body trembling.

"Barrow," she said, tucking some of his golden locks away from his face. He smiled and kissed her.

Blissful within her arms, heat radiated through his body as they shared each other's embrace. Slowly burning together, as they grasped the sheets and Barrow kissing her neck. Brendolyn dug her nails deep into his skin as he swallowed all her moans with his mouth as he kissed her. Shuddering and dancing around the edge of ecstasy, before tumbling over in a wonderful melt of passion.

They lay, cooling in the after bliss of passion. Barrow felt his eyelids drifting closed as Brendolyn's fingers trailed languidly over the lines of his chest, her warm breath cooling across his sweaty skin.

"Will you go out riding with us tomorrow?" Brendolyn asked, her tone sleepy.

He smiled, in his dozing haze, bringing his hands to caress her, delving into her onyx hair. "Of course."

She leant up, kissing his chin. "Will you tell your father about us?"

"I would prefer not to think of my father after what we have just done." Barrow's words were laced with humor. He chuckled but there was no laughter. Barrow opened his eyes to see Brendolyn looking down at him.

"I am serious, Barrow. He should know that we have been married." She touched the line of his lips.

Slowly, Barrow leant up on his elbows. "I will return in a few days' time. It will not be easy to bring it up, but I will tell him. He might be angry."

"Because you broke the treaty?" Brendolyn asked. Her eyes were bright, and she was still so young. Barrow leaned in and kissed her, trailing his fingers over the soft skin of her shoulder.

"Let me worry about my father and his wrath...after I have explained it all, he will understand." Barrow warmed at the sight of her smile and he kissed her again, her lips receptive to his wanton praise.

"Barrow," Brendolyn breathed. Her eyelids fluttered shut as he trailed his mouth along her neck. He made a noise and felt her chuckle. Brendolyn's fingers raked through his hair. "Will you make love to me again before morning?"

He smiled, pressing her back adoring the way she yelped in surprise, followed by her soft chuckle. Looking up to him where he leant above her. "I will wait until the sun glistens in the morning dew and the songbirds welcome the new day."

"I love you," she said, touching his cheek, tracing a line down his lips with the flat of her thumb. Barrow just smiled, kissing her again, and again.

Eero leaned against the tree at the center of the garden, keeping a careful eye on Barrow and Princess Brendolyn as they picnicked. Barrow resting his head in the princess' lap as she laughed and fed him grapes. The picture of love and devotion. He felt a pang in his chest, knowing it could not last.

There was a rustle of skirts beside him and he knew Lady Elsa had come to rest on the other side of the tree. He resisted the urge to turn and look at her, knowing she was wearing the green dress that brought out the color of her eyes and that her hair would be down, brushing tantalizingly against her shoulders and waist. Elsa was too young for Eero to have such thoughts about her, but the vision Eugene had told him about was clouding his judgement. Was she his match? Eugene had not seen the man Elsa married but he insisted Elsa and Eero's fates were intertwined.

Finally, he looked over at her, noting again that she was beautiful. That her red hair caught the sunlight and seemed to glow. Her lips were set in a perfectly kissable pout.

Eero shook off the thought. She was only eighteen, barely old enough to consider love, let alone understand the advances of a knight who was reaching his prime. Any action he took to woo her would be inappropriate. It would be taking advantage of her naivety and inexperience. Perhaps when she was older, but not now.

"King Beaumont will annul their marriage, won't he?"

"Yes."

Elsa frowned. "Will Barrow fight for her? Or will he simply leave and break her heart?"

"I cannot say. He will not want to hurt her."

"Because he loves her?"

"You've heard him speak. Read his poems. Do you not believe him to love your princess?"

He turned toward Elsa again, watching her twist her hands together, eyes downcast.

"I know men speak easily of love when they believe it is the key to gaining what they desire. But I am not foolish enough to believe words are where love is truly revealed."

"And how is love revealed, Lady Elsa?"

She glared at him with those sharp hazel eyes, they almost made his breath catch. "In actions." She let out a sigh, turning her gaze back to the couple in the grass. "Barrow has had her as his wife and I do not doubt that he cares for her but...will he prove his devotion when it is no longer easy to choose her? Or will he cast her aside and leave her to be ruined when protecting her is no longer convenient? Will he love her truly or is he, like so many men, only words?"

Eero studied Elsa's face, the sadness that welled up inside of her causing him to laugh. "How is it that someone so young and beautiful came to speak such bitter words?"

"I may be young but I am not naive. Nor am I inexperienced in the ways of men."

"You're speaking of that knight. The one your brother warned me about. Alaric." He watched her flinch when he said the name. "What did he do that turned you so cold?"

"It doesn't matter. It is in the past."

Eero reached out before Elsa could turn away, tucking a hand beneath her chin.

"It matters to me." He realized when she looked up at him that he had been wrong. Elsa was young, but she was not naive. She would not swoon at a handsome face or kind words.

"He spoke easily of love but when words did not bring him what he wanted...his actions were not those of a man in love. And that is all I wish to say on the matter."

Eugene had said Alaric was not the sort to take no easily. Eero wondered if, when he failed to seduce Elsa with words he had turned to force and taken what he desired from her. Then he wondered if she would recognize real love when it found her. With a guilty twist of his stomach, Eero realized how much he longed to show her, this beautiful, broken girl who had allowed herself to become so hard.

He licked his lips before speaking, eyes darting to her mouth again, then forcing his gaze to return to her eyes. "And what actions would a man in love take, Lady Elsa?"

"I'm sure I do not know. For Bren's sake, I hope it will be an action to protect her heart."

"What about you?"

Elsa's eyes widened.

"What actions might a man take to convince you of his love?" He was standing too close to her. It would be too easy to lean into her and kiss her. Eero could already smell the citrus in her hair. "Ought he send you flowers or challenge any man who dared look at you to a duel?"

She stiffened. "No. I would not accept the love of any man who treated me as a possession."

"Then what? What would you have me do, if I wished to show you that I cared for you?"

Without thinking, Eero leaned forward, kissing her. It was not something he planned to do or ever let himself consider until that very moment. All he knew was he cared for Elsa and he wished to show her. A heady magick threaded around them and Eero could feel it like an inky black cloud of smoke. It was cloying and suffocating, burning his skin.

Elsa shoved him back, gasping as if his touch burned. "Please stop." Her features were pinched with pain.

"Elsa, what's wrong? Did I hurt you?"

"Don't touch me! Please don't touch me." She backed away from him, frantic, like a fox cornered by a hunter. Her eyes darted across the garden to Bren and Barrow, tears welling in her eyes. "I must go." Then she was running, running away from him.

"Elsa, wait!" Eero glanced at his charge before deciding to follow her.

The door to the library opened but Elsa ignored it, continuing to shelve books and fluff pillows on oversized reading chairs. A task that she did not necessarily have to do but it needed to be done. Anger flooded her bones as her lips burned. Angry at Sir Eero for his impudence.

Eero stepped inside, letting the door bang shut behind him but she kept her back to him. After a moment he let out a long suffering sigh. "What are you doing, Lady Elsa?"

"Reshelving the books." She slid a worn leather volume of poetry back into place. "The library is in a terrible disarray."

"Yes, I can see that is what you are doing but what I meant was why…why are *you* doing this?" Out of the corner of her eye she saw him gesture uselessly around him.

"Alnwick does not have enough servants to keep everything in order, especially with a royal visitor, so I am trying to be useful."

"Are you being coy on purpose?"

Finally, Elsa turned to look at Eero. He stood casually by the door, annoyance emanating off his shoulders and sharp gaze.

"I'm sure I do not know what you are talking about. You asked me a question and I answered. I am reshelving the books because it needs doing and I am just as capable of doing so as anyone else."

Eero's jaw tightened. "That is not what I meant and you know it."

She dropped the last three books onto the table with a dull thud. "Then let's say I do not know what you mean, Sir Eero. Did you mean why am I accomplishing this task at this moment? Perhaps it was because I did not wish to spend any more time with you lest you decide to kiss me again. Or do you mean why am I arranging the library instead of watching over Bren and the prince whose intentions you yourself have insisted I needn't worry about?"

"I don't know why I did that…" He looked horrified and Elsa knew he meant it. She knew the horrible curse that Alaric had embedded into their bond, that made those nearest to her desire her as he did. "It won't happen again."

"See that you keep your promise."

"Why are you here in Alnwick playing at being a lady's maid when you and I both know you have other options. *Better* options."

"Better options?" Elsa felt her skin heat with anger. "What better options do you think I have than serving my king by protecting princess Brendolyn?" She jabbed a finger at Eero's chest. "You of all people should understand the importance of what I am doing."

"I understand that that is a task that should be undertaken by the daughter of a low lord. A viscount at the very highest. Your father is a duke. You have a dowry. You have land and titles set aside for you. Why do you choose to stay here? Why do you refuse to marry or even read the letters of suitors?"

Elsa blanched, taking a step back so one of the overstuffed chairs stood between her and the large knight. "How do you know that?"

"You forget, I have known your brothers a long time. I was there at Eugene's wedding. He wished for me to meet you. To dance with you."

"Then you already know the answer you seek."

Elsa felt her face growing hot, looking into the gray eyes of Sir Eero. She remembered the night, she could never forget. A mist of tears threatened to break her composure. Elsa refused to touch her side where the brand tingled at the thought of the man who had claimed her.

"I don't. Even if I did, I would like to hear it from you. Why do you stay here, barely a step above a servant at the mercy of the king when you could take your dowry and be a real lady."

"Bren needs me." The half lie felt flat. "I cannot abandon her."

"And when she marries and no longer needs you?"

Elsa glared. "If there comes a day when Bren no longer requires my services, I will go to Divna and join the Silent Sisters, where I shall take the Oath." Though that thought left a sour twisting feeling in Elsa's stomach. "Not that it is any business of yours."

Elsa turned back to the books, snatching them up and throwing one onto the shelf. It was in the wrong place but she didn't care.

"I don't understand you. You could be anything you like and yet you choose to be..."

Elsa spun around, anger crackling against her skin. "No! I cannot *be* anything I like! Do you think my dowry belongs to me? No! It belongs to my father and my brothers until such time as I marry and it will become the property of my husband. As will every other piece of me! He'll take my body to bear his children. He'll take my bed for his pleasure. Even my thoughts and opinions will belong to *him*." Tears burned in her eyes, the kind that could be blinked back if she was careful. She turned her face away, just in case.

"It would not be like that."

"It would," she snapped back. "Even if I opened those letters and found a gentleman who was kind, who loved me, my marriage can only ever be that." She held back the fact that she chose never to open the letters because she did not want to find someone she cared about who cared for her only for Alaric to claim her. "You don't know anything." Elsa threw the books back onto the table, shoving past Sir Eero toward the door.

"I know you left home because you were afraid of a man, that even here you're afraid of him. Did he do something to you, Elsa? Something that makes you believe it is better to be alone? Something that makes you afraid to even try to love?"

Her fingers hovered over the door handle. Frozen.

Eero took a step toward her. He was so near, Elsa could feel his breath against her ear. "Did he claim you so no one else could ever touch you?"

Elsa's fingers curled into a loose fist, hand falling at her side. "What did my brothers tell you?"

"They did not have to. I can feel it, there is a magick burned into your skin, every time I get close to you." His hand snaked around her waist, palm pressing into her ribs, right in the place Alaric had branded her. She hissed at the sudden burning pain but Sir Eero did not release her. "Please tell me I am wrong."

Elsa pulled out of his grip, spinning around to find him standing dangerously close. Gray eyes full of concern staring into her.

"I can't." She gripped the door handle so hard it dug into her fingers, wrenching it open and running from the library.

CHAPTER

16

Jorn City, Realm of Jorn.

Elated in his travels, the journey home was swift. Barrow commended the sails of the ship, and the hastened arrival of the horses not long after making port in Denorn. Taking the king's road to Jorn City beside Eero and the escort of guards behind, they were home quicker than many other times of travel.

Sir Eero, as they neared the castle gates, put a dampening spirit into Barrow.

"You must prepare yourself for disappointment."

"How can I be disappointed, Eero, when I am in love?" Barrow pulled back on the reins, guiding his mare into the shelter of the stables, glaring at the knight who had been pensive and moody since they had left Alnwick.

"I have a terrible feeling we were not detained longer, but our hastened return has me suspicious of what transpired the past month," Eero spoke in a low tone.

Barrow scoffed. "Luck is on our side, Eero."

"You went against your father and your king, to seek the company of a girl of a neighboring realm. It shall not be favorable should your father be displeased with your absence of duty."

"So you have told me before this journey and again when we remained in Alnwick longer than I had intended. But can you honestly tell me that my father would be so displeased when he learns that I am in love?"

Eero frowned, drawing up his horse.

"You know I served your father before he was king. As his guard and as his first sworn protection I followed him in his own travels. I was beside him in his own rebellions against your grandfather, King Broderick."

He had heard this story before. Eero was always reminding Barrow that he was not the first of the kingdom to break away from their duty.

"Then he would understand what it means to fall in love with one their father does not approve of." Barrow dismounted, handing his horse to the nearest stable hand.

Eero did the same. "Is that how you wish to win his approval of your courting Brendolyn? Perhaps, I should also remind you that Lahrs had told you to not entangle yourself."

"I am in love with her, Eero, I cannot change how I feel about her."

Annoyance traveled up Barrow's spine, twinging in the back of his teeth. Yanking off his riding coat as he stormed out of the stables, Eero was close at his heels.

"You cannot change your feelings, but you can honor her maidenhood." Eero spoke freely, as he always did, keeping his voice lowered so they were not overheard. "Brendolyn is still young, Barrow."

Barrow rolled his eyes, stopping at the narrow fence leading into the side door to the lower parts of the castle. It was eerily quiet, clouds looming overhead. Barrow looked into the gray eyes of the knight.

Eero looked hard at him, his jaw clenching. "You took her to your bed?"

There was a beat, a moment of calm before the thick glob of rain splattered over Barrow's cheek. Swallowing hard against the rise of shame that made him hot.

"She came to my room, Eero. How could I resist her?"

Eero folded his arms over his broad chest, creasing the stiff leather of his jacket, water dribbled along the leather. Before long the sky would open up and the gardens would be drenched. Eero was a formidable force that stood in his way.

"She is a child."

"Is that why you turn your face away from Lady Elsa?" Barrow snapped, his anger unsettling between them. "I have seen the way you look at her."

"There is nothing but mutual compliance between me and Elsa Laronn. But it is not of importance should her father be seeking her as a marriage partner." Eero sharpened his look as he glared at Barrow. "I have not fucked the daughter of the neighboring king before the contract of treaty had been signed."

"You cannot speak to me that way."

Eero stepped closer, he wasn't much taller than Barrow, but he was broad, with tight muscles that filled out his frame. Barrow knew he could not defeat Eero in a fight, but would the man strike the prince? He gulped, not wanting to find out the answer.

"My duty is to speak to you exactly how I always have, Barrow. I cannot command you, but I have been given the permission to tell you when you go too far." Eero's voice was a deep resonating sound. "You go too far, Barrow."

Barrow gulped again.

"Come," Sir Eero sighed. "You should rest before being summoned by your father."

"Of course." Barrow felt like turning on his heels and disappearing into the rain but he knew they would find him eventually.

Entering the castle, one of King Beaumont's servants approached them. "Your father requests your audience, sire."

Barrow smiled. "I shall as soon as I have disrobed my travel attire."

As they walked away the servant spoke up, "He requests it immediately, without delay. Sir Eero is summoned as well, Your Majesty."

Walking side by side, they take the shortest path through the castle up the side staircase. Barrow was suddenly uneasy, as the words Eero had warned gave him the suspicion of truth. It was livelier in the castle, and many of the servants they walked past hardly looked up. It was unusual to see so many on this side of the castle.

After a swift knock on the door of the king's study, Eero pushed open the great door, allowing them entrance. King Beaumont stood tall, looking out of his large window as the rain drizzled over the glass, obscuring the courtyard below.

"Shut the door," he commanded, without turning around.

Barrow stood before his father's large desk, while Sir Eero shut the door. At the sound of the great bolt clicking into place, did his father turn towards him. Beaumont was frowning, his usual spirit diminished to worry.

"You were expected in Nord but I received a letter from our patron that you were never accepted to their house."

Fear trembled through Barrow, sheepishly looking down to his feet.

"Look at me when I speak."

Barrow's eyes snapped up at his father's command.

"You also did not accept the banner in Aavin...which has been a tradition in our family for generations. These three years hence have been planned accordingly for your ceremony of charge on your name day, when you take the seat of Brac as I had before you. Without it...without the blessing of your people how do you expect to be a great king? When I am gone would your people flock to your aide or take heed of your words if you do not act in accordance with your duty?"

A tightness filled Barrow's throat, trying to form words when his father spoke but nothing came. Beside him Sir Eero stood like a statue, patiently waiting and watching.

Beaumont softened slightly, his hand gliding over the papers that lay out on his desk. Then he spoke again, "The House of Moreau is here within our castle walls, do you have any notion why?"

Barrow gulped. "I do not."

"If you had arrived in Aavin, as was the arrangement, you would have received my letter, but as you were not there to receive it, here it is in my hand now." Beaumont extended a letter to his son, but Barrow couldn't move.

Quickly Eero stepped forward, taking it from the king to hand it to the prince. Barrow glanced down, his face growing hot as the words he read filled him with trepidation.

Return to Jorn City before the week is out...the council has made a decision that cannot be delayed.

Barrow looked up to his father.

"It can't be..." Barrow breathed, his heart thumping in his throat.

Beaumont clenched his jaw. "When I received by letter of your absence from Aavin and then in Nord, I assumed the worst." The king shifted on his feet, trying to form words and keep his emotions in check. "I assumed my son and heir to my throne had been murdered in his sleep. What am I to learn instead?"

Barrow's stomach lurched as the king picked up a letter from his desk. His heart was hammering hard in his chest as his hands began to sweat.

King Beaumont spoke, reading the letter aloud. "Many tidings, Your Majesty King of Jorn, Beaumont Aubin. As my sources report upon the findings of your son, Prince of Jorn, Barrow Aubin has been seen within the realm of Corad. Not three days hence my informer within the realm has given me cause to believe he was seen alive and well in the village of Alnwick. My sources also report he was seen in the arms of a dark-haired maiden in the ceremonial Festival of Fertility."

Beaumont let the paper fall. Looking at his son, the look was unlike any Barrow has ever seen. Barrow's breath was ragged, his neck hot and throat tight. Reading the fury in his father like a fourth man in the room breathing down his neck.

"The Castle of Alnwick has been the summer home to the house of Moreau for centuries and as I am to understand it, has been the home of a one dark haired maiden for the past three years."

Barrow felt ill, his stomach churning, his head spinning.

"You married her, in secret?" Beaumont seethed.

"Yes. In short of the events that transpired. Yes, I married her." Barrow could feel the hot tears forming in his eyes.

Beaumont slumped, bracing himself over his desk as he heard the confirmation from his own sons' lips. A fist came down hard against the wood, shaking everything upon it, sending a jolt of shock through Barrow. Witnessing the fury that Barrow had only ever seen spare in his father.

"Was the marriage consummated?"

Barrow's face burned under his father's gaze, his throat closing. He dared not look at Eero, for fear of what the knight would admit openly in one glance.

"Did you put your seed within Brendolyn Moreau?"

Fighting back tears, Barrow shook his head. "I did not…"

He looked away, shame flooding him as he lied to his father. To the king. Tears silently fell down his cheeks as Beaumont stood, scooping up the letters upon his desk, walking the length of the room and throwing the letters into the burning fire.

Turning at last to his son.

"I have paid my informers handsomely for their silence. You will tell no one. This event never happened. Within the month you shall be married to Lisetta Moreau. After the contract is signed and you have been united, you shall live in Brac to begin your house. That is where you shall remain." Beaumont walked to the door, pausing briefly before looking back towards Barrow. "A letter was sent to Alnwick. I personally invited Brendolyn to be my guest. When she arrives, I don't care what you say but you will end it. You will put an end to this and then you will never see her again."

Swiftly the door was opened and the king was gone.

Barrow stood on the spot, unable to move. Numbness overpowering his limbs as tears fell unwanted down his cheeks in silent triumph.

"Come Barrow, you must take rest."

He shook his head, unable to comply with the words his knight whispered at his side. After everything, there was compassion in Eero. Turning his gaze to the fire where the parchment burned, watching the rolled letters of betrayal turn into nothing but ash. Barrow was heavy with shame, feeling the weight of what was discovered. He was a fool before to believe it could be kept secret.

"Barrow." Eero roused his thoughts, taking hold of his arm in a strong grasp.

King Beaumont stormed through the winding corridors of his castle, his rage like a tempest roaring within him. The heavy, echoing footsteps of his boots reverberated off the cold stone walls, each step a testament to his boiling fury. His chest heaved with the weight of betrayal, his mind replaying the devastating news on a relentless loop.

He could no longer contain the storm within him. Stopping abruptly, he pressed his back against a timeworn stone wall. The cold surface did nothing to quell the heat surging through his veins as tears of frustration and anguish blurred his vision. He buried his face in his trembling hands, each sob a raw expression of the profound hurt he felt. The news of the marriage was a dagger to his heart, but the necessity of tearing them apart was a burden far heavier.

With an effort of will, Beaumont dragged himself to his bedchamber, each stride a battle against the weight of despair. He sank into the imposing chair by the window, his frame dwarfing the seat. The room was bathed in the dim, golden light of the setting sun, casting long shadows that seemed to echo his torment.

He reached for a crisp parchment, his fingers trembling as he unfolded it with the care of a man grappling with the gravity of his actions. He dipped his pen into the ink, the scratch of the quill against the parchment a stark contrast to the silence of the room. His thoughts were a maelstrom of fury and determination as he penned a letter, the words forming a lifeline to the resolution he needed.

With deliberate precision, he sealed the letter with a wax stamp, the impression of the royal crest embedding his authority into the missive. Beaumont leaned back in the chair, his shoulders slumped and rubbed the weariness from his eyes. The crushing weight of his decisions bore down on him, his breaths deep and shuddering as he fought against the encroaching darkness of despair. Magick thrummed beneath the surface of his consciousness, a volatile undercurrent that threatened to break free.

Exhaustion clung to him like a second skin, the result of sleepless nights plagued by relentless nightmares. With a weary groan, he stood and made his way to the window. The cool air from the open window was a brief respite from his inner turmoil.

His gaze swept over the lush expanse of the castle gardens below, where the manicured lawns stretched out in a tapestry of greens and golds. His attention was drawn to a figure emerging from the storerooms beneath the castle and making his way to the stables. The man was clad in a leather apron, and his bright copper hair caught in the breeze, catching the last rays of the setting sun. Beaumont's eyes narrowed in contemplative focus as he watched the stable hand, the seemingly mundane sight becoming a moment of clarity amidst his chaotic thoughts.

The image of the stable hand walking purposefully toward the stables was a brief, grounding presence in the swirl of Beaumont's world. He watched in silence, the turmoil in his heart momentarily stilled by the simple, ordinary rhythm of life continuing beneath him.

CHAPTER

17

Denorn, Realm of Jorn

After three days on the open sea, the ship finally approached the bustling city of Jorn, its silhouette rising against the horizon like a steadfast sentinel. As the vessel docked, Brendolyn peered out over the side, her heart tightening with a mix of nostalgia and anticipation.

The familiar sights of Denorn, the port city on the edge of Jorn, greeted them. The once-new shops and vibrant stalls near the harbor were unchanged, their colors and bustle exactly as she remembered from four years past. The same merchants called out their wares, and the scents of fresh bread and sea salt mingled in the air, evoking memories that stirred a pang in her chest.

They would not linger here, however. Lahrs, ever resourceful, had arranged a temporary haven for them. Guided by his extensive knowledge of the city's less-traveled paths, he led them to a serene retreat. This sanctuary was nestled on the outskirts of town, a tranquil abode known for its devotion to the Goddess Ehnarea, the patron deity of light and purity.

Under the auspices of King Beaumont, this place was sanctified and respected, a haven where weary travelers and seekers of solace could find refuge. The women who tended to this sacred space were known for their grace and dedication, their lives entwined with the goddess's teachings. As the carriage prepared to continue their journey into the heart of Jorn City, Brendolyn felt a sense of calm wash over her, knowing they were about to step into a space where the light of Ehnarea would offer them comfort and peace.

"You will be safe there, until we can have a king's escort to the royal palace," Lahrs had told her.

"You believe the faie to be in danger here?" Elsa asked, she voiced what Bren had been thinking.

Lahrs looked stern, he had smiled less in the last few weeks.

"She is safest where I can see her. Now, no more questions, we are arriving."

Lady Arienne was a tall elf, who welcomed them to Jorn upon their arrival. It was there in the chapel, they were to remain until the king's guard would come to escort them to the great city. She was beautiful, Brendolyn observed, patient and well spoken. Guiding them through the silent chapel, into the comfortable library.

Brendolyn was drawn to the stained-glass windows, the ones that overlooked the gardens as lavender bushes waved in the breeze.

"You are free to familiarize yourself with these halls, and the gardens are freshly in bloom. Be at peace, favor find you," Arienne spoke kindly, bowing to them all.

"Stay within the gates," Lahrs told them before he excused himself. He would be directing a letter to the City of Jorn, to inform them of their arrival.

Brendolyn took Elsa's hand and after taking refreshment, they walked the gardens—a large lush plantation of trees and well curated flowers. They took a few turns, in silence. Brendolyn felt tired from the long journey, but if she sat her thoughts began to wander.

"Are you alright?" Elsa asked, catching sight of Brendolyn gazing towards the tall spire of the chapel.

Brendolyn forced a smile. "It is strange to be here again."

"You were invited by the king personally...do you think he found out about you and Barrow?"

She shuddered. "I hope not."

"Lahrs has not mentioned why we have come, surely he would have heard of the king as to this meeting," Elsa added.

They turned, standing in the shade of a large tree, resting their eyes from the bright sun above them. Admiring the view, watching the patrons of the goddess take their blessing at the door of the chapel, where Arienne stood dutifully giving small bunches of lavender to those that sought her out.

Brendolyn let her eyes fall upon one particular patron who stood before the great elf lady receiving his blessing.

"That man, do you see him...the one speaking with the elf lady?" Brendolyn asked Elsa as they stood under the shade of a tree.

Her companion looked that way, before smiling. "The tall handsome one?"

"Yes, how extraordinarily tall and handsome. There is something familiar about him to me," Brendolyn remarked.

Elsa looked back at the stranger, eyeing him warily. "He does not look like a courtier, nor of Corad. Are you certain?"

She looked again. Brendolyn noted the broad shoulders, dressed in black silk, embroidered with intricate leaves of emerald. From the place hidden within the shade of the tree, she could look openly. Admiring his height, the fall of his dark hair that curled slightly. He smiled a brief kind of smile, speaking in a low voice to the elf Arienne, and Brendolyn felt her cheeks go hot.

"It is hard to tell, but there is something..."

Panic rattled through Brendolyn, scampering from sight, as the man in dark clothes stepped along the path towards them. Carrying a bundle of lavender in his hands, he turned a lingering eye up to gaze at the outer walls of the cathedral. Safe out of his direct line of sight, Brendolyn watched from her spot. Her heart hammered as something within her began to stir as she gazed upon the stranger.

"I should ask him," Brendolyn stated.

Elsa gripped her arm, holding her back. "That is unwise, Bren. We do not know him. Wait for Lahrs."

He walked so near, soon he would pass her and then he would be out of sight, it would be impossible to speak to him, or call after him. Her heartbeat quickened as magick fluttered within her. Brendolyn stepped forward.

"I just need to know his name," Brendolyn said, slipping from Elsa's tight grasp. Brendolyn rushed around the tree without looking forward. She turned just as the man crossed her path, colliding with his solid chest.

She gasped and lavender fell around their feet. Gazing up and up Brendolyn gulped—the stranger had wide green eyes.

"Forgive me," she stammered, her face incredibly hot. She knelt down to pick up the little stems of lavender, the man crouching down to do the same.

"No harm done," he spoke, his voice deep and mellow.

Brendolyn gazed into his face. Magick flitted in her throat, light and effervescent, and Brendolyn swallowed hard to settle her nerves. Brendolyn's heart thumped wildly in her chest, unable to break away her gaze. Those eyes a shimmering green watched her as they returned to stand. It felt an eternity, but at last Brendolyn raised her trembling hands, extending to him the lavender that belonged to him.

"Thank you." He smiled, taking the bundle she offered.

"Do I know you?" Words fell from her lips in a rush.

He smiled again, dipping his head. "I do not believe we have ever been introduced."

Brendolyn felt her skin begin to itch, magick shimmering beneath the surface. It was the smell of the sea that invigorated the change, causing her to feel flush. He was watching her, carefully, trying to place pieces together, like a puzzle.

"My name is Bren..." she spoke softly, extending her hand towards him.

"Hello, Bren." His voice was smooth, softening the anxiety that began to pound against her chest. His fingers were soft in her grasp.

He pulled back too soon, his smile fading. Bowing at once, looking behind her warily before he excused himself, stepping away. Brendolyn watched him leave, each step taking him farther away, until he reached the open gates of the churchyard. There, she saw a man with dark copper hair waiting for him and they walked off together.

Brendolyn felt lost, blinking as she began to breathe again. Her face cooling, turning back to where Elsa stood beneath the shade of the tree. Seeing her approach with a questioning gaze.

"Well?" Elsa inquired.

"I must not know him, after all."

Eero resumed his duties in the stables, the familiar rhythm of work providing a soothing counterpoint to the turmoil that had unsettled him. He meticulously returned harnesses to their hooks, the steady, repetitive motions a balm to his restless mind. The rich, earthy scent of the stables, mingling with the musk of horses, was a constant comfort amidst the chaos of the royal court.

"Take these to the front stall, Eero," called Rhys, the stable hand with a mop of unruly reddish hair and a perpetually sun-kissed complexion. He tossed a bale of hay onto the cart with a grin, his eyes crinkling at the corners. "I'll handle the paddock."

"Very well," Eero replied, adjusting the leather straps on his sleeves. He grasped one bale in each hand and nodded to Rhys as they went their separate ways.

Eero found it remarkable how Rhys, despite his cheerful demeanor, worked with a diligence that often surpassed that of the stable master. He remembered meeting Rhys during his early days in Jorn, a time when Rhys had taught him the intricate art of shoeing horses and calming the wildest of beasts. Eero knew that Rhys had once been a soldier—a past life that spoke of courage and battle scars—but those days seemed far behind him now.

He approached the black mare in the last stall, her glossy coat gleaming in the muted light. As she skittered away, Eero took up the rake and began to stir the bedding, preparing a fresh, soft layer for the mare.

"Your mistress isn't here yet, Ciar," Eero murmured, reaching up to stroke the mare's sleek mane. Her dark eyes met his with a hint of curiosity. A gentle puff of warm air against his face made him chuckle, and he nuzzled her coat affectionately.

"Remarkable how you know how to calm them," came Barrow's voice, surprising Eero. He turned to see the prince standing just outside the stall, his expression troubled. Eero noted the prince's usual apprehension around horses; it was clear Ciar's uneasy stance betrayed the prince's presence.

"I was making her ready," Eero said, his voice steady despite the unease dancing through his body. "Princess Brendolyn is set to arrive in Jorn City, and I know she'll want to go riding."

Barrow's face darkened. "I've confessed my mistakes to you, Eero."

"And I've given my opinion," Eero said, brushing his hand over the mare's coat. "We need not revisit it."

"But I cannot forget it," Barrow retorted, his voice rising. "My father's orders are clear. I must end it with her." The agitation in his voice caused Ciar to shift nervously.

Eero's hands tightened around the stallion's coarse neck, his voice a soothing whisper. "Calm now, Ciar." Once the mare quieted, Eero led Barrow out of the stall and into the storage room where saddles were kept. They moved through the room to the large door leading to the back garden paths.

"She has not arrived yet," Eero reassured him. "There is still time before you must meet her."

Barrow's frustration flared. "Ride away with me, Eero. Let us escape to Brac. How long has it been since you've seen my sister?" The prince's suggestion was a plea for escape.

Eero knew that Barrow was struggling to face his responsibilities. It was easier for the prince to flee from his troubles than confront them. Once, Eero would have eagerly joined such an adventure, but now he felt the weight of duty and the necessity for Barrow to remain steadfast. With a resigned sigh, Eero crossed his arms over his chest.

"We cannot," Eero said firmly.

Barrow's anger boiled over, a new, turbulent energy emanating from him. Eero followed the prince as he stormed down the gravel path, his frustration palpable.

"I cannot remain here, Eero," Barrow lamented, his voice a mix of desperation and defiance. "I cannot be forced to marry that venomous woman."

Eero grasped Barrow's upper arm, trying to steady him. In a fit of fury, Barrow swung at Eero, striking him ineffectively in the chest. Eero, unphased by the weak blows, quickly subdued the prince with a firm headlock. The pressure on Barrow's throat and the control over his arm was a stark reminder of Eero's strength.

"I do not want this, Barrow," Eero hissed, his voice low and intense. "I do not want to see your pride wounded or your heart shattered. But you must let her go...you must rally yourself for your kingdom."

"I will not bow to others' will," Barrow growled, struggling against Eero's hold. His resistance was futile; the prince had never known the trials of battle or the weight of real conflict.

Eero released him, stepping back as Barrow sat heavily on the path, his anger still simmering. The air around them crackled with tension, and Eero could hear the restless stamping of the horses in the stables, sensing the unrest.

"You are the Prince of Jorn, Barrow Aubin," Eero said firmly. "You are destined to sit upon your father's throne, just as he inherited it from his own father. As long as this house stands, so too shall the line of kings."

Barrow ground his teeth in frustration. "I don't want the throne."

Eero sat beside him, his expression softening. "The ones who crave the throne are often the least suited to hold it. Those who accept the burden protect it from those who would sow chaos. You will be a great king, Barrow. You must believe in yourself and your ability to lead against the darkness threatening to destroy what has been built."

"I can't be a great king," Barrow said, his voice cracking. "I'm not my father. He fought in the great war, riding into battle with his sword drawn. I've only heard stories of his bravery."

Eero's gaze grew distant as he remembered his own experiences. "War is a lie, a justification for the violence we inflict on those we wish to conquer. I've seen the senseless bloodshed, the young men cut down in their prime. There is no honor in war, only suffering."

Barrow looked at him, eyes wet with emotion. "Lord Bannon tells a different story. He believes that strength must be shown through battle. That's why he persuaded my father to make peace with Entheas—so he could use their forces to conquer the uncharted lands."

A shudder ran through Eero. "Lord Simeon Bannon is a man to be wary of, Barrow. Be cautious with how much you heed his advice."

"But my father trusts him," Barrow protested.

Eero sighed heavily. "Your father keeps Bannon close, but trust is not the same as belief. There are many truths yet to be revealed to you."

Barrow's shoulders slumped in resignation. Eero stayed by his side, offering silent support as the prince struggled to reconcile his duties with his desires. The weight of responsibility and the shadows of looming conflicts were heavy, but Eero hoped that, in time, Barrow would find his path and embrace the role he was born to play.

CHAPTER

18

Jorn City, Realm of Jorn.

Lord Simeon Bannon strode into the private offices of King Beaumont, having been summoned to him in the early hours, well before the start of the king's morning routine. Working through papers when he stopped as the servant knocked on his doors.

Now, the warmth of the room filled him as he made his way to where the king sat upon his lush high-backed chair, sipping from a glass.

"Come, come. I wish a word with you, Lord Bannon." Beaumont instructed him to sit across from him in the matching high-backed chair.

Simeon sat and waited.

Finally, Beaumont spoke. "All is in order for the ceremony, correct?"

Simeon smiled. "Everything is as it should be, Your Majesty."

Beaumont nodded, sipping some more. "Good, that is good to hear...and for the banquet afterwards? What is our entertainment?"

A frown came over Simeon, shifting in his chair.

"Entertainment, Your Majesty?" Simeon looked at the king, who sat forward in his chair.

"Yes, precisely. We have food and music to fill our bellies and plague our ears with their constant droning, we could very well dance all evening, but what of our enjoyment? I had dozens of fire dancers, men who spoke riddles...find me those to celebrate and entertain me."

Beaumont shifted further to face Simeon. All evidence of his rosy cheeks became clear very quickly to Simeon that the king was drunk. A deprivation of sleep mixed with the strong wine from Taastra had been enough to dampen the large man's constitution.

Simeon cleared his throat.

"Perhaps I can inquire about the village. I hear them talk of such things in Denorn." He paused, looking the king over once more. "Are you certain you are alright, Your Majesty? You seem...out of sorts."

Beaumont sat up, his expression very plain, emptying his glass.

"I have never been better," he hissed through clenched teeth.

After all these years, Simeon knew the king well. Knowing how these habits would come about when there was stress, it was also easy to fill the king's head with nonsense of treaties and lovers, but in recent years there was a strong resistance to his magick. Simeon felt the strain of his own hold upon the king.

"Would I ring for a servant, to fetch you some tea?"

To this the king rolled his eyes, standing to his feet, but staggering sideways.

"Tea? At a time like this? Don't be absurd." Beaumont walked over to the chest where the king kept his liquor—imports from every realm.

Simeon stood.

"What hour do you believe it to be, my king, for it is now morning."

The king, who had his back to Simeon, slumped, the chalice hitting down as the drink was abandoned. Beaumont turned to him, eyes darkened, mouth forming into a frown. His cheek hair grew out exceedingly in the last weeks. Beaumont had refused to be groomed and had cast aside all of his personal assistants. Simeon was beginning to see the madness settle in, just as it had done for King Broderick.

"Do not question me on the hour I drink, for I am king, or has the early morning dew made you forget who called you here?" Beaumont's voice was full of malice, spitting his words at Simeon with great haste.

"Forgive me." Simeon bowed.

"Leave me, Simeon, I am tired." His voice was distant, a hand cradling his head. Beaumont shifted, staggering again to the chairs, where he sat his tall frame within.

Simeon walked around to kneel before the king, to be nearly face to face with the man. A slithering danced up his spine, to be near enough to taste the sting of magick.

"Your Majesty." He kept his voice soft.

Beaumont let his hand fall, looking up with large round eyes.

"Do not linger your thoughts upon what is between yourself and the king of the southern realm. He remains dutiful to uphold the treaty. Barrow shall be married and the realms shall be united at last." These words settled over them both.

Beaumont clenched his jaw, shifting in the chair. "His return is not what plagues me. I have not slept. I can feel the darkness looming over my people."

It was delicious, to taste the bitter contempt perfuming the air around them. Simeon had to remind himself to refrain from seeking it, but the sudden urge caught him off guard. Reading a hand out, Simeon pressed his palm against the king's knee, feeling the warmth beneath his touch.

"Let me assist you in whatever you need of me, Your Majesty. Just give me the word and I can give you what you desire." Simeon leaned closer, desperate.

"You know nothing of what I desire, now leave me." Beaumont was hostile.

Simeon did not want to test the king in this state, so he took his leave.

Beaumont stood in the stillness of the chamber, his mind heavy, his body weary from the weight of the crown. The flickering light from the hearth danced along the stone walls, casting shadows that seemed alive, whispering secrets of his solitude. He staggered toward the bell pull, ringing it with a lethargic motion before leaning against the frame of the door, his vision blurred for a moment as he awaited a response.

When the door creaked open, a young maid stepped through, her eyes widening in surprise at the sight of him. His hair was tousled, his face drawn, and exhaustion radiated from him like a palpable aura.

"Would you have some tea brought up…" His voice was rough, laden with the weight of the day, but then a thought pierced through his haze. "Have Rhys bring the tray."

The maid hesitated, confusion etched across her features. "Rhys, Your Majesty?"

"Yes. Rhys, the stable hand. Call him to the kitchens and have him bring the tea up. I have a task for him." His tone left no room for argument, and though the maid seemed perplexed, she scurried away, leaving Beaumont alone once more in the oppressive quiet.

He trudged the length of the room, his boots scuffing against the polished stone floor. Reaching the door that connected his private office to his chambers, he pushed it open and stumbled to his bed. Sitting heavily, he tore off his boots and collapsed backward onto the sheets. The spinning room and relentless pounding in his head overtook him, pulling him into a restless doze.

He awoke to the faint murmur of a voice drifting from the adjoining office. Disoriented but alert, he propped himself up on his elbows. "In my chamber," he called out, his voice hoarse.

Moments later, a figure appeared in the doorway, carrying a tray. Beaumont's gaze fell upon Rhys, who stepped inside with a careful grace. The elf's reddish hair was tied back neatly, his face clean-shaven, revealing a strong jaw and a smattering of freckles across his pale skin. His pointed ears betrayed his heritage, peeking out from beneath the strands of hair. He was dressed plainly, wearing an apron over his tunic and leather arm guards stained from his labor in the stables.

"My head, it pounds relentlessly," Beaumont said, pressing his fingers to his temples as if trying to dull the ache.

Rhys set the tray on a nearby table, his voice soft and deferential. "Forgive me, Your Majesty. Should I call for a healer?"

"No healers. They're useless," Beaumont grumbled. "I need a remedy of the elven kind. Do you know such magick?"

The question brought a faint blush to Rhys' freckled cheeks. He hesitated, then nodded. "I…I could offer you relief, if it pleases you, my king."

"Remove your apron," Beaumont instructed, watching as the stable hand obeyed, draping the garment over the back of a chair. "Come closer."

Rhys approached tentatively, standing before the king with a mixture of apprehension and determination. "May I?" he asked, his hands trembling slightly as he raised them.

"Please," Beaumont sighed, his voice carrying the weariness of someone desperate for solace.

Rhys' hands, calloused from years of labor, were surprisingly gentle as they cupped Beaumont's temples. The coolness of his touch spread like a soothing balm, and his whispered incantations carried an almost melodic cadence. Beaumont felt the magick work through him, sweet and serene, dispelling the storm within his head. A long, relieved breath escaped him, and his eyes fluttered shut.

"Thank you," he murmured, his voice softer now, tinged with genuine gratitude.

Rhys stepped back, pouring tea with practiced ease before returning to offer a steaming cup. Beaumont accepted it, watching the elf move with a grace that seemed almost out of place for a stable hand.

"You have skill," Beaumont remarked, taking a careful sip. The tea was strong and fragrant, grounding him further.

"I am glad to be of service to my king," Rhys replied, his tone humble but steady.

"Stop that," Beaumont said with a faint groan, waving his hand dismissively. "Call me Beaumont."

The declaration left Rhys visibly startled. "I...I couldn't, Your Majesty."

Beaumont's lips curved into a smirk. "How old are you?"

"Three and forty, Your Majesty."

"And how long have you served me?"

"Fifteen years." Rhys' hands fidgeted at his sides, his gaze unwavering.

"Fifteen years is a long time for a stable hand. You've not sought advancement?"

"I am content where I am," Rhys admitted, his voice steady but quiet.

Beaumont stood, towering over the elf, who stepped back slightly. The king drained his tea in two swift gulps, setting the cup aside. "You've been dutiful and well-respected. If it wouldn't take you from your duties, I would call upon you more often for these... remedies."

"At all hours, if you wish it," Rhys replied, a blush creeping up his neck.

Beaumont stepped closer, his gaze lingering on the elf's delicate features. "When we are together, we are equals. I give you my name. Say it."

Rhys' voice was a whisper, yet it carried the weight of a promise. "Beaumont."

Rhys smiled, a radiant expression that quickened the rhythm of Beaumont's heart. His gaze lingered on the elf's softened features—the elegant line of his jaw, the gentle curve of his lips. A breathtaking beauty, so youthful and captivating, that it stirred something deep within him. For a fleeting moment, it reminded Beaumont of another, a figure from his past whose orange hair blazed like fire and whose vibrant eyes were unforgettable. He shook the thought away; it was foolish to let old dreams resurface.

"Is there something else you need of me?" Rhys asked.

Beaumont sighed, forcing down the yearning that clawed at him. It was wrong to desire him, as it had been wrong so many times before. He could never admit to the moments spent watching from his library window—how he had glimpsed Rhys in the stables, or how his gaze often strayed to the gardens below. From that vantage, he'd witnessed countless trysts within the labyrinth of hedges, courtly secrets laid bare.

"*Beaumont*," Rhys said softly.

The sound of his name drew him back. Beaumont looked up to find Rhys studying him intently. Flustered, he turned away, laughing under his breath. "Forgive me, Rhys. My thoughts wander lately. Perhaps it's the headaches—they bring on these bouts of introspection."

He crossed the room to the window, as he often did, seeking the familiar solace of the view. The sprawling gardens stretched below, their centerpiece the intricate maze that so often captured his idle attention.

"I wish to help, if I can," Rhys offered, his voice steady.

"It is nothing," Beaumont replied. "You've done more than enough already."

The faint shuffle of footsteps reached him, and soon Rhys stood beside him at the window. Together, they gazed out over the labyrinth, the warm glow of the afternoon sun casting soft shadows.

"You can see the maze's center from here," Rhys observed. "The view is quite revealing."

Beaumont's heart hammered in his chest and he fought to steady his voice. "Few have reached the center. It's said only the brave or clever ever manage it."

A faint smirk touched Rhys's lips as he glanced at Beaumont. "The young maids call it the Kissing Spot, do they not? I hear it's all they whisper about."

Beaumont chuckled, the sound light and unguarded. "So, the name has spread, after all. But it's not an easy feat. Only the tenacious among us can navigate its winding paths."

"It's far simpler than they believe," Rhys replied, his eyes glinting with mischief. "The steps of a waltz guide the way."

"Clever," Beaumont murmured, his gaze drawn to Rhys's. Those violet-flecked eyes seemed to hold secrets of their own, drawing him deeper into the storm of emotions stirring within.

Rhys leaned closer, the distance between them shrinking until Beaumont could feel the warmth radiating from him. The elf's fingers brushed his hand, light as a whisper, sending a thrill through his body.

"I've seen you watching, Beaumont," Rhys said, his voice low, intimate. "I've often wondered why it's taken so long for you to call me to your side."

Beaumont swallowed hard, his composure unraveling. "It wouldn't have been proper—to take you from your duties."

"My duty is to you, *my king*, and no other."

Beaumont's breath hitched as Rhys's hand slid up his arm, coming to rest against the collar of his shirt. The elf's touch was tentative yet deliberate, his gaze fixed on Beaumont's, searching for any hint of resistance. Beaumont offered none; he was mesmerized, his thoughts and defenses crumbling.

"Rhys," Beaumont whispered, his voice trembling.

"I'll call you whatever you wish," Rhys replied, his tone a caress. The raw intensity in his words sent a shiver through Beaumont, igniting a longing he hadn't felt in years. This was not the steady, noble love he had once shared with Sabian; this was desperation, a yearning born of loneliness and a hunger for solace.

"If you wish to leave, you may," Beaumont said hoarsely. "But if you stay—"

"I would like to kiss you," Rhys interrupted, his voice firm.

The king could not resist. In a rush of desire, he pulled Rhys into his arms, their lips meeting in a fervent embrace. Beaumont pressed him back against the cool glass of the window, the world outside forgotten. He sought refuge in the elf's touch, in the warmth and passion that banished the shadows of his grief, if only for a moment.

For the night, it was enough.

The carriage rolled to a stop in front of the castle, its polished wood gleaming in the midday sun. Jorn was a living tapestry of color, its gardens overflowing with blooms that seemed to celebrate the arrival of spring. Trees stood resplendent in their emerald canopies, while blossoms in every hue painted the grounds with brilliance. The air carried the sweet fragrance of lilacs and roses, mingled with the crisp freshness of newly turned earth.

Lahrs stepped down first, his movements precise and composed as always. Turning, he offered his hand to Brendolyn, who accepted with a graceful nod. She stepped lightly from the carriage, her dress whispering against the stone path as she adjusted to her surroundings. Lahrs remained poised, waiting for Elsa to join them. When she emerged, she inhaled sharply, her eyes wide with delight.

"You weren't exaggerating about the gardens," Elsa breathed, her voice carrying a note of awe. Her lips curved into a soft smile as she turned to take in the vibrant display.

Brendolyn glanced at her companion and returned the smile, though her own expression held a trace of apprehension. Lahrs led the way up the grand steps, his footsteps echoing against the marble as they entered the castle through its imposing front doors.

Inside, the air shifted, cool and still. The grand entry hall of Jorn Castle unfolded before them, a testament to regal splendor. Every detail spoke of the kingdom's wealth and heritage—from the vaulted ceilings adorned with intricate carvings to the magnificent paintings that graced the walls, their subjects seemingly alive under the light filtering through high, arched windows. Brendolyn's eyes adjusted to the dim interior, and a smile tugged at her lips as memories stirred within her. This castle had once been her sanctuary, its towering halls and storied past a part of her history.

"It's even more breathtaking than I remember," she murmured, her gaze lingering on a vast mural depicting the kingdom's legendary founders. Elsa said nothing, her attention fixed on the grandeur surrounding them.

Lahrs guided them through a series of corridors and halls, each more opulent than the last. Finally, they entered a sprawling chamber furnished with richly upholstered chairs and gilded accents. Brendolyn and Elsa waited silently as Lahrs stood sentinel, his elven composure unwavering.

Moments later, a door at the far end of the room opened with purpose.

King Sabian strode in, his expression shifting from curiosity to shock as his eyes fell on his youngest daughter. His pace quickened, urgency in every step. "Sir Lahrs," he began sharply, his voice tight. "I believe there has been a grave miscommunication. What is the meaning of this? Did my instructions not explicitly state she was to remain in Alnwick until summer?"

Lahrs moved smoothly to stand between Sabian and Brendolyn, his calm demeanor a stark contrast to the king's rising agitation. "Your Majesty," he began, his tone measured, "there was a change in circumstances. I assure you, this matter can be resolved without incident."

But Sabian would not be placated so easily. "Resolved? This is hardly the appropriate place for such matters! I gave specific orders—"

Before he could continue, the great doors at the far side of the hall swung open with deliberate grandeur. All heads turned as King Beaumont entered, his stride confident and commanding. Tall and striking, he exuded the effortless charisma of a ruler accustomed to admiration. His arms spread wide in a gesture of welcome as his gaze fell upon Brendolyn.

"Ah, forgive me, Beaumont," Sabian said hastily, stepping forward as if to shield his daughter from view. "I can explain this unexpected—"

Beaumont silenced him with a raised hand, his smile disarming yet firm. "No need, Sabian. I am quite aware of Princess Brendolyn's presence. After all, I was the one who invited her."

Brendolyn's cheeks flushed a delicate pink as Beaumont approached, his gaze warm and appraising. He bowed deeply before her, an action that made her feel both honored and slightly flustered.

"But..." Sabian stammered, his face reddening with frustration. "Perhaps this could have been handled more appropriately. There was no need for such...formality."

Beaumont's smile widened, his tone teasing yet resolute. "Do not fret, Sabian. It is my greatest delight to have all of your illustrious kingdom represented here. Princess Brendolyn's presence is an honor."

Sabian's expression froze, his gaze darting between Beaumont and Brendolyn. Lahrs seized the moment to intervene. "If I may, Your Majesties, I believe it would be best to allow the princess and her companion to rest after their journey."

Without waiting for a response, Lahrs inclined his head respectfully and gestured for Brendolyn and Elsa to follow. He escorted them swiftly from the hall, his steps purposeful as he led them to the private chambers prepared for Brendolyn's stay.

As they walked, Brendolyn cast one last glance over her shoulder. Beaumont's gaze lingered on her, his expression unreadable but undeniably intense. She quickly turned back, her heart fluttering with a mix of unease and anticipation.

CHAPTER 19

You went behind my back and invited my own daughter?" Sabian's voice thundered through the grand chamber, his anger crackling like lightning.

Beaumont remained seated, his demeanor calm and collected despite the storm raging before him. His eyes were cool as they met Sabian's fiery gaze. "What good will it do to shut Princess Brendolyn out of your life, Sabian? She has done nothing but fulfill every demand you've placed upon her. In return, you've cast her aside, leaving her isolated and estranged from her family."

Sabian's face reddened as he placed his hands on his hips. "No disrespect, Your Majesty, but I hardly see how this is any of your concern."

Beaumont's patience frayed, and he rose to his feet, his jaw clenched. "She was not allowed to mourn her mother's passing, nor was she granted permission to return to her home. I know the injustices you've inflicted upon her. I have heard from her own lips the coldness and neglect you've shown."

The room fell into a heavy silence, the air thick with unresolved tensions.

Sabian turned away, his fists clenched tightly at his sides. "You do not understand the shame of it..."

Beaumont's chest tightened with pain. "There is no shame in loving your own child," he said, but his words seemed to drift away, unheard.

Sabian spun back around, his eyes burning with fury and tears. "She carries her mother's illness, the deceitful legacy of her lineage. I cannot bring such dishonor upon the home of my fathers. Her mother and Natalia...they conspired together and tricked me into their bed. Brendolyn is the price I pay for that deceit, and her very presence is a constant reminder of that betrayal. She will be my greatest regret, Beaumont. Why can't you see that?" Sabian's tears flowed freely now, but Beaumont's heart remained unyielding.

"There is nothing to pity here, Sabian," Beaumont said, his voice hardening. "She is a child. Her birth was not her fault. You were entrusted with her care, and yet you stand here, disgracing her honor." Beaumont's words hit their mark.

Sabian flinched as if struck by an unseen blow. "What of your own blood? Fiona has been absent from your court for over a decade. Have you forgotten her?"

"I have visited her every year since her birth. I spent months with her, watching her grow into a remarkable young woman. She will return to court on her own terms. I wish for her to choose her own path." Beaumont's anger surged, and he felt the weight of heartbreak as the love he once held for Sabian began to crumble.

Sabian snorted derisively. "A king who cannot enforce the rules of his own kingdom."

Beaumont's jaw tightened. "She is not without rules, Sabian. But I believe in allowing my children to determine their own destinies. Perhaps you've forgotten the constraints imposed upon us in our youth. Do you not wish for those you love to have the freedom to be themselves and choose whom they love?"

The words hung heavy between them, echoing through the chamber.

Sabian straightened, his resolve hardening. "We have waited years for this union. We cannot abandon the hope that it will succeed."

Beaumont's heart ached with the weight of lost dreams. "I will not sacrifice my son's happiness for a promise made long ago."

Panic flashed in Sabian's eyes. "We cannot renege on the treaty now, Monty. To break our word could unravel everything we've built. In time, they will learn to love. Can you not see the benefit of what must be?"

Sabian reached for Beaumont's hand, his desperation evident. Beaumont, however, pulled away, stepping back from the man he once loved.

"I cannot be a part of a world built on lies, Sabian," Beaumont said firmly. "We've spent too long hiding in darkness. How many years did we spend wishing for change?"

"This is the very change we need," Sabian countered, his voice rising.

Beaumont shook his head, his expression resolute. "This treaty is no different from the ones our fathers made. We are forcing Barrow and Lisetta into a union to appease the council, dictating the fates of our children."

Sabian paced the room, the weight of Beaumont's words evident in his stride. "They will build an empire."

The chamber fell into a profound silence. Beaumont's heart hurt as he looked at the man Sabian had become, a shadow of the partner he once knew.

"I will not stand by and watch the world burn," Beaumont declared, his voice resolute and final.

As Beaumont turned to leave, the cold, dim light of the chamber seemed to grow darker, reflecting the deep rift between the two men. Sabian's face was a mask of frustration and despair, but Beaumont's path was clear. He walked away, leaving behind a legacy of shattered dreams and a future now uncertain, his heart heavy with the burden of choices made and sacrifices to come.

CHAPTER 20

Eir, Realm of Jorn

A carriage arrives in Eir, one that was gilded with fine workmanship, and not one that usually passed through the village, not even the lords that would venture into their midst from the neighboring towns. This carriage was distinct. This carriage brought fear. Drawing up to the great estate and home to Hugo Jax.

Pavan and Thad, recently returned from the little grassy yard, where the men that trained in combat spent their days learning practical skills at Thad's instruction. They saw Juliette, and the three other children of Hugo Jax crowded near the door to their fathers great library.

"What is going on?" Thad asked, catching the glance of Juliette, a lively girl, who was beaming from ear to ear as they approached.

"Father has a distinguished guest, all the way from Denorn."

One of the younger children, Felix, stood and scowled. "It is that odious man, the one who barred the crossing into the channel."

"No, you idiot, that was Lord Vhenderfoux…Father is talking to Lord Bannon, the hand of the king," the other boy scolded and at once, there was an argument.

Thad became inpatient. "Boys, that is enough."

They all quieted, immediately. Looking up at Thad with rounded eyes, it was rare the faie lost his patience, and a swift fear settled over them, whenever it was present.

"Go back to your studies, boys," Pavan advised, his eyes quickly looking at Juliette, who was very silent, watching them.

"Shall you instruct me in my dance lesson, Pavan?"

Behind them, the door opened, and Hugo Jax stood observing them both. The man was agitated, his mouth set in a firm line.

"No lesson today, Juliette...go see the kitchens. Have Lauryn bring up the tea things." Dismissing his daughter, the lord then motioned to both Pavan and Thad, who remained at the door. "Come in, there is a gentleman here who wishes to speak with us."

Pavan felt the fear ripple in Thad, but the faie remained as he ever looked. They entered, following Hugo Jax into the library. Pavan had heard much of Lord Bannon, knew him to be a hard man and one that many within Eir feared. Stepping through the door, they were greeted by the tall figure, dressed in fine garments of embroidered crimson and blue.

"Lord Bannon, allow me to introduce Pavan—" Hugo began, but a hand raised, and Hugo was inclined to be silent.

Those shifting blue-grey eyes lingering uncomfortably long over Pavan. Watching him with an imperious air, before stepping forward to address him personally.

"Yes, I do believe I have heard of you...*Pavan.*"

His voice gave Pavan chills, calming his nerves, feeling the thick roll of magick that slithered over the man who was like a vulture, circling in front of them.

He knew this man, Pavan felt it in his bones.

"Have you?" Pavan spoke with easy calm, masking his emotions, shadowing his magick, shielding himself from the hovering eyes, the lingering gaze of the Lord of Denorn.

A thin smile, more teeth than mirth. "Savior of Eir...you have hailed the failing city to former glories. Of your legacy have I heard repeated again and again in my streets of Denorn."

Pavan felt his lungs burning for air, the room stifling in an uncomfortable heat. Feeling the lord watching him, those eyes boring into him, feeling for a weak point. Pavan remained blank, knowing he was protected. By the magick shield of the pin at his tunic, and the magick he honed through the last few years.

"We are humbled and gratified to have him here, my lord…" Hugo was speaking, but Lord Bannon did not seem to pay the man any mind, focusing on Pavan with such intensity, it took a sudden cough from Thad to break the harsh look.

"I see you keep a faie pet." Lord Bannon was bitter, his words wrinkling in Pavan's nerves. "Have we met?" Those blue-grey eyes lingering on Thad.

Pavan stepped to the side, his large frame coming between Lord Bannon and Thad, who was still, unmoving, and radiating such hatred, Pavan wanted to rush the faie out of the room at once.

"What is your business, my lord?" Pavan asked, firmly.

Suddenly returning to himself, Lord Bannon sniffed, nodding, at least giving the presentation of civility.

"Fortune has smiled upon your little visage of poverty, Lord Pavan. King Beaumont wishes to extend his hospitality upon those of your humble dwellings a place at court, for the duration of the celebrations." He looked pained to give this obviously rehearsed message. Being the Lord of Denorn, he was also the holder of the neighboring towns.

"He honors us." Pavan nods his head and there is a shift, as the tension sharpens around them all.

Lord Bannon's teeth gleam in the glint of the chandeliers.

"Have you such men and women worthy of the king's vision, and the royal families to witness? It was your great talents in Denorn that has whispered your names to my ear."

Hugo was startled to speak. "You mean as entertainment?"

"There is no other form to which I speak, Lord Hugo. As a province of a small matter within the kingdom, there would be no object in bringing your mixed heritage into the king's house." After a long uncomfortable pause, Lord Bannon spoke on, with a wave of his hand. "No matter, the king has offered this grace, so shall it be done. Twelve performers shall be roomed, you may choose among your best to comply. But limit your number to partial magick users…elves and human are welcome."

Pavan's fist clenched, locking his magick deeper beneath the surface. This man was dangerous, he could smell the danger seeping from every pore. Watching those shifting blue-grey eyes as Lord Bannon lingered his gaze over Thad.

"Of course," Hugo Jax drew the sudden attention of the Lord. "Shall we take tea? I believe it is just being brought in."

As he spoke, the door opened, a young maid hurried in carrying a tray, but there were only two cups neatly placed beside the kettle. Pavan glanced from the tray, then to Hugo, who was looking at him, there was a flutter of anxiety in the man.

"Forgive us, my lord, we have training to tend to..." Pavan spoke at once, earning a quick glare from Lord Bannon.

Lord Bannon smiled, mostly teeth. "I shall send a servant to call tomorrow, to retrieve your list of twelve persons. List them all by name, and by race...so there shall be no confusion."

Pavan felt the slithering magick sharply through his hands. A coiling in the pit of his stomach, suddenly it struck Pavan—detection of something deep in Lord Bannon. He could feel revulsion, taste it on the back of his tongue. Pavan felt the magick that the older man clung to with desperation. Lord Bannon was not shielding his magick, was not suspect to anyone being able to detect such craft, but as Pavan watched, he became aware. In his awareness, there was a fleeting form of dread that overtook him.

Death withered its decaying touch deep into Pavan's soul. Feeling the dripping blood that haunted this man's past seep deeper within the touch. Within the fleeting moment, Pavan knew how many victims were lost to this man. He could feel their deaths and he despaired of their souls barred from life and the Veil.

"Of course." Pavan bowed, turning to issue Thad from the room, when a chuckle was heard behind him.

A sharp, cutting sound. Pavan stopped and looked back but Lord Bannon was already turned away from them, his attention now solely upon Hugo Jax, and the tea ready to be shared.

This sudden look went unnoticed, as Pavan watched the man over with sudden renewed interest, watching in the moments it took to walk from where they were to the door. But it was enough for Pavan to realize without denial who Lord Bannon really was. Magick and age had made him nearly unrecognizable.

Needing to be away, Pavan gripped Thad's wrist, practically dragging the faie from the room. Panic suddenly flushing his skin, unable to hold his magick for long as he hurried them from the estate. Out into the fresh air he dragged them into the nearby gardens. This is when Thad refused to go any further.

"Pavan...where are you going, the training yard is that way," Thad said, but Pavan simply shook his head.

"I have no intention of going there…not now."

"Calm yourself, Pavan. Your magick—"

But Pavan could not let these words stop him. Pavan was nearly lost in his own shock, pacing the quiet of the small garden. Looking up momentarily at Thad, who watched him with worry. "This is impossible…"

"What is the matter? You don't look well at all, Pavan."

Pavan gulps. "He should not be here."

There is perplexity in Thad, but the faie grows pale. "What are you talking about, Pavan? Do you mean Lord Bannon?"

"Meilyr told me he was gone…Thad, he lied to me." Bitterness overwhelmed him, glaring at the faie. His chest ached as he realized now what Meilyr had meant. Every utterance of his name was a warning.

"Lord Bannon is not a man to be crossed, should he hear us—"

Pavan shook his head. "Lord Bannon is Charles Maison. That man is my *father*."

Thad grasped hard to Pavan's arm, dragging him deeper into the garden walk, pushing him through a tall hedge. Gaping for break, Pavan leaned his back against the cold stone wall behind. His body felt wrong, it was too much at once to think clearly.

"Stop this, Pavan…" Thad instructed, pushing hard at Pavan's shoulders. "You are not thinking clearly."

"I know him, Thad…I can feel the putrid magick that clouds his senses." Pavan breathed, trying to focus his breathing enough to calm. "He doesn't remember, he couldn't see my magick, but I know him. I remember his abuse, all the years of punishment that I took to shield them from his hand."

Thad touched Pavan's neck, his shoulders, his neck, running his hand through Pavan's hair. Trying everything to keep Pavan in the moment, to not slip back into his magick. "He is no longer that man, Pavan. Whatever you feel now…whatever you may think about him he is no longer your father. He is much worse. Please, you must not give in to your magick. Not now."

Pavan felt the clawing of magick burn its way up his spine, desperate to draw forth from the forbidden well. Trying to breathe slower, to soften the overwhelming heat that eclipsed the calm. He looked into Thad's orange eyes, wild with worry.

"Hit me," Pavan hissed, his hands forming into fists.

Thad shook his head. "I cannot do that."

Pavan's heartbeat was thick in his ears, as sound began to drown out into a murmured hush. His body is on fire, feeling the magick tight in his bones.

Thwap! Pavan gasped as Thad's fist collided with the soft tissue at his side, directly into the diaphragm and shooting pain vibrated through him. His eyes snapped open, and he grasped Thad by the throat, slamming him against the wall. Thad was breathless, speaking but Pavan could not hear him above the thunderous rush of blood in his ears.

A second blow to the left and Pavan heard ringing, releasing Thad to cover his ears in front of the roaring sounds. Counting out the seconds as his body shifted, his magick lingering over the shooting pain in his sides. Bruises would form, Pavan knew Thad had used his full strength with every blow.

It was the sounds of birds that roused Pavan, opening his eyes to be kneeling in the grass. Holding himself as he rocked slightly. Cold washing through him.

"I've got you," Thad whispered, warm arms wrapped around his shoulders, holding him close. Thad was trembling. "You're alright."

Simeon Bannon remained with the leader of Eir for as long as he could stand.

Returned in time to take his meal alone, just as he liked. Simeon hated the sight of the half bred man that claimed a seat on the king's good graces. After the death of the former leader, at the hands of his most trusted assassin, Simeon was disappointed when the people had risen up to elect Hugo Jax as their next in succession. There was little he could do to stop it, in the end.

Heavily taxing the people was Simeon's only consolation, but even after all these years of starving the failing people, they still thrived. Now, it was worse as Hugo had found an unlikely successor. Pavan was low in magick, he barely felt anything from the man with strange green eyes. *Possibly faie touched, or of little elven birth*, Simeon concluded.

He held a greater interest in the faie that accompanied him. Simeon recalled his first instinct when the pair of them walked into the room. There was something forbidden about the magick that was so untouched in the faie's blood. Bannon could feel it thrum with every pulse. He wished to claim the power for his own. But he could not readily purchase the faie from Pavan, not when Hugo Jax had claimed the possession to his young apprentice, and not his own.

"My lord." There was a shouting voice that drew Simeon's attention from the deepest of his thoughts as he looked up at the approach of Leuthere.

But his knight was not alone Simeon was quick to discern. Eyeing the newcomer with scrutiny as Leuthere dragged the man through the dining room. He was dressed in sailors clothes, his blonde hair a disheveled mess.

"I loathe to be disturbed at my meal," Simeon hissed, taking up his goblet to take a drink of the thick wine, a mixture the cook made with red wine of Taastra aerated with the blood of an ewe. It's copper tang sating his hunger.

"Yes, my lord." Leuthere bowed, and shoved the young man forward. "But this man was found lurking in your storehouses. Wearing this..."

There was a heavy clunk as Leuthere dropped a metal pendant onto the table, Bannon leaned forward with some curiosity, spying the familiar insignia of the Signe crest. His eyes flickered up to the man.

"You are a knight of Corad."

Yanking his arm free, the blonde man sneered, spitting at Leuthere who laughed through clenched teeth. "I was not stealing."

"Of course not, but please...have a seat." Simeon motioned to the chair nearest to the knight. "I wish to ask you a question."

Slowly, the man moved to sit. Clearly unperturbed as Leuthere stood behind him, a hand resting on the hilt of his sword. There was a fluttering of nerves in the knight, but not of fear of him. Not yet, anyway.

"Tell me your name."

The knight scoffed. "You wasted your one question to know who I am?"

Simeon sneered, leaning forward, glaring hard at the petulant knight. "That was not a question. I have little patience for ignorance at my table."

He watched the knight gulp, a flicker of fear trembled through him.

"Alaric, of the Signe Brotherhood."

Simeon made no effort to be impressed. "What would a knight of Signe want in Denorn, so far from your Brotherhood?"

He sensed hesitation in the man, much to Simeon's annoyance. Glaring at the knight and without prompt, Leuthere grasped the handle of his dagger, drawing it to press the blade at the throat of the knight.

"My lord asked you a question," he hissed in Alaric's ear.

"I-I am searching for someone. I heard that she was coming to Jorn, so I followed," Alaric stammered, fear heightened the room with a delicious scent that perfumed the air.

"You seek a woman?"

A hardness darkened the knight's eyes, glaring at Simeon. "I am in search of what is mine," he hissed.

There was heat, a fiery passion that dazzled Simeon's senses. Searching the knight. "Show me your arm."

Alaric didn't move. Relenting, Simeon nodded to Leuthere, who removed the blade, but kept it tucked up ready for use if need be.

Now free to move, Alaric rolled up the sleeve of his jacket, pushing up the material of his tunic to reveal the flat of his forearm. Simeon examined the flesh, following the smooth skin of the wrist, to the triangle scar that lay bright and red, above it were old scars of varying ages, slashed in the upper forearm.

"You are bonded, in the old way, to your woman?"

Alaric sneered, pulling down his sleeve. "She was meant to be mine, but her brothers sent her away to have service with the princess."

Fire ignited within Simeon at hearing these words. "Your property is Lady Elsa Laronn?"

"Her father took the land my family held for centuries until the war, when the new edict was proclaimed under King Sabian's rule. After the war my family's land was divided, given to his sons for their own. Now, I have Elsa's hand. She belongs to me as does her dowry," Alaric hissed, angry.

Leuthere rested the tip of his dagger on Alaric's shoulder. "You are of the old people. Was your family the Cairn?"

"My grandfather was Adenos Cairn."

"What do you need of me, young Cairn?" Simeon asked, taking up his goblet to drink the thickened wine. His mouth thirsted for it as he felt the rolling magick flicker within the man before him.

"I want what is mine," Alaric whispered.

"What will you give me, in exchange for this great favor?" Simeon asked, the tang of copper hot in his mouth.

"Anything." His words were shimmering and Simeon stood, striding around the table to appear before the knight.

Leuthere maneuvered the chair back, the wood scraping on the stone floor. Simeon knelt to be just at the eye level of the man who trembled in fear and he grasped Alaric by the throat, drawing him close.

"I require loyalty, Alaric," Simeon soothed, running a finger along the curve of the knight's cheek, his nail scraping the flesh. "Can you give your loyalty to me, in exchange for my services in procuring what is rightfully yours?"

Alaric's pulse beat faster beneath Simeon's touch. He could already feel the pull as the man was quick to comply. All of Simeon's sensations heightened, hearing the whisper in his mind, the desperation to possess the soul that lay pliant beneath his grasp.

"I give you my loyalty, my lord."

Simeon smiled, tightening his hold on Aleric's throat and shifting his hold to expose the side. The knight's pulse quickened and Alaric grasped at his arm, as Simeon restricted his airway by pressing the flat of his thumb over the center of the knight's larynx. Leuthere was quick to restrain him, holding Alaric as Bannon drew closer.

"Submit to me, Alaric," Simeon hissed, leaning between the knight's thrashing legs, the knight immobilized under Leuthere's grasp, and the pressure of Simeon's hand upon his throat.

Leuthere pressed the tip of the dagger he held into the tender flesh of Alaric's neck, in one swift motion he sliced the skin. Blood dribbled free in spurts and Simeon latched on, his mouth hot with the tang of blood, gulping down until he felt lightheaded, his mind hazy with the faint magick that pulsed over his tongue.

"Enough my lord." Leuthere's voice was distant.

Drawing back, Simeon gasped, watching Leuthere heal the wound upon the knight's neck, sheathing his dagger. Clarity was slow to return to Simeon, as he watched two men emerge from the darkest parts of the room to drag Alaric away. Knowing the knight would awaken in agony, writhing for respite of the transference of magick that bound them together.

"Simeon." Leuthere was kneeling, grasping Simeon by the arm to help him to stand.

He wished to push him away, unable to bear the touch of the man, but he clung to Leuthere, leaning on the man as he was led away from the dining room, up the great steps and into his chambers. Simeon felt the heat of the room, as the large fire burned hot in the hearth. Hatred boiled in his blood, tasting the wrath of the knight.

Simeon rounded on Leuthere slapping him hard.

A darkened look shadowed the knight's gaze, the shadows of his face shifted in the light of the fire. Simeon knew it was Alaric's blood as it mixed with his own that made him so hot. His body aching with the desire that coursed through the bond the knight shared with the Signe girl. It was just a taste. A sampling of how much Simeon could utilize in controlling the knight.

"My lord." Leuthere stepped closer.

Strong hands yanked hard at the thick jacket that clung to Simeon's frame. Every touch sending shoots of desire coursing through him. He grasped Leuthere's throat as the man had successfully removed the outer layer, revealing the scarred and thin body beneath. Looking into those wet eyes so darkened by lust, Simeon could see the faintest of white around them.

"You wish for me to take you?" Simeon seethed, tasting the remnants of blood on his teeth and standing inches from the knight. "So broken by your last master that pain heightens your pleasure?"

Leuthere groaned. "Yes."

Simeon smirksed tightening his hold, much like he had when he held Alaric's in his hand. But Leuthere was strong, he was faie but so whittled down there was hardly anything left but the shell of the man. Simeon could mold the killer into whatever he wanted. Force him to strangle the knight of Signe, to drown the princess, or to rape and kill every last member of the royal houses. Leuthere would do so gladly, with pleasure, all because of Orin Gaur. His sadistic nature had broken the man before him to shape the perfect slave.

"Get on your knees," Simeon hissed.

Without hesitation, Leuthere did as he was told. Fully dressed in his armor, Leuthere bent and did as he was commanded. Lust overpowering Simeon as he let the blood shift through him, melding with the power it gave him. His thoughts raced at the possibilities, to use this man in his power to control Denorn, to bring Eir to its knees.

Moaning loudly, Simeon thought of the many ways he wanted to seize the power of the realms. His mind danced around the bloodshed that would bathe the city streets if there was a coming war. Day by day, he was getting closer to that power, Simeon could feel it in his grasp. As his hands sought the warm neck of the man before him now, Simeon was almost lost, his mind clouded with bloodshed.

CHAPTER

21

Seated in the carriage, it was quiet in the plush noble coach as it rolled along through the streets of Jorn City. Pavan looked out the single paned window at the passing shops, and wagons, and walking passersby. There was so much difference between the inland people to the variant of those in the seafaring town of Denorn. These were the height of the fashionable world, where the wealthiest lived and roomed.

"I do not think this is wise."

Pavan looked across from him, where Thad rocked side to side with the movement of the carriage. They were alone, as the small carriage seated only a few. Behind them, in another of the wagons was the rest of their party.

"We have agreed to make an appearance, Thad. Hugo has sanctioned our charge."

Thad leaned forward, desperately grasping at Pavan's hand. "To step foot in that royal house. There are many things that could happen there."

"You speak of your time in court, with your master." Pavan was not ignorant of what haunted Thad, knowing the reservation the faie held in returning to a place of his past. "It is not the same, for you shall be by my side."

Thad's lip twitched. "My glamour may not be enough to shield my face from those that would recognize me from my past."

Pavan brought Thad's hand to his lips.

"I shall shield you from the world, Thad. No harm shall come to you. Do you trust me?" Pavan asked, lowering his tone.

Reaching out, Thad sat at the edge of the bench seat, slotting his legs with Pavan's to be nearer to him. Pressing his forehead to his, wrapping his free hand to grasp the hair at the nape of Pavan's neck.

"I trust you completely."

Bringing their faces closer, Pavan wanted to kiss him, but the carriage lurched, sending them apart. Pavan looked out the window as the carriage was rounding a barricade, slipping through a gate and into the long stretch of stone, before emerging into the courtyard.

They did not approach the front door, but instead the carriage was driven to the left, towards the outer edge and Thad sighed.

"They are taking us to the side entrance, nearest the kitchens." Thad looked out, worry pressing his brows together.

The door opened, and they stepped out into the small courtyard just outside the kitchen doors. As they emerged, the door to the kitchens opened and a servant hurried out, breathless.

"Apologies, sir...you are requested to present before his majesty."

Pavan blinked and glanced at Thad for a moment.

"You need Pavan so soon?" Thad asked and the servant nodded.

"As representative of the Silverans of Eir, you are to be roomed in the guest wing and brought before his majesty, King Beaumont, for his dinner service." Shaken, the servant read from a slip of parchment he had crumpled in his hand.

"My other companions have yet to arrive." Pavan looked to the gates, but the wagon had not been driven through.

"They are welcome and shall be roomed above the kitchens." The servant glanced at Thad, a blush spreading over his cheeks. "Your personal attendant shall be put up in a room beside yours, unless you would rather him sleep in your dressing room. The apartments are fitted with servants' cots."

Pavan nodded. "That will do, thank you."

They parted ways on the second landing, walking in through the kitchens to the staircase. Thad was led away by a maid, to be escorted to their rooms to make sure it was prepared for his master. Pavan reluctantly watched the faie walk away.

"This way, my lord," the servant roused Pavan to follow. Taking them down a longer corridor, to a room that was large and steamy. Fresh steam rising from the copper basin, as a maid pushed open the drapes, letting in a stream of evening light through the window.

"I am to bathe?" Pavan asked.

"His majesty is very keen on cleanliness," a second voice sounded and Pavan turned to see who had entered the room. All the hairs on his neck stood on end as Lord Bannon waltzed into the chamber, looking Pavan over with a sneer.

"There are bathhouses in Eir. Is my smell so repulsive?"

There was no reply, nor an acknowledgement of having listened, as Lord Bannon inspected the garments that were brought out by a maid for him to inspect. Nodding his approval before rounding on Pavan a second time, looking him once over.

"Perhaps a shave, as well." Lord Bannon spoke only to the servant and he left just as quickly as he had arrived.

"Will you need assistance in bathing, my lord?"

Pavan waved off the servant. "No, I can manage. Thank you."

The servant nodded, bowing himself away and shutting the door behind him.

Pavan stripped of his dirtied tunic and dust settled breeches letting them fall to a pile, placing his boots off to the side and finally stepping into the water, hissing at the warmth and sting under his feet. Around him, the water fizzled, a scent of lavender filling his nostrils as he bent his large frame to sit within the basin.

Pavan's hands dipped beneath the dark water, lifting up a violet hue within his hands, washing away the dirt and grime and sweat of travel, his hands grazing over the taught flesh over his scars. Pavan leaned back, letting his body ease into the comfort of the water, eyelids drooping as sleepiness found him.

Jerking up, his mind suddenly alert, a sense of some familiar magick filling him. Pavan looked around, but there was nothing.

Stepping from the basin, Pavan dried himself with the provided linen. Standing for a moment, looking down at the garments placed before him. His fingertips traced along the intricate weave of embroidery upon the deep burgundy tunic. He set it aside, finding the undergarments beneath. Cotton breeches, and cotton linen shirt. Silk stockings and black velvet trousers.

He dressed, frowning as the garments pulled, tucking in the cotton shirt to the trousers. His chest felt tight beneath the confines of the cloth.

At last, he wrapped a silver scarf around his neck, tucking and tying it, before picking up the burgundy doublet. It was snug over his shoulders and straining over the width of his chest. He could only fasten the bottom half of the buttons.

He frowned at his reflection and opened the door to find the servant standing there, waiting.

"Will I do for the kings liking?" Pavan asked.

"Adequately, but I must shave your cheek."

Pavan nodded, following the servant back into the room and sitting upon the chair near the window, where a table was set out with shaving things.

There was hesitation in the servant, who eyed Pavan warily. Preparing the blade of the straight razor against the leather strap tied at his belt. The *shink, shink* of the blade was all that filled the little room.

Setting out the small little bowl, the servant placed white powder from a little vial into it, followed by a dab of oil, and a small amount of water from a goblet, he mixed the contents with a meticulously made brush until a foam began to emerge.

"Is my lord ready?" he asked.

Pavan cringed but nodded. "I am not a lord."

There was a soft chuckle, as the servant draped a towel over Pavan's chest, bringing the foam brush to Pavan's jaw, and slathering it over the stubble that had begun to grow there.

"You are distinguished as the Lord of Eir. You shall sit at the king's table. That is an honor. There are not many who hold that power." He smiled.

Pavan looked up, as the blade of the straight edge of the razor rested against the curve of his cheek. Cold and dangerous to the touch, one wrong move and the blade would slice through his skin. A dangerous thrill echoed through him.

"You hold a blade to my flesh. That is power not many have held."

The eyes shimmered. "But to take that power shall render my soul barren. Should I slice your throat, it shall damn me to torment upon this realm."

"We wouldn't want that."

Pavan tilted his head back, the edge of the blade gliding down, feeling it cut an inch of hair from his cheek. He felt chills climb up his back as he watched the servant's eyes grow wide.

"You have excellent control, I trust you completely but we must make haste. We shouldn't keep the king waiting."

A sigh escaped the servant. "Very good, my lord."

Entering the small dining hall, Pavan was suddenly aware that the eyes now settled upon him. Feeling out of place, in his freshly starched undergarments, and too tight of tunic, Pavan walked through the room, where lords and ladies already sat. Keenly aware of the scrutinous gaze of Lord Bannon, whom Pavan could see out of the corner of his eye, lingering about in the farthest turn of the room.

"Welcome, Pavan," a soft, timbre tone came and Pavan looked across the table, where the empty space was reserved, at the familiar face of a known elf.

"Sir Lahrs." Pavan nodded as his heart leapt into his throat.

"You know this gentleman?" With a thick, heavy accent of a man with dark graying hair and a full beard upon his chin, he was seated to Pavan's right, at the head of the table.

"I was introduced to him as he arrived, Your Majesty." Lahrs smiled, looking from the man to where Pavan sat.

"You mean to insult us, Your Majesty, with having a meal with the likes of him?"

Pavan looked to the man who spoke, a cross expression on his face as he looked Pavan over. Pavan's face felt hot in the stifled room.

"Sir Behras." At once, the man in question turned his eye to the opposite end of the table. Pavan followed his gaze and his blood ran cold.

Pavan did not know how it was possible, but the very presence of the man made his chest tighten. Recognition in Pavan's eyes at the King of Jorn, looking at the man he knew so many years ago. The man who had loved his mother.

"You are guests in my home, just as much as the Silverans." His tone was cold and Pavan felt the glare the king gave to the lord, Sir Behras.

"He is of Eir...thieves, con artist...we cannot trust them in our homes let alone—"

King Beaumont lifted a hand, silencing the room, locking eyes with each of those seated at his table. "Insulting my honored guests is an insult to me, Sir Behras. I trust the man seated here tonight yet you accuse him of crimes abhorrent to the crown. Where is your proof, sir, of this man's slight against your honor?"

The room went quiet and all eyes turned to Sir Behras.

"As I thought." King Beaumont smirked, taking his glass in hand and offering it up in salute. All others followed, drinking as the king did.

Pavan looked down at the place setting before him. His mind raced but grew more terrified as he looked at the many spoons, forks, and knives placed before him. Around him, the talk commenced, polite conversation of lords of state as the first course was brought through.

He stared at the bowl before him, a thin gray soup swirling before his eyes. He looked up, as a thin hand was placed on the table beside his own. Looking at the nails tapping on the tablecloth delicately he looked over, into a very fine, pretty face. She was young, with dark hair that was pinned back. Her lips painted rouge, smiled at him.

"Charming soup tastes a lot like licorice." She lifted a thin handled spoon from her right-hand side which glinted in the light before she dipped it in the shimmering bowl.

Pavan smiled, doing as she did. Sipping the soup, but he stopped as the rancid taste left a bitter tang on his tongue. He turned, catching her eye and she laughed.

He took a quick sip of his wine.

"It is an acquired taste. But then again, I always enjoy the mint soup better when it is in season." She kept her tone light, going back to her meal for a few more sips.

"How many courses are there?" he whispered.

"I think tonight..." She took a look at the talking lords and ladies around her, as she inspected their glasses. "Twelve. But they may begin to come quicker the faster they take their wine."

Pavan clenched his jaw, looking down at the soup before him. As everyone around him sipped comfortably, he stared at the liquid as it began to darken in his bowl.

"Are you familiar with the family of Dern?" A woman spoke from across the way. She was seated beside Sir Lahrs, her matted hair powdered and pinned beneath a small tilted cap.

Pavan smiled. "Yes. They are but a few miles from Eir."

The woman smirked, appeased. "It is a shame Lord Hugo broke the engagement with the lord, I understand it would have been a fine match."

His teeth clenched, but he kept his smile neat.

"Lord Arvel is nearly sixty years old and has three wives already. I do not see a benefit in a young girl of nineteen being married to such a man."

The table grew quiet, as Pavan spoke.

"I believe Lady Helen means there would be mutual benefits to the economics of Eir, with the wealth and high status that Dern possessed," a man seated to the other side of her interjected, his high, nasally voice grating on Pavan's ears.

"Certainly. But the exploitation of a girl, used as a pawn in a scheme between grown men." Pavan felt the simmering heat of the room's anger in his bones as he spoke. "It was not a benefit worth seeing come to fruition."

Lady Helen looked sour.

"You speak for Lord Hugo, upon this matter?" She spoke almost shrill.

Pavan smirked, taking up his cup to drink away the sour taste of the bitterness from his mouth—the air was thick with it. "It is, after all, my authority upon the matter. I was the benefactor that raised Eir from the trenches."

A clamor of spoons, Pavan smirked into his glass as he read the room correctly. All eyes looked upon him with astonishment.

"You?" Lord Behras was going red, the vein on his forehead bulging.

"Benefactor of Eir? It was your own doing; what kind of man are you? What people have you swindled to afford such a sum?"

"There was no swindling, sir. I was not born in Eir, nor in Denorn. My breeding was across the sea. Entheas." Pavan could feel the simmering heat. Catching Lahrs' eye, he could see the elf looked ready to burst into laughter, but he hid it well behind a sip of wine.

"Entheas?" Lady Helen felt faint.

"Perhaps it is not best to talk about such things," King Beaumont interrupted, catching the eye of everyone at the table. He looked upon Pavan the longest and Pavan felt his eyes look straight at him, but there was no recognition there.

"Lahrs is an elf, I do not see the difference if our guest of Eir should not be entirely human, either," the girl beside him spoke up.

The dark-haired king, seated at the end beside her, sat forward, whispering harshly under his breath at the girl beside him. Pavan realized he was the King of Corad. He was King Sabian.

"Very well said, Lisetta," Beaumont agreed, raising a glass.

The room drank as a quiet shifted around them in uncomfortable silence. Pavan cooled his composure, pushing aside the heightened sense of emotions from around him. He would need to be more careful if he wanted to last all twelve courses with the room before him.

It was the tenth course, after sitting through talks of riots, breed of horses, the best dress makers, and who had been swindled of fabric prices that Pavan felt his chest tighten, suddenly overwhelmed by the constant talk and feeling through every shiver of emotion that pricked his magick. Pavan wanted to run.

Laughter set his teeth on edge, forks scraping against plates made nausea roll in his stomach. He stood, abruptly ignoring the looks of astonishment as he gasped, looking around at all the faces. His mouth went dry. His stomach is uneasy.

"Forgive me." He bowed slightly, hurrying the way he had entered, ignoring the laughter that followed, but the lingering pain behind his eyes followed.

Out in the hallway, Pavan stumbled, pausing to brace himself on the nearest wall.

"Pavan," a familiar voice echoed behind him.

Lahrs' strong hand was on his. Guiding him, Pavan followed blindly as the elf locked them away into the nearest door—it was an unused parlor, draped with linen to protect the furniture from dust. Pavan pressed his hands into the sockets of his eyes.

Pavan was gasping, trying to catch his breath but his lungs burned.

"Calm." Lahrs was speaking, but he sounded far away. A firm hand was pressed to the base of Pavan's neck. "You are in control, Pavan."

There was a chill that came over him, Pavan gulped in the lung fills of air as his mind shifted. Easing himself to sit on the nearest draped chair, his body becoming heavy, as he blinked in the near darkness to look upon the elf who was crouched before him.

"What are you doing here?" Pavan spoke as his eyelids grew as heavy as his body. Lahrs shook him, forcing Pavan to remain awake.

"I could ask you the same thing," he said.

"I need to return." Pavan forced himself to stand.

Lahrs pushed him back down. "You need to sit. I cannot let you return to that room. Not with your...predicament."

Pavan scoffed, rolling his eyes.

"I can manage...this is important." Pavan went to stand again, but Lahrs pushed him back with force this time and Pavan scowled at the man's strength.

"Not as important as keeping you alive. Do you have any idea what would happen if they were to see your markings? If they knew what you were?" Lahrs hissed.

"They shall never discover me."

Lahrs reached forward, showing the pendant that lay beneath Pavan's tunic, the one shielding him from sight. "This is not a catch all, Pavan. You cannot rely upon this alone to protect you from the sight of unwanted eyes."

"My magick is grown, Lahrs."

"You are playing a dangerous game, to be here instead of following Svein." Lahrs was cross, his undertones were sour. "Bringing Thad here was foolishness."

"He is safe in my room, no one can touch him there."

Lahrs grasped Pavan hard. "This plan of folly, whatever brought you here to the castle will be your ruin if you stay."

"I'm playing the part, Lahrs...they want a monkey to jump through their hoops, that is what they shall get." His mind was slowly clearing, his alertness returned.

"You just informed the room you are the benefactor of Eir...There were rumors amongst the realms. Your doings in Eir have not gone unnoticed."

"I do not see the significance." Pavan shook his head.

Lahrs knelt, taking Pavan's shoulders to look him in the eyes. "What you gave to Eir, the wealth, the notoriety...it is worth more than anything the lords and ladies at that table have ever seen in their lifetimes."

Pavan looked away.

"You must be careful, Pavan. These people are not to be trusted."

"Why are you here, Lahrs?" There was hesitation in the elf as Pavan asked. "You do not belong here, yet you remain in Corad to play as the king's puppet."

"That is not a story for today."

"Am I fit to return?" He felt cold but his mind was now clear.

Lahrs stood up, straightening his jacket and gave a nod.

Pavan stood, rolling back his shoulders to straighten his composure, leaving Lahrs in the room as he walked back to the dining hall. He arrived, just in time, as the lords, ladies, and the two kings were standing, moving to the next room.

More drinks and conversation.

Pavan sighed but forced a smile on his lips as he watched Lady Helen and another lady he did not know be escorted through the doors. At once, Pavan stood beside Princess Lisetta, offering his arm.

"I do not know if it is proper but allow me." He smiled, earning a smile in return as she took his arm.

"You are quite the gentleman," she applauded, as they entered the long drawing room.

Brighter than the dining hall, but smaller by half, velvet couches and embroidered chairs sat in two equally portioned sitting areas before a large hearth. Pavan gladly left Lisetta at the chairs with the waiting ladies to maneuver around the room to be far away from them.

"Very nicely done, Lord Pavan," a deep voice said, causing Pavan's head to turn.

"I am not a lord." Pavan shook his head, glancing warily at the king. "But I thank you for the sentiment."

Beaumont chuckled. "You are more of a lord than many of those here."

"My mother raised me to be a gentleman." Pavan saw the corner of Beaumont's mouth twitch. He was testing the taller man, trying to spark recognition in him.

Pavan was disappointed.

"She has done a fine job." Beaumont offered him a drink and Pavan held the glass in his hand, casually noticing the lords watching him. He tried to ignore them as he drank.

"Forgive me, for earlier…I am sometimes overwhelmed by crowds." Pavan tried to remain calm, his heart beating faster in his chest.

"I envy you. Sometimes I wish to rush from a room when the crowd becomes unbearable, but alas a king is a little leisure of hysteria." Beaumont hid a smile behind his glass.

Pavan chuckled.

"Ah, here comes one of those moments," Beaumont mumbled, forcing a smile as he turned to the approaching lord. One who took all of the king's attention.

Pavan followed the line of the room, seeing Lahrs enter the room. Without seeming too eager, Pavan made his way in his direction. Taking up a full drink from an open tray, offering it to the elf as he approached.

"Thank you." Lahrs nodded, but did not readily take a drink.

"And thank you for your assistance earlier, sir. It is not often I become ill from so many courses of food," Pavan forced a louder voice, catching the hint of prying eyes around his shoulder from one of the ladies seated nearby.

They drank in silence.

"Let us rouse one of the servants, Your Majesty. There must be one amongst them to play for us!" Came a shrill voice of one of the ladies who sat upon the chair at the furthest wall.

Pavan glanced at the king, who now sat in one of the high backed chairs near the fire, his long legs outstretched, drinking from his glass. Pavan could feel the stirrings of annoyance flicker in the noble breast of the large man.

"I do not frequently disturb my servants when they prefer the solitude of an evening for their supper." Beaumont waved a hand airily.

The lady laughed, fanning herself with a feather fan. "They should be expecting your call at every hour, Your Majesty." Her remark was chilling and Pavan glared at her impudence.

Beaumont sat straighter. "I shall not rouse them."

"Let us retire, my dear," came the lady's pompous husband, leaning closer to take his wife's hand in his own.

"It is not late enough to retire, husband. Let us call for the servant and have a man brought up to play for us..."

Pavan was gripping tightly to the glass in his hand, glaring at the scene as the lady insisted upon going herself. Pavan saw the instrument, at the far corner of the room, an older version of a piano. He boldly strode across the room, ignoring the eyes, pushing past a few of the lords who idled by the corner. Setting his glass down hard, he sat. Unable to stand the shrill voice he struck down upon the piano keys in the beginnings of a strong prelude of the first Rachmaninoff he could remember. His fingers pressed deep into each note, drowning out the words of the lady.

At once the room fell into silence, as every eye within the room looked his way, listening intently as Pavan continued with the force of the song. Each vibration sending shockwaves through his hands, his emotions flowing into the keys.

It ended too soon and the magick dissipated leaving him empty once again. Glancing up to look at the king, Pavan saw him smiling. Astonishment cast a silence over the room, but it was princess Lisetta who stepped forward to sit beside him at the bench.

"You play so beautifully." She drew his eyes from the whispers of the room. "Will you play more of your passionate songs?"

Nodding, he turned, but this time, there was no harsh vigor, he had their full attention now. Allowing the drift of the tune that emerged from the instrument to speak for itself, playing the elegant music he had memorized long ago, hearing Chopin's elegant nocturnes resonate with them. All the while, Lisetta sat listening, watching his hands move across the keys.

Pavan glanced up to look at the king. Beaumont's face was unreadable, sitting in thought, his finger pressed to his mouth as he gazed intently at the fire beside him. Pavan longed to speak to him, to understand the man from his childhood who was unchanged, unaged from the first time he met him in the village of Ledenjour. Caring for his mother, his brother.

Late in the hours, Pavan began to feel the fatigue of playing. He watched bitterly as the lords and ladies began to depart, tired from the lateness of the evening. Pavan was sorry to see Lisetta be guided away by her father, who thanked Pavan again for the wonderful playing. They were all gone as he finished the last of the song.

Looking up at King Beaumont, who was the last to remain.

"Are you alright, Your Majesty?" Pavan asked, his voice trying to stay calm.

The king stood, downing the remainder of his glass before approaching the instrument, his features remaining blank. "You play very well. Another lesson you have learned from your mother?"

Pavan froze, staring openly at the king.

"My mother did not play the piano. She was a cellist. But she taught me the love of music from a very young age. Matched with my ability to memorize whatever sheet of music I could find, it is impossible to forget." Pavan slowed the pacing on the keys, slowing the song, his heart beating faster.

"I am also fond of music." Beaumont nodded, his eyes shifted, catching Pavan's. There was the man Pavan once knew and recognition flared to life. "As I was very fond of your mother."

Pavan's hand froze, unable to complete the notes that ended the song.

"You never told me you were a king."

"I was not a king, then," Beaumont whispered, and Pavan could hear the same emotion in the man's voice. "But your mother knew what I was when I asked her to return to Jorn with me. She came willingly, gladly…"

Pavan gulped, letting his hands fall into his lap as the tears formed unwelcome in his eyes. "From the history I have learned here she died not long after childbirth."

"Isaac."

"You cannot call me that again. Not here."

Shifting his large frame, Beaumont sat on the bench beside him at the piano, invading his space so they touched shoulders.

"This place is not safe for you, Pavan," Beaumont whispered harshly, glancing up to the open door as if he expected someone to enter at any moment. A chill ran up Pavan's spine at the probable possibility.

"Because my father remains as your hand?"

"There is much I wish to speak with you, but not tonight," Beaumont reassured him, keeping his voice low and Pavan noted the anxiety fluttering in the great man's chest. Grasping Pavan by the shoulder, a sudden overwhelming sensation being embraced by the king.

CHAPTER

22

Brendolyn sat beneath the great trees planted in the king's gardens. It had been her favorite spot when last she visited Jorn, and now she sat beneath the swaying branches watching the fluttering of the leaves with Elsa by her side. Along the path, Brendolyn saw the party from her sister, and her four ladies were waiting—three more women than Brendolyn had remembered. Each ignored Brendolyn and Elsa as they waltzed along the path, but Lisetta paused.

"Well, what a delightful surprise." There was a look, Brendolyn knew her sister well—it was one that was full of delight. Lisetta had won a battle only the elder princess was informed upon and irritation prickled Brendolyn's skin.

"I am happy for you, Lisetta, but I have been invited by King Beaumont."

The lady's maids giggled and Lisetta shot them a look. Keeping her smile firmly in place, returning to look back at Brendolyn.

"Enjoy your time in Jorn, Bren, perhaps I shall think kindly upon you after my coronation."

"That is kind of you sister, but unwarranted." Brendolyn stood, eyeing her sister. "You will make a wonderful queen, Lisetta."

Satisfied, Lisetta turned without a farewell, waltzing up the path away from them, her ladies following after and Brendolyn straightened, seeing Varick moving up the path along the way.

"It has been far too long, Bren." His brown eyes looked her over. At once, Elsa stood, pressing against Brendolyn's side. "Look at you, so grown up and with a new companion. We have yet to be introduced."

Elsa snatched Brendolyn's hand, pulling her back.

"There is yet anyone who can do so, sir, so I advise you seek after your princess," Elsa snapped and Brendolyn laced her fingers with hers.

Those cold calculated eyes slid towards Elsa, reflexively Brendolyn stepped back, yanking Elsa with her but her companion stood her ground, glaring at the knight, watching him wordlessly.

"I see no rush, Lisetta is well looked after by Clara." Varick's brown eyes lingered far too long over Brendolyn.

"Leave us, sir," Elsa commanded.

Fire ignited in the knight, his eyes blazing in the direction of Elsa, his lip curling back. "You command me?"

"I am Lady Elsa, of the family Laronn. My station is above your knighthood," Elsa stated firmly. "You have stated your pleasantries to Princess Brendolyn, which is respect for your king's house, but now it is time for you to leave us. Your presence is not welcomed here."

Brendolyn clung tighter to the hand within her own, desperately trying to calm the beating of her racing heart. At last, they heard his name called from Lisetta down the path. Varick smirked, eyeing Brendolyn once more.

"Good evening, Bren." He bowed, before turning as he was bidden and rejoining the ladies along the path.

Sighing, Brendolyn relaxed and grasped Elsa tightly in a hug.

"He is gone," Elsa reassured her, rubbing her back.

Straightening, Brendolyn grasped at Elsa's hand, kissing it fervently. "Come, let us leave our picnic and seek the places which no courtier dare visit."

Starting down the little gravel path, Brendolyn pulled Elsa along with her. They hastened straight towards the large wall, then diverting from the path Elsa soon saw they arrived at the gate leading into the grassy paddock where the horses grazed.

"Are you certain this is allowed?" Elsa asked, nervously eyeing the three young geldings grazing out at the far fence line.

"That is where I had climbed the wall." Brendolyn stopped to point at the exact spot where large hedges now grew. "I had fallen ten feet when Eero had found me."

Elsa rolled her eyes. "Sir Valiant rescuing a princess, how poetic."

"He is the true knight, Elsa."

"He is insufferable." Elsa shrugged.

Brendolyn pulled her along the path. They cut through the grassy hill and slipped between the slats of the fence and entering into the stable at the side door.

Giggling, Brendolyn hurried further into the stables to the last stall, opening the wooden door to look in at the great black stallion within. Upon her entrance, the stallion's head was raised, flicking his tail and blowing air forcefully from his nostrils.

"Hello, Ciar." She raised her hand to press her palm against the warmth of the great horse's nose. "Shall I take you for a ride today?"

"We do not have long before you are to be dressed for dinner," Elsa reminded her, keeping herself at the door of the stall.

Brendolyn sighed heavily.

"Another day, perhaps." She rested her head upon the great neck.

Lahrs was uncertain as he took the stairs to the upper rooms where he was told Thad was roomed. Seeking out the information from a chambermaid who looked at the list of those guests from Eir and had delivered the information to Lahrs gladly. After the dinner with Pavan, Lahrs was increasingly interested in the purpose of their coming.

Stepping up to the door, Lahrs knocked loudly.

"Lahrs, I thought you were in Corad?" Thad was surprised.

"I am where my ward goes. Since she was invited here by King Beaumont, here shall I be too." Without invitation, Lahrs strode into the room looking around at the unmade bed, and the tray of food set upon the center table, with two cups emptied.

Apprehensive of someone walking in at any moment, Thad's eyes drifted towards the door. Lahrs noted the nervousness in his brother.

Lahrs crossed his arms. "Waiting for someone?"

"This is Pavan's room." Thad looked down, a hint of a blush splashed across the faie's freckled skin.

Lahrs knew the look. "You share his room? You share his *bed*?"

"I have no shame in our companionship."

Lahrs sighed, pacing the room to the window before looking back at Thad, who had not moved an inch. "I knew you to be reckless, Thaddeus, but I did not imagine you to be a simpleton."

"We are performing for the king."

"You are playing a dangerous game. What do you seek to accomplish by bringing him here? Already he has shown his magick is unchecked. You cannot deny that it is not dangerous for him to remain in this realm." Taking in deep breaths to slow his breathing, to calm his anger, Lahrs began again, more calmly. "He is here, why has he not travelled to Rhun? There he has been called to, where he is meant to be for his safety."

Thad sneered. "His safety would not fare better in the hands of that witch. Pavan is stronger than he ever was, he has no need of her teaching. I am certain he must make his own choice in the matter, Lahrs."

"I warned Meilyr when he arrived in Tauf without you that things would not be as they should."

Thad became tight. "I know your concern for me in this realm has little to do with my security, Lahrs. You think I am blind to your opinions?"

"That is not what I meant—"

"You meant to keep me out of the way. To keep me away from this realm and those that I have history with."

"You have meddled enough, Thad. Three years have come and gone, with no change in the magick Pavan is guarding. I expect news of him in Rhun, but instead there is silence. Here I have returned to Jorn, where a treaty is to be signed and I instead find you here...What will you do if you are discovered?"

Thad scowled, crossing his arms defiantly. "I won't be."

"Leuthere is captain of Bannon's soldiers," Lahrs bites sharply. "He is familiar with your glamour, no matter the form, Thad. Shall you resign yourself to being suspected in treason upon discovery, or will you leave the realm and let Pavan to his due course."

"I will not yield." Resilient force pushed back with every word.

Lahrs looked sharply at the faie, seeing the unchecked fury written in his orange eyes. "Pavan is in danger here, Thad. You do not understand just how much he is…"

"I know he is in danger wherever he walks. But that does not signify against the truth of the matter, Lahrs. This realm is in danger, because of Pavan's father. How long would you have kept it in the dark that Charles Maison walked free, in the name of Simeon Bannon?"

Lahrs frowned. "You cannot know for certain."

"Pavan told me from his own lips. He recognized Bannon when the hand came to Eir. Before Bannon came to power beside the throne, he was Charles Maison. I have met him countless times in my masters meetings. Charles was a frequent businessman of Orin Gaur who appeared with so much recommendation, when no one had ever heard his name."

Lahrs shook his head.

"You know who his father had become and you told no one?" Thad hissed.

Lahrs was close to Thad now, enough that he could smell the distinct oils of Corad in his hair. The scent to mask, the magick that acted as a barrier. Thad gulped, the smell tickling his nostril, threatening a sneeze.

"It was entrusted to me, this secret."

Thad felt ill, glaring up into gray eyes hardened by years of knowledge. "Who has kept you in their ear?"

"Eleanore."

Thad scoffed. "Perhaps fortunate, that she has been dead these last fifteen years. To keep such a secret that could have kept so many from death at the hands of her deranged husband."

Pain was thick, unyielding and Thad felt the heat of it crawl along his spine. Pushing himself back to be free of it, Lahrs caught his arm, yanking him towards himself. They were so close now that Thad felt the warmth of breath on his face.

"You have spoken enough, Thad. For your next words could very well divide yourself from him forever…"

Thad yanked himself free, grimacing, angry. "My life was hell, because of that man. Bannon kept my master in business, I knew enough of the letters I wrote for him. It was not just the ships of stone, nor the barrels of salt that he sold, it was living people. He sold slaves, bought slaves from the pirates of the northern seas. It was written in my master's ledgers, ledgers that he forced me to burn when the king's men came searching for proof of the black market..."

Lahrs felt the sharpened edge of Thad's words, each cutting him deeper. He knew of Sir Orin Gaur, knew the treachery he had been dealing with for years before the man was hanged in Denorn square, for crimes against the crown, for murdering a member of the high council. Lord Simeon Bannon had been the one to deliver the sentence, Lahrs also knew it was also under Simeon Bannon that the man kept personal business.

"Eleanore had known who Bannon truly was, yet she did nothing...and you..." Thad's chin trembled, tears filling his eyes and dripping along the line of his cheek. "You knew who he was and did *nothing*."

Lahrs touched his cheek. "I wish to have spared you, Thad. Truly it grieves my heart to know how you have suffered, because of Lord Gaur, because of Lord Bannon...but there are so many things at work, so many lives hang in the balance while that man lives...but trust me, Thaddeus, trust that it is what needs to be done."

"I cannot lie to Pavan." Thad's chin quivers. "I cannot pretend that I do not know what that man has done, I cannot pretend it never happened. I am not like you, Lahrs, I am not as strong as you believe me to be."

Lahrs shivered, emotion dragging daggers through his heart.

Thad tried to compose himself, straightening. "Pavan cannot remain ignorant of his father's true nature, of what Bannon has done. He will learn the truth, and it will consume him. You think he is dangerous now, but you cannot imagine what he will be should he discover the truth."

"Then we shall do what we must to protect him." Lahrs touched Thad's cheek. "Help him understand he must leave this place."

"I can't." Thad shook his head. "Not when I am so close."

"Thaddeus, do not let yourself fall into that route. Revenge shall not be your path."

Thad pulled his arm free. "I think it is time you leave."

CHAPTER 23

Varick's knuckles rapped sharply on the door, the echo of his knock reverberating through the dimly lit corridor. He cast furtive glances around the shadowed hallway as the door creaked open, revealing a dim, flickering light from within. A rough hand shot out, grabbing him with surprising strength and yanking him into the chamber. The door closed with an eerie hush, sealing him inside.

The room was stark, its walls lined with shelves of old tomes and curious artifacts that whispered of forgotten lore. Lord Simeon Bannon stood at the far end, his dark tunic disheveled and a crimson-stained cloth in his hand. His eyes, sharp and calculating, appraised Varick with an almost predatory scrutiny. Varick's heart raced, his gaze flitting nervously around the room.

Simeon wiped his hands clean with a practiced, deliberate motion, the red stains merging with the dark fabric. Tossing the cloth aside, he turned with an air of detached authority to his ornate desk, cluttered with ancient manuscripts and strange, arcane symbols.

"What is your meaning of this, Varick?" Simeon's voice cut through the tension like a blade, his tone laced with impatience.

Varick stammered as he approached the desk, his eyes darting around the empty room, searching for any sign of a second presence. "It has been done, just as you asked," he said, his voice trembling slightly as he dared to peer into Simeon's inscrutable face.

Simeon, with an air of disinterest, remained absorbed in a large, leather-bound book inscribed with cryptic runes. His eyes remained fixed on the pages, unreadable. "You have done well," he said finally, his voice devoid of warmth. Varick's lips twitched into a hesitant smile, a fleeting glimmer of hope in his eyes. "Perhaps there is hope for you yet."

Varick leaned closer, his palms clammy and his breath uneven. "I saw her, my lord. She is here in the castle, and she is even more beautiful than before."

At this, Simeon's hand paused over the book. His gaze lifted, piercing through Varick with sudden intensity. "You speak of young Brendolyn?"

Varick nodded, his expression a mixture of eagerness and anxiety.

"What good will she do you," Simeon's voice was almost mocking, "when your reward could be a queen?" He arched an eyebrow, his dark eyes glittering with cold amusement. "Lisetta has been in your charge for most of her womanhood, and yet you turn your gaze away. She will inherit the kingdom."

Varick's face contorted with revulsion. "Lisetta is not like her sister," he spat. "Not in the least. I want Brendolyn. She was what was agreed upon."

Simeon's expression darkened. With a swift, almost predatory movement, he rounded the desk, his hand closing around Varick's throat with a grip like iron. Varick's eyes widened in terror as he felt the crushing pressure. "You will not touch the faie girl until you have completed your task. Sabian is paranoid. The potion you administered is working. We must wait for the ensuing chaos to ignite another war."

Varick's eyes bulged, his breath coming in ragged gasps as Simeon's grip tightened. The lord's cold gaze bore into him, unyielding. Then, with a twisted smile, Simeon released him, and Varick fell back, coughing and gasping.

"But what if it does not? Sabian and Beaumont might never declare war upon each other," Varick wheezed, desperation creeping into his voice.

Simeon's smile was sickly and assured, his gaze condescending. "Then I shall assist them in making that decision." His words hung in the air, heavy with ominous certainty, as the room's shadows seemed to deepen, swallowing Varick's hope whole.

It was colder in the long stone corridors, far colder than Elsa had thought it could be. Walking beside Brendolyn as they took the great stairs, wandered the upper galleries, and began to descend into the lower rooms in search of entertainment. It was easy for Elsa to discern that the princess was actively avoiding the larger areas of the castle where they knew courtiers to be, and more than once did Brendolyn quickly turn when they saw the approach of a courtier.

"We can walk the gardens again."

Brendolyn sighed. "Lahrs has forbidden it. They shall not call another bath to my room. He does not wish for me to get dirty."

"Then let us go to the library, we can read more of the poems that Lahrs was reading to us yesterday," Elsa offered, as they began to walk along a corridor lined with many stained glass windows, color danced upon the marbled floor.

"The libraries are being used for the courtiers to play cards and gamble on racing bets. I overheard the lord talking over the balcony."

Ahead of them, emerging from the opposite end of the corridor, Prince Barrow stopped in the cascade of shimmering color. His blonde hair a blaze of gold but his cheeks an unmistakable red. Elsa realized he was retreating, averting his gaze as he turned on his heel. Elsa had many choice words for the prince but held her tongue. Looking over at Brendolyn, whose soft golden eyes glistened the tears.

"Bren." Elsa reached out, taking her hand.

But Brendolyn was unusually quiet.

"He does that now, Elsa. Whenever I see him across the room, or we happen upon each other, he always turns away," her voice whispered quietly.

Elsa could see the dampened spirits, and dejection in her friend. It was heartbreaking to hear the pain in Brendolyn's voice and Elsa squeezed her hand tighter.

"He is worse than a scoundrel."

Her tears fell at last and Elsa watched the silent torment cascade along the contours of Brendolyn's cheeks. In haste, the princess turned, gripping tightly to Elsa's hand as she hastened her steps. Elsa let herself be pulled along, letting Brendolyn feel in the moment, preparing herself for the torrent of words to spill forth. It wasn't until they were safely secured back in her bed chamber did the tidal wave break through the barrier.

"How could he be so cruel, Elsa?" Brendolyn turned on her, pacing the length of the chamber, stopping just before the window, before returning to stand before the little sitting area before the unlit hearth.

"I cannot say." Elsa was lost for words.

Brendolyn bit her fingers, pacing a second and third time to the window and back, her tears long gone, but her face still wretched with anguish. Elsa felt the pangs in her chest watching her.

"He told me he loved me..." Brendolyn muttered. "He told me that he would stand up beside me and face his father. That he would love me..."

Fear coiled in the pit of Elsa's stomach as she heard Brendolyn muttering to herself and working through the violent thoughts that began to unravel within her. A familiar pang in her ribs, even after three years the brand had never faded. Elsa reacted, reaching out to grasp Brendolyn by the shoulders.

"Brendolyn, you must stop."

Golden eyes glistened. "Why doesn't he love me?"

Elsa had no answer. There was little comfort she was capable of to ease the princess but Elsa began to feel angry. Not only to Barrow, and his unfaithful heart, but for herself in allowing the courtship between the prince and her princess. She was not as a friend should have been to keep Brendolyn from such heartache.

"Please sit." Elsa was soft in her request, helping Brendolyn to sit on the chaise, thankful when the princess went willingly. "He will speak to you, Brendolyn. But give him time to collect himself. There must be a reason for his delay."

"He cannot even look at me."

Elsa brought Brendolyn's hands to her lips, kissing the soft fingers. "Let the shock of your separation lessen in his eyes. You shall hear from him soon."

It felt wrong to speak words she did not believe, but there was something wrong in the narrative. Being invited by the king to Jorn, and Barrow not seeing Brendolyn at all in the last week. There was something they were not being told.

"Shall I make you some tea," Elsa said suddenly, standing to her feet to hasten to the wall where she raised her hand to pull the bell.

"No," Brendolyn said softly. "I think I shall rest before the banquet tonight."

Forcing a smile, Elsa agreed that would probably be best. Making certain that the princess was lying down and fast asleep before Elsa snatched up the letter from her trunk, swiftly slipping from the room and hastening with as much speed her slippers could carry her down the corridor and down the steps. Remembering the path they took down to the gardens, forcefully pushing between a group of walking courtiers without a second glance and bounding down the graveled path to the little gate.

Elsa was halfway down the stable yard when a tall elf with copper hair came up the path towards her. She recognized the stable hand.

"Are you lost my lady?" Rhys asked, holding a rake over his shoulder.

"No, I have come to request a favor from Sir Eero. I know he is in the stables in the evenings," Elsa stated, glancing beyond the elf to the building in question.

"Certainly, you shall find him within." Rhys smiled, motioning her on with a bow.

"Thank you." Elsa curtsied, ignoring the pinch in her side from exertion and grasping the letter tighter in her hand as she continued on to her destination.

It was quiet in the stables, as most of the horses were out in the far paddock. Elsa buzzed with nerves as she looked in at the first storage room, but there was no one there. Hastening down the long line of stalls to the front of the stable where the main offices were housed. Checking one door, then the next before entering into the last room with a fire blazing in the hearth.

She gazed at the tapestry that hung on the furthest wall, one of the last battles of Thourns. She had seen a similar depiction in her father's study in Signe. Elsa's eyes searched the landscape of lavender, at the twisted trees. Her vision flickered over the remnants of a cathedral and sorrow filled her chest.

"Looking for something?"

His deep voice startled her and she gasped, whirling around with a ready arm, but Sir Eero caught it mid swing, a widened smile on his face.

"Do not sneak up on me." She frowned, yanking her arm away.

"Of course, my apologies." Sir Eero bowed. He looked unusual to Elsa, not dressed in his armor or the thick leather apron. Instead the knight wore a simple grey tunic and doublet. "What do I owe this honor for meeting you in my office?"

Elsa took in a breath to calm her nerves before extending the crumpled letter she held out to him. "I have a letter."

He did not take it but raised an eyebrow, smirking at her with that full mouth.

"We have messengers at the gate who see the letters of court," Eero told her, clasping his hands behind his back.

Elsa frowned. "This is an important letter. One I only trust in your hands."

Intrigued, the knight took the crumbled letter, examining it closely. His eyes darted from it up to Elsa and suddenly his features were serious.

"It is not sealed," he stated flatly.

"Yes." Her cheeks felt hot. "I trust you in getting it to its destination without opening it."

There was a change, a shift in the knight as he watched her. He grew serious and looked almost angry, glaring at her with an intensity that began to make Elsa more uncomfortable. She fidgeted, standing in the silence for far too long.

"Will you deliver my letter?"

"Of course." He pocketed the parchment but crossed his arms over his broad chest. "Now, I will ask you again. What do I owe the honor of meeting you here?"

Elsa scoffed. "I told you."

"A lie," Sir Eero stated. "You brought me a letter, when you could have given it to me at any moment, Elsa. Please don't make me ask again."

"Your prince refuses to speak to Brendolyn."

A long painful silence stretched out between them and Elsa hated the unsurprised look in the knight's face, the undeniable from his lips. Elsa's anger began to grow, transferring a little to the knight.

"He has broken her heart, Eero."

Eero still said nothing.

Elsa stepped forward, confronting the knight. "Barrow has taken advantage of her, and now she is heartbroken. Can you hear what I am saying?"

Cold grey eyes slid towards hers. "Perfectly clear, Elsa."

She wanted to hit him, to strike his face, to make him understand her furry. Hot tears began to burn in her eyes, glaring at the knight who stood motionless before her, his emotions unmoved, unchallenged. He was like stone.

"He refuses to talk to her, he has not explained to her what is happening…Is she only here so that Barrow can flaunt his victory over her to her face? I cannot see what purpose there is in bringing Brendolyn to Jorn if it is not to make King Beaumont see they love each other. That they are meant to be together. Does Barrow know that he is breaking Brendolyn's heart by keeping away?"

Eero examined her. "He knows what he is doing."

Grinding her teeth, Elsa scowled.

"He does not know what he is doing, because he cannot understand the heartbreak I have seen in her, nor the loss she had felt in his denying her an audience." Elsa's eyes burn with tears. "He cannot understand the damage he has done by casting her aside."

"Barrow has committed treason against his king and your own, Elsa," Eero began with a somber tone. "It is not something he can ignore. Nor can his father. King Beaumont was gracious in his discovery, he has quieted any rumors that the violation has occurred. In time, Barrow will speak with Brendolyn as he should, but for him he is likewise heartbroken. Knowing to be separated from her forever is more than Barrow can endure."

"He has no intention of keeping his promise to Brendolyn…" Elsa felt the drop in her stomach at hearing what Sir Eero was really telling her. "Barrow will marry Lisetta."

"Prince Santino is in good health. He shall become king after his father and with it all of the titles will pass to him. Lisetta shall have her dowry and the means of an alliance with Jorn. Joining the Three Realms shall strengthen our borders."

"You speak of the Scalanis pirates? They are nothing more than thugs that burn ships and steal traded goods." Elsa scowled.

Eero clenched his jaw, biting back words he wanted to say. Elsa saw the tension in the knight's neck, his uneasy demeanor. She gulped but attempted to remain tough with her head held high.

"Those pirates have raided more than ships that make the great crossing. They have burned down villages, killed hundreds of elven kin and faie alike," Eero spoke gruffly. "But it is not only the pirates that we must be wary of…there are shores beyond the eastern borders, where our ships cannot cross but our looking glasses have seen on the horizon."

"Myths of the expanse of the east. My father believes it cannot be done."

Eero sighed, uncrossing his arms. "There is much that many do not know. But an alliance is a benefit to our strength."

"You believe it is right that Barrow should begin his rule with a lie?"

"He was promised to Lisetta since infancy, Elsa," Eero told her. "It had been kept secret from them for too long. It allowed for Barrow to hope that he would fall in love with whomever he wished, but it has been known this union would happen."

Elsa narrowed her eyes. "How long have you known?"

"I have been the guardian of Barrow since he was five years old, Elsa. Of course I knew about the match."

"Advise your prince to explain everything to Brendolyn. She needs to hear it from him. Then I can help her heal and move past him as best as I can."

Eero nodded. "As you wish."

Swirls of colors graced the dance floor as the courtiers danced the royal dances on the marbled floor of the great hall. From the table at the top of the hall, Brendolyn sat with the guests of Corad but seated further away from her family. Lahrs was seated next to her, to keep her company when those nearest refused to acknowledge her presence. It was after their meal, when the dancers began. Soon there would be entertainment. Brendolyn had heard it would be a spectacle, with fire and dancing like they had never seen before.

"You are looking forlorn again." Lahrs' voice cut through her thoughts.

She looked away from the swirling color of skirts and jewels that mesmerized her. In truth, her eyes had remained puffy, even after Elsa had placed a cold compress on her eyes while she got ready for the evening. Brendolyn was tired of crying, but the question from her close companion made her want to hide. Her temples ached and her throat was thick, swallowing back the urge to weep.

"I am missing Elsa," Brendolyn admitted to the half-truth. She disliked these formal meals when Elsa was not permitted to join them. Desperate for the evenings when the king took his meals privately so they could enjoy banquets in less formal settings.

"You did not touch your food. It is not like you to turn away such well-prepared courses." Lahrs kept his voice low, watching her with uncanny grey eyes.

Brendolyn saw the look and knew the kindness behind them. So much care was being pressed upon her, as her guardian should, but the comfort from her dearest friend was unbearable. She glared at the half drunk glass of thinned down wine before her.

"I am tired."

"I have known you your whole life, Brendolyn." Lahrs reached over, taking hold of her hand. "Something troubles you."

Opening her mouth to speak, Brendolyn froze, her eyes glossing over as she looked across the hall to see a familiar head of golden hair slipping from the room out onto the garden terrace. Her heart pounded heavily.

"I need some air." Brendolyn's hand slipped away. Standing from her chair, she hastened away. Her gown feeling too heavy and her hair feeling too tight. Gulping back tears Brendolyn emerged onto the terrace.

It was cool in the evening air, a welcomed balm to her warm, flushed skin.

"Brendolyn."

Casting her eyes towards him, Brendolyn gazed at the lovely presence of Barrow, standing at the edge of the stone steps leading down to the gardens below. He must have been beginning his descent when he heard her feet approach. He looked surprised, delighted and Brendolyn could feel the flutter of anxiety overwhelm the prince, followed by an uneasiness that provoked a flare of annoyance in Brendolyn.

"Your Majesty." She curtsied slightly.

Prince Barrow took a step forward, then stopped. His eyes darting from her, to the door, unable to decide if he should come forward or remain. Perhaps he meant to flee, but Brendolyn was prepared for him to vanish as he had all those other times they had met in the time she had returned to Jorn.

"Are you well?" she asked, stepping the distance between them.

"Very well." Barrow flushed, stumbling back slightly and gripping so tightly to the stone railing, his knuckles had gone white. Brendolyn smiled, hiding her pain and anguish, reaching out to touch the soft skin of his hand.

"Do not hide from me, Barrow," she whispered, catching the terrified look in his clear blue eyes. His transparency was evident, she needed no magick to discern his fear of speaking to her. "I am here waiting for your word to banish my fears."

Barrow gulped. "Forgive me...Brendolyn, I am sorry to have brought such shame upon your honor."

"Shame?" Brendolyn took hold of his hand more firmly, stepping down the first step, so they were eye to eye. "I have no shame in what has come between us, Barrow."

"The treaty." Any pretense of Barrow's calm composure was breaking. Brendolyn could see it now as the emotions began to pass through her.

"Your father did not approve of our union?"

Barrow hesitated. "He did not approve of our secrecy. I did not tell him what he did not already know. It was foolish to believe I would not be followed."

"And you must marry Lisetta?" It was painful, as she began to understand what her heart had already suspected. A little bit of her heart began to crumple, a deep rooted anguish that would fester if she allowed it to deepen.

"I don't want to." Barrow lowered his head, drawing his hand away. "But for the realms I must satisfy the treaty."

"Barrow." Brendolyn touched the prince upon the cheek, lifting his chin to look into his teary blue eyes, leaning closer until she was close to his chest and kissing his lips with a soft kiss. "I will always love you."

"Prince Barrow," a voice cut in from the doorway leading out onto the terrace.

Standing behind them, at the door was Sir Eero, his arms crossed in front of his chest, watching them closely. Hearing the loud clamor from within but there was coolness and calm on the terrace, Brendolyn reluctantly took a step back, dropping her hand from the prince as he stepped forward.

She was soon to follow, but Sir Eero placed a hand out, holding her by the waist. His gray eyes tender, his features softened. Brendolyn touched his chest, feeling the flutter of anxiety beneath the breastplate. The calm exterior of the knight was unreadable, but the magick that flared to life in his blood was unmistakable.

"Are you alright, Brendolyn?" he asked in a low voice.

"I will be," she reassured him.

Letting her hand fall away she entered the hall, the spectacle that played out before her drew her breath away—standing at the center of the room was a man dressed in black, the leather slick with an oily sheen and his dark hair pulled away from his face.

Breathing fire from his mouth, the crowd gasped in awe. Music shrilled the room as whips of fire swirled like snakes in midair, coiling into a dance that swirled around the man's limbs. He danced with fire, his movement shifting languidly as he dragged the fire over the marbled floor. Brendolyn wondered if the stone would become black, but it remained smooth and untouched. He was marvelous. Each movement creating a story with fire.

It made her think of Augusta, to the home of her mother. Hearing stories of the fire dances that they performed, in her lessons with Lahrs, that told stories of the victories and told the future. Brendolyn looked around at the courtiers who watched in amazement, some speculating their superstitions of such magick, but none of them heard the words in the movements. They did not understand the story within the fire.

It was a tragedy that burns brightest in the dance, as the man in black blew more fire into his hands. She watched the snake like vines curl and wave around him. Turning around a final time as the fire was extinguished, his chest heaving and bowing to the courtiers who clapped. Brendolyn's breath caught.

It was the man from Denorn.

Others began to dance, emerging from behind him, but the man in black walked forward. Brendolyn felt his eyes watching her closely as he drew nearer and her heart began to pound hard in her chest.

"Brendolyn.," Eero whispered, pressing a hand to her back.

Wiping her cheeks. "Yes?"

"You were crying," he whispered, looking around. "Shall I take you to Lahrs? He must be looking for you."

"No, I am alright. I can see him from here, he talks with Lord Anval."

Anxiously she looked around, seeking the man in black but he was gone.

"I believe I know that man, who breathed fire." She was almost certain it was him.

Sir Eero nodded. "He is a performer from Eir, they arrived yesterday at special request by King Beaumont."

"Is he faie?"

Eero maneuvered them through a group of courtiers who laughed at the drunken follies of a nearby man who frequently made sport with the shortcomings of those that knew him. Brendolyn felt uneasy standing in their sights but they ignored her completely.

"I do not know if he is faie, or elven kin. But he holds magick with a charming grace," Sir Eero was now saying, keeping his conversation light.

"He must be faie, to speak with fire as he did. Not many would dare bring this sort of magick here. I understand it is forbidden to use fire magick in Jorn."

Eero sighed, glancing sideways at her. "It is not forbidden, but there is a limit of who may utilize that certain talent if they are registered."

Shrugging off the remnants of sadness, Brendolyn took Eero by the arm, walking beside him around the outer edge of the hall, until they reached a quieter section near the archway leading towards the stairs. Desperately she wished to retreat and find Elsa, but she must remain dutiful to the feast and stay for the remainder of the festivities. They stood closest to a window, to keep from the unbearable heat of the room.

Brendolyn stopped. "I wish he remained, so I might speak with him."

"Do you speak of Prince Barrow?" Sir Eero asked and she saw the gentle concern in the knight's eyes, gazing down upon her. "Or the mysterious stranger from Eir?"

"I do not believe there is anything more to be said with Barrow. He still loves me, but he must marry another. It is beyond our powers to forget our duties." She wished her voice sounded confident, that her voice didn't tremble but her heart was weakened and she felt it dampen the heart she once held.

"You are considerate in your thoughtfulness, princess. But perhaps even your strength has been dampened by the weight of such a truth." Eero gazed around the room, his calculating eyes scanning the faces of the courtiers that began to mingle about the room, hanging languidly on each other's arms, laughing dangerously loud.

"I am grieved." Brendolyn shrugged. Her eyes, still puffy, could cry no more tears this night, she refused to let herself be swept away. "But I am not damaged."

Eero smiled, patting her arm, turning them away towards the stairs. "Let me escort you to your chaperone, the night grows late and the kings have left for the evening. It is in these twilight hours that the ladies and lords of court behave in unusual ways."

"Let him stay." She caught a glimpse of the elf at the further end of the hall in conversation with another lord. A chill ran through her, perhaps a draft from the window. "It grows cold, I wish to return to Elsa."

"As you wish."

CHAPTER

24

After performing, his blood hot from the fire and his breathing coming sharp, he saw her. At first, he believed he imagined her. But she was real. At the farthest end of the hall she stood, dressed in silk, her hair pinned away from her face and her pointed ears catching the light.

She was a faie and she was beautiful.

This scared Pavan, looking at the same girl he had seen in the village and in the gardens of the churchyard. His wrist began to itch, touching the ribbon secured under the line of his tunic. In one moment, their eyes connected and a jolt went through him, electrifying. Then he saw Lahrs, the elf that healed him in Ledenjour.

Pavan became haunted by memories, walking away from the group of courtiers now swarming to dance.

He made his way through the crowd, needing air. He emerged onto the terrace, gasping as the swarm of heat overflowed through his body. Breathing back the heightened emotions, moonlight washed over him and slowly the magick calmed.

Swiftly taking to the steps of the terrace at the sound of approaching footsteps and descending into the darkened garden below one of the great windows of the hall, Pavan shifted beneath the vines that overgrew the stone, hearing her softened voice through the cold windowpane.

"I wish he remained, so I might speak with him."

Hearing her voice sent shivers along his spine. Trembling against the cold stone behind him, Pavan wanted to run but his heart yearned to hear her speak.

"Do you speak of Prince Barrow?" Now he could hear the voice of the knight, Sir Eero. "Or the mysterious stranger from Eir?"

Pavan closed his eyes, desperately wishing to melt into the stone wall. If only he could hear them clearly, but the sounds were muffled. Pressing himself up further along the vines to secure a foothold, peeking in through the glass at the pair that stood so near to the window Pavan could just make out the outline of her silhouette.

"I am grieved, but I am not damaged."

The air was thick with a tension that gnawed at the edges of Pavan's resolve. Brendolyn's voice trembled, each quiver sending ripples through the atmosphere, as if her very words carried the weight of an ancient sorrow. Pavan felt it in the pit of his stomach, a slow, twisting ache that mirrored the turmoil in her voice. Remembering the tome that Arienne had given him, its pages filled with arcane knowledge that he had only begun to decipher. The words held secrets of how to shield oneself from the onslaught of emotions, but Pavan had yet to master them.

Instead, he found himself vulnerable to the storm of feelings that crashed against his mind. He had learned to suppress his own emotions, to bury them deep where they couldn't reach him. But these were not his own—they were hers, seeping into his consciousness like a creeping fog. The sheer intensity of it was exhausting, a torrent of emotions too vast and powerful to simply dispel. Pavan's connection to her magick was his weakness, a siren's call that lured him into the depths of her despair. He could feel it in every fiber of his being, an unspoken plea that resonated within him, echoing his own silent agony.

"Let me escort you to your chaperone, the night grows late and the kings have left for the evening..."

He shut out her tenderness, lowering himself away, Pavan leant back upon the stone. Unwanted feelings soured his tongue with bitterness. Pavan wanted them gone, clenching his fists he felt the ice begin to crystalize beneath his feet, creeping up the vines around him.

All at once, the two that spoke so near were gone. Like a sudden weight had been lifted from his chest, Pavan could breathe again. Taking his chance, he stole away into the night. Taking the path he had memorized soon after arriving here, learning the paths and turns of the gardens in his many wanderings to a voice the mass within, Pavan managed to find his way back into the castle. In the underbelly of the stone beast, taking the servants narrow corridors until he was well out of danger of seeing her again.

Pavan's heart pounded with a restless urgency as he longed to speak to her, to reveal himself as the man imprisoned behind the façade. Yet the chasm between them felt insurmountable—she was royalty, free to traverse the world as she wished, while he was bound by the chains of his own making. The mere thought of approaching her would send ripples through the court, and the fear of being exposed for who he truly was gripped him with icy fingers. Visions of the sea and a dark-haired girl's haunting song swirled in his mind, calling to him with an undeniable intensity.

"Pavan," Thad's voice cut through the haze, grounding him.

Startled, Pavan blinked, his surroundings coming back into focus. He barely recalled the journey to his chamber, but there was Thad, waiting for him with a concern etched deeply into those bright orange eyes. Tender hands reached out, offering the solace Pavan desperately needed.

"I am exhausted," Pavan admitted, his voice a weary sigh as he pinched the bridge of his nose. His fingers fumbled with the buckles of his leather jacket, slick with protective oils designed to guard against flames.

Thad was immediately at his side, his skilled fingers working with gentle precision to remove the jacket. Warmth spread through Pavan as Thad's hands massaged his aching muscles, their touch a soothing balm. Pavan leaned into the embrace, inhaling the calming citrus scent that enveloped him, momentarily erasing the sea's haunting call and drawing him into a cocoon of comfort. Thad smoothed Pavan's disheveled hair, pressing a soft kiss to his jaw.

"Sleep, you need rest," Thad's voice was a soft murmur, but Pavan struggled to focus, his body sinking into the nearest chair under the weight of exhaustion.

"I saw her," Pavan mumbled, his voice barely audible.

Thad knelt before him, tracing the lines of Pavan's scars with a reverent touch that ignited a fierce warmth within him. Pavan tilted his head back, sleep encroaching with relentless persistence.

"Who did you see, Pavan?" Thad's voice seemed distant, a gentle echo in the encroaching darkness.

"My goddess," Pavan whispered, his words drifting between consciousness and slumber as he absently touched the ribbon on his wrist.

Thad took Pavan's hands in his own pressing firm, reassuring kisses to each one. "Sleep, Pavan...you must sleep."

As the embrace of sleep took hold, the world around Pavan faded, leaving him cocooned in the warmth of Thad's care and the faintest echoes of the sea's call.

Thad left Pavan slumped in the chair, wrapped in a cocoon of slumber while he cast protective wards over the room, the runes glowing softly as they sealed the space. The tension coiling within him was palpable, a storm brewing in his chest that demanded release. He needed to clear his mind, and as the night deepened, he descended the labyrinthine corridors, slipping through narrow servant's stairs that wound their way to the humble quarters above the kitchens. He paused before the third door, knuckles rapping sharply against it, eyes scanning the flickering light that seeped beneath.

"What?" The gruff voice from within was unmistakable.

A smirk touched Thad's lips as he watched Svein's half-asleep frown transform into reluctant recognition. The half-giant, a towering figure of muscle and strength, sighed and stepped aside, his massive frame blocking the doorway. He lit a candle, its soft glow casting a warm light over their faces.

"I know it's late," Thad began, suddenly acutely aware of how his desperation must have seemed.

Svein settled onto the bed with a groan, the ancient frame creaking beneath his weight. "Troubles, Thad? It's been years since you've come to me like this, with that look in your eyes."

Thad's cheeks flushed, his words tumbling out in a rush. "It's not that...I've made a grave mistake."

Svein's interest was piqued. He leaned forward, his eyes narrowing with a mix of curiosity and concern. "Not like you to admit to mistakes, Thaddeus."

"It was a mistake to bring him here," Thad's voice grew frantic, his heart hammering in his chest. "There's danger...there's something that could change everything."

Svein raised a hand, his expression stern but patient. "Slow down. I need to understand what's happening."

Thad drew a deep breath, fighting to steady his voice. "It was a mistake to bring him here. There's something here—a presence that unsettles me." The pangs in his chest were sharp, a wildfire of jealousy and regret igniting with every word.

Svein's eyes narrowed, intrigued. "Something or someone? The man whom the people fear?"

Thad's face flushed crimson, the heat spreading to his cheeks. "You mustn't tell Pavan...please, Svein. Don't let him know I was wrong." The pit in his heart felt like a dark, expanding void, threatening to swallow him whole.

"Wrong about what, Thad?" Svein's question was gentle but firm, urging Thad to confront his turmoil.

The tears began to prick at Thad's eyes, his anger bubbling into a storm of regret. His magick pulsed violently, responding to the emotional tempest within. "It was never Isaac I saw crossing the Treacherous Sea. He's not the one who haunts my thoughts, nor the one who has called to me since childhood."

Svein's eyes widened with realization. "Not Isaac...then—"

Thad's anguish deepened, his heart beating erratically, as though it were trying to escape its cage. He sank heavily into a chair, his body trembling with the weight of his revelations. Tears streamed hotly down his cheeks, the guilt searing through him. "He is gone, like all the others. I sent him to his doom, thinking he would return to save me from my burdened heart."

Svein scratched his scruff thoughtfully, his expression somber. "You once told me about the boy from Denorn, the one you sent north across the sea. Eleanore's other son."

Thad nodded, a grim determination in his eyes. "I deluded myself into believing that Pavan could be his replacement. From the myths, I thought the sons were destined to be linked. Sons born hand in hand."

"That is impossible, Thad," Svein said, shaking his head in disbelief.

Thad's frustration boiled over. "But I've seen them! Not together, but I swear by the Blessed One that they are equal in appearance and spirit."

"Pavan loves you, Thad. Perhaps if you explain—"

"Pavan is not mine!" Thad's voice cut through the room, raw and accusing. "He never was. The faie…" He paused, the anger cooling to a bitter edge. "It was always her."

Svein's frown deepened. "What faie?"

Thad's gaze was hard, his voice a harsh whisper. "Brendolyn."

"The princess Sir Lahrs is sworn to?"

Thad's fists clenched as he faced Svein, the weight of his fears and regrets pressing down upon him. "Brendolyn is here, Svein. A girl who comes to Pavan's dreams. I have seen it myself, when we have crossed that pathway of our minds. I have seen her with my own eyes as she stands upon the sands to call to him. Just as I had seen since I was young. It is the same call, the same pull…"

Svein cut him off with a raised hand, his gaze steady and penetrating. "They are only visions. It is not known for certain if those with the gift of sight speak the truth."

Thad's eyes flared with a mix of anger and desperation. "You don't understand. He is not some witch, or an elf with a wary gift. Pavan is Ehlfern, with the capability of so much more than any of us can truly understand. If he is born hand in hand with another that is a deeper power none of us have ever seen."

Svein's expression softened, though his voice remained firm. "I do understand more than you think. I know the burden you carry, the way Henry's shadow looms over your decisions. But acting out of this deep-seated anger and fear could lead to more harm than good."

Thad's face twisted with frustration. "What am I supposed to do, then? Stand by and wait for it all to unravel? To lose him to that girl? Does she deserve his love after all the pain he has endured to reach this point?"

"That is not your choice. You told me once there was never a choice given to you."

Thad hesitated, his throat burned with agony. "He would choose her over me."

"Do you not wish Pavan to live a happy fulfilled life?"

"I cannot live in this world without him. What point is there to this life, when I am so far from the Veil? I am so far from the goddess, there is nothing left of my life after this one but eternal darkness."

"There is always the Tree of Sanctity."

"Now who is speaking of legends?" Thad smirked, a hint of his former self flickering to life at the half giants words. There was some truth to the myths of the tree that grew within the great northern realms, at the doorway to the Veil. Thad knew it was impossible to reach such a doorway.

Svein sighed deeply, his large hand resting on Thad's shoulder in a gesture of calm reassurance. "Think of your past, Thad. When you endured too much at the hands of so many that wished to burden you with pain, it was not through reckless confrontation but through understanding and strategy. You must confront your past, not with violence, but with clarity. There is always hope for those who seek it."

Thad shook his head, his voice trembling. "I'm not sure I have that clarity. All I see is a web of deception and danger, and I'm trapped in the center."

Svein's eyes were filled with sympathy. "You're not alone in this. You have allies, and you have your own strengths. Pavan, despite everything, is a part of your world now. He has his own role to play. Don't let your past dictate your future actions."

"There is only one way to finish this score and stop the pain. There is no tree that can claim my soul, I am lost already, Svein."

"You do not speak of the girl now, but of revenge upon the one that began this turmoil."

"I must put an end to the wrongs committed against my people. I shall storm the great fortress of Hilvaer and slit the throat of the man that murdered my future."

Svein rubbed his beard thoughtfully. "Eske is not a strong man, but he has many men that follow in his name. You shall need more than a slender blade and faie words to end that line."

"Come with me." Thad was stern, excited at the possibilities. "Sail with me to Tauf for those that would follow us. We shall siege the fortress and take over that which has endured so much agony. There shall be nothing to stop us, they shall fall because I shall have killed the man behind the great design."

"You cannot kill Bannon," Svein whispered.

"He is *Charles Maison*, Svein. It was destiny that my path should return me to Jorn. To put an end to all his wrongs."

Svein shook his head, rubbing a hand along the great thick ginger beard. "This is not reasonable, Thad. There are other ways."

Thad's gaze dropped to the floor, his mind racing with conflicting thoughts. "What if confronting Bannon is the only way to protect everyone? What if I can't protect those I care about? If I don't act, will the danger only grow?"

Svein's voice was steady and measured. "There are other ways to address the threat without succumbing to the same mistakes that have haunted you. Speak with Meilyr and take Hilvaer. Your path forward should be guided by wisdom, not merely by the shadows of your past."

Thad looked up, his eyes red-rimmed but resolved. "And what if I fail?"

Svein gave him a reassuring nod. "Then you must find the strength to rise again, Thad. Do not let fear root you to the ground where indecision breeds regret. It is not just Hilvaer that's at stake. The rot runs deep through the very veins of our cities, festering in the dark corners we dare not speak of. We cannot afford for our error to be exposed."

Thad took a deep breath, the storm within him slowly settling. "You're right."

Svein's face softened into a rare smile. "Good," he murmured. "We'll speak of this again on calmer shores. But for now, you should return to your rooms. If you do not wish to share my bed tonight, then it is best to seek the solace you find with Pavan. I'll see to the preparations for our journey to Tauf when we return to Eir."

Thad rose from the chair. "Thank you, Svein."

Svein watched him with a mixture of concern and pride.

As Thad left the room, the candle's flame flickering behind him, wiping at the wayward tear and drawing up the dark hood over his head as he disappeared into the corridor on silent feet in search of the best possible outcome.

Elsa stepped into the darkened kitchens, drawing her shawl tighter around her shoulders. She suddenly regretted making the walk into the kitchens, to make herself some tea.

In Alnwick, the distance was never this great. Her bare feet ached from the cold stone and miles of corridors.

Tiptoeing across the quiet, Elsa reached for the copper teapot on the higher shelf. Searching the wall of cupboards in the darkness, only a sliver of moonlight shimmered in through the windows. Elsa found the large barrels of water beneath the window, next to the great sink that housed a pump that drew from the wells far beneath the castle in the catacombs.

She dunked the ladle into the first barrel, filling her kettle.

"Well look what we have here." A voice behind her startled Elsa as she dropped the kettle onto the table, water spilling over the edge onto the floor. "A little kitchen mouse scurrying about. What are you doing down here, girl?"

Elsa spun around to see one of the knights of Jorn leaning in the doorway.

He was not wearing a uniform but she recognized him. One of the wolves under Lord Bannon's employ. Leuthere.

She lifted her chin. "Princess Brendolyn desired some tea to help her sleep," she lied. Just a small lie to show she belonged and that someone might be waiting on her.

The man's eyes roamed up and down over her body, drinking in her thin nightgown. Elsa crossed her arms over herself, pulling her shawl tighter around her body. The way Leuthere studied her pricked her skin.

"You're not one of the servants," he cooed.

"No. I am a member of King Sabian's court and a guest of the king."

"A mouse of Corad, with long auburn hair and beautiful pale skin." He stepped into the kitchen, circling Elsa like a cat cornering its prey. "You should have called for a servant, little mouse."

"I didn't see a need. I'm more than capable of brewing tea."

"I'm sure you are. I'm sure you are capable of a great many things. But Lord Bannon does not like strangers wandering the palace at night. I ought to take you to him so he can make sure you're not a spy." He leaned against the table, penning her in with his arms.

Elsa swallowed the cold fear that rose up in her. The hand of the king was a dangerous man. Brendolyn had told her about the sense of danger she felt whenever she was near him.

"Of course, I could be convinced to forget I saw you, for the right price." Leuthere gripped her chin with a rough hand, studying her face now. His lips curled in a smile.

"Perhaps a kiss might convince me." His gaze dropped to her curves again. "Or something a bit more."

"Sir, I believe you have me mistaken for someone else. I am Princess Brendolyn's lady in waiting and I…"

"I know exactly who you are, Elsa Laronn." He shoved her down so hard her teeth rattled, back pressed to the table. "You're that little lady Sir Eero is sweet on, I have seen you together conspiring."

Elsa trembled. "I'm not conspiring."

"Silence, little whore. I am going to fuck you just so I can see his face when he finds out you are ruined," Leuthere seethed, shaking Elsa violently.

Fear coiled inside of Elsa as she struggled to free herself from his grip, but the man pinned her down with one hand to her throat. She had been here before and knew exactly what was to come but there was something different about this than when Alaric had forced himself on her—a sense of control. Elsa had never been able to fight Alaric when he demanded things of her as if the magick binding them together stripped her of her will. Or perhaps something inside of her had simply snapped at the prospect of being used by one more man. At being used as an object of physical pleasure. She kicked and scratched at the knight, trying to free herself, fingers grasping for anything she could use as a weapon as a teacup skittered out of her grip.

"Stop! Get your hands off of me!"

"You're a bold little mouse. Will you scream for me?" The knight held her down with ease, his grip on her throat slowly depriving her of oxygen. With the other hand he pushed up her nightgown, baring legs and stomach and…He paused, fingers brushing over the brand on her ribs. It burned the way it always did when it was touched.

She tried to jerk away.

"Blood magick. Did the man who marked you fuck you when he bound you to him? Will it burn red hot when I do?" He smiled a cruel, menacing smile at her. "Does Sir Eero know that you already belong to someone else."

"I don't belong to anyone!" Elsa's fingers finally wrapped around the kettle and she swung as hard as she could, smashing it against the knight's head. He stumbled back and Elsa kicked him, scrambling off the table and running up the small narrow stairs.

A hand clamped over her mouth, dragging her into the shadows of a doorway. "Don't scream. You'll get us both killed." A ginger haired man stood over her, hand clamped to her mouth. "What are you doing here?"

She recognized him with dark clothes, but his image shifted, as though her eyes tried to look beyond him when she tried to focus. Elsa started to cry. It had been a very long time since she had cried in earnest but she was scared and shaking.

He pressed his hand harder against her mouth. "For fuck's sake girl. I'm not going to hurt you now stop that."

Something in his voice compelled her to stop, but it wasn't kindness. She realized with a start that it was magick, he'd used his faie voice on her. Her sobs subsided unwillingly.

"That's better. I'm going to let you go. Do not scream." He slid his hand away from her mouth. "Now, tell me what you are doing here."

Elsa couldn't answer. He glanced up and down at her rumpled nightgown and hair. Not in the leering way the knight or Alaric did. Already in her mind the knight had Alaric's face. She was never going to escape him. The faie reached out, wiping away her tears, his touch was surprising in tenderness, bringing his fingertips to her temple.

"It's all right girl. He cannot hurt you now. I won't let him." His words were wrapped in magick, his bright orange eyes glowing like embers in the darkened space hidden in the doorway.

Elsa crumpled.

He caught her, bracing her against his chest, swearing under his breath. "It's all right, girl. You're safe, no one will hurt you in the royal wing, but you must go back to your rooms and stay there for the rest of the night, do you understand me?"

Elsa nodded.

"Good. Forget my face." His voice was tinted with the familiar taste of magick and Elsa felt it settle on her skin. "Wait until I am gone then go back where it is safe. I will find the man who hurt you."

He stepped out of the shadows and Elsa immediately lost the man's face. His image became shrouded. She counted to a hundred, waiting for the knight to find her. When he didn't she peered down the corridor. This was the royal wing which meant Eero was not far away. She let out a breath, Elsa would go where it was safe. The safest place in the palace.

She stepped out into the hall and ran, not stopping until she reached the doors to Eero's room, pounding her fist against it.

Anxiety coiled inside of Elsa as she waited for the door to open.

Eero was still dressed for the day when he opened the door. He startled back when he saw her, no doubt taking in her appearance. But he never looked at her that way, even when he kissed her there had been no lust in it. He was the only man she trusted.

"Elsa, what are you doing here?"

"There's a man in the royal wing! He had magick. He made me forget his face." Elsa rushed into the room as her mind tried to remember every detail.

Eero was near her, wrapping a blanket around her shoulder.

She rounded on the knight, glaring at his calmness. "You must act, Eero! You must see to the king, he could be in danger!"

Smiling gently, Eero touched Elsa's hair, guiding her back to sit upon the nearest chair. She sat, reluctantly, her heart racing wildly.

"I shall go, Elsa, but not until I have certainty you are unharmed."

She shook her head, trembling. "I am fine."

Eero raised her hands, looking down at the deep gash in the center of her palm. It was not deep, but the deep red blood had begun to dry. She felt flush, not knowing when it was she had gotten the wound. Her thoughts raced through the moments.

"I'm fine," she breathed.

His fingers were warm to the touch, lingering over the center of her palm. Elsa winced, feeling the magick tighten her skin, wincing as the skin closed, leaving no evidence of a scar. She was crumpling, her body crawling as the harsh memories began to swim. Leuthere's hands on her, making her skin crawl.

Eero touched her cheek. "I will return to you, Elsa. Please, stay here until I have ensured it is safe."

Nodding, Elsa watched him go, leaving her in the seclusion of his chambers. It was warm, she looked at the fire that began to burn brighter in the hearth. Wrapping the blanket tighter around her shoulders, it smelled of the knight, a woodsy musk that lingered when he was near. It made her chest ache, the brand upon her ribs reminding her of her bond. Elsa frowned, lowering her hands into her lap.

Eero returned, quietly shutting the door behind him.

Sitting up straighter, Elsa was eager to hear of the news. "The king, is he alright?"

He sat beside her. "He is well and sleeping."

"That can't be right, I saw a man in the corridor. He grabbed me, and warned me away. He used magick to make me forget his face, but I remember his words, I can see his copper hair."

"Rhys was in the corridor, administering his services to the king." Eero smiled, but there was something in his look that was disheartening. "Rhys is an elf and helps Beaumont with remedies to help him sleep."

Elsa was baffled. "I have seen the stable hand, this man was not of elven birth."

Eero stood, his brows drawn together, as his mouth frowned. Stepping over to a cabinet where glasses stood. "Would you like a drink?"

"I cannot!" Elsa shifted, fear began to prickle into her mind as she watched the knight pour into the glass.

Eero turned. "It is water, Elsa. I do not take wine...it does not agree with my temperament."

She relaxed, if only slightly, carefully watching the knight as he approached with the glass. Indeed there was water within, clear and cold. Elsa drank gratefully, gulping down the cool liquid until the glass was empty.

"Thank you." She offered back the glass.

He returned the glass to his cabinet, before walking to the door and pulling on the cord that rung for the servant. Casting his eyes back at Elsa.

"I have called for an escort," he told her. "You must return to Brendolyn."

Elsa shot up. "I cannot, Eero. He is still out there!"

Eero was there to comfort her, standing so close she felt the pangs in her chest as the brand began to burn, causing the tears to form in her eyes.

"He is gone, Elsa...you must return to your princess. You must return to the safety of Lahrs' care," he spoke gently. "You can trust the girl who shall take you."

Elsa trembled, her chin quivering. "I can feel him touching me. He was in the kitchens...he saw me there alone. Lahrs warned me not to go out alone."

"Audry shall take you, he shall not approach you with Audry by your side," He encouraged Elsa, touching her chin to raise her eyes to meet his. "Was it Leuthere that attacked you, Elsa? Was he in the corridor?"

Tears slipped hard from her eyes and she hate how powerless she felt.

"Elsa, you must tell me if he has harmed you. You must tell me if he has raped you."

Vigorously, she shook her head.

Eero drew her in against his chest, wrapping his strong arms around her to draw her into his warmth. She grasped tightly to him, letting the bitter emotions out, weeping into his chest until the maid would arrive.

CHAPTER

25

Brendolyn stepped into the garden, a place where the scent of honeysuckles and the rustling leaves whispered of freedom, a stark contrast to the oppressive walls of seclusion in Alnwick. Here, beneath the open sky, where the world felt vast and unbound, she could breathe again. The servants moved silently around her, their presence comforting in its simplicity—they neither stared nor whispered, unlike those within the castle walls.

"Lahrs is bound to lecture us if we return late," Elsa murmured beside her, a hint of mischief in her voice as they walked along the garden's shaded path.

Brendolyn sighed, linking her arm with Elsa's as the cool shade wrapped around them like a gentle embrace. "He'll have to find it in his heart to forgive us. If I remain in that castle another moment, I fear I shall go mad."

The path ahead wound through tall hedges and past ancient trees, their leaves whispering secrets of olden days, of forgotten love and lost battles. The air was thick with the scent of earth and flowers, a heady mix that filled her senses and drowned out the memories of her confinement.

"Perhaps we could talk about what happened between you and the prince," Elsa suggested, her voice tentative, as if treading on delicate ground.

Brendolyn's expression darkened, her steps faltering. "There's nothing more to say. It's over."

Elsa stopped, pulling away from Brendolyn, her eyes searching her friend's face for any sign of the pain she knew lay beneath the surface. "You speak with such calmness about your separation."

Brendolyn turned to face her, the breeze ruffling her hair as she forced a smile. "Knowing that he still loves me is enough, even if we can never be together."

"That isn't love, Bren," Elsa said softly, her voice laced with concern.

Brendolyn's gaze fell to the ground, her calm façade cracking as she spoke. "He cannot break the treaty, Elsa. His duty to the realms demands sacrifice." Her voice trembled, the words leaving her lips like shards of glass. Deep within her, a gnawing agony stirred, clawing at her insides, threatening to break free and consume her. The garden, once a sanctuary, now seemed to close in around her, the weight of her emotions pressing down on her chest.

Elsa stepped closer, her eyes softening as she reached out to touch Brendolyn's arm. "And what of your sacrifice? What of the cost to your heart?"

Brendolyn looked up, her eyes glistening with unshed tears. "That is the price of love in this world, Elsa. We are all bound by duty, no matter the pain it causes."

The garden, with its silent beauty and hidden corners, seemed to echo her words, the truth of them hanging heavy in the air. In this world of treaties and alliances, of duty and sacrifice, love was a luxury few could afford, and those who did often paid the highest price.

"He is asking you to sacrifice your own happiness to appease his vanity. To know he holds your devotion shall keep him satisfied, but what happens when he stops loving you Bren...your heart shall not endure the heartbreak."

"It is enough for me to have his heart."

She quickened her steps as they moved further along the garden path, taking the sloped turn on the graveled path, leading towards the castle. Not looking where she was going, Brendolyn was too late to hear the warning of Elsa behind her and colliding with a tall figure. Brendolyn fell back onto her backside on the graveled walk.

Looking up as the man in dark clothes turned.

"Daydreaming can be a dangerous activity while walking." He smiled, outstretching a hand and he helped her stand, not waiting for her approval.

A warmth overcame Brendolyn, she smiled up at him, with the stranger's hand in her own, but he was hardly a stranger.

"We should really stop meeting like this," Brendolyn admitted.

She felt the hard calluses, the roughness in those gentle hands but he pulled away suddenly, his hands retreating to the safety behind his back as he looked her over, giving a faint smile that sparked something within Brendolyn.

"You are mistaken, I do not believe we have ever met."

She scoffed. "You deny it, sir, when I have met you in Denorn."

"I have never been to Denorn, I am from Eir," he said, raising his eyebrow, those green eyes watching her closely.

"For shame!" Brendolyn exclaimed, looking at Elsa who stood nearby her. "Elsa can second in my favor that we saw you in the cathedral in Denorn. You were speaking to Lady Arienne, with a bouquet of lavender in hand."

"She could not have seen me, I believe she was hiding behind the tree."

Brendolyn chuckled, triumphantly. "There. You admit to having seen us."

"See who?" The stranger's eyes darkened, his mouth slanting in a faint smile.

"*Us*, sir, in Denorn." Her playfulness delighted in his banter, sparking mischief that was undeniably faie.

"I come from Eir."

"Bren, you must be careful," Elsa whispered, grasping at her elbow.

Realizing their formality, Brendolyn remembered her etiquette. This was not Lahrs, and she could not speak so openly as she was used to with the elf. But speaking to this stranger was as easy as breathing. Gazing up into his magnificent green eyes, Brendolyn smiled again.

"Forgive me, sir, I believe I must have been mistaken. We have been lingering too long and shall let you do your duties." She pressed forward, taking Elsa by the hand to hurry along the path.

He turned aside, allowing them to pass. It wasn't but a few steps that she realized that the man was walking behind them.

"Following us now?" She looked at him over her shoulder.

"I was also walking in this direction, unless knocking into me has made you lose your memories." His words were sharp, sending a thrill through her, those uncanny eyes held something, a secret.

Brendolyn knew she was to find Lahrs to escort them through the gardens. She did not know this man, they had never been formally introduced and Brendolyn blushed, catching the stranger's eye watching her thoughtfully but he remained at a distance.

"Then I believe we shall walk together, in silence of course."

She continued to walk with Elsa by her side. They walked arm in arm as they made for the intended grove of trees. Brendolyn felt the presence of the man who kept a very safe distance with them. Feeling the breeze shift against the green of the trees, Brendolyn was saddened to miss their bloom. Her memories reawakened with the memories of the last visit to this grove. She sighed heavily. At last she stopped, turning about to see the man was not far off, he observed the trees, but as Brendolyn watched his gaze soon shifted back. Glancing her way, sending a shiver through her. Leaving Elsa's side, Brendolyn stomped after the stranger.

"What is your name?" she demanded.

He smiled but said nothing. He walked in the opposite way, hiding himself behind the nearest tree. She followed, embracing the large trunk, gazing up at the dark-haired man.

"Come now, they must call you something." Brendolyn followed, her curiosity growing for the man.

He stood beside the tree, he was nearly as tall, if not taller, than King Beaumont, reaching up to touch the lowest branches. Brendolyn watched with amazement as he plucked a lonely bloom, late in arrival from the leaves.

His eyes cast a glance at Brendolyn. "You demand we remain silent and yet you require I answer your silly questions, princess."

She smiled. "So you do know me."

"It would be impossible not to recognize you, princess." He smirked, outreaching his hand to offer the bloom to her. "They call me Pavan. Does this please you?"

Brendolyn took the bloom, it felt so light in her hands.

"*Pavan*, like the dance?"

This made him smile again, he nodded. "Like the dance."

Brendolyn outstretched her hand.

But he did not take it, he only bowed. "It was lovely to make your acquaintance, princess. Now, if you will excuse me, I really should return."

With that he turned, walking away from her. Brendolyn blinked, her mouth falling open. He knew her after all. She ran to catch up with him, he had a long stride.

"Wait a minute. I am not done with you yet." She followed closely at his heels.

Pavan didn't slow his steps, but side glanced in her direction.

"Such a princess, always demanding to be looked at. Perhaps it would work on the courtiers, but I am below your station, princess. It is not proper for me to speak with you."

"Please, don't call me that. I am a princess, but please, call me Bren. And I am allowed to speak to whomever I want."

"I cannot, princess. I am forbidden." He turned, ready to leave but Brendolyn grasped his arm. Opening her mouth to speak, but across the yard, coming straight at her was Sir Varick.

"Brendolyn! Brendolyn, your father is requesting for you." He arrived in a huff, his breathing ragged as he looked Pavan over, clearly put off by the presence.

Brendolyn sidestepped, moving closer to Pavan without realizing, as the knight approached. Her expression became cold.

"I shall go up to him, Varick, thank you." But the knight did not leave.

Varick was looking Pavan up and down. Brendolyn could see the knight's look of puzzlement, before looking then to Brendolyn.

"I shall walk you."

But Brendolyn didn't move and Varick clenched his jaw.

"Your father insisted." He tried to reach for Brendolyn, but a hand grasped the man's wrist.

Varick looked up to Pavan, shock filled him.

"It is not polite to handle a woman in such a way, sir. She will go to him as she said…you cannot force her." Pavan's voice was deep, guttural, making Varick's face color.

Pulling his hand away, Varick looked at his wrist, grasping it, as if the touch of the other man burned him. Varick was clenching his jaw as he stormed away.

After a moment, Brendolyn relaxed, finally looking up to meet Pavan's gaze.

"He has a habit of making me uncomfortable," she whispered, looking after the direction the knight had stormed away.

Pavan didn't move, his eyes remained locked on her.

"Would you like me to walk you the remainder of the path?" Pavan's voice made her shiver, the cool calm tone the exact opposite of the deep tone given to the knight. "I do not see your companion."

"Yes." She nodded, looking around the gardens. Her excitement had gotten the better of her, losing sight of Elsa. "Where has she gone?"

"She shall be along the path shortly, princess. Perhaps it is best to wait near the castle, where you shall be seen by the servants."

Nervously Brendolyn nodded, her heart hammering in her chest by the interruption of Varick. Together they walked the path, in complete silence. As they neared the castle, the stairs in view, Pavan stopped.

"Thank you." She curtsied slightly, before hurrying up the steps, leading to the doors leading into the castle. Looking back as she neared the doorway, seeing him watching her.

She waved, smiling to herself when he returned the gesture.

Elsa walked along the garden path, keeping a careful eye on Brendolyn and the mysterious man, Pavan, in the distance. She watched them circle the trees, smiling in a way she had never seen the princess look before. But it was improper, and she did not want to leave them alone, Elsa stepped forward to follow them, but a shadow crossed in front of her. Instinctively, Elsa clutched to her bodice.

She stiffened looking up at Leuthere, though she wasn't certain why. He was one of the king's knights and there was no reason to fear him. Though something in her bones told her she should. Something to do with the kitchens. She shook the dark thought away.

"Elsa Laronn." His lips curled into a smile that reminded Elsa too much of a cat cornering a mouse. He had a long cut and the muddled remnants of a bruise on the side of his face. "All alone while your princess flirts? Where is that loyal dog that follows you around?"

"I rather like being alone, Sir Leuthere." She lifted her book from the basket on the bench beside her, pretending she had always planned on reading it.

He plucked the book from her hands. "I rather like being alone with you as well." Leuthere leaned close to her and the near touch crackled over her skin like a flash of lightning.

Elsa jumped to her feet, stumbling away from the man she was not sure why she was afraid.

"Relax, little mouse. I have no intention of defiling you here in the gardens." He rose, half cornering her with his large body. "Though, I certainly wouldn't mind finishing what we started in the kitchens last night. Perhaps tonight. I'll touch you in all the ways Eero won't. All the ways you secretly desire."

Elsa shoved his hand away. She had never spoken to this man before. "I'm sorry, you must have confused me with someone else. Now, if you'll excuse me, I really must catch up with Princess Brendolyn." She held out a hand for her book.

Leuthere studied her for a long moment, gripping on her book tightening. "Let us dispense with the games, Lady Elsa." He spoke her title like it dripped with sarcasm. "We both know you are not so pure and chaste as that shocked look would have me believe. That mark on your ribs proves it."

Elsa's hand instinctively flew to her ribs, knowing the brand was covered by miles of silk. Flinching when Leuther smiled. "How—I don't know what you're talking about."

"But you do. Just like you know that all I have to do is tell King Sabian about that little mark and suddenly your comfortable little life as the princess's companion, not to mention the attention of Sir Eero, would simply evaporate."

"You wouldn't."

"I might."

"Then why haven't you?" And how did he know in the first place? Her mind reached for any interaction she had with this man, certain there was something, but it was as if the space was empty.

Leuthere curled his arm around Elsa's waist, starting to guide her down the path, walking slowly. "I'm weighing my options. King Sabian might offer me a small reward for informing him that his daughter's companion is a whore but I'm guessing you, and perhaps the princess herself, will offer a great deal more to keep it secret."

She lowered her gaze. "What do you want?"

"First I want to know where you got that mark and who gave it to you."

Elsa stiffened trying to pull away but the man's grip tightened. "Why?"

"I have my reasons. Perhaps I wish to purchase you from him."

"Alaric will never release me from the bond." Too late she realized what she had said and Elsa silently cursed.

Leuthere smiled. "And why is that?"

Her shoulders inched lower. She may as well tell him or else he would tell the king, though she hated the idea of him knowing her secrets. "Because he wants to claim me as his wife." She shoved her way out of the knight's grip. "Now tell me what it is you want from me."

That wicked grin curved his mouth again, giving the knight a sinister look. "Right to the point. An admirable quality in a lady." He brushed his fingers over her cheek and neck, eyes watching her in a predatory fashion. "Originally I had considered requesting something rather carnal. To take something Sir Eero desires."

Elsa's eyes blazed with defiance as she shoved the knight's hand away. "Eero doesn't desire me," she growled, her voice a mix of anger and fear.

Leuthere's lips curled into a cruel smile, his eyes cold and calculating. "No? Are you so certain? It hardly matters. He'll cast you aside when he learns of your...indiscretions. And what I want is far more valuable. I want your favor." His chuckle was low and menacing, echoing through the moonlit garden. "One day, I will come to you with a request, and you must not refuse me."

Elsa's heart raced as she glared at him. "What sort of request?"

"That is for me to decide," Leuthere said smoothly, his gaze flicking toward the path where the King walked alongside Lahrs, the nobleman's rich cloak billowing behind him. "Do we have an arrangement, little lady? Or shall I inform his majesty that there is a whore within his household?"

Elsa's throat tightened, her mouth dry. The weight of the decision pressing down on her. "One favor?"

"One favor," Leuthere confirmed, his tone final.

With a shuddering breath, Elsa nodded. "Fine."

Leuthere's smile broadened, a glint of satisfaction in his eyes. "An excellent choice, my lady." With a dismissive nod, he turned on his heel and strode down the garden path toward the palace, his footsteps fading into the distance.

As he disappeared from view, Elsa felt a wave of dizziness wash over her. Her legs trembled as she turned to face the king and his companion. She locked eyes with Lahrs, feeling a surge of desperation.

Summoning all her remaining strength, Elsa dipped into a deep curtsy, her eyes fixed on Lahrs with an earnest plea. "Forgive me, Your Majesty," she said, her voice quavering but resolute. "Might I have a word with Sir Lahrs?"

The king and Lahrs halted, their attention shifting to her. Lahrs's eyes narrowed, a flicker of curiosity and caution crossing his face. The king's expression remained inscrutable, but there was a subtle shift in his demeanor, an indication of his awareness of the gravity of the moment.

Lahrs's brow furrowed as he assessed Elsa's distressed state. "Very well. What is it you wish to discuss?" His voice remained steady, but his eyes betrayed a flicker of concern.

Elsa's mind was a storm of frantic thoughts, her pulse quickening with the weight of her predicament. As she rose from her curtsy, her gaze locked onto Lahrs with a mix of desperation and resolve. The garden, bathed in light, felt like a cruel contrast to the turmoil churning inside her. The rustling leaves seemed to whisper mocking secrets as she struggled to find her voice.

"I have a—" Elsa started, but her throat felt constricted, the words catching as if ensnared by an unseen force. Her determination to confide in Lahrs was thwarted by a mysterious barrier, a sensation of magick pressing against her lips. She could see Leuthere's taunting smile in her mind, his dark power lingering like a shadow over her.

Lahrs's eyes sharpened with concern. "Are you ill, Elsa?" His features, though pleasant, were now marred by a genuine worry. His voice softened as he reached out with his own subtle magick, a gentle pulse of energy that brushed against Elsa's skin, probing for signs of enchantment or affliction.

"No," Elsa managed to croak out, shaking her head vigorously. She watched the king and his entourage take the long path back toward the castle, their figures growing smaller in the distance. Her heart raced, her fear nearly overwhelming her. "I saw Varick in the gardens...Bren was walking with the man from Eir."

Lahrs's expression shifted, a pallor crossing his face before he regained his composure. His demeanor remained stoic, but Elsa could feel the anger radiating from him, a powerful force that momentarily disrupted the calm façade he maintained. The mention of Varick and the Eirian stirred something deep within him, an undercurrent of rage that he struggled to contain.

Lahrs's voice dropped to a low, urgent tone. "What did you see? Tell me everything."

Elsa took a shuddering breath, trying to force the words out despite the lingering pressure of magical interference. "Leuthere...he forced me into a bargain. He wants a favor, but I-I need to warn you about him. He's dangerous. He—" She faltered, the words trapped by the same unseen force that had plagued her.

Lahrs's eyes narrowed as he sensed the frustration and fear in Elsa's voice. His own magick flared subtly, a countermeasure against whatever enchantment was stifling her words. "Focus, Elsa. Concentrate. I need to understand what happened."

Elsa's vision swam as she fought against the magical barrier, her resolve hardening. She glanced back toward the direction of the palace, her thoughts a whirlwind of urgency. "Leuthere touched me. He-he wants something from me, but I can't remember what...and that night, in the corridor there was a man with orange eyes. He made me forget."

Lahrs's face grew grim as he processed her fragmented message. The undercurrent of anger and worry was palpable in the air, mingling with the faint echo of magick that rippled through the garden. His hand gripped Elsa's shoulder firmly, offering both support and a silent promise of protection.

"Thank you for coming to me," Lahrs said, his voice now steely with determination. "I will address this matter with utmost urgency. Do not worry—your warning will not go unheeded."

Elsa nodded, relief mingling with lingering fear. As Lahrs turned and began to stride toward the castle, she watched him go, her heart still pounding with the weight of the revelations. The garden, once a serene refuge, now felt like a battleground of secrets and danger.

Simeon Bannon traversed the labyrinthine corridors of the castle with the assured stride of a man who knew his presence commanded both fear and respect. The ladies of court, as if sensing his approach, hurriedly averted their gazes and scurried away, their rustling skirts a soft, hurried whisper against the cold stone. The lords, meanwhile, regarded him with a mix of caution and disdain, their eyes darting away as if to avoid catching the malevolent gleam of a predator.

Simeon revealed this atmosphere of dread. The mere knowledge that his letters of summons had sent shivers through the court was a power he savored. Each encounter, each fleeting glance of fear, was a draught of exhilaration. The scent of apprehension, so palpable in these hallowed halls, was a fuel that invigorated him.

Yet, there was one figure that eluded his comprehension, a new arrival from Eir who had become a persistent enigma. Simeon's meticulous scrutiny of the Eir newcomers had revealed them all as mere shadows of magic, lacking in the potency he usually feared or manipulated. But this one, this dark-clad man with eyes like polished emeralds, was different. He was a puzzle that gnawed at Simeon's patience.

As he meandered through the lower corridors, nearing the kitchens, Simeon spotted the man again. Clad in obsidian garments that seemed to swallow the flickering torchlight, the stranger's expression was as impenetrable as his dark attire. Their eyes met—his were unyielding, a stark contrast to the subservient or deceitful gazes Simeon was accustomed to. It was as if this man had no faults to exploit, no cracks to worm through.

"Lord Bannon," the man's voice cut through Simeon's contemplation with unsettling calm. The green eyes locked onto him, unflinching and devoid of fear.

"Are all your preparations ready for tonight's banquet?" Simeon inquired, his mind already probing for vulnerabilities.

"Everything is prepared, Lord Bannon. Though I am not performing tonight, there will be no disappointment." His tone was polite, his demeanor coolly assured.

"Good. Very good," Simeon replied, his gaze narrowing with interest. He moved closer, feeling the air hum with a subtle, almost imperceptible energy. If this man possessed any magick, it was contained with such mastery that it was invisible to Simeon's senses. This level of control intrigued and unsettled him.

Before Simeon could respond further, the man from Eir bowed slightly and departed, leaving Simeon alone in the dim corridor. Moments later, Leuthere, his most trusted knight, appeared, his expression a mask of barely contained excitement.

"I have news of the one you seek," Leuthere announced, his voice a low, eager rumble.

Simeon's eyes gleamed with interest. "Speak. What have you uncovered?"

Leuthere's smile was thin but triumphant. "I have located the woman bonded to Alaric. She has agreed to grant one favor."

Simeon scrutinized his knight, noting the barely suppressed agitation that rippled beneath Leuthere's surface. It was clear the task had stirred something deep within him, a mix of desire and frustration.

"You've managed not to tarnish her reputation or your own in the process," Simeon commended. "You've done well."

Leuthere's lip curled in a sneer. "She carries the taint of her bond. I would find satisfaction in tearing it from her."

Simeon's hand rested briefly on Leuthere's bronze-clad shoulder, a gesture of both camaraderie and authority. "Your reward will come in due time. Our greater purpose will not be hindered by such trifles." He traced a finger gently along the curve of Leuthere's cheek. "Find the fallen knight in the brothel. Let him revel in the news of his wife's impending return. Tell him we will deliver her soon."

"Yes, my lord." Leuthere bowed and departed, his figure fading into the shadows as he set off on his new mission.

As Simeon watched him leave, he turned his thoughts back to the illusive man from Eir, feeling a dark thrill at the mysteries yet to unfold.

CHAPTER
26

As Pavan made his way through the winding corridors of the castle, he nearly collided with Lord Bannon. The older man's brow was furrowed, his mind clearly occupied with something heavy. Pavan kept his silence, his eyes studying Simeon's distracted demeanor. He could feel the tension radiating off the lord, a subtle disturbance in the air that hinted at troubles unspoken. Without a word, Pavan slipped away, his footsteps echoing through the stone halls as he ventured deeper into the heart of the castle.

The passageways twisted and turned, a labyrinth of stone and shadow, where each corner seemed to lead to another identical hallway. Just as he felt the familiar tug of uncertainty about his direction, Pavan saw a figure approaching from the opposite end. It was King Beaumont. The king's steps slowed as he recognized Pavan, surprise flickering across his features.

"I'm sorry," Pavan began, feeling a touch of embarrassment as he moved to turn away. "I seem to have lost my way."

Beaumont's surprise melted into a warm smile as he approached. "You're not the first, nor will you be the last. I doubt a week goes by that I don't find myself turned around in this place."

Their steps naturally fell into rhythm as they walked side by side through the ancient halls. Pavan laughed softly, but the sound faded as a more serious thought took hold of him. "You mentioned before that you knew something about my father."

At this, Beaumont halted abruptly. His gaze fixed on Pavan, his expression shifting to one of gravity. "There is much I wish to tell you, Pavan. And one day, I believe you will come to understand the full truth. But for now, know this: within these walls, you are safe." His hand tightened on Pavan's arm, a gesture of reassurance, but also of urgency.

Pavan nodded slowly, feeling the weight of the king's words. "I believe there's a reason I came here, to the castle... Not just to find answers about my father, but perhaps to protect you. The magick he wields—it isn't truly his own."

Beaumont's brow furrowed in confusion. "What do you mean? He is like you, Pavan. His magick is the same as yours."

Pavan shook his head, his voice dropping to a whisper. "No, it's not. When I saw him, I could feel his magick, just as I can sense it in everyone here. But with him, it's different. I can shield myself from being seen, from being touched by others' magick. But his...it doesn't flow as it should. His magick waxes and wanes, like the phases of the moon. It's strongest when full, but then it fades, as if it must be replenished."

Beaumont's face darkened as he pondered Pavan's words. "I don't understand," he admitted.

"There are darker ways to acquire magick," Pavan explained, his voice barely above a whisper. "Ways that are unstable, chaotic. Drawing power from another's soul, stealing their magick to make it your own...If he is siphoning magick, there may be little left of the person he once was."

Beaumont's eyes widened as the implications settled over him. "You think he's learned this dark magick?"

Pavan's expression was grim as he replied, "It's not a common practice—far from it. This kind of magick is forbidden, written only in the oldest tomes that were supposed to have been destroyed by Venora long ago. But someone must have taught him."

Beaumont's gaze grew sharper. "Could they be here, within this kingdom?"

"The magick is too powerful to be contained by ordinary means," Pavan said, his voice laced with concern. "The kind of power we're talking about...those who wield it have been extinct for centuries."

"You believe there is another Ehlfern—another like you?"

Pavan nodded, the truth heavy on his tongue. "It's the only explanation. He's dangerous, but to what end? What purpose does he serve, and what dark design does he follow?"

Beaumont's face reflected a dawning realization, a connection forming that gave Pavan a spark of hope. The king opened his mouth to speak, but before he could utter a word, a piercing scream cut through the silence, shattering their moment of revelation.

The scream tore through Pavan, seizing his heart with a force that stole his breath. It was a cry of such raw, soul-wrenching agony that it resonated deep within him, as if the very fabric of his being was unraveling. Beaumont heard it too, but where Pavan felt the pull of the scream in his very soul, the king's reaction was one of alarm.

Their eyes met, and in Beaumont's, Pavan saw panic—a fear that mirrored his own.

"Brendolyn," Beaumont whispered, his voice trembling with dread.

Pavan's blood ran cold. The name alone carried a weight of unspeakable terror, and without a word, they both turned and raced down the corridors, the sound of the scream echoing in their minds, guiding them to where the danger lay.

"Father?" Brendolyn's voice was a soft murmur as she stepped into the private chambers of her father, the southern king, Sabian. The room was bathed in the warm glow of the setting sun, and the air was thick with the scent of roses, their fragrance lingering like a bittersweet memory. Yet the room was empty, eerily still.

She hesitated, her eyes scanning the familiar surroundings, the ornate tapestries, and the flickering shadows cast by the candelabras. "Father, are you here?" she called again, her voice wavering as she moved toward the smaller bedchamber beyond. The silence pressed against her, heavy and foreboding, until she saw him.

Sabian sat slumped in a grand chair, his hand loosely holding a glass. His face, once full of warmth and vitality, was now ghostly pale, his eyes sunken and dark as if shadowed by some unseen force. Brendolyn's heart tightened with fear as she rushed to his side, falling to her knees before him.

"Father, what is the matter?" she whispered, her voice trembling as she took his hand. It was icy cold, a sharp contrast to the warmth that filled the room. Something deep and primal stirred within her, a gnawing dread that something was terribly, irreversibly wrong.

Sabian stirred at the sound of her voice, a faint smile tugging at the corners of his mouth as his gaze found hers. "There you are, *mi amore*," he muttered, his voice a shadow of its former strength, as his hand gently touched her cheek.

Brendolyn held his hand tighter, pressing it to her face, desperate to bring warmth back to his clammy skin. "Are you alright?" she asked, her voice barely above a whisper, laced with growing panic.

His eyelids fluttered, his expression slackening as his mouth began to droop, drool slipping from the corners of his lips. In a terrifyingly brief moment, his body went limp, sliding out of the chair before she could catch him. Brendolyn screamed, her faie voice reverberating with a haunting resonance that echoed through the chamber.

"Father!" she cried out, her hands trembling as she grasped his cravat, frantically loosening it as his body convulsed beneath her. Tears streamed down her face, hot and relentless, as she watched her father struggle for breath, choking on something unseen, something she couldn't fight.

Suddenly, the doors to the chamber burst open, and two figures rushed in. Beaumont, the northern king, was the first to reach them, his eyes wide with alarm. Pavan was close behind, his expression calm but intense, as he took in the scene before him.

"What happened?" Pavan's voice was steady, almost unnervingly so.

"I came to him as he called," Brendolyn sobbed, her voice thick with fear. "He was pale and wasn't himself. He collapsed, and—I believe it's poison." Her shaking hand pointed to the fallen cup, the spilled liquid spreading across the floor like a dark stain.

Beaumont's face contorted with grief and rage, his thick brows knitting together as he reached for Sabian, his large hands grasping the southern king's tunic. He tilted Sabian's head back, leaning down as if to offer aid, but Pavan's hand shot out, stopping him.

"Wait," Pavan commanded, his hand hovering above Sabian's mouth. "If it's poison, there could be traces on his lips. It could kill you, too."

"Save him," Beaumont pleaded, his voice breaking with desperation. "Pavan, please, save him."

Brendolyn looked between them, her vision blurred by tears, but she caught the silent exchange between the two men. She felt Beaumont's hands gently pull her back, his grip firm but reassuring. Pavan stepped closer to her father, his expression darkening as he placed a hand over Sabian's chest.

"Pavan…" Brendolyn whispered, but her words were lost as the air around them seemed to shift, the very air trembling as Pavan began to murmur ancient words of magick. The language was powerful, resonating with the very bones of the castle.

She gasped as Pavan's eyes fluttered closed, his skin beginning to glow with faint, intricate patterns, lines of energy that pulsed and twisted like living runes. The designs were unlike anything she had ever seen, ancient and otherworldly. A long moment stretched out as Pavan pressed his hand against her father's chest, channeling his magick into Sabian's failing body.

The transformation was almost immediate. Color returned to Sabian's ashen skin, his convulsions slowed, then stopped entirely. Pavan's breathing grew labored as the ritual took its toll on him, but he didn't falter. With a final, shuddering breath, he pulled away, gasping as Sabian's chest rose with a deep, steady inhalation.

"Father," Brendolyn whispered, rushing to her father's side as his eyes fluttered open, the dark circles beneath them fading. She took his hand in hers, feeling the warmth return to his skin.

Sabian's gaze was clearer now, though weakened, and he managed a faint smile. "*Mi amore*," he murmured, his voice barely audible but full of relief.

Brendolyn clung to him, tears of gratitude spilling down her cheeks as she looked up at Pavan. He stood nearby, his face pale, drained from the effort, but his eyes were filled with quiet determination.

Beaumont released Brendolyn's hands, his own shaking with a mix of fear and relief. "Thank you, Pavan," he said, his voice thick with emotion. "You've done more than I could ever ask."

But Pavan's gaze remained on Sabian, a flicker of concern still lingering in his eyes. "This was no ordinary poison," he said quietly. "We must find out who did this. And why."

Brendolyn nodded, her heart still racing, but for now, all she could do was hold her father's hand and pray that the worst was over.

Beaumont stood in the dim chamber, his gaze locked on Pavan, who staggered back, gripping the edge of the bed for support. The air was thick with magick, an oppressive force that seemed to weigh down the room, making it hard to breathe. The lines and markings on Pavan's skin began to fade, the remnants of the powerful spell he had just cast. As Beaumont approached, he noticed something that made his heart skip a beat—Pavan's eyes were entirely white, void of pupils, and glowing with an eerie light.

"Pavan?" Beaumont's voice was cautious, filled with concern as he advanced slowly.

"Don't touch me..." Pavan hissed, his voice a deep, gravelly sound that didn't seem entirely his own. He was shaking, his breath coming in labored gasps as he tried to regain control. Beaumont knelt nearby, careful not to make contact, his eyes flicking to Sabian, who lay on the floor, his color slowly returning.

"You took all the poison from him," Beaumont whispered, the realization hitting him hard. He could see the pain etched into Pavan's features, his body trembling with the effort it took to contain the deadly toxin.

"There was no other way to save him," Pavan groaned, collapsing back against the bed, his body wracked with spasms. Behind him, Brendolyn stood frozen, her eyes wide with fear and confusion. Sabian, though still weak, was breathing steadily—a small comfort in the chaos.

Beaumont quickly raised a hand to stop Brendolyn from rushing forward. "What is wrong with him?" she asked, her voice shaking with worry.

Pavan's muscles tensed and strained, his skin beading with sweat as he groaned in agony. Beaumont winced as he watched Pavan's body convulse violently against the bed.

"He's taken the poison into himself...it's in his body now," Beaumont explained, his voice tight with fear. He wiped a tear from Brendolyn's cheek, his heart heavy with the weight of the situation.

"Is there nothing we can do?" she asked, her eyes locked on Pavan, who was clearly in unbearable pain. A guttural groan tore from Pavan's chest, reverberating through the room.

"Get Lahrs," Beaumont whispered urgently. Brendolyn nodded and quickly left the room, her footsteps echoing in the corridor. Beaumont turned back to Pavan, who was now convulsing, drool spilling from his clenched teeth. The magick in the room intensified, a cold, sharp force that seemed to push Beaumont back. He stumbled, struggling to stay upright.

He hurried to Sabian, pulling him into his arms and carrying him across the hall to an adjoining room. After placing the southern king on the bed, he stumbled into the corridor and grabbed the arm of a passing servant. "Call for Rhys and bring hot water to this chamber," Beaumont ordered, his voice firm despite the turmoil inside him. "No one is allowed to enter the other room. Do you understand?"

The servant bowed deeply and rushed off.

Lahrs entered the room, Brendolyn close behind him. Servants hurried past, bringing water to the adjacent chamber, where Rhys, the stable hand, was shouting for more. Lahrs recognized the elf from previous meetings but focused on the task at hand as he stepped into the guarded room.

Beaumont stood at the foot of the bed, his head bowed, but he looked up as Lahrs approached. "He took the poison from Sabian," Beaumont said, his voice heavy with the implications.

Pavan lay on the bed, writhing in pain, his body contorting as if trying to expel the poison by sheer force of will.

Lahrs moved toward Pavan but stopped short, encountering an invisible barrier that surrounded the bed. "Let down the barrier, Pavan," Lahrs instructed, pressing his hand against the air, which resisted his touch. The magick was strong, thick in the room, and Pavan had clearly erected the barrier to contain whatever ailed him.

Pavan's eyes fluttered open, his brow slick with sweat. He saw Lahrs standing there, and with a strained shake of his head, he refused to let the barrier drop. His skin was marred with dark, inky shadows, the poison coursing through his veins like a living curse.

"The poison will kill you, Pavan. Let me in," Lahrs urged, his voice firm but compassionate.

Pavan's eyes flicked toward Beaumont and Brendolyn, who stood together, Beaumont's arm around the princess. Reluctantly, Pavan allowed the barrier to fall, and Lahrs stepped forward.

"Go to Elsa," Lahrs said to Brendolyn gently. "I'll call you when it's over."

"I can't...I can't leave him," she replied, her voice trembling as she watched Pavan struggle. His cries of agony tore at her heart.

Lahrs sighed, recognizing that she would not leave. "Very well. Bring me the water basin," he instructed, rolling up his sleeves as Brendolyn hurried to comply.

Pavan groaned, his hand trembling as he indicated a spot on his chest. Lahrs understood and moved swiftly, prying open Pavan's jacket, the buttons scattering across the room. With a firm tug, he tore open the shirt, revealing Pavan's chest. The sight made Brendolyn gasp.

Deep purple scars crisscrossed Pavan's otherwise smooth flesh, old wounds that told of battles long past. But Lahrs focused on the dark pool of shadow beneath Pavan's sternum, where the poison had gathered, slithering and inky like a living entity.

"He's out of danger, Your Majesty," Lahrs said, his tone assured as he pointed to the dark pooling beneath Pavan's skin.

"You can know that for certain?" Beaumont asked, his voice tinged with doubt.

"He's a fool," Lahrs muttered, casting a harsh look at Pavan. "But he has some skill with magick. He's trapped the poison here." He pointed again, this time causing the inky shadow to recoil, sending a wave of pain through Pavan's body.

Beaumont grimaced at the sight of Pavan's scars. "Those scars...?"

"Old wounds, Your Majesty," Lahrs replied. "Now, I need a blade." He extended his hand to Beaumont, who stared in disbelief.

"Excuse me?"

Lahrs remained serious. "A dagger, Beaumont. I need to bleed him to drain the poison, so I can extract it. It's quite safe."

Brendolyn shifted, producing a small blade concealed in the slits of her gown.

"You carry a blade?" Beaumont asked, astonished.

"Lahrs has taught me many things, Your Majesty. Including how to wield a dagger," Brendolyn said with a smirk, eyeing the northern king, who stood dumbfounded.

"Bren, place this in his mouth," Lahrs said, cutting a thick cord from the bedclothes and handing it to Brendolyn.

Lahrs placed the tip of the dagger against Pavan's sternum, holding it there as Brendolyn moved to the head of the bed. Pavan flinched, trying to pull away, but Lahrs placed a firm hand on his chest. "Let her," he soothed, and Pavan stilled, watching as Brendolyn gently placed the cord between his teeth.

"Brace yourself, Pavan," Lahrs warned, his hand steady as he readied the dagger.

Pavan gripped the bedsheets, his knuckles white as he bit down on the cord. The dagger pierced his skin, and Pavan choked on his scream, his body tensing as thick, gelatinous, ink-colored blood oozed from the wound. Lahrs quickly extracted the dagger, his hand hovering above the dark liquid as it flowed out.

Muttering incantations, Lahrs manipulated the slithering poison, drawing it from Pavan's body and suspending it in the air. The dark substance writhed, resisting, but Lahrs's will was stronger. He guided it into the basin of water, where it hissed and dissolved.

Pavan's body relaxed, his head heavy against the pillow as his eyelids fluttered shut. He breathed heavily, the worst of the ordeal seemingly over.

"Is that it?" Beaumont asked, his voice filled with tentative hope.

"He'll need to rest to recover his strength, but I believe that's all," Lahrs replied, his tone reassuring as he glanced at Brendolyn, who was still watching Pavan with concern.

Brendolyn nodded, her eyes filled with tears as she turned to Lahrs. "I came when I was called, but when I entered the room, he wasn't himself. He looked so pale…and then he began to shake, his mouth foaming…that's when you came in. I'm sorry, I used my faie voice. I didn't know if anyone would hear me."

Lahrs took her hand, his expression gentle. "You did the right thing, Bren. You saved his life."

CHAPTER

27

Varick hissed at the pain from his wrist, seated before Lord Bannon as the man prodded at the raw flesh of the wound burned into his skin.

"You are certain it was the fire thrower?" Bannon asked, inspecting the burned skin closer. The red skin now raw and blistering, in a perfect shape of a hand.

Varick clenched around the pain. "There is no denying, he grabbed my arm and it felt as though my entire body was lit ablaze."

Bannon said nothing, but searched through tinctures upon his desk, coming upon a vile and removing the stopper, pouring it over the wound.

Varick cried out, trying to pull away but the man held his arm tight against the table, he was immovable. Looking down as the skin bubbled, turning a sickly yellow, the pus began to thicken and Bannon sniffed, then scraped the thickened yellow substance with a knife. Standing then he strode around the desk, depositing the substance into an empty jar. Bringing it to the light to see it, the oozing liquid began to solidify. Shifting from the putrid yellow into a darkened amber, before changing to a deep crimson red.

"What was that?" Varick hissed, coddling his arm now stinging anew.

"Just a simple extraction, this is the remnants of magick." Bannon smiled at the pus that sludge around within the jar. Returning to his desk, the jar was placed between them.

Varick looked through, the look of it churning his stomach.

"What kind of magick can do this?" he asked, watching the lord flit about his room, opening boxes and reading through different vials and papers, before returning with a small green bottle.

"A very strong, substantial magick." Bannon knelt before the glass jar, watching closely as he let a drop into the jar of pus, watching carefully as the substance began to rot, decaying before them and a rancid smell perfumed the air.

Varick covered his nose, but Bannon inhaled.

"Can you heal my arm?" Varick muffled through his arm.

Bannon glanced at the burn, sneering. "It will scar. There is nothing to be done. Bandage it and keep it clean."

Varick stood, letting his arm drop. His nose was scrunching at the horrible stench. "You have to heal my arm...how will I explain this to my lords?"

"You're a smart man, I am sure you will think of something."

Varick stood his ground. "You could heal it, but you won't."

Bannon's lips curved into a thin, sardonic smile as he regarded Varick's pained expression. "Why would I waste my precious magick on a fool who cannot even keep himself out of trouble?" he drawled. The candlelight in the room flickered, casting long shadows that danced menacingly across the walls, echoing Bannon's words. "Your incompetence could draw the attention of those who might shatter all of my carefully laid plans."

Varick's face twisted with frustration and pain. "He grabbed me for nothing!" he shouted, his voice echoing off the stone walls of the dimly lit study.

Bannon's eyes gleamed with a cold, calculating light. "The magick wielded by this fire thrower is no ordinary sorcery, Varick. It is not the kind of spellcraft one finds in dusty tomes or practiced by mere apprentices. It is ancient and primal, a power that courses through his very veins—a magick to be feared and respected. You should consider yourself fortunate that his wrath only manifested as a burn. For him to risk exposing himself..." Bannon's smile grew, sending an unsettling chill down Varick's spine. "You must have done something to provoke him."

Varick's throat tightened under the weight of Bannon's piercing gaze. He shifted uneasily, struggling to maintain composure. "I was just doing my job," he stammered, feeling the heat of the burn and the heat of Bannon's scrutiny.

Bannon's laughter was a low, dangerous rumble. "Ah, yes. He was seen with Brendolyn, wasn't he? The young woman who so often defies her father's commands. It is my duty to ensure she is brought to heel when summoned."

The mention of Brendolyn made Bannon pause, his eyes narrowing thoughtfully. A deep, contemplative silence fell over the room as he processed this new piece of information. His gaze lingered on Varick, a calculating expression in his eyes. "Perhaps there is more to this than I initially surmised," he murmured, his tone rich with intrigue.

At that moment, a sharp knock resonated through the chamber, slicing through the tense silence. The heavy oak door creaked open, and Leuthere entered, his presence imposing and commanding. His dark armor glinted faintly in the candlelight, adding to the aura of authority he carried.

"Leave us, Varick. Return to your duties," Bannon instructed, his voice brooking no argument.

Varick nodded, his face a mask of frustration and pain as he gathered himself and exited the room. The door closed behind him with a decisive thud, leaving Bannon and Leuthere alone in the dimly lit study.

Leuthere's gaze flicked briefly to the jar of decaying pus on Bannon's desk before meeting his lord's eyes. "What is our next move?" he asked, his voice low and steady. The dark corridors of the castle seemed to hum with an unspoken tension as he awaited Bannon's response.

Bannon's expression was thoughtful, his mind already racing.

"We cannot risk the knight, he shall be dealt with soon enough."

"And the Signe slut?" Leuthere hissed, his cold eyes gleaming.

Bannon touched the cold glinting metal on Leuthere's arm. "She shall be given to her lord husband in time, but first I must deal with this new magick. He is more powerful than I thought."

Leuthere hesitated. "A faie of Augusta?"

"Perhaps, Leuthere, but there is only one true way of knowing...but we must be cautious. While the king of the south is taken ill, it must not be expected of treason until the appropriate moment."

Leuthere bowed.

Pavan awoke with a start, the searing pain in his chest now reduced to a dull throb. He blinked, disoriented, his fingers grazing the soft silk that now cloaked his body. The room around him was vast, unfamiliar, bathed in warm light streaming through wide-open curtains. He was no longer in the cramped bedchamber of the King of Corad. This place felt different—less like a prison, more like a sanctuary.

The door creaked open, and Pavan's heart leaped as a dark-haired girl entered, carrying a tray. She was slender, her movements delicate but purposeful. A small smile lit her face when she saw him awake. It was strange to see a girl dressed in such finery walking across the room carrying a tray with such elegance.

"I caught the maid as she was bringing up your tea," she said softly, her voice a melody that matched the serene atmosphere of the room. "We didn't know when you would wake, so they kept bringing meals."

Pavan breathed in deeply, trying to find his voice, unsure if it would betray his weakness. The girl set the tray aside and took a seat in the small chair by his bedside, her golden eyes locking onto his with an intensity that made his pulse quicken.

"You saved my father," she said, reaching for his hand. Her touch was light, yet it sent a shiver through him. "Thank you."

The whisper of her gratitude carried a weight that was more than just words. Her magick, subtle and raw, danced along his skin where their hands met. Pavan pulled away, sitting up straighter despite the soreness that slowed him.

"You don't need to thank me," he said, his voice rougher than he intended.

She tilted her head slightly, a soft smile playing on her lips. "You seem to make a habit of rescuing me."

"And you," Pavan countered with a smirk, "seem to make a habit of getting into trouble."

She laughed lightly, a sound that warmed him more than the sunlight pouring into the room. "When you're well enough to walk, I'll take you to the gardens."

"You're optimistic," he replied, his tone teasing.

"Guilty," she admitted with a grin, rising to pour tea from a delicate porcelain teapot. She brought the cup to him, her hands steady, but Pavan's own hands trembled as he reached for it. He tried to refuse her help, but she insisted, guiding the cup to his lips. The hot liquid was bitter, and he grimaced.

"That's terrible," he said, frowning.

She chuckled, setting the cup aside. "It's made of ground peppercorn and willow bark. Lahrs brews it to heal inner wounds."

Pavan groaned. "Of course he does. That elf is always prepared."

Her eyes sparkled with curiosity. "You know Lahrs?"

Pavan shifted uncomfortably, the tea beginning to spread warmth through his aching limbs. "I've met him. I used to live in Entheas."

Her expression brightened. "Are you an elf?"

Pavan looked away, his gaze falling to his hands. "I am not."

"Not faie, nor human…" Her voice was soft but insistent. "What are you?"

"You ask so many questions," Pavan said, meeting her gaze again, his chest tightening. Her curiosity was disarming, her young magick a beacon that drew him in despite his better judgment.

"I only ask what I don't understand," she said unapologetically. "I know I have magick, but I've never met another faie. You…you have so much magick around you, but I can't tell where it comes from."

Her words sent a chill through him. The way she spoke, with such wonder and innocence, stirred something deep inside. He shook his head. "It's unimportant, Bren."

"Everything has importance," she insisted, reaching for his hand again. Her fingers were warm, her touch gentle, but it felt like fire against his skin. He pulled away, a cold knot forming in his stomach.

"It's dangerous to try to understand my magick," Pavan warned. "It's best not to ask so many questions."

"Are you afraid?" she asked, her golden eyes searching his.

Pavan's heart pounded in his chest. He could lose himself in those eyes, in the depth of the magick that thrummed within her. But the fear of what he might become—of what he might do—held him back. A knock at the door broke the moment, and Brendolyn quickly stood, straightening her skirts as a familiar figure entered the room.

Thad paused, his sharp gaze taking in the scene. "I've come to check on you, Pavan, but it seems I've interrupted."

"It's no trouble, sir," Brendolyn said quickly, moving to leave but Pavan shifted suddenly, reaching out to grasp her wrist. Magick flared between them, and he released her just as quickly.

"Don't go," he said, glancing at Thad. "I'd like to introduce you to my companion."

Ignoring the protests of both Thad and Brendolyn, Pavan swung his legs over the side of the bed, forcing himself to stand. Pain shot through him, but he waved them off, determination burning in his eyes.

"You shouldn't push yourself," Thad warned, stepping forward to support him. Pavan accepted the help, but his attention remained on Brendolyn.

"I'm fine," he insisted, though his voice was strained. "This is Princess Brendolyn, as I'm sure you've realized."

Brendolyn curtsied, smiling up at Pavan before turning to Thad. "An honor. You are a close friend of Pavan's?"

Thad returned the smile, his keen eyes observing her closely.

Pavan chuckled as Thad blushed slightly. "Very particular, yes. But you'd be more interested to know he's faie, just like you."

Brendolyn's eyes widened with excitement. "I have so many questions!" she exclaimed, clasping her hands together in delight.

Thad dipped his head graciously. "I'm sure you do."

"I'll fetch Elsa," Brendolyn said eagerly, "we can take tea in the library." She squeezed Thad's arm affectionately before hurrying out of the room, leaving behind a swirl of silk and a lingering scent of lavender.

As soon as she was gone, Thad turned to Pavan, a knowing look in his orange eyes. "You're in a lot of pain, aren't you?"

Pavan exhaled, wincing. "More than I'd like to admit."

Thad helped him back onto the bed, his hands gentle but firm. "Must you be so stubborn?"

"Always," Pavan muttered, settling back against the pillows. "But she needs your help, Thad."

Thad sighed, sitting beside him. He inspected the bandage on Pavan's chest before taking his hand, squeezing it reassuringly. "A favor from your particular friend? You're incorrigible."

Pavan blushed. "Oh, shut it…"

"Very well, I'll do this for you. Does she know much about her gifts?"

"Hardly anything," Pavan admitted. "Lahrs told me she's just beginning to understand them. You're the best person to guide her, Thad. Her magick is so new, so raw."

Thad brushed a lock of hair from Pavan's forehead, his touch tender. "You care for her?"

Pavan's expression darkened. "She's a child."

"That doesn't mean you don't care," Thad replied softly. "You took a great risk for her."

Pavan flinched, trying to push away the memory of the king convulsing on the ground, of Brendolyn's terrified face. He couldn't let her lose her father, not like that. "She saw my markings."

Thad's expression hardened. "And what about King Beaumont?"

"He can be trusted," Pavan said firmly, reaching up to caress Thad's cheek. "We'll be gone in a few days. Back to Eir, back to our lives. There's no danger in staying a little longer."

Thad shook his head. "Don't fool yourself, Pavan. There's always danger. Sabian was poisoned the same way his wife was…"

Pavan grimaced. "I know."

Thad studied him for a moment. "There's something about her, isn't there? You see something in her."

Pavan couldn't stop the shiver of magick that coursed through him. He glanced down at his wrist, where a tattered ribbon was tied—a relic from a life he'd tried to leave behind. Thad's fingers traced over it gently, his orange eyes filled with understanding.

"Your goddess," Thad said quietly, his gaze piercing.

"Don't," Pavan whispered, closing his eyes. "I wasn't myself."

"There's no shame in it," Thad replied, his voice steady. "Being here, so close to her… you must feel the bond you share. The special pull that guides you to her."

Pavan shook his head, his heart heavy. "I can't have her, Thad. I can't have anyone."

Thad's grip tightened. "But you want her. I've felt the link between you two. If you could, would you choose her over me?"

Pavan looked away, his throat tight. "That's not what I meant. My magick is dangerous, Thad. I could kill her. I could kill you."

Thad sighed, leaning into Pavan's touch, his breath warm against Pavan's skin. "You've come so far," he murmured, his voice a soft caress. "You've learned so much after all this time. How many nights have we shared? How many moments have we crossed paths within the shared mind space?"

Pavan's chest burned with an ache that wasn't just physical. The remnants of the poison still lingered, pulsing through his veins like a slow-moving fire. "But I have not touched you, Thad," he whispered, his voice raw. "I cannot touch when I yearn to caress your skin. How can I satisfy you when I can offer you nothing?"

"Pavan," Thad breathed, his lips brushing against Pavan's jaw as he held him close. His fingers wove through Pavan's dark hair, each movement gentle, reverent. "I am touching you now. Believe me when I tell you that I am satisfied. Believe me when I tell you how many pleasurable nights I've had in our minds, enough to satisfy me for a lifetime."

Tears welled in Pavan's eyes, slipping down his cheeks as he gazed desperately into Thad's kind, soft orange eyes. There was tenderness there, a warmth that made Pavan's heart ache even more. But the air around them was thick with magick, a stifling presence that perfumed the room with the reality Pavan couldn't escape. He raised his hand, trembling, to trace the thick vein in Thad's neck. He knew that vein held the strongest pulse, the richest source of life. It would be easy to take it, especially now, with Thad so vulnerable and willing.

Isaac. The name whispered in Pavan's mind like a curse.

"Your magick pulses beneath the skin, begging me to take it from you," Pavan inhaled sharply, his voice trembling as he leaned closer to Thad. "And Brendolyn...her magick calls to me the most. Young and blossoming, it's like a beacon. I can feel it whenever I'm near. It makes me desperately hungry."

Thad tilted Pavan's chin up, forcing him to meet his gaze. "Can you feel her magick blooming?"

"She has so much," Pavan murmured, his voice laced with longing. "She is strong, but if I am not guarded...if I become too close—"

Thad's grip tightened on Pavan's neck, pulling him closer. "You are good, Pavan. You are strong, and you can stop it."

"Sometimes," Pavan admitted, his body trembling with the effort to hold back the dark hunger that lurked within him. "Thad, I fear I don't want to stop it."

Thad's eyes hardened with resolve. "And if it comes to that, when you lose control, I will be here. Who is better suited than me or Lahrs to sedate you? I've been taught the spell, Pavan. I remember my promise to you."

Pavan's resolve wavered, and he finally nodded, his body easing slightly. He leaned his forehead against Thad's, breathing in his familiar scent—the musk of his skin, the oils in his hair. There was a comfort in Thad's presence, a balm to the fear and pain that threatened to overwhelm him.

Gently, Pavan reached up to touch Thad's cheek, and a rush of euphoria washed over him as he welcomed Thad's magick. It flowed between them like honey, warm and rich, scented with sandalwood and something uniquely Thad. The world outside faded away, leaving only the two of them in that moment.

Pavan kissed him, desperate and eager, seeking solace in the familiar taste of Thad's lips. The pain, the fear, the hunger—they all melted away, leaving only the warmth of Thad's embrace and the sweet, intoxicating magick that bound them together.

Pavan watched as Thad left the room, the door closing softly behind him. The silence that followed was oppressive, a stark contrast to the warmth Thad had brought with him. Pavan sighed, leaning back against the pillows, his thoughts a tangled mess of fear and longing.

He stared at the ceiling, his mind drifting back to Brendolyn's wide-eyed curiosity, her eager questions, and the powerful connection they shared. It terrified him how much he wanted to protect her, to be near her, even as he knew he couldn't. His chest tightened with the burden of the choice he would eventually have to make.

But for now, Pavan allowed himself a moment of weakness, a moment of imagining a world where he wasn't bound by the past, where he could have both love and loyalty, where he could be free from the chains of his own magick.

And in that fleeting dream, he could almost believe it was possible.

Brendolyn's smile greeted Thad as he approached the small table set in the ornate corner of the castle library. "Forgive me, Pavan was reluctant to rest," he said, bowing his head slightly.

"Sounds like him," Brendolyn replied, nodding in understanding and motioning for Thad to take a seat across from her. She studied him curiously. His orange eyes, flecked with gold like an autumn sunrise, and the pointed peaks of his ears, half-hidden beneath a sweep of dark copper hair, hinted at the faie heritage that defined him.

"This is my lady's maid, Elsa," Brendolyn introduced, gesturing towards a nearby chaise where Elsa had been engrossed in a book. Elsa's gaze was sharp as she looked up from her reading.

"I am here to ensure this is a cordial affair," Elsa said, her voice clipped yet polite. Brendolyn giggled at Elsa's stern demeanor.

"Don't mind her, Thad," Brendolyn said, her attention shifting back to the older faie. She had seen him in passing before, but her gaze had always seemed to slide over him, as if her eyes were enchanted to overlook him. She knew it was some form of magick, though its purpose remained a mystery.

"How old are you?" Thad asked suddenly, his voice breaking through her thoughts.

"Nearly eighteen," Brendolyn replied, placing her hands gracefully on the table. "And you?"

"Eight and thirty," Thad said with a smirk.

Brendolyn's eyes widened. "You are older than Lahrs?!"

Thad leaned in closer, his eyes intense as they held hers. Flecks of gold danced amidst the orange of his irises, like embers in a low flame. His magick felt warm and comforting, like cinnamon-infused milk. Brendolyn couldn't help but admire the flawless, freckled skin of the faie, and the soft, clean sheen of his copper hair. She felt herself getting lost in the magick of his gaze.

Elsa's voice broke the spell. "You barely look past twenty."

Thad smirked, flashing his straight white teeth. "Hazard of the charm."

"Do you use charms and glamours?" Brendolyn asked, curiosity piqued.

"All in good time, princess," Thad replied, looking at her hands. He extended his palms, facing upwards. "May I touch you?"

Brendolyn hesitated. "Is it necessary?"

"It shall last but a moment," Thad reassured her. "I have a gift of sight. It will show me your magick, and in turn, you will see mine. But only if you permit it."

Brendolyn placed her hands in his, feeling the warmth of his touch. As his fingers closed around hers, she experienced a brief rush of images. The vision was fleeting but vivid: a grand court adorned with white flowers, a young bride with plum hair standing at an altar. She saw a dark-haired man close, their bodies almost touching, his breath against her face. The vision shifted quickly, and Brendolyn was back in her own mind, her face flushed with the intensity of what she had witnessed.

"Extraordinary," Thad exhaled, observing her with a penetrating gaze. "I sense deep magick in you, Brendolyn. You are undeniably faie, but there is a stronger magick within your blood."

"Is that a good thing?" Brendolyn asked, her curiosity tinged with apprehension.

Thad smiled. "It is remarkable. When I entered your mind, I felt resistance. I could sense your thoughts brushing against mine."

Brendolyn blushed. "I did not mean to pry."

"You are perfectly fine, Brendolyn," Thad said, waving away her concern. "I suspected your sight would be strong. Your mother hailed from Augusta, of the Athrun people?"

Brendolyn nodded. "I know my mother was from Augusta, but I've been told little beyond that."

"The Athrun are faie with strong magickal intuition," Thad explained. "They never ventured further south than Augusta for fear of severing their connection to the Blood Tree. There is so much faie in you, but a deeper magick as well."

"The Blood Tree, like the barren tree in the courtyard?" Elsa interrupted, her book forgotten in her lap as she leaned in with interest.

"Yes," Thad confirmed. "The Athrun are one of the three faie lineages from the Veil, alongside the Euphron and the Dusan. They ruled Nyr beyond the treacherous seas, an ancient bloodline with abilities ranging from elemental magick to changeling powers and the manipulation of emotions."

"I thought the ancient bloodlines had died out," Elsa interjected.

"Many have," Thad said, his tone growing somber. "Or so we believed."

Brendolyn noted the wariness in Thad's expression as he looked at her with an unreadable intensity. "What magick do you have, Thad?" she asked, eager to learn more about the faie's abilities.

"I can change my shape, but I am limited to only one other form," Thad explained. With a flick of his wrist, a small flame danced in his open palm. Brendolyn marveled at it, her mouth falling open before the flame extinguished. "I've also learned healing magick, though it's constrained by my alchemist training."

"What about your faie voice? Can you sing?" Brendolyn asked, her curiosity getting the better of her.

A shadow crossed Thad's eyes, and he glanced away for a moment before meeting her gaze again. Brendolyn sensed a sudden shift in his demeanor, a darkness that seemed to weigh heavily on him. She worried she had overstepped, but then Thad smiled.

"Your faie voice is powerful, Brendolyn," he said softly. "Be cautious in how it is used, and how others may attempt to take it from you."

Brendolyn frowned, her throat tightening with emotion. "You no longer sing?"

"Not since I was a boy," Thad said, a touch of melancholy in his voice.

As the distant toll of the chapel bell signaled the hour, Brendolyn knew their teatime was ending. She watched as Thad stood, leaving the untouched tea behind. She followed suit, preparing to depart with Elsa when she suddenly stopped, glancing back at Thad as he turned towards the servants' corridor.

"Is Pavan really a faie?" she blurted out. "There's talk in the servants' hall, though nothing beyond that. They wonder about his magick."

Thad approached her, taking her hand in his. This time, no magick flowed between them; she felt a tingle of suppression as her own magick was subtly dampened by his. There was a sad smile on Thad's face.

"It is beyond my power to tell you about Pavan," he said softly.

Brendolyn sighed. "As I thought."

Thad pulled his hand away, leaving a small, slender book in her grasp. Its cover was tattered black leather with yellowing parchment and Brendolyn ran her thumbs over the blank cover.

"You may keep my book," Thad said. "Inside, I've recorded all forms of magick I've encountered, including spells to ward off prying eyes and recipes for healing potions."

Excited, Brendolyn flipped through the pages but quickly realized the language was an older dialect of Elven she had yet to master, but much of it was understood.

"I believe Lahrs is teaching you the older dialects," Thad said, his smile warming his whole face. "When you've worked hard at your studies, this book will help you master the magick here."

"Thank you," Brendolyn said, her smile genuine as she looked up at him.

"Favor find you, princess," Thad said, touching her arm. "May the goddess shine her light upon your path."

As Thad walked away, Brendolyn sensed a strange undercurrent in his blessing. Despite his warmth, there was an unmistakable pity in his eyes, and she felt his hesitation.

"He seemed nice," Elsa remarked, joining Brendolyn as they made their way to their chamber. "A bit odd, but his heart was good."

"Yes, there is goodness in Thad," Brendolyn agreed, though her thoughts were clouded with uncertainty.

"You don't seem confident in his lesson. Perhaps it was too brief, but given the circumstances in Jorn, where being faie is nearly illegal, it's understandable," Elsa said, her tone sympathetic.

"He was sad," Brendolyn reflected, her gaze drifting to the expansive lawn outside. She clutched the book to her chest, the weight of its ancient knowledge heavy with possibility. "I saw glimpses of his past and future, filled with pain, yet he wouldn't let me see more. He's powerful but holds back."

"Do you think he was trying to mislead you?" Elsa asked.

Brendolyn shook her head. "No, he was honest. Perhaps he didn't want to overwhelm me. After all, he and Pavan are here under limited invitation. I'd hate to see them punished for their association with me."

As they walked towards their rooms, Brendolyn couldn't shake the feeling that Thad's presence and his gift held deeper significance. The book in her hands was a key to understanding not just her own magick but the hidden truths of a world she was only beginning to uncover.

His body ached from the strain, but the garden's tranquil embrace was exactly what Pavan needed. After three long nights confined in the stifling room, bound to the bed by Lahrs' insistence, every moment of freedom felt like a gift. The healing potions, though necessary, had left an unpleasant taste in his mouth, and their effects had been more debilitating than beneficial. But now, the open greenery of the garden, with its high hedges and meandering gravel paths, soothed his restless spirit.

As Pavan meandered through the garden, the scent of blooming flowers filled the air, the garden was a haven of old-world charm. It wasn't surprising when he spotted Brendolyn lounging near the fountain, her presence a soft note in the garden's symphony.

The fountain was an intricate piece of art, with cascading waters that shimmered under the sunlight. The basin was home to exotic fish that sparkled like liquid jewels, swimming through the waters. Brendolyn lay on the edge of the fountain, a small book held delicately in her hands. Her dark hair caught the light, creating a halo effect that made her look like a figure out of a faie tale Meilyr had once told him.

Pavan approached with quiet steps, his gaze drawn to the book she held. It was unmistakably Thad's, a precious artifact of knowledge and mystery. The sight of it stirred a smile on his lips. Thad's generosity was as unexpected as it was touching; giving such a personal and valuable item to the princess spoke volumes about his trust.

Brendolyn lifted her gaze as Pavan approached, her expression a serene blend of curiosity and quiet delight. The garden's natural magick seemed to mirror her calm, its vibrant energy amplifying the warmth in her golden eyes. She offered him a welcoming smile.

"Pavan," she said, her voice soft and melodic, blending effortlessly with the garden's gentle whispers. "How are you feeling?" She snapped a small book shut and slipped it into her pocket with practiced ease.

"Better now, thank you," Pavan replied, his eyes briefly lingering on the faded cover. "I see you've been enjoying a rare find."

Brendolyn nodded, her fingers brushing over the worn edges of the book. "Thad's notes are fascinating. I can read only fragments of Elven, but what I understand is remarkable. They speak of ancient magicks and lost arts—it's like holding a piece of history in my hands."

As he moved closer, the garden seemed to hum with subtle energy, the air growing warmer and tinged with a soft, golden glow. It was as if the very essence of the place was welcoming their reunion.

Brendolyn gestured to the edge of the fountain where she sat. "Would you join me?"

Pavan smiled gently but shook his head. "I've rested enough. Shall we walk? The grove should offer us some shade from the sun."

They began to stroll along the winding path leading to the grove. The shaded trees stretched their verdant arms over them, casting a dappled light on the ground.

"Thad has shared much about the faie," Brendolyn said, her tone light but inquisitive.

"He's a gifted teacher," Pavan replied, his voice steady and measured. "I've learned many things from him over the years."

Brendolyn glanced sideways at him, her curiosity unabated. "Are you married?"

Pavan faltered momentarily, caught off guard. "No, I am not."

"How old are you?"

"Eight and twenty," he replied, offering her a brief, sideways glance before resuming his measured pace.

A thoughtful silence settled between them, broken only by the rustling of leaves and the distant murmur of water.

"Have you ever been in love?" she asked suddenly.

The question brought a faint smile to Pavan's lips. "There have been moments," he admitted, his gaze shifting to the dark-haired princess beside him. "Times when I could say I was in love."

Brendolyn tilted her head, her expression puzzled. "Your answer...it's honest, but not what I expected."

"Were you hoping for a tale of unwavering devotion to a single, destined love?" Pavan asked, his tone playful as they reached the shade of an ivy-covered pavilion.

"Do not mock me," Brendolyn countered, her cheeks warming to a soft pink.

"I would not dare," Pavan replied, his smile broadening. "But honesty compels me to say I have loved many, and I will love many more. Love is not finite, Brendolyn." He plucked a small flower from the vines above.

Brendolyn took the bloom from his fingers, her touch lingering briefly on his rough hand, sending an unexpected shiver through him. "And have you kissed them, these loves of yours?"

His smirk deepened. "Yes, a kiss to seal my affection. But," he added, leaning slightly closer, "you assume too much if you think I have only kissed women."

Her mouth fell open in shock, her wide eyes locking onto his. Pavan straightened, the corners of his lips twitching into a knowing smile.

"You mock me, sir," Brendolyn said, her tone flustered as she tried to regain composure.

"Because to kiss alone is a chaste thing," Pavan replied, tucking her hand under his arm as they began to walk once more. "And it speaks to the delicacy of your innocence."

They strolled in silence again, the garden's tranquil charm weaving its spell around them. After a time, Brendolyn broke the silence. "You love Thad."

Pavan paused mid-step, his expression softening as he turned to her. "You are perceptive."

"I remember how he looked when he saw me in your chambers," Brendolyn said. "At first, I didn't understand it. But when you called him a particular friend, it became clear."

"Does this trouble you?"

Brendolyn's smile was gentle, her blush deepening. "Not at all. It's endearing to see love without fear. How did you meet him?"

"He saved my life," Pavan admitted, his voice low and reflective.

Her smile widened, radiant warmth lighting her features. The subtle hum of magick stirred in Pavan's blood as he looked at her, her presence resonating in the deepest parts of himself. For a moment, he fought to suppress the longing he sensed within her—a sweetness that struck a quiet yet powerful chord in him.

"Tell me about your prince," he said softly. "He is deeply in love with you. I would like to hear your thoughts."

"Do not call him my prince," Brendolyn mumbled as they walked on. Her smile faded, the change in topic clouding her mood.

"If I may be bold, princess," Pavan began, "your curiosity about love only confirms your yearning to understand it better. Now, he is your prince—because I have not seen him look upon any woman at court as he looks at you. He is utterly captivated by you. But...do *you* love *him*?"

Brendolyn cast him a sharp look, a faint smile tugging at her lips. "And now who is the perceptive one?"

Pavan chuckled. "He doesn't hide his emotions well. Nor does he bother to spare a glance for the other women of the court—despite how many there are."

Her cheeks flushed a delicate pink, her skin glowing faintly as sunlight broke through the trees. Pavan averted his eyes, suddenly self-conscious, and led them toward the shaded alcove of a marble statue.

"He is to marry my sister, Lisetta," Brendolyn murmured, the brightness fading from her voice. "The council arranged it, with the approval of both kings. But he told me he loved me...and I believed I loved him."

She stopped walking, her expression clouding with sadness.

Pavan's smile faltered. He let her hand fall to her side, watching as melancholy softened her features. Regret tasted bitter in the air, and he longed to smooth away the edges of her sorrow, to touch her cheek and assure her it would be alright. Instead, he straightened, locking his magick deep within, shielding his heart.

Her golden eyes glimmered as she looked up at him. "We were married...in secret," she admitted, her voice barely audible. "It was during the Festival of Fertility in Corad. We didn't realize it at first, but the rites were binding. We..." She faltered, her cheeks reddening as her gaze fell to her hands.

Understanding dawned on Pavan. "You consummated the marriage," he said gently.

Brendolyn nodded, her voice trembling. "I was the happiest I'd ever been. But when he returned here, it all fell apart. I was summoned to Jorn not long after, and when I arrived, Barrow declared the marriage void. He said our union never happened. And yet...he told me he still loved me." Her voice cracked, a single tear slipping down her cheek. "Would he not fight for me? Would he not..." She trailed off, wiping the tear away angrily.

"He's an idiot," Pavan muttered.

Brendolyn's head snapped up. "You cannot call the prince that."

"I most certainly can." Pavan's tone was resolute. "An idiot, respectfully. To claim your love, to marry you, and then abandon you—that's the greatest folly I've ever known."

"He has his duties as the crown prince," she argued weakly. "His responsibilities—"

"He knew those responsibilities before he promised you his love," Pavan interrupted, his voice firm but kind. "Don't try to excuse his cold heart for breaking yours."

Her sadness deepened, and it pained him to see her so burdened.

"He promised me..." she whispered. "He said he'd make it right."

"I believe he promised that because he wished it were true for himself. But love—" Pavan's voice tightened, his throat constricting. "Love is painful, sometimes."

Brendolyn looked at him, her eyes shimmering with unshed tears. "Are you speaking of Prince Barrow, Pavan...or yourself?"

For a moment, he was caught off guard by her insight. Her gentle concern shone through her own heartbreak, a quiet, steady light.

"We speak of your troubles, princess, not mine," he said, forcing a smile.

Her hand tightened on his arm, her golden eyes piercing. "You're always so eager to comfort others, but you won't let anyone comfort you, will you?"

"It is unwise to dwell on the past," he said, swallowing hard. His magick stirred, bitter and hot beneath his skin.

"What was her name?"

The question froze him. He looked away, but Brendolyn's touch remained, soft yet insistent.

"Penelope," he whispered. The name slipped from him like a sigh, carrying the weight of buried grief.

Brendolyn smiled faintly. "What a beautiful name. Was she your greatest love?"

Pavan's lips curved upward, though his eyes reflected only sorrow. "She was dearly loved. She was my wife, long ago."

As his smile faded, Brendolyn reached out, taking his hand in both of hers. "Did she leave you?" she asked softly.

Pavan nodded, his voice raw. "In the worst way. Even my love could not save her. She...died."

Without hesitation, Brendolyn wrapped her arms around his neck, pulling him into an embrace. The warmth of her gesture was startling, and he found himself holding her briefly before stepping back as the laughter of ladies echoed nearby.

"We should go," he said quietly, his voice distant.

She nodded, dabbing at her eyes. Together, they walked in silence, each carrying unspoken burdens.

As they passed a group of ladies, Pavan felt their gazes linger on him, their words sharp and unfamiliar in Jornedian dialect.

"They find you handsome," Brendolyn said, breaking the silence.

He grimaced, unimpressed.

"But they also find it repulsive that you walk with me," she added, her tone calm but resigned.

"Repulsive? Why?"

"I am faie," she said simply. "In Jorn, prejudice runs deep. I am fortunate to be born to my father's house, but others of my kind...they suffer greatly."

Her honesty stunned him. She reached for his hand, her smile soft. "Will you have tea with me tomorrow?"

"I do not think that wise," Pavan replied, his voice tight.

Her smile faltered. "I see."

"I am below your station, princess. It would not be proper." He knew he was making excuses, knew he needed to protect her from himself.

Her gaze lingered on him, thoughtful. "Then will you escort me to the upper galleries?"

"Is that a command?" he asked, arching a brow.

"A request," she said, her smile returning.

With a sigh, Pavan offered her his arm. Together, they ascended the steps, the weight of their unspoken emotions hanging between them like a fragile truce.

Brendolyn's hand fell reluctantly from Pavan's arm as she gracefully adjusted the heft of her skirts, leading the way up the grand staircase. The steps, crafted from polished marble, ascended to the quieter, more private levels of the palace. Pavan followed a few steps behind, feeling the weight of his racing heart and the sharp prickle of his own magick under his skin.

The second floor was a realm of tranquility compared to the bustling lower levels. Here, the grandeur was subdued, replaced by an atmosphere of serene elegance. The halls were lined with rich tapestries depicting scenes of long-forgotten battles and idyllic landscapes, their vibrant colors illuminated by the soft light of enchanted chandeliers.

The only sounds were the echo of their footsteps and the distant murmur of palace servants going about their duties.

As they reached the gallery, Pavan marveled at the sight before him. The hall was a vast expanse of smooth, polished stone, its walls adorned with portraits and landscapes that seemed to breathe with life. The paintings were masterpieces, each brushstroke meticulously applied to create scenes of breathtaking beauty. The gallery was a testament to the artistic heritage of the faie, surpassing even the famed collections of Paris.

"This one is of the Field of Thourns, it is within Rhun," Brendolyn's voice was soft, almost reverent, as she stood beside Pavan, her sleeve brushing against his arm.

Pavan stepped closer to the first portrait, his eyes drinking in the details. The painting depicted a rolling hillside bathed in golden light, the grasses swaying gently under an azure sky. It was an image of serene beauty, but as Brendolyn spoke, a shadow fell over her expression.

"Rhun is between the Realms, is it not?" Pavan asked, his gaze lingering on the sweeping grass.

"Yes," Brendolyn nodded, her voice trembling slightly. "It was once a part of Corad, before the wars ravaged its beauty. Scorched by dragon fire."

The term 'dragon fire' struck a chord with Pavan, and he felt a chill run down his spine. He tried to keep his voice steady. "Dragon fire?"

"It was a magick so intense it turned everything to ash. Men of Jorn, men of Corad—none survived," she said, her voice breaking with the weight of her grief. Her tears glistened in the light of the chandeliers, reflecting the sorrow of a past too painful to forget.

Pavan's heart ached for her. "War is a dangerous burden."

Brendolyn moved to the next painting, depicting a majestic tree line, its branches heavy with the weight of ancient wisdom. She paused, gathering her composure. "My mother was Hana DeFay. Few speak of her, but she was one of Princess Kryana's ladies. As was my Queen Mother, Natalia, and Lady Aletta..."

Pavan listened with rapt attention, his gaze following Brendolyn as she moved from one painting to the next. The gallery's magick seemed to hold its breath, amplifying the emotional weight of their conversation.

Her voice grew softer, touched with sadness. "Princess Kryana was betrothed to Beaumont. His arrival in Corad the year before the war was supposed to be a union of peace. But Kryana fell ill and passed into the Veil."

"Lady Aletta married Beaumont instead?" Pavan's memory served him well, and he caught a fleeting smile on Brendolyn's lips.

"Yes," Brendolyn said, her voice steadying. "Natalia, my mother, married my father. The unrest between the kingdoms fueled the war, and the Field of Thourns became a symbol of its devastation. My mother was young, and my Queen Mother couldn't bear the thought of Hana returning to Augusta."

Pavan halted, his eyes widening with realization. "Augusta was destroyed."

Brendolyn nodded, her expression a tapestry of grief and resilience. "It was once a haven, a thriving city for the faie. But it was razed—its people either killed or scattered. My father refuses to speak of it, as if that part of me were erased along with the city."

"Your mother's legacy endures in you, Brendolyn," Pavan said softly. "Though the place is lost, her strength and story live on through you."

Brendolyn's smile was laced with sorrow, but a faint glimmer of hope warmed her eyes. "You are very kind, Pavan."

"I am honest," he replied, as they resumed their walk down the gallery. Their steps brought them before a grand painting, its scene an ethereal landscape steeped in twilight hues.

"Will you always be honest with me?" Her voice was barely above a whisper, mingling with the distant murmurs from the far reaches of the gallery.

Pavan studied her, noting how her gaze darted briefly toward the sound. "I shall always try, princess."

Brendolyn shot him a stern look, her expression softened by amusement. "I wish you wouldn't call me that," she said, a playful smirk tugging at her lips.

"But you are a princess," he countered with a teasing lilt.

She sighed and turned back to the painting, her eyes tracing its vivid strokes. A small smile surfaced, tender and unguarded. "Please, call me Brendolyn."

Pavan's lips curved into a wider grin. "Brendolyn."

Her bright eyes met his, brimming with warmth and curiosity. "Pavan."

"I suspect you are the source of much mischief," he teased, his tone light yet tempered by the way her presence seemed to amplify the faint hum of magick in the air.

Brendolyn tilted her head, studying him as though trying to solve a puzzle. "You're a mystery, Pavan. I can't seem to understand you."

"Some things are meant to be felt, not understood," he replied, his voice quieter now as he glanced around the secluded alcove of the gallery. "You should return to your chaperone, Bren. We're alone."

She stepped closer, her hand brushing lightly against his chest. "Then there is no one to interrupt us."

Pavan's pulse quickened, his composure tested by the nearness of her. "You shouldn't be alone," he murmured.

"I am not alone," Brendolyn whispered, her hand trailing upward to rest against his neck. Her gaze lingered on his lips, and he could feel the magnetic pull of her intent.

He caught her hand gently, pressing a kiss to her palm, savoring the spark of magick that danced faintly between them. Desire surged, but he held himself steady. Smiling down at her, he said, "You shouldn't be alone with *me*, Bren."

Pavan stepped back, letting her hand fall slowly from his. His expression softened, but the tension in his shoulders betrayed the storm brewing inside him. "Bren," he began, his voice weighted, "you don't understand what you're inviting. Being close to me...it isn't safe."

Brendolyn frowned, confusion mingling with frustration. "Safe? Pavan, you've saved countless lives and endured things I can't even imagine. Why would I fear you?"

"It's not fear you should worry about," he replied.

Brendolyn's breath hitched at the vulnerability in his voice. Tentatively, she placed a hand on his arm, urging him to look at her. "Don't shut me out, Pavan. Maybe I can help—"

"You already do," he interrupted, his tone gentle but firm. "I couldn't live with myself if I hurt you."

Before Brendolyn could respond, the sound of hurried footsteps echoed from the far side of the gallery. A maid appeared, her cheeks flushed from exertion.

"Princess Brendolyn," the maid said, dipping into a quick curtsy. "Sir Lahrs is waiting for you. He sent me to fetch you at once."

Brendolyn hesitated, her gaze lingering on Pavan as if reluctant to leave. "Tell Lahrs I'll be there shortly," she said, her tone polite but firm.

The maid nodded and scurried off, leaving the two alone once more.

With a reluctant glance over her shoulder, she turned and walked away, leaving Pavan alone amidst the flickering light of the gallery. He exhaled slowly, closing his eyes as he tried to steady the turmoil within.

"Favor find you, Bren."

CHAPTER 28

Eero found Elsa standing alone on the balcony of the tower's upper room, her figure framed against the starlit sky. Below, the gardens stretched out in shadowy tranquility, the faint strains of music drifting up from the great hall where courtiers reveled in celebration. He approached with measured steps, careful not to disturb her quiet reflection. Her posture, rigid yet delicate, spoke of a deep, contemplative sorrow. As he drew closer, the glimmer of tears on her cheeks caught the light.

"The hour is late," she murmured, her voice a soft melody carried by the night breeze, yet she did not turn to face him.

Eero paused beside her, his gaze tracing the elegant lines of her profile. "It is," he replied gently. "Would you not prefer to be in your chambers, reading, or playing your lute?" He noted the tears with a pang in his chest.

"I find solace in the music tonight," Elsa said, her tone tinged with a quiet sadness that echoed in her words. "The musicians from Eir...their skill is unmatched."

Eero leaned on the stone railing beside her, his eyes following hers over the moonlit gardens. "I believe they're playing a composition by the one they call Pavan."

At the mention of the name, Elsa turned to him, her eyes suddenly alight with warmth. "Pavan, the firebreather?"

A faint smile touched Eero's lips. "So they say. The maids speak of him often in the servants' hall. Audry, in particular, has a fondness for him—she's always had a weakness for brooding men who whisper poetry in the quiet moments."

Elsa laughed softly, the sound like a delicate bell in the stillness. "Perhaps that's why she enjoys your company."

Eero chuckled, a rueful smile crossing his face. "Audry is a charming girl, but I am far too old for her affections."

Elsa's expression grew more serious, her brow furrowing slightly. "Yet that hasn't stopped you from offering me your hand."

His smile faded, replaced by a solemn gravity. "That's different, Elsa," he said, the words heavy with regret. "My duty to your family—my duty to you—is to offer protection."

Elsa's hand rested gently on his arm, her touch warm despite the chill in the air. "I will never marry, Sir Eero," she said with quiet resolve. "Not even to a man of such honor as yourself."

Eero felt the heat of her hand seep into his skin, igniting a fierce protectiveness deep within him. Urgency quickened his heartbeat as he leaned closer, his voice low and intense. "Then take the great ships, Elsa. Take your princess under my men's guardianship and sail to Tauf. Leave these shores behind—there's danger here, whispers of a threat that grows each day."

Elsa's brow furrowed in concern, her fingers lightly tracing the tense curve of his shoulder. "Danger?" she asked, her voice tinged with sudden fear. "Is this about that night with Leuthere? I promise you, Eero, I am unharmed."

He shook his head, the weight of his fears pressing down on him. "It's not just the captain, Elsa. There's a darkness spreading in this realm. I can feel it," he said, his hands gripping the balcony rail, the stone beneath his fingers thrumming with latent magick.

Her eyes searched his, seeking answers to questions she had not yet voiced. "You've hidden your elven heritage even from those closest to you?"

Eero laughed bitterly, a sound devoid of humor. "There's much I've hidden, Elsa. But that's not what matters now." He took her hand, his grip firm, his voice filled with determination. "My heart is bound to you, whether you accept it or not. My devotion to you is unwavering. I wouldn't speak of it if not for the need to offer you comfort and protection. Whatever happens, I will never leave your side."

Elsa's heartbeat quickened, a flutter of fear and something deeper sparking to life within her. "What are you saying, Eero?"

"Alaric is in Jorn," he said, his voice dropping to a grave whisper. "Audry saw him within the castle, speaking with Leuthere and Lord Bannon. Whatever their plans, it bodes ill for us all. As soon as these celebrations end, I will personally see you and Brendolyn safely to Entheas."

Elsa pulled her hand away, a defiant fire in her eyes. "No, I will not leave this realm."

Eero's frustration boiled over, his voice hardening. "Alaric has come to claim your hand, Elsa. He's allied with Leuthere and Lord Bannon, men who wield power that could shatter Jorn. He's more dangerous than any knighthood Corad could muster."

Though fear flickered in Elsa's eyes, she held herself with an icy composure, blinking back the tears that threatened to fall. "I cannot leave this realm, Eero," she said, her voice steady despite the tremor in her heart. "Not while the bond remains. The blood magick ties me to him—enduring this agony is all I can manage. To be separated by such a distance...it would destroy me."

Eero's heart ached at her words, his desperation to protect her growing. "Then you must return to Corad at the earliest opportunity."

Elsa shook her head, her resolve unwavering. "Where my princess goes, so too will I be," she said softly, a tear slipping down her cheek. Eero's hand twitched, longing to brush it away, to pull her close and banish her fears with a kiss.

Instead, he took her hand once more, his grip firm but tender. "I will speak to Lahrs," he said with quiet resolve. "He will ensure you return home safely."

Elsa's gaze held his, a silent understanding passing between them. She nodded, her hand squeezing his in a wordless promise.

"You were gone last night," Pavan's voice cut through the quiet of the workroom, where Thad was seated at a low bench, painstakingly repairing the flowing fabric of Juliette's gown. The once-vibrant silk had come apart during one of the evening's dances.

Thad's hands moved deftly, but his eyes remained fixed on his work, avoiding Pavan's gaze. "I was in the gardens," he said, his tone laced with a tension that belied the simple statement.

Pavan's instincts were on high alert. He could feel a knot of unease tightening in his chest. Kneeling before Thad, he searched the faie's orange eyes for any hint of truth. "Tell me truthfully, Thad. You've been different since we arrived here. I need to understand."

Thad sighed, lowering the garment into his lap. He met Pavan's gaze with an intensity that nearly took his breath away. "I was in the gardens, and the library, and the courtyard, and the stables. I have been everywhere and nowhere, Pavan. Perhaps you simply failed to notice my presence."

Pavan was taken aback by the sharpness in Thad's tone. "Thad, I don't understand. Why are you—"

Standing abruptly, Thad tossed aside the unfinished gown and stormed towards the adjoining chamber. Pavan followed, watching as Thad angrily rearranged his clothes for the evening. The room seemed to grow warmer with Thad's rising frustration.

"Thad," Pavan called out, his voice tinged with desperation.

Thad's movements were jerky, his anger palpable. He grabbed for his doublet, the fabric rustling violently. Pavan stepped forward and grasped Thad's hand firmly. "Tell me what I've done wrong. Has someone said something to you in the castle while I was unwell?"

Thad's face flickered with a mix of irritation and pain. "Unwell? You poisoned yourself recklessly, without a thought for the consequences. You endangered yourself for a king's life."

"It was a desperate act," Pavan replied, his voice soft but firm. "I couldn't stand by and watch when I could have done something to help."

Thad's eyes narrowed, the orange glow within them intensifying. "Desperate to save a man you barely know? What did she say to you? Did she beg you, promise you something in return?"

Pavan's face flushed with anger. "Thad, enough. This is not about what anyone said. It's about what I felt was right."

A surge of heat seemed to radiate from Thad, filling the room with a palpable tension. "Enough of watching you in her company? Enough of seeing you share dinners, walk arm in arm, and flirt openly with her?"

"I don't flirt with her," Pavan shot back, his voice rising. "I am simply showing gratitude for her hospitality."

Thad's face darkened. "Your goddess is nothing but a spoiled child. The flames of her power are but a flicker compared to the storms she stirs."

The temperature in the room seemed to rise with Thad's anger, his eyes blazing with a fiery intensity that matched the heat. "You speak unfairly, Thad. You once told me she was—"

Thad stepped closer, his voice low and dangerous. "I told you what you wanted to hear, Pavan. She is ignorant of the world and her own feelings. She may never master magick before it consumes her."

Pavan, filled with a mix of rage and despair, grabbed Thad by the front of his tunic. The faie's smirk was a bitter contrast to the fire in his eyes. "She is your fated match, Pavan. I've seen her visions, her cries for you across the waves. You cannot deny her, no matter how much you may wish to."

Pavan's heart wavered, torn between his feelings for Thad and his duty to Brendolyn. "I love you, Thad," he whispered, his voice breaking. "*Only* you."

Thad's face remained hardened, a mask of anger and sorrow. "You cannot change fate."

"I choose to love you," Pavan insisted, reaching out to pull Thad closer. "I cannot love her while I am faithful to you."

"You cannot love me," Thad said, his voice cold. "I've told you before not to…"

"You've never told me not to love you," Pavan interjected. "After all these years, how could I not? How can I look at her when my heart belongs to you?"

Thad shook his head, pushing Pavan away. "Do not speak of magick you do not understand. There are things beyond your control."

"There's little magick left that I do not know, Thad. This isn't about magick but about choice. I refuse to be bound by a goddess's will when it ignores my heart. How can I choose her over you?"

"You will choose her," Thad said firmly, his tone final.

"I will not," Pavan declared, his voice filled with determination.

Thad, now visibly agitated, yanked a fresh silk shirt from the pile. He pulled it on, the fabric shimmering against his pale skin. Pavan could feel the vibrant mix of emotions emanating from Thad—jealousy, anger, and a deep, unspoken pain. The scent of Thad's cologne, a mix of exotic spices, lingered in the air, stirring memories and longing.

"I must attend to the girls as they dance," Thad said, his voice resolute. "I advise you to remain here."

Anxiety clawed at Pavan's insides. "I am not a danger to anyone."

Thad's sharp eyes met his. "I do not wish for you to be a distraction."

Thad moved to the table, retrieving the gown he had been mending. His steps were heavy as he approached Pavan, their closeness allowing Pavan to feel the heat of Thad's anger and the subtle spices of his cologne.

"I will return to you," Thad said quietly. "Wait for me."

Pavan leaned into the tender touch of Thad's hand on his cheek, his heart pounding with a mix of hope and despair. Thad turned away, closing the door behind him with a finality that left Pavan in a heavy silence.

Pavan walked to the window, his gaze fixed on the darkened lawn below. The castle was alive with distant sounds of the banquet and dance, but the halls around him were empty and still. As he wandered, his eyes were drawn to a familiar sight—a grand piano in a corner, draped in dust-covered plants.

He approached with a mixture of amusement and nostalgia, pulling the coverings away to reveal the dusty keys. A smile touched his lips as he wiped the dust away and took a seat before the instrument. The keys vibrated under his fingertips, the familiar feel of the piano a soothing balm to his troubled heart.

In the midst of the turmoil, Pavan found a moment of solace, letting the music flow and easing the tension that had gripped him so tightly.

Brendolyn slipped into the great hall under the veil of darkness, her heart racing from the argument with Lahrs about not attending the night's revelry. Lahrs' insistence that Elsa's absence be concealed for reasons beyond her own health gnawed at her nerves. The opulent chamber, lit by chandeliers casting shimmering light over golden walls, was alive with the bustling excitement of high society.

Her eyes darted warily through the crowd, seeking any trace of the hidden threat she sensed in the air. The courtiers, adorned in lavish attire that sparkled like stars, swirled gracefully across the dance floor. Their laughter and conversation blended into a symphony of elegance and excess, masking the undercurrent of tension that Brendolyn felt keenly.

Brendolyn edged towards the grand windows, their gossamer curtains swaying lightly in the draft. Behind their delicate drapes, she took refuge, her breaths coming in quick, shallow gasps. She pressed her back against the cool, stone wall, trying to steady her pulse.

King Beaumont held court at the hall's apex, seated on an ornate dais surrounded by his closest advisors and the pinnacle of societal rank. His regal presence commanded the space, and despite his apparent ease, Brendolyn could not shake the sense of danger lurking within the revelry.

Gingerly, she peered through the translucent fabric, catching glimpses of the King's interaction with his courtiers. They moved with practiced grace, their voices a melodious hum that only underscored her apprehension. Brendolyn's fingers tightened around the edge of the curtain, her resolve wavering. She knew she should approach him, but the oppressive atmosphere and her own growing unease made every step toward him feel like a monumental task.

"Hello pigeon." The voice behind her was nauseating. A strong hand slipped around her waist, pressing up against her back, those hands caressing the bodice of her gown.

Brendolyn froze, trying to pull away, but Varick held her closer. His other hand clamping over her mouth and pressing his mouth to the curve of her ear.

"Don't be so shy, pigeon…they shall hear you if you squirm…what would your prince say, hm?" Varick smiled, pressing against her, his free hand tight against the curve of her bodice.

Brendolyn shifted, her hands clawing at his hands, but he was immoveable, then she remembered the dagger. Scrambling in the folds of her gown, listening to Varick chuckle in her ear. Grasping the hilt, Brendolyn bit hard against the hand at her mouth.

Varick hissed, swearing, yanking free. Brendolyn turned, the dagger drawn up, the point of the small blade at the curve of his throat. The knight froze, pressing himself back against the windowpane, eyeing Brendolyn with a smile.

"Such spirit," he purred, eyeing her. Brendolyn pressed harder on the blade, the tip dimpled against the freshly shaven skin of the man's neck.

"Do not follow me," she hissed. Stepping out of the curtain and turning on her heel she dashed back the way she had entered, desperately wishing to be free of this place. Wanting to return to her rooms, Brendolyn quickly returned the dagger to the hilt of her pocket.

Just as her fingers brushed the cool, gilded handles, a firm hand closed around her wrist. She turned sharply, her breath catching in her throat. Barrow's striking blue eyes met hers, their intensity catching her off guard.

"Leaving without the honor of a dance?" His gaze was both piercing and inviting.

Brendolyn's composure faltered. She gasped, her face flushing a deep crimson. "Of course," she stammered, forcing herself to regain her poise. With an unsteady breath, she allowed herself to be led to the center of the hall, her steps feeling heavier with each passing moment. The murmurs and curious glances of the assembled courtiers made her feel as though she were under a magnifying glass.

"Do you think this is wise, dancing together?" she whispered, her voice trembling slightly.

Barrow's smile was warm, his confidence palpable. "They cannot control whom I choose to dance with. This is my party, after all."

As Brendolyn settled into his embrace, she couldn't help but blush, the sensation of being held by him bringing a fleeting sense of comfort. "They will talk," she murmured, feeling the reassuring warmth of his hand on her lower back.

Barrow's expression grew serious. "Let them talk. I want to savor every moment with you, regardless of their whispers." He leaned in closer, his breath warm against her ear.

The dance began, and Brendolyn felt a strange sense of liberation as they moved together. The room spun around them in a mesmerizing blur of color and light, each step perfectly synchronized with Barrow's. She allowed herself to smile, the tension easing from her shoulders.

"You've improved," she said, her eyes sparkling with genuine admiration.

Barrow's smirk widened. "I took lessons specifically to dance every dance with you."

The final spin of their dance brought them face-to-face with Lisetta. The dark-haired princess stood in their path, her expression a mask of unreadable fury. Her hands were firmly planted on her hips, and the room fell into a stunned silence.

"Lisetta?" Barrow's voice was a low, controlled growl as he addressed her. The courtiers, now frozen mid-step, watched the scene unfold with bated breath.

Lisetta's gaze was locked on Brendolyn, her eyes flashing with an intensity that sent a shiver down Brendolyn's spine. Without a word, she drew back her hand and slapped Brendolyn across the face.

A collective gasp rippled through the crowd as Brendolyn's cheek stung from the blow. Her hand flew to her face, her eyes wide with shock and pain.

Barrow moved swiftly, positioning himself between the sisters. "Lisetta, what is the meaning of this?" His voice was sharp, but he maintained a facade of calm.

Lisetta's eyes filled with tears, but her voice was cold and steely. "Don't play the fool, sir. You court the princess while secretly indulging in your affair. You will be ruined, Barrow."

Barrow's posture grew even more rigid. "You forget yourself, Lisetta. You will be queen only if I am king. Without me, without the throne I offer you, you will have nothing."

The words hit Lisetta with palpable force, her face shifting from fury to stunned hurt. She looked between Barrow and Brendolyn, her resolve wavering.

"I suggest you retire to your apartments," Barrow continued, his voice a low, commanding growl. "I have no wish to see you tonight."

Lisetta's cheeks flamed with anger and humiliation as she turned on her heel and stormed away, the echoes of her footsteps fading into the silence.

Barrow's gaze softened as he turned to Brendolyn, who stood there with tears streaming down her face and her cheek reddened from the slap. Embarrassment and sadness mingled in her expression.

In a flurry of emotion, Brendolyn tried to escape, slipping through the crowd with desperate haste. She heard Barrow calling after her, but her voice cracked with suppressed sobs. "Do not follow me..."

Barrow's expression was one of wounded confusion as he watched her retreat. His heart ached at the sight of her distress.

Brendolyn's pace quickened as she fled through the corridors, her tears blending with the rain that began to fall from the darkened sky outside. She found solace only when she reached a quiet, shadowed room filled with portraits. The room was dim, lit only by the flickering glow of a single candle.

It was there she saw Pavan, seated at a table with strange white markings. His fingers danced across the surface, producing a melody that was both haunting and enchanting. The music flowed with a complexity and depth that Brendolyn had never encountered.

The sound stopped abruptly as Pavan noticed her presence. He stood, knocking his chair to the floor in his surprise. Their eyes met, and he seemed momentarily lost.

"I am sorry," Brendolyn said softly, her voice trembling as she approached. "I didn't mean to intrude. I heard the music and followed it...What were you playing?"

Pavan looked down at her, his voice gentle. "Have you ever heard this tone before?"

Brendolyn shook her head, her curiosity piqued. "There has never been a song like this."

Pavan resumed his place at the table, his hands gliding over the keys with a delicate touch. "This melody can be played softly, or with more force..." His fingers struck the keys with a dramatic flair, causing Brendolyn to jump as a powerful resonance filled the air.

Pavan smiled at her reaction. "But when played together, they create a new sound..." The music swelled with a blend of soft and dramatic tones, creating a unique, haunting harmony.

As Brendolyn watched him, she noticed a worn, stained ribbon tied around his wrist. Her hand reached out, touching the fabric with a mix of wonder and recognition.

Pavan's expression shifted to one of surprise and discomfort as he pulled his hand away. "You lied to me," Brendolyn whispered, her voice trembling with revelation. "You're the man from the cages. All these years...I thought you were dead."

Pavan's eyes softened as he met her gaze. "I am not the same man you remember. I never intended to deceive you, princess, but I believed I would never see you again. Your kindness gave me strength when I was at my lowest."

Tears welled in Brendolyn's eyes as Pavan continued, his voice breaking slightly. "It was your spirit that kept me going. When I saw you in Denorn, I wanted to thank you, but fear held me back. Now, the fates have brought us together once more, and I owe you my life."

Brendolyn's heart raced. "You saved my father and my realm. You've given me so much more than I could ever repay. You owe me nothing."

Pavan's features tightened with concern. She placed her hand gently on his chest, where Lahrs had removed the poison. The touch made her gasp as a searing heat surged through her.

Pavan's eyes widened in alarm. "The magick I wield...it comes with a price." He pressed his lips to her hand, attempting to ease the pain. His touch was cool and soothing, but Brendolyn was overwhelmed by a sudden, intense urge.

Pavan pulled away abruptly, his expression hardening. "I cannot have this...Forgive me." His voice was filled with anguish as he fled the room, leaving Brendolyn alone with the tumultuous feelings and the fading echoes of the haunting melody.

Pavan's body was a tempest of desire and agony, aching for the magick that surged within her, so tantalizingly close. It beckoned to him, a magnetic force that pulsed with raw power, demanding to be possessed. Each moment of her nearness intensified the storm raging within him, an insidious craving that twisted his insides with its ferocity.

He staggered through the castle's corridors, the cold stone walls bearing silent witness to his torment. The darkness seemed to close in around him, a suffocating shroud that mirrored the conflict tearing at his soul. The very air felt charged, vibrating with his inner turmoil as if the castle itself could sense his struggle.

Bursting into the chill of the night, Pavan gasped for the frigid air, his breath coming out in ragged clouds that mingled with the rising mist. The garden before him was a shadowy expanse, the once manicured flower beds now wild and overgrown, their delicate blooms lost to the encroaching chaos of the storm.

Lightning sliced through the darkened sky, illuminating the gardens in stark, blinding flashes. Thunder followed with a deafening roar that seemed to resonate with the storm inside him, shaking him to his very core. Each crash of thunder felt like a violent echo of his own internal strife, amplifying his desperation.

His legs trembled uncontrollably as he plunged into the garden's heart, forcing his way through tangled foliage and drenched earth. He screamed into the storm, his voice a raw, ragged sound that was swallowed by the roaring wind and booming thunder. The heavens themselves seemed to weep with him, as the sky unleashed a torrential downpour that battered him with relentless intensity.

Pavan sank to his knees in the muddy garden, the cold rain hammering down on him with a relentless force. It soaked through his clothes, the chill seeping into his very bones. His hair plastered to his face, the rain streaming down his cheeks like tears. He felt the earth's embrace, its cold and unforgiving, mirroring the emotional wreckage within him.

As the storm raged on, Pavan let the rain wash over him, its icy touch a bitter balm to the feverish chaos inside. His anguished cries faded into the storm's embrace, leaving him alone in the wild, primal beauty of the tempest.

CHAPTER
29

Thad's gaze followed the stormy exit of the princess, her elegant gown swirling behind her like a tempest. His sharp eyes tracked the prince as he attempted to follow but returned with a storm cloud of his own. Prince Barrow, typically the picture of regal confidence, now exuded a simmering frustration.

Barrow's stride was forceful, his shoulders tense as he navigated the vast expanse of the great hall. The hall, a grand testament to opulence, boasted towering arches and walls adorned with tapestries depicting the rich history of the realm. Chandeliers cast a soft, golden glow over the polished marble floor, but tonight, their light did little to warm the chill in the air.

Stopping before a servant who held out a goblet of deep red wine, Barrow accepted it with a curt nod. Thad, lingering close by, caught the fleeting scent of the prince's cologne—a heady mix of cedar and musk—an aroma that spoke of both elegance and vitality.

Prince Barrow was indeed a striking figure. Tall and broad-shouldered, he cut an imposing silhouette against the backdrop of the hall. His blonde hair, styled in an effortless yet sophisticated manner, framed a face that was both youthful and commanding. There was a vigor in his eyes, a fire that reminded Thad of the best qualities of his father—qualities that clearly captivated Brendolyn.

As Barrow took a deep draught from his goblet, Thad couldn't help but notice the contrast between the prince's robust exterior and the turmoil that clouded his gaze. Thad's own feelings were a swirl of complex emotions. He saw why Brendolyn was drawn to Barrow: the prince's presence was magnetic, his charisma undeniable. Yet, Thad's own discontent simmered just below the surface. He was acutely aware of the prince's imperfections, the flaws hidden behind his polished exterior.

Thad's attention returned to Barrow, who was now engaged in a terse conversation with a few courtiers. The prince's gestures were animated, but his words carried a sharp edge. His frustration was palpable, a stark contrast to the usually graceful and composed demeanor he presented to the public.

Thad leaned in closer, his senses sharpened by the proximity. The sound of laughter and music from the banquet seemed distant and hollow, a stark contrast to the inner turbulence of the prince and the echoing silence of the hall. The grandeur of the setting, with its gilded accents and intricate details, seemed almost to mock the emotional storm unfolding within its confines.

As Barrow's eyes flickered towards Thad, the prince's usual charm was overshadowed by a hint of vulnerability. Thad, with his keen perception, recognized the subtle shift. There was more to the prince's demeanor than mere irritation; it was the weight of responsibility and unspoken conflict that now settled upon his shoulders. The hall, with its lavish decor and high ceilings, felt suddenly oppressive, as if the grandeur itself were bearing witness to the prince's unvoiced struggles. Being betrothed to a woman he held no interest in.

Thad, standing on the periphery, took a deep breath. The scent of the cologne, the distant strains of music, and the sight of Barrow's troubled expression all converged into a moment of profound realization.

"Women." Thad's smirk lingered as he watched Prince Barrow, the echoes of laughter and clinking glasses from the grand hall fading into the background. Standing beside the prince so close he could see the sparkle in his blue eyes.

Barrow's scowl cut through the festive atmosphere like a blade. "I do not believe we have been introduced. Take care how you speak of the royal family of Corad."

Thad's eyes twinkled with a mixture of mischief and challenge as he raised his glass. "Yes, forgive me. I meant no offense, Your Majesty."

Barrow's irritation was evident as he walked the length of the hall with purposeful strides, the polished marble floor echoing with each step. Thad, undeterred, matched his pace until they reached a tall window overlooking the castle gardens, where the night was alive with the soft glow of moonlight and the distant hum of magickal creatures.

Barrow leaned against the window frame, his expression darkening as he took a long drink from his glass. The garden below was a maze of intricate pathways and lush flora, illuminated by bioluminescent flowers that bathed the scene in an ethereal light.

"Women are better when they do not make you love them," Barrow muttered, his voice tinged with bitterness. He glared out at the garden, as if seeking solace in its serene beauty.

Thad raised an eyebrow, his gaze shifting to the prince's nearly empty goblet. "You have made a great alliance. Princess Lisetta is remarkable—"

Barrow cut him off with a dismissive snort. "Lisetta is spoiled, but she is the exact woman to be a great queen. At least that is what my father and his council have determined."

"And Brendolyn?" Thad's voice held an edge of restrained jealousy, a pang of emotion that flared to life at the mention of her name.

Barrow's face darkened, his eyes shifting as he searched the darkened landscape below. "She is goodness itself." His tone, however, quickly soured. "Ehnarea bless me, I married her in secret."

Thad's heart raced, his skin prickling with a mix of surprise. The prince, now visibly drunk, was divulging secrets he shouldn't. "You married her?"

Barrow's laughter was bitter, a hollow sound. "I had her for a night...it was perfection itself. Now, I shall share my bed with her sister." He tossed back the remainder of his drink with a careless flourish.

Thad struggled to process the revelation, the weight of Barrow's words sinking in amidst the revelry of the hall. He saw the prince's glossy eyes, his unsteady movements, and realized the gravity of what was being confessed.

"What did you say your name was?" Barrow's gaze snapped back to Thad, his scrutiny sharp despite the alcohol clouding his judgment.

"Thaddeus," Thad replied smoothly, though his attention was momentarily drawn to the figure of Leuthere moving through the crowd.

Barrow sighed heavily, the frustration evident in his voice. "Never fall in love with a woman, Thaddeus. They shall only break your heart."

Thad's smile remained, though it was tinged with a trace of sadness. "Oh, I never do that." He reached out to gently take the prince's cup, their hands brushing briefly. Thad's gaze lingered on Barrow's striking blue eyes, taking in the handsome features marred by inebriation. "You should go to bed, Your Majesty. You're drunk."

Barrow's expression was a mix of defiance and weariness. "I am not drunk."

Thad tilted the cup, holding it up to catch the light. "Three glasses of elvish wine...you must be a brave man."

As Thad's eyes flicked towards the guard beyond the crowd, a subtle shift in the atmosphere alerted him to the need for caution. With a graceful nod, he excused himself from the conversation, his smile masking the urgency beneath.

Barrow watched him go, a touch of confusion in his gaze, but too weary to protest.

Thad slipped away into the depths of the hall.

CHAPTER
30

Entering through the kitchens, Pavan smiled sheepishly at the scullery maid, when the young elf jumped at his entrance. She was attending to the large pots, where they cook many of the meals they serve. She was alone and at once, Pavan stepped back.

"Forgive me." He bowed, shifting himself to exit through the door.

"Wait." Her timid voice was urgent.

Pavan stopped, looking back, the maid was standing, pointing at Pavan's feet. Her face pale and Pavan realized his boots tracked in mud.

"Oh." Pavan blushed. His clothing dripping, his boots muddy and leaving a trail along the stone floor. At once, he locks eyes with the maid.

"Forgive me, sir, but I cannot get the scuff again. Madam would not like mud tracked through her kitchen…" The maid spoke calmly, eyeing Pavan warily.

He quickly removed his boots. Glancing up at the maid who watched him closely. Setting them aside, Pavan stood to shift himself out of his outer jacket, and doublet that were soaked through and draping the dripping garments over the back of a chair. Looking to the maid, who was astonished, blushing faintly.

"T-thank you," she stammered, eyeing Pavan.

Curtsying in a gentle manner, shifting herself to take the jacket and boots, quickly depositing them into the basin at the counter. Turning her attentions to the floor, waving her hand in a delicate manner, Pavan watched the water dribble up from the stone, floating in little bubbles that bounced and blobbed, the maid quickly sending them into the basin as well, leaving no trace of water to be found.

Pavan smiled. "I suppose your magick does not apply to dripping hair?"

The maid blushed, shaking her head, but hurried to a cabinet on the opposite wall, bringing him a linen towel from within. Pavan smirked, accepting the offering.

"Thank you."

He was glad of the towel, blotting at his damp hair, leaving the kitchens with the maid's promise of returning his jacket and boots when they had dried. Pavan cared little for the items he left in her care, there were others in his room, more suited to his own style, but for now, he walked the darkened corridors in solitude. Basking in the chill that ran through him with every step on the cold floor.

Magick fizzled, drawing his attention up, there was something in the air. Something dangerous nagging in his gut. Pavan slinked, holding the linen towel so tight in each hand he began to feel the material rip. So familiar was the tang on his tongue, the shift within him. It took Pavan a long moment to realize the danger.

"Thad," he whispered, his heart skipping a beat.

Dropping the towel, discarding it as he ran the length of the long corridor, bounding up the stone steps to the upper levels. Searching each opened door, eyeing every darkened corner, until he stopped at the door held slightly ajar. Slipping through, without a sound, into the darkened library.

He began to hear voices—the slithering, shifting voice of Simeon Bannon. Pavan's heart quickened. Quieting his magick with a cold shutter, Pavan slunk around the wall, listening intently to the sound of his father's voice.

"Have you found him, Leuthere?" Bannon spoke low, a shift in his voice that was unlike Pavan had heard before.

A second voice, from the man to whom Lord Bannon spoke was smooth, like liquid. "Not yet, my lord...but he cannot hide from us for long."

Pavan's skin shivered, all the hairs raising on his arms, looking along the darkened shelves. Magick prickled under his skin, familiar magick was near. At once, Pavan crouched, hiding himself away as he rounded towards it.

Lord Bannon spoke fervently. "You must return to Denorn, Leuthere...wait for my letter, should your assistance be needed..." Pavan heard the hushed tones grow fainter, drawing closer to the magick that was nearby.

The sound of heavy footfalls echoed down the stone corridor, marking the departure of Sir Leuthere. The silence that followed was thick and unsettling, leaving Lord Bannon alone in the dimly lit hallway. Pavan, hidden in the shadows, felt a cold shiver run down his spine, the prickling sensation of dark magick brushing against his senses. He caught sight of a familiar figure lurking in the gloom. Without a second thought, he lunged forward, clamping his hand tightly over the figure's mouth and gripping the wrist that held a dagger poised for an attack.

Thad struggled against Pavan's iron hold, his movements frantic and desperate. But Pavan's grip was unyielding, his muscles coiled with tension as he forced the man into stillness. They both froze as Lord Bannon's gaze swept over the darkened alcove where they hid, the nobleman's eyes narrowing as if sensing something amiss. Pavan held his breath, his heart pounding in his ears, praying that the shadows would keep them concealed.

After what felt like an eternity, Lord Bannon's attention drifted away, and he slithered down the corridor, disappearing into the darkness. The moment he was gone, Pavan wasted no time. He dragged Thad backward, pushing through a nearby door and shutting it firmly behind them. They found themselves in a small, claustrophobic room tucked away just off the library, the air thick with the scent of aged parchment and dust.

Thad thrashed violently, his panic driving him to fight with all his strength but Pavan held him fast, his grip as unyielding as steel. "Be still, Thad," Pavan hissed, his voice a low growl.

Thad was strong, elbowing Pavan in the gut to wiggle away.

"How dare you," Thad spat, turning, with a great kick, landing the blow in Pavan's stomach.

Pavan stumbled, gasping at the force, but kept his footing. Glaring at Thad, who's orange eyes shone with malice, contempt.

"I have saved your life, Thad...you cannot kill Bannon," Pavan hissed, raking his dark locks out of his face.

Thad scoffed. "I would have taken off that old fucks head."

Pavan gripped Thad's jacket front, slamming him back against the wall with an audible thud. "He would have killed you, Thad."

Thad struggled. "Get your hands off me."

With his strength, Thad punched Pavan, leaving a mark on the edge of his cheek. Pavan swore, dropping Thad, staggering back against the blow.

"Do you not understand what he has done to my life. He has caused it all, Pavan," Thad hissed, tears slithering down his cheek, clenching his hands into fists.

Pavan ignored the ringing in his ears, calming the magick that began to race in his heart, prickling the expanse of his skin, glaring up at Thad.

"Don't be a fool." He shook, staggering closer to Thad, ignoring his own danger of magick overwhelming him and eying the faie who was heightened with rage.

Thad scoffed. "Protecting your *father*?"

Pavan shook. "He was that once, but no longer. I am not ignorant of what he has done, Thad. I have known the destruction he is capable of committing."

Thad grimaced. "Charles was there with my master. He took advantage of the resources he had...he was there..."

Something in Pavan was dark, feeling the anguish in the faie, drawing nearer. Knowing what Thad had been through, seeing through the faie's eyes, and feeling the moments of pain between them.

"I know, Thad..." Pavan touched the smooth fabric of Thad's tunic.

"I have to kill him, Pavan." Thad was trembling. "To end the torment."

Pavan leaned in close, his breath warm against Thad's skin, the anguish and sorrow he felt creeping toward him like a dark tide. His fingers traced the curve of Thad's cheek, feeling the blood pulse beneath his touch, alive and vibrant. He knew he should pull away, but the connection between them was too strong, too intoxicating. His hand slid down to caress the faie's neck, his lips brushing against Thad's in a tender, almost reverent kiss.

"He is Ehlfern, Thad," Pavan whispered against his lips, his voice tinged with a sorrowful resignation. "A blade will not kill him." He pressed Thad back against the wall, their bodies aligning, the warmth of Thad's trembling frame seeping into his own. Pavan's breath shuddered as he continued, "His magick is stronger than mine. If you attempt this assassination, it will be your life that is forfeit...and I cannot allow that."

Pavan kissed Thad's cheek, feeling the magick within him swirl and claw its way to the surface. It pulsed in his belly, dark and demanding, as he raised his hand to Thad's throat, his senses attuned to the thickening blood just beneath the surface. Desire coiled tightly within him, a potent mix of need and protectiveness.

"Thad," he murmured, his voice a low, guttural sound. Thad whimpered in response, and Pavan could feel the fear and vulnerability in that small sound. "It is agony, knowing it was my own father who caused you such pain." Pavan's magick shifted, reaching out instinctively as he scraped his teeth over the stubble of Thad's jaw, inhaling the scent of citrus that clung to him. "I want to rip his heart out, to devour his soul...Thad, for you, I would burn down the world for the torment he's caused."

Thad was trembling now, his breath coming in soft, uneven gasps, and Pavan could feel the sharp edge of desire cutting through his restraint. He tightened his grip on Thad's throat, pulling him closer, his arm wrapping around the faie's waist as if anchoring them both in the storm of emotions.

"Pavan," Thad whispered, his voice a fragile thread. "You must stop."

But Pavan only chuckled softly, a dark sound that vibrated against Thad's skin. He tightened his hold even more, a fierce protectiveness mingling with his need. "Do not threaten your own life again, Thad," he warned, his tone both tender and possessive. "He will devour you...to take away your pain."

The magick within Pavan burned hotter, desire twisting through him as he pressed his thumb into the pulse point of Thad's throat, feeling the quickening beat beneath his touch. Thad gasped softly, the sound sending a shiver of satisfaction through Pavan as he leaned in closer, his lips brushing over Thad's skin, claiming him in this moment of raw, undeniable connection.

Cold, sharp pain was sudden.

Pavan's eyes snapped open, and he gasped as the reality of what had just happened hit him with brutal clarity. He took a step back, staring into Thad's wild orange eyes, now brimming with tears. Pavan felt a sudden, searing pain in his side. He looked down, his breath catching as he saw the hilt of a bone-handled dagger protruding from between his bottom ribs. The blade was buried deep, and his magick flared in sharp agitation around it.

"I'm sorry," Thad whimpered, his voice breaking as he clung to Pavan, their bodies trembling in unison. Pavan could see the fear and regret in Thad's eyes, but the pain radiating from the wound demanded his attention. He stumbled back, trying to steady himself as the world seemed to tilt around him.

"Thad..." Pavan hissed through gritted teeth, blinking rapidly as a ringing began to fill his ears. His hand fell away from Thad, and he could feel the warmth of his own blood seeping through his tunic. "It's alright...I—"

He staggered against a nearby chair, the sound of it scraping loudly against the floor. Pavan breathed hard, fighting against the wave of lightheadedness that threatened to overwhelm him. His magick, usually a steady pulse beneath his skin, was now surging wildly, trying to redirect itself to the wound, agitated by the foreign object lodged in his flesh.

Thad was at his side in an instant, his hands moving frantically over the blood that dripped down Pavan's leg. Pavan gasped, his knees buckling as he collapsed to the floor.

"Leave it," Pavan ground out through clenched teeth, his voice raw with pain.

Tears streamed down Thad's face as he leaned over Pavan, his hands trembling uncontrollably. "I must remove the dagger so you can heal the wound..."

But Pavan was already shaking his head, his expression grim. "If you remove it, I cannot heal my wound and contain my magick...I will bleed out."

Thad's terror was palpable, his hands hovering uncertainty over Pavan's injury. He was trembling, caught between desperation and fear. Blood seeping into the fine silk of Thad's shirt.

Pavan reached up, grasping Thad's cheeks with both hands, forcing the faie to focus on him. He looked deep into Thad's orange eyes, trying to steady the chaos swirling between them. "You must get Lahrs...He can help me contain my magick while you heal the wound..."

Thad hesitated, his breath hitching in his throat, but Pavan leaned forward, pressing a desperate kiss to his lips. He could taste the salt of Thad's tears, but soon the bitter tang of his own blood followed, sharp and metallic. Pavan gasped, pulling back, the effort sending another jolt of pain through his side.

"Find him, quickly," Pavan urged, his voice barely above a whisper as he fought to hold himself together, to stay conscious. His grip on Thad's cheeks faltered, but his gaze remained steady, filled with a mixture of urgency and determination. He knew that time was running out.

Thad moved through the unfamiliar corridor, each step calculated to avoid detection as he followed the vague directions Pavan had given him. His heart pounded in his chest, the urgency of the situation driving him forward. It was late, and the castle had long since quieted. When he finally reached the door, he hesitated only for a moment before knocking lightly, hoping against hope that Lahrs, known for his late-night reading habits, would still be awake.

The door creaked open, and to Thad's surprise, it wasn't Lahrs who greeted him, but a young woman with dark hair cascading over her shoulders—Princess Brendolyn. Thad's cheeks flushed with embarrassment as he quickly looked down, not expecting to encounter her here.

"Forgive me, princess," he stammered, his voice barely above a whisper. "I was looking for Lahrs...Sir Lahrs."

For a moment, she seemed as surprised as he was, but then a gentle smile crossed her lips. "Lahrs is in the second door to the right, not left..." Her voice was calm, almost soothing, and Thad nodded gratefully, turning to correct his mistake.

He raised his hand to knock again but froze as he noticed the blood staining his skin. The sight of it brought the reality of the situation crashing down on him once more. He gulped, trying to steady his nerves.

"Are you injured?" Brendolyn's voice, now tinged with concern, cut through his thoughts. She stepped into the corridor, her eyes wide with worry.

Thad quickly wiped his hand on his jacket, trying to erase the evidence. "I'm—I need to speak to Lahrs..." He turned back to the correct door just as it opened, revealing Lahrs standing there, his expression one of bemused concern.

"Thad?" Lahrs asked, his gaze sweeping over Thad's disheveled appearance.

Thad flushed again, acutely aware of the princess's presence behind him. But the urgency of Pavan's situation pushed him to speak. "It's Pavan...he's hurt."

Behind him, Brendolyn gasped, the recent trauma of her father's poisoning still fresh in her mind. The mention of Pavan's injury sent a ripple of anxiety through her, but Lahrs, ever composed, immediately became serious.

"I can explain on the way," Thad continued, his voice firm as he tried to convey the gravity of the situation. "He cannot heal his own injury and control his magick at the same time."

Without hesitation, Lahrs stepped out of his room, his focus shifting entirely to the task at hand. He turned to Brendolyn, his tone commanding in a way that left no room for argument. "Stay."

The princess did not follow as Lahrs and Thad hurried away, their footsteps echoing softly through the dimly lit corridor. Thad led them down stone steps and through darkened halls, the weight of his earlier actions pressing heavily on his shoulders. As they moved, Thad explained in a breathless whisper what had transpired.

When they finally reached the library, Lahrs halted abruptly, his gaze hardening as he turned to Thad. "Thad, of all your follies..."

Thad's face burned with shame. "I know it was wrong, Lahrs...but Pavan's magick came on so suddenly, it was dark...I couldn't think..."

Lahrs didn't respond, his focus shifting back to the task at hand. They pressed on, entering the passage that led to the chamber where Thad had left Pavan. As they rounded a large shelf, Thad's breath caught in his throat.

Pavan sat slumped in a chaise, blood dripping steadily onto the floor, the deep red pooling beneath him. The trail of blood leading from the overturned chair told the story of his struggle to reach this spot. His face was pale, beads of sweat dotting his forehead as he fought to maintain control over his wild magick.

Lahrs didn't waste a moment. He quickly crossed the room, kneeling beside Pavan and placing a hand over the wound. The elf's face tightened with concentration as he began to channel his own magick, stabilizing the chaotic energy that threatened to overwhelm Pavan. Thad stood back, helpless but watching with wide, anxious eyes, praying silently for Pavan's survival.

Lahrs knelt in front of Pavan, his expression tight with concern as he assessed the diminished, vacant look in his friend's eyes. Pavan was still breathing, but his skin was ashen, and a thin trickle of blood ran from the corner of his mouth. Gently, Lahrs touched Pavan's face, trying to draw his focus.

"Pavan," Lahrs spoke softly, his voice steady and calm. Pavan blinked slowly, his gaze drifting down to meet Lahrs'.

Thad, his heart pounding with fear and regret, knelt beside them. "I got him as fast as I could," he whispered urgently. "Tell me it's not too late."

Pavan's bright green eyes flickered, and with a bloodied hand, he reached up to caress Thad's cheek, his touch weak but filled with a strange tenderness. His chest heaved with effort as he took in a labored, pained breath.

"It is not easy to kill me, Thad..." Pavan's voice was a strained rasp, but he managed a faint, reassuring smile.

Lahrs sat up straighter, his face determined. "We must remove the dagger. Thad, you'll close the wound, and I'll be here to contain the magick's recoil. Can you do that, Pavan?"

Pavan nodded firmly, though his strength was clearly waning. Thad repositioned himself, his hands trembling as he prepared to extract the dagger. One hand hovered over the hilt, the other pressed down on Pavan's blood-soaked tunic. The sheer amount of blood made Thad's heart race with dread, and tears welled up in his eyes, blurring his vision. This was his doing, his mistake, and the guilt gnawed at him relentlessly.

"Thad..." Pavan's whisper cut through the haze of Thad's emotions, drawing his gaze upward. Those unnaturally green eyes were locked onto his, filled with a pain that was almost unbearable to witness. Yet, despite the agony, Pavan managed to reach up again, wiping away Thad's tears with a gentleness that made Thad's chest ache.

"It will be alright," Pavan murmured, forcing a smile despite his pain. He then turned his gaze to Lahrs and gave a curt nod, signaling that he was ready.

"Remove the dagger, Thad," Lahrs instructed, his voice steady and commanding.

Taking a deep breath, Thad gripped the handle tightly and yanked the lodged weapon free. Blood immediately poured from the wound, darkened and thick with the influence of corrupted magick. Thad's hand quickly moved to cover the wound, his magick surging beneath his fingertips as he worked to slow the blood flow. His other hand clamped down on Pavan's thigh, trying to keep him still as the healing process began.

As Thad worked, Lahrs held Pavan down, his voice rising as he vocalized the enchantment they both knew well. The room filled with the sound of their combined efforts—Lahrs' commanding incantations, Pavan's agonized groans, and Thad's ragged breathing as he poured every ounce of energy into closing the wound.

"Almost there," Thad winced, his arms trembling from the strain. The blood flow had slowed, but he needed to stitch the skin back together as quickly as possible. Every groan from Pavan was like a dagger to his own heart, and the man's thrashing made the task even more difficult.

Suddenly, Pavan's body surged with a violent burst of magick, pushing Lahrs back with incredible force. Thad barely had time to react before Pavan's hand shot out, seizing him by the throat and lifting him off the ground. The faie struggled, but the magick had drained his strength, leaving him helpless in Pavan's relentless grip.

"Pavan, stop..." Lahrs pleaded, trying to pry Pavan's hand from Thad's throat. But Pavan's eyes had shifted, the green replaced by a terrifying white as the magick took full control. Runes began to etch themselves across Pavan's skin, glowing with an ominous light as his power threatened to consume him.

Thad's vision began to blur as he gasped for air, his lungs burning, his fingers clawing desperately at Pavan's hands. Just as the world started to fade, Lahrs acted, punching Pavan hard across the face. The impact broke the spell, and Thad crumpled to the ground, gasping for breath.

Pavan staggered back, his eyes wide with horror as they returned to their normal green. Tears streamed down his face as he realized what he had done. "Thad..." he breathed, his voice breaking with anguish.

Thad, still trembling from the near-death experience, struggled to his feet, ready to embrace Pavan and reassure him. But Pavan stiffened, recoiling as if afraid to cause more harm. Thad's heart ached as he saw the torment in Pavan's eyes, but there was nothing he could do.

Lahrs, breathing heavily from the exertion, spoke with quiet authority. "We should clean this up and get you to your chamber, Thad." He looked pointedly at the faie, but Thad couldn't tear his gaze away from Pavan, who now stood trembling, unable to meet his eyes.

"Right," Thad murmured, finally looking down at the blood on his hands, the full weight of what had happened settling heavily on his shoulders.

As Thad and Pavan made their way back to the bedchamber, the silence between them was thick with unspoken words and lingering tension. Thad's footsteps were slow, each one dragging as if the weight of what had just transpired was too much to bear. The blood on his hands had dried to a dark crust, but he couldn't shake the feeling of it, couldn't forget the sensation of Pavan's hand around his throat.

Pavan walked beside him, his expression a mask. He kept his distance, hesitant to reach out as if to fear of causing Thad more pain. Every glance he stole in Thad's direction only deepened the ache in his chest, a gnawing guilt that he didn't know how to soothe.

When they reached the chamber, Pavan pushed the door open gently, standing aside to let Thad enter first. The faie moved mechanically, his movements stiff and reluctant as he stepped into the room. Pavan followed, closing the door softly behind them, the quiet click of the latch sounding louder than it should have in the stillness.

Thad hesitated in the middle of the room, his eyes distant as he stared at the floor. He didn't know where to go, didn't know what to do with himself. The bed, with its soft, inviting linens, suddenly felt like a distant island he couldn't reach.

Pavan watched him, his heart heavy with the need to comfort Thad but unsure how to bridge the chasm that had opened between them. He stepped closer, but not too close, his voice gentle and low as he finally broke the silence.

"Thad..." Pavan began, his tone filled with an earnest tenderness.

Thad turned his head slightly, just enough to acknowledge Pavan's words, but he didn't move. His hands twitched at his sides, the remnants of blood making his skin feel tight and uncomfortable. His throat was still sore, the memory of Pavan's grip fresh and raw. Feeling the blood oozing between his fingers as he had pressed into the wound. Glancing up at the gaping hole in Pavan's tunic, the blood soaked material heavy with drying blood a deep red.

Pavan took a careful step forward. "I didn't mean to hurt you," he said, his voice trembling with the weight of his remorse. "I would never—"

"I know," Thad interrupted quietly, his voice almost too soft to hear. He finally looked up, meeting Pavan's gaze with eyes that were dark and troubled. "I know you didn't mean to. It's not...it's not your fault."

But despite his words, Thad's body remained tense, his posture rigid. He didn't reach out to Pavan, didn't close the distance between them. Pavan's heart sank, the rejection subtle but clear.

Pavan took another step forward, his hands itching to pull Thad into his arms, to hold him and assure him that everything would be alright. But he stopped himself, sensing Thad's unease. Instead, he spoke softly, trying to reach past the barriers that had sprung up between them.

"I wish I could take it all back," Pavan murmured. "The dagger, the magick...everything. I hate seeing you like this, Thad, *mo ghrá*."

Thad's eyes softened, but there was still a guardedness in his expression. He looked away, his voice distant as he replied, "It's just...it was too much, too fast. Everything that happened...I didn't think. I didn't realize what I was doing."

Pavan shook his head, his expression pained. "You were scared. I understand that. But I don't want you to be afraid of me. Not after everything we've been through together."

Thad finally sat down on the edge of the bed, his hands clasped tightly in his lap. He didn't look at Pavan, his gaze fixed on the floor. "I'm not afraid of you, Pavan. I'm afraid of what this could mean...What might happen if we lose control again."

Pavan knelt in front of him, careful to keep a respectful distance. He reached out slowly, his hand hovering near Thad's knee, but he didn't touch him, waiting for permission. "We won't let it happen again," Pavan promised, his voice filled with quiet determination. "I'll do everything in my power to protect you, to protect us. But I can't do that if you push me away."

Thad's breath hitched, and he finally looked down at Pavan, his eyes glistening with unshed tears. He wanted to believe him, wanted to reach out and take the comfort Pavan was offering. But the fear lingered, a shadow that wouldn't easily be dispelled.

Slowly, almost hesitantly, Thad placed his hand over Pavan's, the touch tentative but meaningful. "I'm not pushing you away," he said, his voice shaking slightly. "I just...I need time. I need to process everything."

Pavan nodded, his hand gently turning to grip Thad's in return, offering what comfort he could. "Take all the time you need," he whispered, his voice thick with emotion. "I'm not going anywhere."

They stayed like that for a long moment, the silence between them no longer heavy with tension but filled with a quiet understanding. Pavan didn't push, didn't ask for more than Thad was ready to give. He simply stayed close, offering his presence, his support, and the promise that he would be there. Thad helped Pavan change, throwing the bloodied garments into the fire. Dressed in clean linens, Thad lay beside Pavan in the large bed. Entwining their legs as they clung together in the darkness, letting the cool blue of the moon shimmer across their skin.

Eventually, Thad sighed, his body relaxing slightly as he let go of some of the fear that had gripped him. He leaned forward, resting his forehead against Pavan's, their breaths mingling in the stillness of the room.

"*Mo ghrá*," Thad whispered, his voice barely audible.

Pavan smiled softly, his eyes closing as he savored the closeness. "I love you..."

Thad's heart clenched as he felt the steady rise and fall of Pavan's chest against his own, the larger man finally succumbing to the deep pull of sleep. Pavan's exhaustion was palpable, his breath warm against Thad's neck, and for a moment, Thad could almost convince himself that everything was fine, that they were safe, that nothing had changed.

But as the room grew quieter, the weight of what had happened began to settle in Thad's mind. The pain he'd pushed aside, the fear he'd buried deep, now crept back, insidious and cold. He held Pavan close, not daring to move, as if releasing him would unravel the fragile peace they'd found in these few moments.

Thad's thoughts churned as he cradled Pavan against his chest. The warmth of the man he loved, now asleep and vulnerable, did little to ease the storm inside him. His hands, though clean of blood, trembled as if stained by guilt. The memory of Princess Brendolyn's innocent eyes and trembling voice clawed at him, stirring a venomous hatred in his heart.

How could she, untouched by heartache, have any claim to Pavan's heart? The thought gnawed at him, coiling his emotions into a knot of bitterness. He resented her purity and the undeserved ease with which she could have Pavan's attention. A surge of revulsion welled up, not just towards her, but towards himself—towards the weakness that made him feel this way, and the fear that crept into his soul as he held Pavan.

The softness of Pavan's breath against his chest should have been comforting, but it only deepened Thad's inner turmoil. The faie swallowed hard, trying to keep the bile of jealousy and self-loathing from rising too high. He hated that stupid girl, hated her innocence, her beauty. She didn't deserve the heart of Pavan, not like he did. Yet here he was, trembling with the fear of losing what he held so dear, and hating himself for it.

Slipping from the warmth, Thad stepped out into the corridor. Heart shadowed by jealousy, he walked the moonlit corridors, hoping to ease his thoughts.

CHAPTER

31

Brendolyn jumped at the thunder, the storm erupted suddenly.

Curling herself closer into the comforts of her warm bed, the light of the dying fire made Brendolyn shiver as it cast unnatural shadows over the walls. It had been hours, and still Lahrs had not returned, worry striking her at every thought. First, seeing Thad who had come so urgently, with blood on his hands, wanting Lahrs to help him.

She had never seen Lahrs so urgent, his command to her to stay was so forceful, Brendolyn became frightened. Knowing something to be wrong, a force of agony residing deep within her ached. Brendolyn pressed at her side, but the pain remained.

Finally, Brendolyn stood, throwing aside the blankets to hurry to the door. On a whim she unlatched it, seeing Lahrs just as the elf reached the door to his chambers. Brendolyn gasped.

There was so much blood.

"Lahrs." She hurried to follow him, eased to find the elf did not stop her, she watched him drag his tall frame across the room. Pouring himself a glass of water before raising a shaking hand to gulp it down. He was disquieted, Brendolyn could feel despair and unease.

Brendolyn's thoughts spiraled as she raced through the dim corridors, her mind fixated on the faie who had come to collect Lahrs. Had they reached Pavan in time? Or had they been too late? A tight, icy coil of panic constricted her chest, forcing her to move faster, her heart hammering with dread.

"Pavan—is he alive?" she demanded, her voice trembling with urgency.

Lahrs looked up slowly, his gaze distant as if just now realizing her presence. His usually sharp grey eyes seemed dulled by exhaustion. "You should be asleep," he murmured, shaking his head as he turned back to the task at hand. He poured water into the basin, the clear liquid instantly darkening with the crimson of blood as he dipped his hands into it.

The metallic scent of blood hung heavily in the air, making Brendolyn's stomach twist in revulsion. Her eyes flickered over the ruined silk that clung to Lahrs, the fabric soaked in blood. She stepped forward, her hands trembling as she reached to unlace his tunic, her fingers moving with a desperate urgency.

"I cannot sleep," she whispered, her voice cracking as she met his weary gaze. "Not until I know Pavan is alive."

Lahrs hesitated, then nodded. "He is alive," he confirmed, his voice barely above a whisper, laced with exhaustion.

Relief surged through her, but it was tempered by the sight of the elf before her. She quickly finished unlacing his tunic, pulling away the blood-soaked fabric and tossing it into the fire. The flames hissed and sputtered as the wet garments began to burn, a slow curl of smoke rising as the fire consumed them.

"Go to bed, Bren," Lahrs urged softly, his voice gentle but firm. He pulled a clean tunic over his head, the simple motion seeming to drain the last of his strength. He slumped into a nearby chair, his shoulders sagging under the weight of unseen burdens.

But Brendolyn couldn't leave him like this. She knelt before him, placing her hands gently on his knees. "You're weary," she whispered, her voice filled with concern. Lahrs, who was always so strong, now looked fragile, and it terrified her.

Lahrs closed his eyes briefly, then placed a hand on her head, his touch light but comforting. When he opened his eyes again, he offered her a faint, tired smile. Brendolyn's heart ached at the sight. She took his hand, kissing it gently and pressing it to her cheek, drawing comfort from the warmth of his skin.

"I need rest," Lahrs said softly, his voice laced with exhaustion.

Brendolyn nodded, her heart heavy. "Let me sing for you, please?" she asked, her voice trembling with emotion.

Lahrs smiled again, this time a bit more warmly. "Of course," he whispered.

Brendolyn began to sing, her voice soft and melodic, a lullaby woven with ancient magick that filled the room with warmth and light. As she sang, she watched Lahrs' eyes flutter shut, his breathing steadying as the tension slowly melted from his body. She continued, her song a soothing balm for both their souls, until at last, Lahrs drifted into a peaceful sleep. Her voice drifted quiet, bathing the room in tranquil silence.

"Thank you, Bren..." His voice was soft.

Brendolyn smiled, leaning up to push back errant hairs from the elf's face. His gray eyes looked up, meeting hers.

"Tell me what happened, please?" she begged.

He sighed, heavily. "I cannot, Bren."

She would not relent, grasping his hand hard. "Please Lahrs, what has happened to him? Do not keep me in the dark about this...not this. Pavan is in danger, isn't he?"

There was heartbreak, Lahrs was restricting his emotions, guarding himself from her senses. Brendolyn felt the angry tears begin, vengeful trailing down her cheeks.

"His magick is strong...there is so much to explain, but I cannot tell you too much. Pavan is in danger, you are very perceptive...so resilient." Lahrs began to drift, his body slumped, his eyes drooping as he began to fight sleep.

Brendolyn shook his arm, "Lahrs, what must be done...what can I do?"

Lahrs grimaced, shaking his head. "So much to be done."

She straightened, touching Lahrs' cheek. "Tell me, what can I do for Pavan...what must be done?"

"He must leave Jorn, he must not remain here..."

Beaumont jolted awake, his breath ragged and uneven. The nightmare that had clawed its way into his slumber lingered at the edge of his consciousness—a monstrous wolt with glistening, dripping fangs seemed poised to consume him whole, devouring not just his flesh but his very soul. Its eyes burned like molten amber, searing into him with an intent that transcended hunger, a wrathful presence that made his pulse hammer in his ears. Shadows curled and stretched around the beast, whispering sinister secrets as it prowled closer, its breath a foul stench of decay and malice.

Even as he woke, gasping for air, the phantom pain of its jagged teeth sinking into his chest remained, an ache that reached beyond his body and into the fragile threads of his spirit.

He sat upright in bed, the shadows of the room pressing in like a suffocating fog. His chest heaved with each breath as he pushed back the dark, tangled locks of hair that clung to his damp forehead. The sweat on his skin had begun to cool, leaving a shiver in its wake. Beaumont's pulse thundered in his ears, the remnants of the dream still clawing at the fringes of his mind.

He swung his legs over the side of the bed, his bare feet touching the cold, stone floor of the chamber. The room was dimly lit by the flickering glow of a single lantern, casting long, wavering shadows across the walls. The furnishings—a grandiose, yet somber array of dark wood and rich fabrics—seemed to close in on him, the silence amplifying the echo of his racing heartbeat.

Beaumont ran a hand over his face, trying to ground himself in the present. Weighted by the nightmare, with its feral terror, felt all too real, leaving an uneasy tension in his limbs. He reached for the nearby goblet of water, his hand trembling slightly as he took a deep sip. The cool liquid did little to dispel the sense of dread that clung to him like a second skin.

His royal chamber, once a sanctuary of solitude, now seemed a realm of shadows and whispers. Beaumont's eyes darted to the window, it was far from morning yet. Returning to bed, he leaned back against the dampened pillows, trying to shake off the lingering fear, but the sensation of those phantom fangs remained, a grim reminder of the terror that had stolen him from the safety of his dreams.

"Are you alright?" a welcomed voice calmed him.

Turning, Beaumont smiled down at the sleeping elf beside him, Rhys, whose presence was a balm against the nightmare's chill. Beaumont settled back onto the bed, his heartbeat gradually slowing as the weight of his panic began to lift.

"It was just a dream," he mumbled, his voice rough with residual unease.

Rhys stirred, his sleepiness quickly replaced by a furrowed brow and an expression of concern that made his delicate features seem even more striking. "You have never dreamt before," he said softly, his tone edged with quiet worry.

Beaumont chuckled, though it sounded hollow. "Yes, you're right..." His smile faltered as guilt gnawed at the edges of his mind. Shutting his eyes, he drew in a shallow breath, willing himself to let go of the dark fragments still clinging to him.

When he opened them again, Rhys's calloused hands were on his cheek, grounding him. The touch was warm and steady, a reminder that he wasn't alone.

"Monty," Rhys murmured, his voice just above a whisper

The chamber was dimly lit, shadows flickering against the stone walls as the fire in the hearth struggled to keep its warmth. The weight of the world seemed to press down on Beaumont, the very air thick with the presence of ancient magick. It pulsed faintly around him, a malevolent force that had been gnawing at his soul for years, slowly eating away at his strength, his spirit. Every breath was a battle, every heartbeat a reminder of the curse that festered within him.

As Beaumont spoke, his voice was laced with a grim acceptance, the words heavy with the burden he had carried for so long. "I am dying," he whispered, the admission like a blade cutting into the silence.

His eyes, dark and intense, met Rhys' gaze, seeing the shock and fear reflected there. The stable hand's wide, tear-brimmed eyes were filled with a mixture of disbelief and sorrow. Beaumont's bitter smile deepened the lines on his weary face as he reached out to brush a stray lock of copper hair from Rhys' brow.

"Magick..." Beaumont continued, his voice barely more than a murmur. "Dark, unholy magick has been ebbing away at my heart, at my mind. I thought I could keep it at bay for a little longer."

"Who?" Rhys' voice was raw with emotion, trembling with the weight of the question. Beaumont could feel the anguish in the elf's trembling body as he pulled him close, wrapping him in a protective embrace. The feel of Rhys' warm skin against his own brought a fleeting comfort, a reminder of the life he still clung to.

"We cannot dwell upon the man who plagues me...he is not master here," Beaumont said, his tone firm despite the underlying pain. His hands pressed gently against Rhys' back, holding him close, feeling the steady rise and fall of the elf's breath.

Rhys trembled in his arms, his tears warm against Beaumont's bare shoulder. The king could feel the heartache in the elf's silent weeping, the sorrow that mirrored his own. He tightened his grip, willing his strength to flow into Rhys, even as his own was steadily drained away.

"Do not be afraid for me, Rhys...I am not dead yet," Beaumont tried to reassure him, though his voice faltered, betraying the truth that lay beneath his words.

He sighed heavily, the weight of his fate pressing down on him once more.

"It is a long way off, dearest Rhys...I shall be here for so much longer." But even as he said the words, Beaumont could feel the lies wrapped around them like a shroud. There was so much left unsaid, so much he longed to reveal, but fear kept his secrets locked tightly within.

"This dark magick...how long have you known?" Rhys' voice was a fragile thing, almost breaking under the weight of the question, his tear-streaked face searching Beaumont's for answers. The king wiped away the drying tears with a gentle touch, his heart aching for the pain he had caused.

Beaumont forced a smile, though it didn't reach his eyes. "Years. It has been such a long while..." His words trailed off, exhaustion creeping in at the edges of his consciousness. The effort of holding back the darkness, of maintaining the facade, was beginning to take its toll. He brought Rhys' hand to his lips, pressing a fervent kiss to the calloused skin, a desperate attempt to anchor himself to the moment, to the life he still had.

"Monty," Rhys whispered, his voice a mix of warning and plea, a single word laden with the depth of their bond.

"I plan to make great use of my time, Rhys," Beaumont replied, his voice growing softer, tinged with a bittersweet determination. "Let us start now...I have no intention of letting you leave this chamber yet." He smiled, a fleeting shadow of the man he once was, and ran his hands through Rhys' hair, drawing him closer.

Rhys smiled back, the sadness still present but overshadowed by the love that shone in his eyes. He leaned forward, closing the distance between them, and pressed a tender, wanting kiss upon his king's lips. It was a kiss that spoke of hope and despair, of love and loss, a kiss that was both a beginning and an end.

In that moment, the world outside the chamber faded away, leaving only the two of them, wrapped in the fragile warmth of each other's embrace, as the dark magick continued to seep into Beaumont's soul, inch by inch.

CHAPTER

32

Thad's footsteps echoed softly in the silent upper gallery, where the shadows of the night stretched long and deep. The moonlight filtered through the high, arched windows, casting a silvery glow over the ancient tapestries that adorned the walls. Each tapestry was a masterpiece, woven with scenes of old battles, legendary creatures, and long-forgotten heroes. The stories they depicted seemed to come alive in the shifting light, as if the figures themselves were moving within the threads, reliving their ancient glories.

His eyes drifted from one image to the next, taking in the tales of valor and sacrifice, of magick and bloodshed. The history woven into these walls felt heavy, almost suffocating. Thad's mind wandered through the labyrinth of history and his own tangled emotions, a web of feelings he could hardly untangle.

It had been so long since he had walked these corridors. Each step felt like a journey into the past, a time when things were simpler, when he was not burdened by the weight of his own decisions. He remembered running through these halls, laughing with abandon, unaware of the dark shadows that would one day cloud his heart.

Now, the memories felt distant, like echoes of a life he could no longer claim as his own. The boy who had once danced in the moonlight here was gone, replaced by a man weighed down by guilt, jealousy, and a longing that he could never fully satisfy. He paused before a tapestry depicting a warrior holding a blazing sword, the light from the weapon casting back the darkness surrounding him. Thad's fingers brushed against the edge of the fabric, as if he could draw some of that light into himself, chase away the shadows that had taken root in his soul.

A voice broke the silence, startling him. "Prowling the moonlight?"

Thad turned sharply, his heart leaping in his chest as he came face to face with Prince Barrow. The prince stood before him, his golden hair tousled and disheveled, the moonlight casting a soft halo around him. The vulnerability in Barrow's appearance was evident, his nightclothes partially obscured by a heavy overcoat. In one hand, he held an empty glass, its surface catching the moon's light and reflecting it in a soft, almost melancholic gleam.

For a moment, the two men regarded each other in silence, the gallery's shadows making the scene almost surreal. Thad's pulse quickened, his emotions a tumultuous mix of surprise and apprehension.

"Your Highness," Thad said, his voice steadier than he felt. "What brings you here at this hour?"

Barrow's eyes met Thad's, their depths shadowed by a weary sadness. He shifted slightly, the empty glass clinking softly in his hand. "I could ask you the same, Thaddeus," Barrow replied, his tone gentle but laced with an underlying tension. "The palace seems even more restless tonight, and the gallery is a place where the echoes of the past seem to linger."

Thad studied the prince's face, noting the lines of fatigue and the haunted look in his eyes. "I needed some air," Thad said quietly. "The weight of the night was too heavy to bear in the confines of my room."

Barrow nodded, as if he understood. "It seems we are both drawn to the same sanctuary in moments of turmoil. The past is a cruel companion, is it not? Always reminding us of our burdens, of what has been lost."

Thad's gaze fell to the empty glass in Barrow's hand. "Are you troubled, Prince Barrow? I thought I warned you against elven wine?"

Barrow's lips curved into a faint, almost sad smile. "More than I care to admit. The shadows of this place have a way of amplifying one's sorrows. The weight of responsibility, the expectations...they are often too much to bear alone. This is just water."

"Perhaps," Thad said softly, "it is the loneliness that makes the shadows feel so heavy. We carry our own pain and try to navigate it in the dark, but sometimes...it's the presence of another that can make the burden a little lighter."

"You are not wrong," Barrow said. "In moments like these, it is the company of another that offers the faintest glimmer of solace."

Thad nodded. "If you need someone to talk to, Your Highness, I am here. Sometimes sharing the weight can make it more bearable. And perhaps a nice cup of tea will set that head of yours right."

Barrow looked at Thad with a mixture of relief and hesitation. "Thank you, Thaddeus. It seems that tonight, the gallery has not only become a sanctuary for the past but also a place where unexpected alliances can be forged."

They stood together in the moonlit gallery, the silence between them no longer uncomfortable but filled with a sense of mutual understanding. The shadows that had seemed so oppressive now felt a little less daunting, if only for a moment.

"It's embarrassing," Barrow admitted, a touch of self-deprecation in his tone. "A promised king who can't even hold his wine."

Thad stepped closer, falling in step beside the prince as he began to walk towards the doors leading into the corridor. "I've known many a lord who doesn't touch wine at all. There's no shame in it."

"Good," Barrow chuckled, the sound light and grateful. "It would be a shame to be laughed out of my own kingdom."

"No man shall ever laugh at you, Barrow," Thad said firmly, his tone laced with a quiet resolve.

Here, the prince stopped, a distant look overtaking his handsome features. A wave of sadness washed over him, dimming the warmth in his eyes.

"Your Majesty, Prince Barrow?" Thad touched his shoulder gently, his concern evident.

Barrow glanced over, blinking hard as if trying to clear the fog of his thoughts. "Perhaps I should take that cup of tea," he muttered, rubbing the bridge of his nose as if to ward off the lingering effects of his earlier indulgence.

Thad's smile widened, a warm yet mischievous glint in his eyes. "It just so happens, I make a marvelous cup."

Barrow looked at him with a mixture of surprise and gratitude.

Thad led the way, guiding Barrow through the corridors. As they walked, the atmosphere between them lightened. Thad's gentle banter and Barrow's occasional chuckle helped to ease the tension that had hung over them both.

Upon reaching the modest kitchen, quieted in the late hours of the night, Thad set about preparing the tea with practiced ease, his movements smooth and deliberate. Barrow watched with a mixture of curiosity and admiration, seemingly comforted by the simplicity of the act. Thad poured the steaming tea into delicate cups, the fragrant steam rising in soft tendrils. He handed one to Barrow with a playful grin. "Careful now, Your Majesty. This tea has been known to bring clarity and calm."

Barrow took the cup, his fingers brushing against Thad's in a brief, unexpected touch. He looked up with a grateful smile. "If it lives up to your claim, I might just make you my official tea brewer."

Thad chuckled, the sound easy and genuine.

Barrow leaned back, rubbing his tired face. His hand raked through the fall of golden hair. Thad saw the smooth skin in the glow of the moonlight streaming in through the window. He had the urge to caress the prince, a familiar touch of desire flared to life in the faie. Thad gulped his tea, hissing at the burn.

"You must be tired," Thad said, taking the prince's empty cup. "You should go to bed. I shall not keep you here all night."

"Come, you can give me advice until the sun burns over the horizon."

Thad stood, following the prince. "As you desire, Your Majesty."

Barrow spoke freely, his words tumbling out in a stream of thoughts about horses, summer hunts, and the simple pleasures that filled his days. Thad listened, his admiration for the prince tempered by an understanding that Barrow, for all his charm and vigor, lacked depth in many things. His skills, if they could be called that, lay in his ability to recite poetry and captivate those around him with a smile.

As they made their way to the small parlor adjacent to the prince's chambers, Thad found himself lost in thought. Barrow's golden hair, the way it caught the flickering torchlight, stirred memories of another—a man from Thad's past whose image had been burned into his heart long ago. Aron Dourn, with his bronzed skin and easy grace, a man who had once filled Thad's life with both joy and pain. The resemblance between the two men was unsettling, tugging at memories Thad had long tried to bury.

Barrow must have sensed the shift in Thad's mood, for he paused in his chatter, glancing over with a slight frown. "I have bored you, forgive me," he said, his voice tinged with concern.

Thad shook his head, snapping back to the present. "No, I must apologize. My thoughts were elsewhere."

Barrow stretched out in his chair, the firelight dancing over his handsome features. "Thinking of a girl back home?" he asked, a teasing smile on his lips.

Thad's gaze softened, his mind briefly returning to the past before he pushed it away. "It was a long time ago...but please, tell me more about Brendolyn. You were saying she enjoys the orchards."

Barrow continued speaking, his voice carrying on about the princess and her love for the orchards. But as he spoke, Thad's attention began to wane, his thoughts drawn elsewhere. The more Barrow talked, the more a dark jealousy began to churn in Thad's chest. Brendolyn could love this prince; they would make a fine couple. But the thought of it stung. Thad knew she was meant for Pavan, not for this charming yet shallow prince. The jealousy gnawed at him, fueled by memories and desires he had long tried to suppress.

Thad watched as Barrow yawned, his long limbs stretching lazily in the chair.

"Your Majesty..." Thad began, his voice taking on a tone of something more intimate, more personal.

Barrow turned his head, a drowsy smile on his lips. "Please, Thaddeus, call me Barrow. I have shared enough secrets with you to warrant formality."

Thad moved to the seat beside the prince, the proximity sending a thrill through him. The golden light of the fire bathed Barrow's hair in a soft glow, highlighting the smooth, pale skin of his face. Thad's jealousy flared, mingling with a hot, sudden desire that took him by surprise. His hand, almost of its own accord, found its way to Barrow's knee, resting on the fabric of his trousers. He leaned in closer, his other hand gently brushing the golden curls that framed Barrow's face.

"You look so much like your father," Thad murmured, his voice thick with emotion. He traced the prince's profile with his gaze, noting the striking resemblance to Beaumont, though softened by the fair golden hair inherited from Lady Aletta.

Barrow's eyelids drooped, the weight of sleep and wine making his voice slow and slurred. "You knew him?" he asked, the words barely more than a whisper.

Thad's smile turned bittersweet, his fingers raking through Barrow's hair with a tenderness that belied the heat growing within him. "I knew him when he was a prince. Just like yourself." His hand slid further up the prince's thigh, the tension between them thickening as Barrow leaned into his touch, his breath hitching.

"Were you...a member of court?" Barrow asked, his brows furrowing as he tried to stay awake, his body instinctively responding to Thad's advances even as his mind began to drift.

Thad chuckled softly, the sound tinged with both amusement and melancholy. "No," he replied, his voice lowering to a hushed whisper. "My introduction to him was more...intimate."

Barrow's eyes widened slightly, a gasp escaping his lips as Thad's hand inched closer to the heat beneath his trousers. The prince's guard was down, his mind clouded by remnants of wine and sleep brewed into the tea, leaving him vulnerable to the older man's advances.

Thad watched the prince closely, a mix of emotions swirling within him—desire, jealousy, and a deep, aching sadness. He knew this moment was a reflection of the past, a shadow of what once was, and yet he couldn't stop himself. The pain of memories long buried surfaced with a raw intensity, driving him closer to the edge of something he wasn't sure he wanted.

Barrow's breath quickened, his body reacting even as his mind struggled to comprehend.

Thad leaned in, his lips brushing against the prince's ear as he whispered, "You remind me so much of him..."

The room was cloaked in a thick, expectant silence, broken only by the soft crackling of the fire and the ragged breaths of the two men. The flames cast flickering shadows across the stone walls, their warm light playing over the tension-filled space between Thad and Barrow. Thad could feel the ghosts of his past pressing in on him, their weight nearly unbearable. The line between memory and reality blurred, leaving him teetering on the edge of something dark and dangerous.

Barrow's breath hitched, his body jerking upright as Thad's hand slid between his thighs, cupping him with a deliberate, intimate pressure. The prince's eyes widened, the sleepy haze that had clouded his mind moments ago now completely shattered. Thad could see the confusion and alarm in those wide blue eyes, the innocence that had moments before made the prince so alluring now turning to a vulnerable fear.

"Thaddeus, this is unexpected."

"Would you like to know my secrets, Barrow?" Thad palmed Barrow through his breeches, earning another startled gasp. "I never let a woman dictate my heart."

"Please," Barrow grasped Thad's hand. "I can't do this."

Thad sneered, leaning closer to Barrow, their foreheads nearly touching. "You can have Brendolyn, Barrow. You can have her and her alone...don't settle for a half love in the arms of Lisetta."

Magick thrummed within Thad, a dark, seductive power that curled around his senses, whispering insidious thoughts into his mind. The taste of it was sharp on his tongue, an intoxicating mix of desire and danger that made him feel both powerful and repulsed. He could see the effect of his touch on Barrow, the way the prince trembled, caught between instinct and confusion. Thad's hand moved with purpose, his fingers pressing against the heat beneath the fabric as he leaned in closer, his breath warm against the prince's ear.

"I can't," Barrow groaned.

Thad's smile was a thin line of predatory intent as he leaned back, his weight pressing down over Barrow's solid frame. His knees braced against the cushions, his hips rolling forward to slot perfectly against the prince's. The heat between them was undeniable, a physical force that seemed to pull them together with a magnetic intensity.

Barrow's groan was laced with both desire and hesitation, his hands gripping the edges of the chair as if trying to anchor himself in the midst of a storm. His breath came in shallow gasps, his blue eyes wide, pupils blown with a mix of lust and confusion. Thad's hand found its way to the prince's jaw, tilting his head so their eyes locked. The rawness of the moment hung between them, heavy and electric, every nerve ending on fire.

"You must have her," Thad murmured, his voice rough with the edge of his own barely-contained desire. His thumb brushed over Barrow's lower lip, feeling the prince's breath hitch beneath his touch. "Whatever the cost, Barrow. She is yours..."

The words were a command, a temptation dripping in his faie voice, but there was something more behind them—an urgency born not just from lust, but from something deeper, darker. Thad could feel it coiling inside him, the agony of want boiling through his veins like molten fire. His own desire was a painful thing, a sharp-edged need that cut through him with every passing second.

Barrow's hands, hesitant at first, slowly came to rest on Thad's hips, fingers digging into the fabric of his trousers as if seeking something solid to hold onto. The prince's resolve was crumbling, Thad could see it in the way his body responded, the way his eyes darkened with the same hunger that Thad felt.

But there was a wariness in Barrow's gaze, a flicker of doubt that Thad recognized all too well. It was the doubt of a man caught between duty and desire, torn between what he wanted and what he knew he should do. Thad could see the battle playing out in those blue eyes, and it only fueled his own desperation.

Thad's lips hovered just above Barrow's, close enough to feel the warmth of his breath, but he didn't close the distance. Not yet. He wanted to savor this moment, the tension, the build-up, the delicious torment of being so close yet not quite giving in. His free hand slid down the prince's chest, feeling the muscles tense beneath his touch, tracing the path of heat that led down to their hips, where the pulse of want was strongest.

"You feel it, don't you?" Thad whispered, his voice a low rasp. "That fire inside you...burning for her, for this."

Barrow's eyes fluttered shut, a soft whimper escaping his lips as Thad's hips rolled again, sending a wave of pleasure rippling through both of them. Thad's control was slipping, the tight leash he had on his own desire fraying with every passing second. But he needed Barrow to break first, needed the prince to give in, to surrender completely to what they both knew was inevitable.

"Take her," Thad urged, his voice trembling with the intensity of his own need. "Claim what's yours...just like this."

"Thaddeus," Barrow whispered. Those hands grasping tightly to Thad's hips, holding tightly to Thad's tunic. Kissing Thad with longing desperation. Lust heavily perfumed between them.

Thad's grip tightened in the fall of Barrow's golden hair, his teeth grazing the prince's neck with a feral intensity. The strangled moan that escaped Barrow's lips only fueled Thad's fire, making him press harder, desperate to taste every inch of the prince's skin. Barrow's hands were clumsy but eager, fumbling at Thad's tunic, working with unsteady fingers to expose the bare flesh beneath. Thad exhaled sharply, his breath mingling with the prince's, his senses swimming in a heady mixture of lust and the dark tendrils of magick that curled around his thoughts.

"Take it, Barrow."

Barrow, once hesitant, was now driven by a primal need, his gentleness giving way to something raw and unrefined. Thad could feel the prince's newfound confidence in the way he pushed him back, in the grip that bruised his arms, in the way Barrow's lips crashed against his with bruising force. The prince's desire was palpable, seeping from his skin like a fever, and Thad could do nothing but respond in kind, following Barrow's lead as they stumbled from the parlor and onto the waiting bed.

Barrow's hands, though unpracticed, roamed with an urgency that set Thad's blood ablaze. His fingers traced over Thad's body, mapping the lines of muscle and the heat beneath his skin. Thad chuckled low in his throat, the sound vibrating against the prince's lips as Barrow kissed him with an almost desperate hunger. The sensation of the prince's hot mouth on his chest, his neck, sent shivers down Thad's spine, the pleasure mounting until it was almost unbearable.

But then, like a cold wind cutting through the heat, a voice echoed from the parlor.

"Barrow?"

Thad froze, the world crashing back into focus with brutal clarity. Barrow, lost in the haze of lust, didn't stop, his lips continuing their journey along Thad's neck, his hand slipping down to palm him through the front of his trousers. Thad bit back a groan, his body betraying him even as his mind screamed for him to stop.

"Stop, you fool," Thad hissed, forcing himself up and pushing the prince away. The sound of the door creaking open drew his gaze, and there stood Eero, the knight's face a mask of cold fury.

"Eero," Barrow gasped, scrambling to conceal his disheveled state, his eyes wide with a mix of shock and guilt. "Thaddeus was...this isn't..."

"Get out," Eero hissed, his voice like steel, pointing a trembling finger toward the door. Thad stood, his skin burning with the aftermath of what had almost happened. He glanced at Barrow, whose face was a portrait of confusion and shame, before turning to leave.

But as soon as Thad stepped into the corridor, Eero was upon him, his hand gripping Thad's neck and slamming him against the wall. Thad's breath caught in his throat as he found himself staring into the knight's eyes, cold and unforgiving.

"Don't think for a moment I will forget this, Thad," Eero growled, his voice low and menacing.

Thad sneered, shoving the knight back. "Like I answer to you, Eero."

Eero's expression didn't change, his eyes narrowing as he leaned closer. "No, you don't. But you're playing with dangerous fire, Thad...You've crossed a line."

Thad's face twisted into a bitter smile. "I tasted his flame, Eero. He will want none but her."

A flicker of doubt passed through Eero's eyes, his grip on Thad's tunic tightening. "What did you do?" he demanded, his voice a mix of fear and anger.

"I did what was necessary to ensure Pavan remains mine," Thad replied, his tone defiant, even as a part of him recoiled at the truth of his words.

Eero released him, stepping back with a look of disgust. "This is beneath you, Thaddeus. I knew you to be stubborn, but I didn't think you'd be cruel."

"You don't know me," Thad spat, the words tasting of ash.

Eero's gaze softened, just for a moment, as if he could see through the armor Thad wore, down to the vulnerable soul beneath. "I knew you once. When you were lost and frightened, hiding behind the mask your master made for you."

Anger flared in Thad's chest, his fists clenching at his sides. "I am no longer my master's slave."

"No," Eero agreed, his voice a quiet whisper, a stark contrast to the tension between them. "But you're still walking the path he set you on. Don't let his poisoned heart taint your goodness."

Thad's breath hitched, the knight's words striking a chord he hadn't expected. "I am better than them," he insisted, though the conviction in his voice wavered.

Eero shook his head, a bitter smile playing on his lips. "You're no better than the man who took you from Monselt, Thad. No better than Eske who violated you in Hilvaer. You took advantage of him, Thad. You used your strength against Monty's son...What would have happened if I hadn't walked in?"

The question hung in the air like a noose, tightening around Thad's throat. He couldn't answer, the weight of his actions pressing down on him with crushing force. His skin flushed hot with shame, his heart pounding in his chest. He would not have stopped, Thad knew he would have taken his fill of the prince with no second thought.

Eero's expression darkened, his lips curling in disdain. "If you had gone any further, I would have had no pleasure in killing you, Thad. But as his protector, I wouldn't have hesitated."

Thad's throat constricted, the reality of what Eero was saying clutched hard at his core. There would have been no going back, should he have crossed the threshold and taken Barrow, the damage would be irreparable.

"You are lost, Thad," Eero continued, his voice cold and hard. "And if you don't find your way back...you'll destroy everything you care about."

Thad's resolve crumbled, the strength that had carried him through so much fading under the weight of Eero's words. "I...I did not touch him. Barrow remains pure by my hands," he whispered, his voice barely audible.

Eero's gaze softened, but the hardness in his eyes remained. "Leave this place before you do something you can't take back."

Thad nodded slowly, his heart heavy with regret.

"I shall return to my chambers."

"I do not speak of this wing, nor this part of the castle, Thad. Leave Jorn, and never return, before those that knew you have discovered the truth of this night..."

Morning arrived, but the rain persisted, draping the castle in a dreary gloom that weighed heavily on Brendolyn's heart. She sat at the breakfast table with Elsa and Lahrs, the food before her untouched as her mind churned over the events of the night before. Her thoughts were clouded with unease, memories of blood and fear haunting her, making the once comforting surroundings feel cold and unfamiliar.

"Brendolyn, did you sleep through the storm?" Lahrs asked gently, his voice breaking through her reverie. He looked at her with his usual vigor, concern etched in his features.

She met his gaze, drawing some comfort from his kindness, but the sadness that clung to her refused to dissipate. The terror from the night lingered, suffocating her, making it hard to find her voice. "It kept me up only briefly," she managed to say, her words heavy with the weight of unspoken fears.

Lahrs paused, his hand hovering over his plate as he studied her. There was a shift in his demeanor, a silent recognition of her distress. "What is it? Are you ill?" he asked, his voice laced with worry.

Brendolyn forced a small smile, shaking her head. "Not ill, Lahrs. I have a bit of a headache. Perhaps I didn't get much sleep after all."

Elsa, who had been quietly observing, turned to Lahrs with a curious look. "What magick does Pavan possess?"

The question hung in the air like a heavy fog, and Lahrs visibly tensed. His fork slipped from his hand, clattering against the plate before he quickly recovered it. "We should not speak of this, Elsa. It is not a topic for conversation."

Brendolyn watched as Lahrs shifted uncomfortably in his seat, his usual calm demeanor shaken. There was something he wasn't telling them, something that gnawed at her insides.

"Pavan is different," Brendolyn pressed, her voice steady. "He is neither faie nor elven, but there is a deeper magick within him. When I'm near him, I can feel its power, Lahrs. I want to understand."

Lahrs took a deep breath, clearly torn. He hesitated before finally speaking, "It is not my place to discuss such matters, Bren. Some things are better left unsaid."

Brendolyn scoffed, her frustration bubbling to the surface. "You've never kept secrets from me before. Does this have anything to do with what happened last night?"

Elsa's eyes widened with sudden interest. "What happened last night?"

Lahrs shot her a pained look, clearly struggling with what to say. His gaze softened as he looked at Brendolyn, but there was a deep sorrow there too. "We will not speak of it, Elsa," he said firmly, his voice tinged with regret.

The silence that followed was thick with tension. Brendolyn could see the strain in Lahrs' face, the conflict tearing at him, but his lips remained sealed.

She pushed back her chair abruptly and stood. "I shall visit my father. Alone." Her voice was clipped, anger lacing her words as she stormed away from the table. The rain pounded against the windows as she ascended the stairs, each step fueled by aggravation. Instead of retreating to her rooms, she made her way to her father's private chambers, her heart heavy with the need for answers.

As she neared the doors, she heard a voice from within. She knocked, and the room fell silent.

The door creaked open, and there stood King Beaumont. Brendolyn's cheeks flushed with surprise. She glanced past him to see her father lying in bed, his face pale and drawn. But what struck her most was the evidence of tears in the king's eyes—he had been crying.

"Good morning, Your Majesty," Brendolyn murmured, dipping into a slight curtsy, trying to compose herself.

The king managed a small smile, though it was tinged with sadness. "Good morning. Your father has not been able to rise from his bed, but his health remains strong." He stepped aside, gesturing for her to enter. "You came to sit with him. He is asleep now, but I believe he would benefit from hearing your voice."

Brendolyn hesitated at the threshold, an inexplicable reluctance rooting her in place. "Perhaps I should wait," she whispered, her voice betraying her uncertainty.

The king's expression shifted to one of concern. "Are you unwell?" he asked gently, closing the door behind him as he stepped into the corridor with her.

Brendolyn fought the tears that threatened to spill over, overwhelmed by a sudden rush of emotion. Without thinking, she reached out and embraced his middle, seeking comfort in his presence. Beaumont didn't move at first, but then his hand came to rest on the top of her head, a gesture of quiet reassurance.

"Brendolyn, are you alright?" His voice was calm, kind, wrapping around her like a warm blanket.

She struggled to speak, her throat tight with the weight of her anguish. Her chest heaved as she fought for breath, desperate for the warmth and safety that Beaumont now offered so freely. She could hear his heartbeat, the rhythm steady and strong.

"You are unwell," he began, his voice laced with gentle concern.

She shook her head, her curls tumbling along her shoulders. "No...I just...I don't know," she whispered, her voice breaking.

Beaumont's eyes softened, his concern deepening. "Allow me to find you a comfortable seat, and some tea. Will you take tea with me, princess?"

Her chin trembled, and she finally managed a silent nod. At once, Beaumont took her hand, placing it on his arm so he could guide her down the hall to a quiet parlor. He seated her gently before settling into a chair beside her.

"Now then," he said softly, his eyes full of warmth and understanding. "Will you tell me your troubles, Brendolyn?"

Brendolyn felt a blush rise to her cheeks under his attentive gaze. She wasn't used to this kind of attention, and it both comforted and unnerved her. "You are very kind," she said, glancing down at her hands as she searched for the right words. "Inviting me here, when my father did not."

A shadow of discomfort passed over Beaumont's face, but he quickly masked it. "You have every right to be here," he whispered, his voice sincere.

Brendolyn hesitated, waging an internal battle with herself. The words she needed to say were heavy, lodged deep within her. "I hardly know where to begin, Your Majesty."

Beaumont reached for her hand, his touch steady and reassuring. "You may begin when you are ready...but first, let us speak as friends. Call me Monty. Think of me not as a king, but as someone who is here for you, as a father, as a friend."

Her eyes welled with tears, thick droplets spilling onto the silk of her gown, leaving dark spots of sorrow. The emotion she had held back for so long broke free, her voice trembling as she spoke. "This place is a torment," she confessed, the words tearing from her with a gasp.

Beaumont remained still, his hand holding hers firmly. "It must be difficult, returning to a place that has caused you so much pain," he said softly, his empathy clear.

The mention of her pain brought the loss of her Queen Mother crashing back into her mind. The grief was still fresh, the wound in her heart as raw as ever. Brendolyn nodded, her voice cracking as she spoke. "I miss her. Even though I was not of her blood, she loved me more than I could have ever dreamed."

She covered her mouth, trying to stifle her sobs, but the grief was too powerful, too overwhelming. The tears flowed freely, each one a testament to the love she had lost.

Beaumont listened quietly, his presence a steady anchor in the storm of her emotions. When she finally found the strength to continue, her voice was hoarse with sorrow. "And now...now I have returned, only to be separated from the man I love."

The king's face softened, but there was a deep sadness in his eyes.

"You know of our secret," she said, her words faltering as she revealed what she had kept hidden for so long. "Barrow told me that you knew...and that you asked him to end it. So he has done as you asked."

Beaumont sighed heavily, his regret palpable. "I am deeply sorry for the pain I have caused you," he murmured, his voice thick with emotion.

Brendolyn shook her head, her resolve strengthening as she spoke. "It was my own doing. You only did what you thought was right for your kingdom. I know your heart, and I know you want Barrow to marry for love. You are a loving father...I have felt it." Her voice trembled, but there was a quiet determination in her words. "Know that I love him. Let that be enough to ease your conscience. I loved him, and I married him. But it is all ended now, for the good of our realms."

A sad smile touched Beaumont's lips, his blue eyes misted with tears. He reached up to wipe them away, his movements tender. "If only I had your fearlessness, Brendolyn," he said, his voice a whisper. "To hold such strength against a hardened world."

"I believe you to be fearless," she replied, her voice filled with conviction.

But as she spoke, she saw a shadow pass over the king's face. His posture slumped, the strength in his frame seeming to drain away. Brendolyn felt the change in him, her own heart quickening as she sensed the fear that gripped him.

Without thinking, she reached out and touched his cheek, her hand trembling. "You are afraid?" she asked softly, her voice laced with concern.

Beaumont pulled back slightly, his hand falling away from hers. His eyes met hers, and for a moment, she saw the depth of his fear. "Perhaps it is best if you left Jorn, Bren," he said, his voice urgent.

His words struck her like a blow, confusion and fear swirling in her mind. "Monty," she began, shaking her head. But the king gripped her hand, his desperation clear.

"There is danger here, Brendolyn," he whispered, his voice tight with fear. "There is a power with dark properties, magick that our world has not seen in centuries. Promise me you will go with Lahrs when he travels to Entheas. Promise me you will leave these shores?"

Her heart pounded in her chest, her throat dry as she struggled to comprehend his words. "Pavan?" she asked, her voice barely a whisper.

The king's eyes widened in alarm. "No, Brendolyn...there is another. There is something more dangerous here, something deeper, darker. An ancient magick that has taken hold of my heart."

"You're frightening me," she gasped.

"Forgive me." He kissed her hands. "But I cannot think of what harm could befall you, should I no longer remain to protect you."

Brendolyn nodded slowly, the gravity of his words sinking in. "I understand," she said, her voice steady despite the turmoil inside her.

Beaumont stood abruptly, his movements hurried. "Forgive me, I must return to dress...but allow me the honor of a dance at the ball this evening."

Brendolyn rose, her mind racing. "Of course."

The king nodded, his expression tense. He bent low to kiss her cheek, then hurried from the room, his footsteps echoing down the corridor as he rushed away.

Brendolyn remained standing, her thoughts a whirlwind of fear and confusion. The rain outside continued to fall, its steady rhythm a somber reminder of the darkness that now threatened to engulf her. She began the slow walk back to her rooms, where Elsa awaited her, perched on the edge of a cushioned chair near the fireplace. The soft glow of the fire cast flickering shadows across her face, but her expression was one of quiet curiosity as Brendolyn entered the room, her gown damp from the mist that had crept through the corridors.

"You're pale, Brendolyn," Elsa said, standing and crossing the room in an instant. Her hands found Brendolyn's shoulders, steadying her. "What happened?"

Brendolyn hesitated, her thoughts still tangled in Beaumont's warning. She shook her head lightly, trying to dismiss the weight of his fear. "King Beaumont is troubled," she murmured. "He spoke of magick...magick that frightens him. I have never seen anyone so frightened."

Elsa's brows knit together, her concern deepening. "What could he mean?"

"He spoke of something ancient, something dark," Brendolyn replied, her voice barely above a whisper. She sank into a chair, her hands clasped tightly in her lap. "He begged me to leave Jorn. To go with Lahrs to Entheas."

Elsa knelt beside her, her face earnest as she searched Brendolyn's troubled expression. "Did he say why? What does he fear?"

Brendolyn shook her head. "He didn't, but I could feel it, Elsa. The weight of it, pressing down on him. He spoke of an ancient magick that has taken hold of his heart."

A long silence stretched between them, broken only by the crackle of the fire. Elsa reached for Brendolyn's hands, holding them tightly. "And what of Pavan?" she asked cautiously. "He holds an old magick...one that Lahrs does not speak of."

At his name, Brendolyn's heart ached. She closed her eyes, trying to block out the memories of his absence and the pain it brought her. "It is not him, there is another, but perhaps it is the same magick."

Elsa sighed, her gaze distant as if piecing together a puzzle. "The magick the king fears...could it have something to do with Pavan's struggles? You said he carries a weight of his own, a darkness that gnaws at him."

"He is tortured by it." Brendolyn nodded. "He hides himself for fear of discovery, how else can we explain why Lahrs does not talk of his magick."

"Perhaps he hides for the same reason that King Beaumont is frightened. Perhaps it is wisest to heed the advice of the king and leave this realm."

Brendolyn blinked back tears, the question cutting deep. "I don't know," she whispered. "I don't know if I can leave Pavan behind."

In the heart of the bustling castle kitchens, the air was thick with the scent of roasting meats and the steam that curled up from the great stoves. Thad sat near a narrow window, tugging at the damp collar of his tunic, his eyes dark with frustration. The heat was unbearable, clinging to his skin like an unwelcome shadow. His gaze followed the maids as they hurried past, arms full of baskets and linens, their movements quick and precise as they navigated the chaos around him.

A soft, hesitant voice broke through the clatter. "My lord?" Thad's head jerked up. A young elven maid stood before him, her auburn hair tied back, her face bearing the kind of quiet beauty that had undoubtedly caught the attention of Sir Eero. Audry was her name, and her resemblance to the princess's companion was uncanny.

"Audry," Thad acknowledged with a nod, his voice low and guarded. "And please, I'm no lord. Is there somewhere we can speak privately?"

She nodded, leading him out of the stifling kitchen and into the cool, dim corridor. The relief from the heat was immediate, and Thad let out a sudden breath. They slipped into a small storage room, it's only light a thin beam filtering through a high window. Audry turned to him, her eyes wide and anxious as she extended a hand holding a folded parchment.

Thad took it with a solemn nod. "I know it was a great risk for you to obtain this."

Audry offered a small, brave smile. "It was no trouble when the cause is so important."

As Thad unfolded the parchment, his eyes flicked over the familiar slanted handwriting—orders for lodgings at the Velvet Crown. His expression darkened as he looked up at Audry, who was trembling slightly.

"You're certain he's being housed at the Velvet Crown?" he asked, his voice a whisper.

She nodded, her eyes glistening with fear. "I saw him being escorted through the city streets by Leuthere himself. If I didn't know of your connection to Iyda, I wouldn't have dared come to you with the unsettling thought of Leuthere taking a Coradian knight. He is of the Brotherhood."

Thad reached out, taking her hands in his. They were cold, trembling with the weight of the danger she had put herself in. "You've done well, Audry," he murmured, his voice softening with a reassuring warmth. "I'll handle it from here."

Her eyes searched his, doubt lingering in the depths of her gaze, but she nodded. "Can you really help them?"

"It shall be done," Thad promised, the words leaving his lips like a vow. He watched her leave, the uncertainty still clinging to her like a cloak. Whether or not she would speak to Sir Eero about their meetings was of little concern to Thad now.

He didn't return to his quarters to gather supplies. Instead, Thad ascended the narrow stairs to the staff sleeping quarters above the kitchens. He made his way down the dim corridor, knocking softly on a door at the far end. It creaked open to reveal Svein, the half-giant's brow furrowed with concern.

Thad entered quietly, the weight of his thoughts pressing down on him as he stared out the small window overlooking the gardens. The parchment felt heavy in his hand as he ran his fingers over it, the significance of its contents sinking in.

"What's troubling you, Thad?" Svein's voice rumbled softly, breaking the silence. "It's not like you to be so quiet."

Thad's gaze lingered on the gardens below before he turned to face Svein, who seemed almost comically large in the small room. "There is something I must do," Thad began, his voice thick with emotion as he looked down at the folded parchment. "An errand...but not for my elven brother."

Svein stepped closer, his eyes narrowing with concern. "Something weighs heavily on your heart."

Thad nodded, his chin trembling as the anticipation of what was to come over-whelmed him. Svein placed a large hand on his shoulder, its warmth and weight ground-ing him.

"Will you not tell me, old friend?"

Thad wiped at the tears that threatened to fall, slipping the parchment into his tunic pocket. "There is so much to say, but I fear you will not approve."

Svein leaned down, pressing a gentle kiss to Thad's forehead. "You have a choice to make, Thaddeus. One that may have far-reaching consequences."

"If I go to the inn, and I find the knight there…" Thad trailed off, his voice breaking with uncertainty.

"You've never hesitated before," Svein observed, his brow creasing with worry.

"This is different," Thad replied, his voice a strained whisper. "I've not been careful in Jorn. Eero has been watching me. If I intervene now, he will know it was me."

"What does Pavan think of your actions?" Svein asked, his voice soft yet probing.

Thad's shame was palpable, his gaze dropping to the floor. "I haven't told him…about the girls I've been freeing, the ones I've taken to Entheas. Pavan wouldn't understand the magick I use to manipulate those who deserve it most."

Svein sighed heavily, his hand a steady weight on Thad's shoulder. "You shouldn't keep secrets from him."

"I can't tell Pavan the means by which I accomplish this. He wouldn't accept the dark magick I use against those with the blackest hearts." Thad's voice was bitter, anger simmering beneath the surface. "But this knight…he uses the Velvet Crown to manipulate these girls, to break them."

"The Velvet Crown…founded by Leuthere," Svein mused, his frown deepening.

Thad gripped the parchment tightly. "I have proof of the man I seek being housed there. I've seen the darkness in his heart reflected in a young maiden within these walls. Can I stand by and let him continue while knowing he's bound to her?"

Svein's hand cupped Thad's cheek, a tender, grounding touch. "You know the dangers of what you do, Thaddeus."

Swallowing hard, Thad fought back the tears, forcing the parchment back into his jacket. He trudged across the room, sitting heavily on the edge of the bed, burying his face in his hands. "He will suffer," Thad whispered, his voice filled with anguish.

"You will save those girls from their servitude," Svein said after a long moment. "But you must find the strength to not become what you despise."

"Will I be able to refrain from killing the knight?" Thad's voice was fragile, laced with desperation. "Will I fall further from Ehnarea's Light?"

"You fear becoming like those who once held you captive?" Svein asked gently.

Thad's eyes burned with the memory, his fists clenching as he forced the emotions back. "Leuthere was once like me, a boy taken from his family, broken again and again until there was little left of goodness. He held me down, laughed as they took me. Am I no better for seeking vengeance against those who wrong these girls? Am I any different, feeling their misery as I carve into their flesh, as I curse them for their evil?"

The silence that followed was thick and heavy.

Finally, Svein knelt before Thad, their eyes meeting. The half-giant took Thad's hand in his own, his grip firm but comforting. "The difference is vast, Thaddeus. You save those who cannot protect themselves. You are a beacon in the darkness, not the shadow itself."

Thad chuckled, a sad, weary sound as he kissed Svein's knuckles. "After the next feast, Svein, take the others and return home. Go to Eir and leave me to my fate if they find me."

"I will protect them until you return," Svein promised, his voice steady. "And then we shall sail to Tauf, together."

CHAPTER
33

Thad was tired, having waited all through the night in search of this place. Glaring across the road at the little inn nestled within the narrowing side streets off the main road of the great city. It was exactly where he remembered it, but it now had a new owner. He waited for it to open, standing in the little alcove hidden out of sight.

It was nearing midday, when he saw the mistress of the Velvet Crown bustle up the side street from her villa not far away to the front door of her establishment. Unlocking the great big lock that secured the front door shut from the outside. A sickening feeling sunk in Thad's stomach as he glared at the woman dressed in richly colored garments.

Ducking out from the alcove, Thad crossed the street, approaching the great front door. Knocking with a closed fist upon the heavy door of which he could feel enchantments.

"What can I do for you, dearie?" came the honeyed voice as the door swung open.

Thad glared down at the severely powdered face of the woman before him. She was old, but Thad could see the lines of magick that de-aged the once wrinkled skin stretched over the edges of her jaw and neck. It was a crude work that would wear off within the month. To which Thad knew she would need more magick as the years progressed.

"I come from the castle, as I have heard your establishment is the best location for certain entertainment." Thad's voice was forced into a deeper tone, as he knew his features were obscured by the limited means of his glamour.

Her face brightened, showing her large yellowing teeth in a broad smile.

"Of course, sir, we have many fine delights here. Come in, come in." She turned to allow him entrance and Thad stepped through to the front entrance.

"Thank you." Thad was quick to remove his outer jacket, giving it to the nearest girl that waited behind her mistress. The young girl's wide grey eyes watched Thad.

"Come to the dining room, I can serve you some refreshment."

Thad's eyes slid to the intense gaze of the woman. "That won't be necessary."

The woman's face faltered, her eyes narrowing as she took him in, now in the light of her parlor. Thad was confident in his magick, knowing the woman held none of her own. Thad looked again to the young girl who stood watching him with wide wondrous eyes. She was faie touched, and much too young for this place.

"What are your particular delights, lord..."

"Lord Dourn, madame. But I shall not be needing any food or refreshment." Thad spoke and his voice became deeper, his words laced with hints of magick.

She smiled. "Of course."

"I should like the company of a red haired girl," Thad stated flatly, looking away from the young girl to the woman. "One with bloom."

The madame gave a nervous laugh. "I am afraid our only red haired girl has been saved for this morning, my lord. But I can offer you one of my blonde girls and the delights of our refreshments that shall heighten our magick incense to give you visions of your mind's delights."

A part of Thad writhed with anger, but he kept the innermost emotions within to not break the character he was placating. He was precise in his stance, keeping himself upright as he looked the woman over. From her heavily powdered hair, to the matted hair beneath the little silk cap she wore to hide the unwashed nest of dulled curls. His scrutiny examined the bodice that was snug against her vivacious curves, to try to keep her once supple bodice in frame as it had once been, but he saw the age of the old styled gown, the worn down silk that was not newly spun. His eyes could take her in at a moment of examination to determine his next steps.

"Perhaps only a brief audience, madame," he used his sweetened tone. One laced with enticing magick as he pulled from his pocket a large purse, showing a portion of his gold within, watching with pleasure as the madame's eyes bulged slightly and changing the way she held herself into a more flirtatious enthralled demure stance. "I have been away from home for too long and wish to have a sampling of...your sweetest girl."

"My Lord Dourn is generous, to honor our humble parlor with your extravagance," she nearly bellowed, trying to contain her excitement and grabbing Thad's arm as she licked her rouged lips. Thad placed the gold back into the little purse.

"But I wish to remain anonymous, for fear of my time here reaching abroad to my estates." His grip tightened upon the purse as the madame grasped it greedily. "I would hate to report your disloyalty to the master whom you serve."

He struck a flutter of fear, as the madame became pale at the utterance of her benefactor, unable to bring herself to mutter his name.

"Good sir," she whispered, her perfume smelling much too strongly of intoxicating flours that held magickal properties of seduction. Thad wrinkled his nose, immune to such mundane parlor tricks. "You shall be unnamed within my books, and I thank you for your generous donations to our humble cause."

Thad gave up the purse. "My room, madame."

Madame straightened, snapping hard at the girl who lingered in the entryway to the parlor. At once the timid girl hurried forward, unable to look up to meet madame's gaze.

"Take Lord Dourn to Dahlia's room."

Thad followed the young girl, his feet falling against the plush carpet that minimized the sound. He saw the frayed edges, smelled the scent of powder used to mask the copper reaction of potion that would linger in the stone well after the potions were made. Thad felt the tingle of it static the air as they walked beyond the velvet curtain that led to the back of the inn. Rooms lined the dark painted walls, each one hung with a wooden carved sign upon the door with a different flower. He was stopped in front of the second door, with a Dahlia carved onto the little plaque.

"Here, my lord..." The young girl did not enter, her feet never leaving the dark carpeted floor of the corridor while Thad stepped through to the plush peachy pink carpet within the room.

"Thank you." Thad stopped, looking down at the little girl whose wide gray eyes watched him with wonder. "What is your name, girl?"

She flushed scarlet, her hands grabbing the apron she wore as her eyes flicked along the hall, expecting the madame to storm down with a raised fist. Thad saw her fear in her eyes, her hesitation.

"Chloe," she whispered timidly.

Thad bowed to her, honoring her with respect. "Thank you, Chloe."

She left him in the room where he began to look about. His senses could smell the magick that burned from the incense that slowly rose from a small metal plate near the fireplace. It tickled his nose, but he could not feel the effect. Turning away to examine the small trinkets that lined the windowsill. Beyond of which he could see nothing, as the glass of the window was distorted, like fractured diamonds that dispelled color throughout the room.

"My lord." He heard her voice and Thad's heart began to beat faster.

Turning to see the fair young girl not much older than Chloe standing before him. She had emerged from behind a dressing screen, where a small door led into a bathing chamber beyond and Thad swallowed thickly.

"Dahlia." Thad bowed his head.

"This is unexpected, you are not my usual." She was trying to keep herself strong but Thad could feel her heart fluttering across the room. "But it is not unwelcome, my lord."

"I have come to deliver this." Thad reached into his pocket, extending a sealed letter in Audry's hand and offering it to the girl whose eyes widened, confusion written in her beautiful eyes.

She slowly stepped forward, taking the letter from him, opening it timidly, and scanning the words that Thad did not know of the contents. But he could see as she read, as her demeanor shifted. Stepping back to sit on the edge of her waiting bed, her hand came up to cover her quivering lips as the tears began to pool.

Thad knelt in front of the crying girl. She was part faie, he could feel her faint magick flickering beneath the surface. It pained a deep wound within himself. She did not pull back away from him, even as her hand fell to her lap, the letter crumpled. Waiting patiently as she dabbed at her eyes.

"Sir Alaric requests you?" Thad asked, seeing the faded bruised upon the girl's arms, hidden beneath the collar of her bodice.

She nodded, wiping at her wet cheeks.

"He is displeased when madame offers another of the girls...the magick works better when it is..." Her lips trembled again.

Thad nodded, remaining at a distance and allowing her to compose herself.

"I know madame holds your debt," he began, eyeing the letter now crumbled in her grasp. "I know what it is you have been through. And I have come to take you away from here, should you choose to accept my offer."

"I cannot, they shall find me," she whispered, eyeing the shut door.

"You shall be protected, Dahlia. Under my care, they cannot find you." He inched closer, to catch her glance, lowering his magick guise to show her his true face.

She gasped. "You are faie?"

"I am Thaddeus Brousevier of Monselt, son of Sefir of Augusta. I have come to take you from this place of torment. To sail you across the sea to the shores of Entheas. Beyond the pillars of Tauf where no one dares enter."

Her expression widened, unable to hide her shock.

"I give you my promise that no harm shall befall you and your sisters."

"How can we leave this place, she locks us in every night?" Dahlia's eyes searched his, seeking for answers.

Taking a vile from his pocket, he offered it to Dahlia.

"It is not poison, but a sleeping draft. One that shall make madame sleep for a long while. Long enough for you to take her keys and travel to Denorn." He took out a second purse, giving it to her other hand. "This shall be enough to get you to the Chapel of Light. Seek Arienne, there she shall keep you safe until I can reach you."

Dahlia clutched tightly to the vile and the purse.

"You will do this willingly?"

Thad reached out, caressing her cheek to swipe away the fallen tears. He could feel her fears, but her hope burned brighter within her chest.

"For you, I would burn down the realms." A seed of grief flickered in himself and he hardened. "Go now, speak to those that are willing to depart of this place. Go and I promise to meet you in Denorn."

She jumped to her feet, clutching the purse and vile to her chest, watching the door warily as Thad stood slowly to his feet.

"What shall you do, when Alaric comes to call? I expect him within the hour."

"Don't worry about him, Dahlia." Thad pressed a kiss to Dahlia's forehead and touching the trembling arm nearest to him. "Go."

Thad waited until she was gone, when he raised his hands to unclasp the buckles of his tunic. Taking off his outer garments, folding them neatly before tucking them under the chair near the door of the room. He turned to the wardrobe, extracting one of the flowing garments, placing it gently over the bedcovers. Thad eyed the silk, letting his fingers trail over the delicate material.

There was a great chill in the room as Thad removed the remainder of his garments. Standing bare within the sweet smelling room, magick pooled in his belly, feeling the familiar pull as he began to shift his form, his skin tingling beneath the shift of his glamour. Stretching his arms up to ruffle his hair that began to tumble down his back in a cascade of orange flame.

In this body, it was easy to slip into the silk dress. The sheer material hung over his shoulders, caressing his arms and shifted cooly over the mounds of his breasts.

Thad sat before the vanity mirror. Using dabs of rouge left upon the tabletop upon his lips and cheeks, and above the cleavage to give his pale freckled skin a healthy glow. Thad examined the tousled hair, it would be impossible to tame the wild tresses, but it gave Thad's glamour a sultry demure look that would satisfy any knight.

Next, Thad moved about the room, reawakening his reflexes to the body that moved lighter, his limbs graceful with each new step as he remembered how this form danced, walked, moved. Thad felt a trembling between his thighs, it had been a long time since he had used this form—all the others had no need of such deception. Now he was reawakened to the last guilty pleasure in this form, imprinted upon his skin as well as the trembling heat between his thighs.

Memories recounted in Thad's mind, his thoughts drifting to the bronzed skin belonging to the familiar large body. His lips remembering the heat of the last kiss and Thad frowned. There would not be the same pleasure, not from Alaric. This was not an act of passion, this was revenge. Waiting in the warmth of the room until the knight arrived.

When he did arrive, Alaric smelled of cedar and damp hay.

It made Thad wrinkle his nose, his back was to the door as it opened. He was busy mixing the fizzing liquid in a glass for his guest to drink.

"You are not Dahlia." He was stern, his voice a puff of young, haughty dislike.

Thad's smile remained, though his insides twisted in discomfort. He watched Alaric with a practiced ease, sensing the knight's underlying tension. Alaric was every bit the imposing figure Thad had envisioned—tall, blonde, and muscular. The raw power exuding from him was palpable, and Thad could feel the dangerous allure the man held. He knew all too well the fear that Alaric could evoke, and in this moment, he was ready to manipulate it to his advantage.

"My name is Theia." Thad smirked.

"I don't care who you are, I requested Dahlia...she knew what I liked."

As Thad stepped closer, his gaze locked onto Alaric's. The scent of the knight—a mix of musk and something deeper, more primal—overwhelmed him. Thad could feel Alaric's desire simmering beneath the surface, a dangerous edge that excited him. He also detected a trace of nervousness in the knight's posture, something that made Thad's smile widen slightly.

"She was a timid girl," Thad said softly, his voice a seductive purr. He reached out, gently touching the thick arm beneath Alaric's padded tunic. The firmness of the muscle under his fingers was a testament to the knight's rigorous training. "I am better practiced at handling a man of your passion."

Alaric's eyes flicked down to Thad's body, lingering on the sheer gown that revealed more than it concealed. Thad could feel the heat radiating off the knight, his arousal palpable. As Alaric's gaze moved over the glamoured form he embodied, Thad took Alaric's large hand in his own, examining it with feigned fascination.

"You must train every day," Thad murmured, his voice laden with a soft, practiced allure. He drew Alaric's hand to the curve of his own throat, letting his fingers graze the knight's roughened skin. "Your hands tell the story of your dedication."

Alaric's blush deepened, and Thad felt a thrill of satisfaction at the knight's reaction. His own pulse quickened as he maintained eye contact, his voice dropping to a husky whisper. "I like to be ridden hard."

The effect was immediate. Alaric drained the drink in quick, thirsty swigs, his desperation now clear. Tossing the cup aside, he seized Thad with a force that took him by surprise. Alaric's lips crashed onto Thad's with a fervent hunger, his hands gripping Thad's slender throat with an intensity that bordered on painful.

Disgust roiled within Thad as Alaric's hot mouth pressed insistently against his, the taste of bitterness—likely from the oranges in the drink—mingling with the knight's fervor. Every part of Thad's being screamed in revulsion. Yet, despite his loathing, the desire he had stirred coiled tightly within him, his glamour amplifying the sensation.

Alaric's hands roamed over Thad's body with rough, demanding touches, palming the curves of the breasts through the sheer gown. Thad fought to suppress his own reaction, trying to focus on the task at hand. The tension between them was electric, and Thad had to remain in control, despite the conflicting emotions churning within him.

Thad's fingers fumbled with the laces of Alaric's tunic, his hands moving with practiced precision to reveal the pale, muscular skin beneath. As he exposed the knight's hardened chest, Thad's touch was both firm and deliberate, caressing the flexing muscles that responded to his every movement.

"Damned magick," Alaric hissed, his voice breaking into a strained growl. His eyes glazed over, struggling to focus as the enchantment began to seize him. The magick, potent and dark, was seeping through him, altering his senses and thoughts.

Thad's smirk widened as he traced his fingers over Alaric's sweaty brow, feeling the heat and tension of the knight's skin. He guided Alaric back towards the bed with a slow, deliberate pace, every step calculated to maintain the illusion of seductive control. The change in Alaric's demeanor was palpable. His eyes, once sharp and commanding, now darkened and grew unfocused as the magick consumed him.

The knight's strength was evident in his rigidity and the tremor of his breath, but Thad knew the enchantment was swiftly taking over.

Thad leaned closer, his voice dropping to a velvety whisper. "Let the magick take you. Surrender to it."

Alaric's eyes, now shadowed with a deepening haze, followed Thad's every move.

Thad continued his delicate manipulation, his hands soothing over Alaric's skin even as the knight's responses became increasingly erratic. The enchantment was blurring the lines between Thad's façade and the knight's desires, making it clear that the knight was no longer seeing Theia, but rather the manifestation of his own need and frustration.

"Elsa," Alaric growled.

Grasping at Thad's narrowed hips, drawing their bodies closer, Thad felt Alaric hard against his stomach and anger danced on Thad's heated skin.

Letting Alaric touch his body, kneading the small of his waist, grasping hard at his rear, his large hands relentless upon the swell of his breast, Thad gasped, his body responding to each brutal attack, flushed from head to toe with desire.

"Will you be gentle?" Thad asked, his words a ploy to push Alaric further into the facade. In his haze of desire, Thad watched Alaric losing control.

"Oh, Elsa...always so timid. This is not our first time." Alaric grabbed Thad's jaw hard, kissing at the pulse point, before lowering his hands to the fabric of the dress.

In one swift movement, the thin fabric ripped in Alaric's hands, it came apart, fluttering to the carpeted floor leaving Thad exposed.

"Glorious," Alaric mused, trailing his fingers down.

Thad's skin prickled at the gentle touch. Looking sharply up when Alaric's fingers stopped over the curve of his ribs, where Thad knew the brand lived upon Elsa's body. Turning his head away, nausea overpowering him as Alaric bent down to kiss him.

A new anger filled the knight. Thrusting Thad back onto the bed, large hands unlacing the belt that held up his trousers, releasing the straining manhood and reaching forward to grab a fist full of 'Theia's' hair.

"Come on, please your husband."

Alaric sunk his hands deeper, gripping hard until Thad hissed. Thad complied, sinking deeper and making the knight gasp. Hatred fueled Thad as he grazed his teeth sharply over tender skin, hearing the pain filled hiss above him.

"Bitch," Alaric hissed, yanking Thad off.

Thad smiled, wiping his mouth off the dribble of spit and glaring up at the knight who was red in the face. "All that cock and you waste it in my mouth. I thought you would have taken me by now."

Slap!

Thad's face stung from the hand that smacked hard across his face, gasping at the sudden sting. He smiled as the familiar heat pooled between his legs and glared up at Alaric's fury.

"Shut up!" Alaric demanded as he gripped the long orange hair, and brought their faces closer together. "You belong to me."

"Then show me, take what is rightfully yours."

Thad knew he was playing a dangerous game, he felt the magick tickle at the back of his throat. His body hot with desire, coaxing the man to take control, desperation to feel it again, even if it was cruel and deceptive. His body thrummed with the desire he craved for so long.

The knight pushed him down, climbing onto the bed to force himself to kneel between Thad's spread thighs. Gripping relentlessly to the thin limbs holding Thad's wrists as he plunged his manhood deep into Thad's glamoured form, moaning.

Thad gasped, the force so sudden it took his breath away. Glaring up at Alaric's face, noticing his eyes black with desire, each thrust brutal. Losing himself for a moment in the carnal desire that radiated through him, Thad began to moan, feeling the budding heat begin to build towards its peak.

"Elsa."

Alaric's breathy moan brought Thad back to the room. Blinking through the haze of pleasure with every thrust sending Thad closer to the brink of completion. Alaric was lost in the moment. Thad hated Alaric and hated each moan that was breathed into his ear. Thad pulled his hands free, reaching for the dagger on Alaric's belt but Thad was pinned—the blade secured out of his reach. Grunting in frustration, Thad threw his head back and above him, Alaric moaned. Gripping Thad's knee to bring his leg up around Alaric's hip, a new angle that sent him deeper.

Thad moaned, grasping at the bedsheets.

Thad bit his lip, desire coiling tighter as the knight sunk deeper and deeper with each erratic thrust. Around him were the sounds of the knight's moans, the muffled huffs in his ear, as Thad's body betrayed him. Heat winding deeper as his body chased the sensations that clouded him, pushing him closer to the edge.

Alaric cried out sharply, spilling his seed deep within Thad's shifted form. The knight began to slump forward and Thad's eyes snapped open, using his strength to flip them, looking down at the shocked and overwhelmed expression on Alaric's face.

"Oh, my lord," Thad sighed, his hand roaming up the expanse of the knight's heaving chest and wrapping around Alaric's throat before thrusting his hips to further deepen his own burning pleasure.

Alaric gasped, trying to break free, when Thad grabbed the dagger at Alaric's hip, bringing the blade to the knight's throat, riding him as the pleasure pooled deep within him, nearly sated.

"What is this?" Alaric hissed, unable to move beneath Thad.

Thad leaned forward, pressing the dagger further into Alaric's throat as he moaned, his orgasm ripping through his body. Thad sighed, his mouth falling into a smile as he trailed the tip of the dagger down to the exposed chest laid before him.

"You don't know me...but you will. When I am finished with you, there won't be anything left of your mind but what I will do to you."

Thad reached with magick—it was easy to enter Alaric's mind, slipping into the earliest memory and finding the first moments of watching a ten year old girl in the orchards. Thad grimaced, feeling the disgusting things Alaric visioned with the young

Elsa. His body was hot with fury as he dug the tip of the blade into the smooth flesh of Alaric's chest, making the first cut.

Eero stepped up to the door of the Velvet Crown, uncertain of what he would find within. He stepped up to the door, nervous as he knocked on the hardwood. Audry had been cautious when she had come to him earlier in the day, her worry had overpowered her secrecy she had kept and now he wondered if it was anything. She could not tell him for certain but gave him the name of the famous den.

A woman opened the door, who looked pale beneath her powdered makeup. He could see the hesitation as she took him in, he was a stranger and not dressed in his palace uniform.

"Come back again, we're not open today." She moved to shut the door, but Eero blocked it with his foot.

"I have come in search of someone, a knight named Alaric," he addressed her firmly.

"No one by that name comes here. None has ever come here answering to that…" She began sourly, but a guttural scream echoed from within.

Eero barged past, knocking the woman aside and following the source of the agonized scream.

"You cannot go back there!"

But Eero frowned, glaring at the woman as he reached the velvet curtain.

"Stay there!" he demanded, his voice laced with magick and leaving her standing at the doorstep.

Eero wasted no time in following the sound, pushing beyond the velvet, magick fogged his senses as the wave of incense plagued him. He reached the door where the sound came from, kicking it in with brutal force. He expected something completely different, his eyes rounded, seeing an orange haired faie straddling Alaric. She held a dagger, carving into the flesh of the knight's chest—ancient magick. Recognition flashed in Eero, seeing the faie's profile and he rushed forward.

"Theia!"

Grabbing the arm of the faie, he pulled her off Alaric and looked into wild orange eyes gone nearly black.

"Stop this," Eero hissed, grasping the hilt of the dagger.

Behind them Alaric howled in agony.

"He deserves to be carved," her voice spat, struggling against Eero's hold.

"Stop this." Eero released the slender wrist and grasped both shoulders to shake the faie, unable to stop the force of his beating heart.

It was sudden, the brutal force of the knee into the flat of Eero's stomach, making him stumble back. Looking at the beautiful faie glistening with sweat, her hands stained with blood, Eero knew her well.

"This isn't right, Thaddeus," he groaned, holding his side.

"You have no right to stand there and tell me what is right. You who knew of Elsa's agony, yet you did nothing but stand aside and watch his miserable life remain untouched."

Eero blinked in surprise. "Elsa told you?"

"She needn't say a word. Not when I can feel the bond between them. Frightening her in the castle. Hushing up an abhorrent act by sending her to be with the Princess of Corad." Thad was spitting, his glamoured face enraged.

"You cannot kill Alaric."

"I don't need to kill him, all I need is to split his mind, curse his body."

Eero saw the bloody dagger, his eyes trailing along the body attached to it. Theia was naked, glistening, flushed and Eero quickly glanced away.

"Will you put something on?" He kept his eyes averted, but he felt the warmth of her body draw closer.

"Would you like to know what he did to me...what he imagined doing to her, Eero?" Thad whispered, his voice returned.

Eero glanced up, the glamour faded as Thad now stood before him.

"Don't do this, Thad."

Thad grasped Eero by the shoulder, pushing him back with magnificent strength and pinning Eero to the wall so close he could see the orange of the faie's eyes get thinner as the black took over.

"You care so much for Elsa, but why haven't you killed him yet? Why haven't you freed her from the bond?" Thad breathed, his hand touching the dip of Eero's chin.

Magick smelled heavy on his words, Eero could feel the effects of the room as the incense burned heavier, clouding his thoughts. It crept up along his spine making it difficult to breathe.

"She is safe," Eero breathed, shaking his head.

Thad tightened his grip, pressing even closer. There was desire swimming between them, mixed with the sour taste of dangerous magick. His heartbeat thumped in his ears, drowning out the pained groans of Alaric upon the bed.

"She will never be safe until his blood spills on the ground at my feet. I have been inside his head. I have seen his darkest thoughts, Eero. His unholy thoughts of a little girl...so young. You expect me to let a man like him go free?" Tears sprang free in Thad's orange eyes. "You expect me to let her hide away in fear of that man coming for her...claiming her?"

Eero gulped back the pain.

"Do not split your soul, Thad."

Thad rasped a laugh, mixed with the despairing cry. "So that's it then. You wish to spare me for the Veil. To keep my soul pure for the goddesses' good light. You cannot save me, Eero. No one can save me from the blackhearts that haunt me. Where was your savior's call when I carved into their flesh, Eero?"

Eero trembled. "I am trying to save you from yourself, Thad. You have been destructive in your own soul. After all these years, you have been hurting yourself."

"I like the pain."

Thad's lips crashed on Eero's in a hot, desperate need. They tasted of honey mixed with the bitter tang of magick. Images crashed with his own, through their touch. Visions of Elsa smiling in the training yard with Eugene, then to the tears in her eyes as she begged Alaric to stop. It was agonizing, to witness them all, to feel her fear. Eero was cold, his cheeks wet from tears but he was not crying.

Yanking back, Eero felt the trembling faie clinging to him. Thad was unable to keep himself hardened to the overwhelming emotions that overtook him and Eero held him in his arms.

"Do not hold onto it, Thad. You must let it go or it will consume you," Eero whispered, pressing a kiss into Thad's damp hair, his own eyes misted with tears.

"It hurts, Eero." Thad clung to him. "To be so helpless."

Sighing softly, Eero ran a hand down the length of Thad's back. Suddenly aware of how naked the faie was and breaking their embrace to snatch up the blanket draped on the nearest chair. Eero wrapped Thad in the warmth before looking deep into Thad's orange eyes.

"You cannot save them all from the darkness that spreads within these realms." His voice was almost a whisper.

"Do you have any idea of how often I have been traversing the great seas with such precious cargo...there are still so many who need my help. Eero..." There was warmth between them and the air cracked with magick.

Thad smelled of honeysuckles and a warm inviting scent that lingered in Eero's nose. The knight drew closer, his senses overwhelmed with the desire that heightened the room.

"So brave, little Thad."

Drawing back slightly, the faie scoffed.

"Little? I believe I am older, Eero. You insufferable ass, to insinuate my height—"

He didn't let the faie finish, crashing his mouth hard to the warm lips with a hunger Eero had never felt before, wanting to consume and be consumed by the fire. Want coiling hot under his skin, Eero began to feel himself getting out of control.

Thad pushed him, glaring at him.

"You are compromised by the incense, Eero."

"I am well enough." Eero smiled, leaning in to bring their lips together again.

Slap!

It stung, the harsh backhand that brought Eero to his senses.

"There now," Thad smoothed his fingers over the reddened skin "there's the Eero I know."

"You slapped me!"

Thad laughed, dropping the blanket as he walked across the room with confidence, snatching up his garments from beneath the chair nearest to the door.

"Yes, I slapped you." Thad chuckled, stepping into his trousers.

Eero breathed with a sense of clarity, looking around the room that smelled of sweat and damp wood. His eyes roamed the less enthralling furniture that no longer held the enticement and charm, ettling his gaze upon the knight that huddled beside the bed, whimpering and in pain.

"You slapped me with magick." Eero glared at Thad, who now pulled his tunic over his head.

"I have cleared your mind. Now, let us forget this place and leave before they come looking for him. There is a backdoor through the kitchens."

Eero narrowed his eyes. "Your magick curse was unsuccessful?"

Thad glared at the wounded knight huddled in despair and Eero could see the clenched jaw. Thad quickly slipped his feet into the soft leather of his boots and glanced up at Eero with a faint blush.

"He shall endure, but the scar shall remain...you stopped the completion of the ritual."

CHAPTER

34

Pavan waking in the comfort of his bed, with a bright morning after the rain, gripped his side in pain. He dressed, wearing basic black garments and needing some air, decided to walk out to the garden. Ignoring everyone, he stopped suddenly, as Lord Bannon stood in his path, returning from his own walk through the gardens.

"Good morrow, sir," Lord Simeon Bannon smiled, pleasantly and Pavan's stomach rolled in nausea.

But his smile returned. "Good morning."

The lord smiled wolfishly, glancing around, his hand reaching up to touch the vines of a nearby trellis. His eyes taking in the quiet gardens, still too early for many to be out.

"Your companion...the faie." The eyes slid over to where Pavan stood and Pavan gulped. "He holds a power...one that is very great and unreserved."

Keeping his features cold, Pavan slid his hands behind his back. "My faie servant is haughty, yes...but I have my ways of handling him."

Again, there was a grin and Lord Bannon turned.

"I should very much like an interview. Magick is my specialty, you see, and there is a great number of things I would like to ask of him." There was a flicker of ire, hidden beneath layers of coldness. Pavan's skin crawled, and magick began to fester, a vile taste in his mouth.

Pavan frowned, showing his displeasure. "There is not much to him, other than his sport of mischief. Simple conjuring, riddles, that sort of thing..."

Lord Bannon came closer, pressing in on Pavan's space, his gaze lingering on Pavan's eyes. Holding back, Pavan shielded his magick, withholding down to his every breath.

"If it's all the same," Bannon cooed, and Pavan felt the coil of magick, an attempt at seducing Pavan's resolve. "I have a little errand for him...one that is very particular to his...talents."

Each second felt an eternity, breathing back the nausea that crept along his spine. Pavan clenched his jaw, eyeing the man coldly. Those dead blue eyes shifted to a mute gray.

Pavan sneered. "He is not for sale, Lord Bannon. I am very protective of what is mine...and he is *mine*."

There was a shimmer of amusement, mixing with the tang of bitter contempt and Lord Bannon chuckled. "Should you change your mind, Sir Pavan, you know where to find me."

"Excuse me, Lord Bannon. I have business to attend to." Pavan bowed stiffly, glaring at the lord as he walked away. His fists clenched so tight blood began to trickle between his fingers.

Pavan did not look back. He did not slow his steps, even as the pain in his side from the tender wound still healing, burned furiously. He needed to find Thad.

As he bound up the steps, entering into a side door leading through the servants corridors, Pavan felt in the curve of his jacket pocket, finding the cold metal and pulling from the contents of his pocket, the pendant. It had once belonged to his mother. Made of a shimmering metal, mined in the deepest chambers of Entheas. Meilyr had been the one to give it to Eleanor.

Pavan rubbed his thumb over the surface of the stone, embedded in the carved surface. Magick hummed, warm and radiant against Pavan's palm.

Thad was hunched over the table, with the little book open before him. This one was new, he worked quietly, as the maids and other servants talked loudly about the dining room, just off the kitchens. Pavan stepped quietly around, sitting beside the faie.

"*We need to talk,*" Pavan spoke, his elven quick on the tongue.

Thad did not look up, his pen scrawled against the page. Pavan caught the eye of one of the maids who sat at the other end of the table as she looked up from her mending work.

Pavan scowled, returning his gaze to Thad. "*Thad stop writing and look at me.*"

A pause of a pen, but the faie did not look up.

Anger boiled under Pavan's skin. Sitting back with a huff, crossing his arms and glaring at Thad, but still the faie would not look at him.

Having had enough, Pavan gripped Thad's collar, yanking him to his feet, the chairs' feet scraping angrily against the stone floor. Behind him, the maid gasped, but Pavan ignored her. Slamming Thad against the wall, there was no resistance.

Pavan spoke again, his words remained in elven.

"*Look at me.*" He growled, pressing the faie back, so his spine dug into the jagged rocks. Thad hissed. "Thad, *LOOK* at me!"

Finally, those orange eyes slid up, meeting Pavan's gaze.

Reaching into the hidden folds of Thad's jacket, Pavan extracted the twin blades, tossing them onto the table. Then, he felt around the padded tunic, caressing Thad's sides, releasing Thad as he felt down to his boots, extracting a third dagger from the hidden sheath in his boot. Pavan tossed it onto the table.

"Satisfied?" Thad hissed.

Pavan was angry, bringing the pendant out of his pocket again, sliding the chain around Thad's neck, glaring into those beautiful eyes, eyeing the faie's frowning mouth. Pavan wanted to kiss him, but he refrained.

"Do not remove this pendant," Pavan stated, his voice harsh and brutal.

Thad scoffed, reaching up to yank the chain off, but Pavan gripped his wrist, leaning into Thad's space, his lips dangerously close to Thad's and the scent of citrus sharp in his senses.

"You will not remove it," Pavan commanded. Thad's gaze shifted, his stubborn defiance flickering with doubt as he lowered his hand.

Thad searched Pavan's eyes. "Has something happened?"

Pavan eased, his tone softened. "He was searching for you, Thad. That night in the library. He was searching for someone...it was *you.*"

Thad's eyes lowered. Pavan tilted his chin up, returning those eyes to look up at him and Pavan felt the flutter of fear.

"He wants your magick, Thad...he knows who you are."

CHAPTER
35

S abian sat at the head of the grand banquet hall, his presence commanding amidst the revelry that surrounded him. The rich tapestries and golden chandeliers cast a warm glow over the scene, the lively music and swirling dancers blending into a tapestry of joy. Laughter and the clinking of glasses filled the air, yet Sabian's mind was elsewhere.

His gaze lingered on Beaumont, who danced with Brendolyn in the center of the hall. Her laughter was bright and unrestrained, a sound that seemed to lift the weight pressing on Sabian's chest, if only for a moment. He felt a rare pang of pride, a deep affection for the princess who had endured so much and yet stood so radiant.

As his eyes shifted across the room, they landed on a darker figure seated three chairs down—the man who had saved him. Pavan. The quiet, brooding figure had become an enigma within the castle walls. When their eyes met, Sabian raised his glass in acknowledgment, a silent thanks for a debt he could never fully repay. Pavan returned the nod, his expression unreadable, his glass raised in solemn respect.

Sabian motioned him, causing the man across the way to stand with compliance, coming down the table's length to sit beside him at the table.

"Your Majesty," Pavan began, his tone measured.

Sabian inclined his head slightly, a small smile gracing his lips. "Lord Pavan," he said warmly. "It is good to see you here tonight."

"I am not a lord, Sabian," Pavan replied, his gaze steady. "Forgive my imprudence, but I believe I must speak with you about what happened that day."

The warmth in Sabian's expression dimmed as the memory of the near-fatal poisoning resurfaced. "Yes," he said gravely, his voice dropping so only Pavan could hear. "For what you did, I owe you my life. I cannot thank you enough for taking the risk upon yourself."

Pavan shook his head, his emerald eyes intense. "I only did what was necessary."

"Your magick, baffles me immensely. Lahrs is a remarkable healer, but even his magick had its limitations, what you were able to accomplish..." Sabian lowered his voice even further at seeing Pavan look more solemn.

"I cannot speak of it, Sabian," there was hesitation in his look as Pavan glanced cautiously around, "but what concerns me deeply is that such a risk was present at all. The poison was no accident."

Sabian sighed, leaning back in his chair. "You believe it was deliberate?"

"I do," Pavan replied without hesitation. "And I suspect the threat comes from within these walls. There is precedent—too many illnesses, too many unexplained deaths within these. Even the queen's passing..." He hesitated, measuring his words.

Sabian stiffened slightly, his eyes narrowing. "You speak of my wife."

"I mean no disrespect," Pavan said quickly, his voice low and urgent. "But her death, so close in context to your own near demise, fits a pattern. Illness has plagued your line too consistently to ignore. Your own father was beset with illness before his death, surmounting yourself to the throne. If we dismiss this attempt on your life as an isolated event, we may miss the larger picture."

Sabian's jaw tightened, his hands gripping the arms of his chair. "I have considered that possibility," he admitted, his voice strained. "But to believe it...to accept that her death was purposeful, the near loss of my heir and son...it is almost unbearable."

Pavan leaned closer, his voice steady but insistent. "Sometimes the truth is what we least wish to confront, but that does not make it any less real. Whoever did this, they intended to start another war."

Sabian closed his eyes briefly, the weight of the conversation bearing down on him. When he opened them, he met Pavan's gaze, a flicker of determination returning to his own. "You are wise in your knowledge. Perhaps an asset to my council."

"Your Majesty," Pavan frowned, shaking his head with dejection, "I am not fit to stand in such regard, but merely wish to belay an outside observation to you."

Sabian observed him. "It is not often I allow the persuasion of those not of Corad in my ear, but I owe you my life. I shall observe this thought further."

"Thank you for your ear," Pavan said firmly. "I also beg you to consider removal of your kin to calmer shores. There is a danger here that lingers too close to the throne."

Sabian nodded slowly, his expression grim.

As the music swelled and the hall's festive energy pressed against their hushed conversation, Sabian reached out, clasping Pavan's shoulder. "Thank you again, Pavan. For your life, your counsel...and your courage."

Just as Sabian began to turn his attention back to the dancing, a tall figure slumped into the chair beside him.

At last, out of breath and flushed from exertion, Beaumont collapsed into the chair beside the King of Corad, his oldest and dearest friend. Sabian greeted him with a warm smile, lifting a cup in silent offering.

"You are in high spirits tonight," Sabian said with a laugh.

Beaumont took the cup and drank deeply, savoring the wine before grinning at his companion. "I celebrate the occasion, Sabian. Tonight, we shall fear no longer." His cheeks were red, and his voice carried a note of relief that seemed to lighten the air.

Sabian chuckled, his gaze flickering briefly to the dancers. "Perhaps when my strength returns, we shall dance again as we once did."

Beaumont placed a firm hand on Sabian's shoulder, his grin softening into something more sincere. "Of course. I have wanted nothing more."

Sabian took Beaumont's hand in his, clasping it tightly. For a moment, the revelry around them faded into the background. His eyes turned toward his daughter, Brendolyn, who moved gracefully through the crowd.

"I was wrong, Monty," Sabian said at last, his voice low, almost hesitant.

Beaumont followed his friend's gaze, his expression softening as he sighed. He leaned closer, his tone gentle but firm. "A good king admits his faults."

Sabian nodded slowly. "And faults I have plenty to spare," he admitted. "I cannot begin to express what a fool I have been." He took a long drink from his cup before lowering it, his gaze darkening with unspoken thoughts. "It is a strange thing to feel…" His words faltered, trailing into silence.

Beaumont's brow furrowed as he leaned in. "You were poisoned, Sabian," he said in a hushed tone, his eyes locking with the other king's.

Sabian nodded gravely. "A strange business…to be afflicted in the same manner and yet survive."

A shadow passed over Beaumont's face as he tightened his grip on Sabian's shoulder. "Do not dwell on the reverse, my friend. It is good that you live, and some thoughts are better left unspoken, untouched."

Sabian exhaled slowly, his gaze steady. "I have spoken to someone I trust—a man who may bring us clarity, help us uncover the truth behind this treachery."

Beaumont, however, was no longer listening. His gaze drifted past Sabian, his expression darkening as it fixed on a figure in the crowd. The man did not dance like the others; he loomed, his presence too close to Brendolyn.

"Monty?" Sabian's voice drew his friend's attention.

Beaumont's jaw tightened, his hand falling away from Sabian's shoulder as his eyes remained locked on the shadowed figure. "Who is that man?" he murmured, his voice tense.

Sabian followed Beaumont's gaze, his expression hardening as he took in the scene before them. "That is Sir Varick."

Sir Varick stood too close to Princess Brendolyn, his grip firm on her arm as she tried to pull away. The sight made Beaumont rise sharply from his seat, his chair scraping loudly against the stone floor before toppling over. His towering figure and outstretched hand cut through the lively chatter of the hall as his voice thundered.

"Unhand her this moment!"

The hall fell silent, all eyes turning toward the commotion. Varick faltered, his hand slipping from Brendolyn's arm as Beaumont began to approach in long, deliberate strides. The crowd parted before him like a tide. By the time Beaumont reached him, the knight had lowered himself in a trembling attempt at contrition.

"Your Majesty, I only—" Varick stammered, his words faltering under Beaumont's withering glare.

"Silence!" Beaumont roared, his voice reverberating through the hall. The air felt thick with tension as the entire court froze, watching the unfolding scene. Beaumont's eyes burned with disdain as he loomed over Varick.

"Your actions are an affront," he said, his tone low and dangerous. "Your presence here is unwelcome, and I suggest you remove yourself from this hall before I have you banished from Jorn. If you dare address either me or Princess Brendolyn again, your life will be forfeit. Do I make myself clear?"

Varick's face turned ashen, his mouth opening and closing wordlessly. Beaumont took another step forward, his imposing figure eclipsing the cowering knight.

"Do. I. Make. Myself. Clear?" he repeated, his words a venomous whisper.

Varick nodded frantically, stumbling backward before retreating from the hall in disgrace.

The silence lingered as Beaumont turned back to Brendolyn, his expression softening. He extended a steady arm to her and though her cheeks were flushed, Brendolyn accepted his offer, allowing him to escort her back to the banquet table. Once there, Beaumont faced the court again, his tone lighter but firm.

"Bring in the entertainment," he commanded. "I wish to be amused."

The musicians hesitated before the first strains of a lively tune filled the air. Slowly, the hall came back to life as the courtiers resumed their revelry. Beaumont, however, clenched the armrest of his chair, his anger still simmering beneath his composed exterior.

"He will be dealt with in the morning," Sabian said quietly, placing a reassuring hand on Beaumont's arm.

Beaumont nodded curtly, his gaze shifting to Brendolyn. Though she sat poised, there was an unmistakable unease in her expression. He longed to ask what Varick had said to her, but his attention was abruptly pulled away by another presence.

Pavan.

Seated beside Brendolyn, Pavan's complexion had paled, his emerald eyes rimmed with an eerie sheen of white as they locked onto Beaumont's. A heavy, oppressive heat radiated from the boy, and Beaumont recognized the tinge magick.

"Excuse me," Beaumont murmured to Sabian before moving toward Pavan.

Taking the vacant seat beside Pavan, Beaumont leaned in, his broad shoulders blocking them from the rest of the hall.

"Breathe," he whispered firmly.

Pavan's clenched fist trembled, the veins in his hand darkening with magick, straining to contain it within himself. Beaumont instinctively reached out, placing his hand over Pavan's and squeezing gently.

"She is safe," Beaumont murmured. "Look—she is safe right there."

Pavan didn't glance at Brendolyn. His gaze stayed fixed on Beaumont, his voice tight and pained. "Her fear, Monty...I can feel it. It's calling to me."

Beaumont's grip tightened on Pavan's arm as he leaned closer, his voice steady. "Do not act on it. I will handle Varick. Focus. Breathe."

Pavan inhaled shakily, a semblance of calm returning to him, but their moment was interrupted by an unfamiliar voice.

"Forgive the intrusion, Your Majesty," a man said, bowing slightly.

Beaumont looked up, his attention snapping to the stranger. There was something disconcerting about him—the way his presence seemed familiar yet elusive, his features difficult to focus on like magick shrouded him from truly being seen.

The man's gaze flicked between Beaumont's hand on Pavan's arm and their proximity, a faint, knowing smirk playing at his lips. Beaumont pulled back sharply, tension prickling his neck. The stranger turned his attention to Pavan. "We are short dancers," he said smoothly.

Pavan's demeanor shifted immediately, concern shadowing his face. "Lianus was just in the servant's hall this morning," he whispered, his words laced with unease.

"Juliette is distraught. She refuses to perform without a partner."

Beaumont watched as the weight of duty clashed with personal desire in Pavan's expression. A fleeting glance toward the princess betrayed his hesitation. Yet, the pull to alleviate the dancers' tension, to fulfill his companion's request, was unmistakable.

"Give me five minutes," Pavan muttered through clenched teeth, resignation heavy in his tone.

Beaumont waited for the copper haired man to retreat into the crowd before leaning closer to Pavan. The younger man hesitated as he moved to stand, but Beaumont seized his wrist, pulling him down to whisper in his ear.

"Come to my chambers after dinner," Beaumont said, his voice low, urgent.

Pavan gave a single, almost imperceptible nod before slipping away, his figure soon lost amidst the swirl of dancers and courtiers. Beaumont remained seated, watching him go, then turned his attention to Sabian.

A strange expression shadowed Sabian's face, and Beaumont reached out, his hand resting lightly on the other king's arm.

"Are you all right?" Beaumont asked, concern softening his tone.

Sabian's demeanor soured as he pulled away, lifting his glass and draining it with deliberate fervor. "You think I don't see what's happening here?"

Beaumont stiffened, withdrawing his hand as Sabian's voice turned sharp, accusatory. "You misunderstand, Sabian. That boy is—"

The goblet hit the table with a heavy thunk, cutting Beaumont off. Sabian's eyes were alight with anger, yet there was something deeper there—betrayal, perhaps.

"I know your type, Monty," Sabian said coldly. "Dark hair. Olive skin. And young—far too young, even for you. What is he? Thirty?"

Beaumont felt a sharp pang in his chest, the words lodging in his throat. "He's not...eight and twenty," he began, his voice faltering.

Sabian's gaze pierced him, demanding answers. Beaumont could say nothing—nothing of the truth that burned to escape. He wanted to tell Sabian who Pavan really was. That the boy was the son of Eleanore, his beloved Eleanore.

But no words came. Instead, Beaumont swallowed the bitter taste of his silence, his gaze shifting across the room. In the far shadows, he spotted a familiar figure—Lord Bannon, deep in conversation with a fellow lord. Moments later, Bannon slipped away, vanishing from the hall like a ghost.

"You whispered in his ear, invited him to your chambers tonight," Sabian said, his voice barely above a whisper yet brimming with accusation.

The words struck Beaumont like a blow, stealing his breath. He turned to Sabian, seeing the pain etched in the face of a scorned lover, a betrayed friend.

Straightening in his chair, Beaumont summoned the mask he had long perfected, the one that concealed the fractures in his soul. His gaze hardened, meeting Sabian's head-on.

"We are both free men, Sabian," Beaumont said, his tone cool and unyielding. "Is it wrong to seek the splendor of youth to invigorate my bed? He is, after all...quite agile."

The words were like shards of glass, cutting both speaker and listener. Sabian flinched, his face crumpling as the band struck up a lively tune. The music filled the room, drowning out the echoes of their conversation.

Beaumont turned away, the light of the hall blurring at the edges as a shift in the atmosphere mirrored the turmoil within him. His heart, though hidden behind his practiced poise, was breaking.

Pavan entered the corridor, glad to be free of the confining restraint. He could not handle feeling her anguish, the rush of anger that flooded through him, seeing her distressed. Now, he sought a different feeling. A demanding gnawing desire in the pit of his stomach. Pavan found Thad, securing a last-minute pin in Juliette's hair.

"Thad," Pavan whispered, touching the curve of his elbow.

Those eyes looked at him and Pavan's stomach flopped. His eyes lingering down to the exposed part of the faie's tunic, where the pendant rested.

"Juliette is ready, thank you for this—"

"I need to speak with you first, please." Pavan intreated, gently pulling on Thad's elbow and breathing easier when the faie nodded. Following Pavan as he led them into the nearest room, it was small, little more than a closet.

"What is it, Pavan?" Thad hesitated.

Pavan sighed, leaning in and capturing Thad's lips in a desperate kiss, pressing him back against the shelves behind them.

"Pavan, not here..." Thad shook his head, pulling away.

Pressing his forehead to the faie's, Pavan inhaled deeply, magick was sharp. His side ached, the pain behind his eyes making him wince but not wanting to leave him.

"I need only this," Pavan whispered.

Thad trembled, but did not push Pavan away. Now, Pavan sighed, kissing Thad's jaw, trailing his lips to the curve of his neck, inhaling the scent of magick that lingered.

"I cannot let this doubt come between us, Thad. Do not let me continue knowing you regret what you did." Pavan took Thad's hand in his, pressing his palm to the curve, where the dagger had stabbed him and Thad let out a shaky breath.

"I hurt you," Thad breathed, unable to meet Pavan's gaze.

"You saved me." Pavan kissed him.

Thad looked away, there was something more. A deeper unsettling feeling that came over him, making Pavan shiver.

"What is it, Thad?" Pavan asked.

"It is nothing." Thad shook his head.

Pavan was firm, taking hold of the faie's hand, pressing it with strength. "Yes, there is...I can feel it upon you Thad...there is doubt. You have doubts about us?"

"I have seen your dreams, Pavan...I know you dream about the princess. She is the one at the seaside, with the dark hair...she sings to you, doesn't she?"

"They are only dreams." Pavan shook his head.

"They are more than dreams, Pavan...they are the visions of the one who is given to your very heartsong...she is your fated match."

Pavan dropped Thad's hand, glaring hard at the faie's guilty eyes.

"That's impossible, Thad. I cannot be the fated match of a silly little girl. I love you, and no one else." Pavan could see the strain for control in Thad as they stood so near to each other. "You don't love me..."

Thad shrunk back. "I will always love you, Pavan."

Hesitation was a strong taste upon Pavan's tongue as the magick burned through him. Pavan could feel the change between them as those orange eyes slowly lifted to stare straight into him.

"Tell me why it's impossible to love me completely, Thad."

"They are waiting." Thad reached for the door but Pavan took hold of his wrist, gripping him hard and holding Thad back.

"They can wait for an eternity...we shall not leave this room until you tell me why you cannot love me, Thad. Why is it impossible to let me into your heart? I know you tell me it is because you are faie, but there is something more...there is something keeping us apart and it has nothing to do with that girl."

"She is your destiny."

"Do not talk to me of destinies, Thad...do not whisper to me of what my mind whispers in the darkest corners. I choose my own path, I choose my own happiness. I made my choice to devote myself to you completely. All I am asking is why you cannot do the same?"

Thad's eyes were glistening with tears.

"It burns me, to know I cannot have you forever," Thad hissed. His words a sharpened edge. "I have fallen for you as I should not have done. After what I have felt for—"

Thad paused long enough to calm his emotions.

"There has not been born to this world brothers born hand in hand. I could not understand it...I *do not* understand it." Thad began after a long moment. "I believed it would be the same, that I could love you with equal heart that I had the moment I saw him in Denorn all those years ago."

Pavan frowned. "You speak of your master?"

"I speak of Henry," Thad hissed, charging the air between them with unseen magick, a sharp spark that sent a thousand shivers through Pavan.

"You knew Hal?" Pavan whispered.

"In the moment I laid eyes upon him, I knew that he was meant for me...it is the bond that one shared with the one they are fated to, but I was afraid of what my master would do to him should he find him there. It is a fate worse than death." Thad looked wretched, his fair skin splotched as tears fell along his cheeks. "I told Henry to run...to go far away and never return to these shores."

Pavan felt numbed as he listened to Thad speak.

"It tore my soul to watch him sail away on that ship...watching him leave these shores to never return. Knowing myself to be separated from him forever."

"Why did you not go with him?"

Thad looked away. "I was bound to my master...the magick would have killed me, should I have gone so far."

A sharp knock on the door sounded and Juliette's voice called from the other side. They were ready for them to dance.

Pavan sighed heavily. "Thad."

"We shall talk again. Pavan, I promise. I love you, *mo ghrá*..."

From the midst of the lively banquet, a hush fell over the crowd as a striking figure emerged from the shadows. The music softened, the dramatic ensemble giving way to a hauntingly delicate tune. A woman, with an ethereal grace, moved to the center of the hall, her presence commanding immediate attention. The courtiers fell silent, their eyes drawn to her as the first notes of the viola floated through the air.

She danced alone, her long skirts flowing like liquid silk around her as she moved in perfect harmony with the music. The candles flickered, casting shimmering patterns of light that danced along with her. The air seemed to hum with an almost tangible magick as the melody swelled and the music deepened with the addition of the cello and a second viola.

Brendolyn, who had been caught in the whirlwind of the evening's events, found her breath catch as a second figure appeared. Pavan entered the hall, his presence a stark contrast to the dark silk doublet he had worn earlier. His attire now matched the woman's gown, a subtle yet elegant shift that left Brendolyn momentarily breathless.

The memory of the earlier confrontation with Sir Varick surged back, mingling with her astonishment. She recalled the knight's urgent whisper to escape with him, only to be interrupted by Beaumont's commanding voice. The tension had been palpable, and she had felt a deep, unsettling anger. Her relief when Beaumont escorted her back to her seat was short-lived, replaced by a disorienting clarity that came only after Pavan's departure from the table. The sensation of feeling his emotions so vividly had unsettled her.

Now, as she watched Pavan and the woman dance together, their movements were mesmerizing. The dance was unlike anything Brendolyn had ever seen—a fluid interplay of elegance and intensity that spoke more than words ever could. They circled each other in a rhythm that seemed to blend the grace of a waltz with the sharp precision of a sword fight. Each step, each turn, was a conversation in motion, a silent exchange of passion and skill.

In a moment of stillness, Pavan's eyes met Brendolyn across the room, his gaze piercing through the dim light. It was a fleeting connection, charged and intense, before the dance resumed. The performance reached its climax as the woman collapsed gracefully to the floor, Pavan's hand outstretched towards her. The music reached a triumphant crescendo, the hall erupted in applause and excited murmurs.

As the courtiers began to mingle and the room buzzed with conversation, Brendolyn found herself drawn to Pavan. She moved through the crowd with purpose, her heart racing as she followed him toward the corridor. She watched him descend the staircase, her breath quickening as she hurried to catch up. Turning a corner, she found herself abruptly pulled into a shadowy alcove beneath the stairs.

Pavan's hand gripped her arm with a surprising firmness, his voice a low, commanding whisper. "You should not follow me, princess."

Brendolyn's eyes widened in the dim light. "I wanted to speak with you. I was concerned after seeing Thad—there was so much blood. I need to know you're alright."

Pavan's frown deepened, his expression one of discomfort and unease. The shadowed space heightened the tension, the flickering light from the distant candles casting shifting patterns over their faces. "It is not a place for idle chatter or concern," he said, his tone edged with a cold determination.

Brendolyn swallowed, her heart pounding as she searched for the right words. The silence between them was heavy, filled with unspoken emotions and the weight of the night's events.

"Not here, we cannot be seen here." His tone was dark, strained and he could not look at her.

"I leave for Entheas in two days' time, Pavan...there may not be another chance to speak with you." Brendolyn reached up, caressing the curve of his jaw. Her breath stilled, feeling the wave of magick, his muscles flexed beneath her touch.

"Then you shall be safe, princess."

"Will you not look at me, Pavan...will you not say goodbye?" Her voice trembled, her heart fluttering.

At last, his green eyes looked up, calming the rush of anxiety that began to build within her and she smiled.

"Goodbye, princess..." he breathed.

Fear rattled her, she shook her head. "Pavan, you must leave Jorn...do not remain here."

His head shook, he was slipping away, drawing back.

"Pavan, it is dangerous." She clung to his middle, wrapping her arms around his middle and the man stiffened. "I can feel danger here, Pavan...I can sense something happening. I don't understand, but I am afraid."

A hand rest calmly against her shoulder.

Brendolyn gasped back her tears. "Please don't stay. Not here...not where there is danger."

"You should return to your party, princess..."

He spoke so calmly, but Brendolyn could feel the race of his heart where her cheek pressed to the flat of his chest, unable to bring herself to let him go.

"It is not my party...I am invisible...no one will miss me there." Her words trembled but his hands grasped her waist, pushing her back. Brendolyn stumbled away from the alcove.

"Brendolyn?"

She froze, her eyes lifting to the graceful steps of Barrow as he descended the steps towards her. It was clear to Brendolyn, why Pavan shoved her. He could hear the approach of the prince, when she could not.

"Barrow," she breathed, wiping at her tears. Fear flickering as she glanced at the alcove.

He stood in front of her now, his back to the alcove where Pavan stood hidden in the darkness.

"I have been looking for you, after what happened..." His hand cupped the curve of her cheek, smiling at her sweetly and Brendolyn smiled.

"I am alright." She nodded, reassuring him.

She gasped, feeling the warmth of his lips on hers, Barrow did not waste the opportunity to embrace her. Brendolyn felt her face grow hot, knowing they were being watched.

"Barrow, not here..." she warned, her gaze drifting to the stairs.

He chuckled. "It is alright, no one followed me. I would kiss you endlessly, Bren..."

Her head was dizzy as his arms embraced her, drawing her close to his chest to kiss her once more. But she felt wrong. Her head ached, there was coldness in her veins, mixing within her blood, and there was a stagnant feeling, flickering to life with a fire of anger.

She gasped, stepping back.

Barrow was confused, watching her closely, with concern.

Tears stung her eyes. "I can't." Her body trembled, stepping back, making distance between them. "I can't torment my heart, Barrow...not like this."

He was wounded, Brendolyn saw the despair in the prince's features, but it was wrong. He was going to marry Lisetta, it was wrong to keep pretending like this.

"But I love you, Bren...only you..." he entreated.

Brendolyn took another step back. "I'm sorry." Her tears fell freely, glancing to the alcove, now empty. Pavan was gone, and her head was on fire. Turning away from Barrow, she hurried up the stairs, grasping her skirts to keep herself from falling.

CHAPTER

36

S imeon slipped into the hall, ascending the steps leading to his private chambers after receiving a note from Leuthere having arrived from Denorn, with a package.

"Lord Hoban..." He leered down at the slumped man that hissed and growled. His bulking frame shackled in magick chains in a chair set close to the fire.

"Let me go, I have done nothing..." the large man shouted but Simeon leaned close, shushing the man who was restrained against the bindings of the chains.

"Tsk tsk, now, my lord...we both know why you are here."

Lord Hoban grimaced, trembling against the crook of Simeon's finger, his nail close to the edge of the large man's throat.

"I don't...I don't know what you want from me." Lord Hoban was whimpering, unlike the man Simeon knew from before and a smile spread wide over his lips.

"I see. That faie has seen you...he has turned your mind." Simeon lowered, kneeling down before the man. Hunkering deep and finding the magick that resided deep within the man.

Seeking, Simeon's magick clawed its way through him, ignoring the shouts of agony as Simeon tore through the man's mind, eyes rolling back, muttering beneath his breath. It was citron, magick that was sweet as honey, strong against his senses. Simeon whined, keening at the exhilaration.

Drawing back, with a gasp, Simeon smiled. Beneath his grasp Lord Hoban wept, his skin pale, his body trembling, sniveling with snot, and blood trickling from the man's nose.

"You are returned, Hoban…What is your redemption?" Simeon asked as he began to feel the crawl of anguish come over the man and drew his magick closer to the surface.

Lord Hoban's eyes widened. Blood dripping out of both nostrils, his eyes watering a tint of red. "Please," he garbled, blood filling his mouth and horror flooding the man's features.

"What did you tell him, Hoban? What did you tell Gaur's cunt of my plans?" Simeon hissed, coming dangerously close to the man's face.

"He only asked…a…n-name…" Hoban rasped.

Hoban's veins bulged, Simeon's fingers slithering forward, tightened around his throat, squeezing the life from him.

"Good." Simeon smiled, snapping the man's neck. The large body heaved, before slumping to the side, restrained by the chains that held him upright.

Simeon smiled down at him, his new surge of energy within his body humming with gratitude.

A flicker of candle and the room grew cold.

A lush voice filled the air, *Your power has grown,* it cooed, a gentle caress on Bannon's cheek.

He smiled. "His essence came without a fight, it was easy to obtain."

A gentle purr flitted through him, the voice caressing the magick he now held.

"We cannot delay, I desire to ensnare the young prince, for his heart is weary. I can read the energy from him, he writhes with anger and longing."

Simeon could sense the excitement embrace around him and the voice grew delighted.

He so young of body and mind shall be the easiest catch but beware the king…he has a true heart that cannot be matched.

To this Simeon snarled, "He will soon bend to my whim, as his father before. Who else but I have made such a king as Broderick beg me to end him? He rotted for years as I whittled away his will to live, now shall be no different from then."

Confidence surged within the man, feeding off of the new-found energy that coursed through his veins. Longing for more soon followed.

Patience, Simeon, the voice whispered, sending shivers up Simeon's spine.

Someone enters. The presence of the voice vanished and the coldness Simeon was left with made him shiver as a knock sounded at the door. He turned, unhooking the latch and the door swung open, standing before him was Varick. A smile creased on Bannon's lips as he invited him in.

"My lord." The man bowed.

"Come, enter, Varick." Simeon smiled, watching the knight enter his chambers.

Seeing the fear and hesitation in the brown eyes, Sir Varick saw Lord Hoban slumped, dead in his chains.

He felt the fear, seeing the sweat glistening off of the knights skin. "Is that man—"

Simeon laughed. "Quite dead."

Varick was a coward, hunkering back, keeping his distance from Simeon. Let the sniveling man have his peace, when no distance could prevent Simeon from killing the man where he stood.

"You have a need for me, sir?"

Now, they have come to it, the reason the man was summoned to this place. Simeon straightened his stance, glaring at Varick with contempt.

"If you ever touch Brendolyn again, I shall snap your neck," he stated, seeing the fear radiate from the knight.

"She is *mine*, by right."

Simeon hissed. "She is Barrow's slut! Your impatience draws his eyes upon your intentions. I have no patience for impudent men, Varick. Touch the slag again, and our contract is forfeit."

True fear radiated, alarm of his doom weighing heavily in Varick's heart. Simeon felt the flutter of magick, the strong taste of it sharp on his tongue and Simeon stepped closer.

"Do we have an understanding, Varick or shall I remind you what awaits you should you fail me?" His hand rest open over the curve of the knight's shoulder. Relaxed, but intentionally fixed, Varick understood.

Trembling, the knight nodded. "I understand, my lord."

Simeon smiled, his lips pulling tight over the curve of his teeth as he glared down at the knight. "Now get out of my sight."

It was dark in the corridor, Pavan maneuvered through the servant's stairs, coming to the door leading out into the royal wing. He had asked the sweet kitchen maid which steps would lead him here. Now as he neared the king's door, Pavan's heart began to pound mercilessly.

He knocked once, leaning his frame against the wall, waiting.

The door opened a fraction, before a hand pulled him inside. Pavan let himself fall into the warmth of the chamber. Turning to see Beaumont standing before him, much as he had seemed before, but his divine silk doublet was replaced by a long dressing gown made of gold and embroidered brocade. Beneath, his shirt lay open slightly, his feet bare against the stone.

"You perform quite well, Isaac. Forgive me...Pavan," Beaumont corrected, giving Pavan a warm smile.

"I was trained at the very best schools in—that doesn't matter," he muttered, finding himself blushing. It was an odd sense of eagerness, seeing the man he had grown attached to as a child, as the man before him now.

"Your mother would be proud."

Pavan's lips twitched, trapped between a smile and the pained expression he always fought to banish. Beaumont walked to the side cabinets, pouring himself a drink from his crystal bottle before turning to offer a drink to Pavan.

"I always believed I had made you up," Pavan admitted, taking a gentle sip of the drink offered. "A knight come to rescue my mother...but here I have come to discover you are a king."

Beaumont chuckled, a charming sound.

"I was not a king then, Pavan. Only a man who was in love with a woman, desperate to live a life not by duty or rules."

Pavan looked away, his throat tight, unable to speak.

"I wish for you to meet Fiona," Beaumont said at last, leaning his large frame upon the back of a dark green velvet couch.

Pavan gulped down another drink. "I am not a courtier...there is no need for me to be introduced to the royal family."

Beaumont shook his head. "As a guest of the king, no one could question the word to tell them who you are."

"It is not that simple, you know it is not." Pavan shook his head, eying the king, looking him over with a knowing glance. "I am aware of the particular status you have about you, Your Highness. Inviting me to your table, so openly, would raise more questions about your honor."

Beaumont chuckled, drinking. "Am I that apparent to you, Pavan?"

"What is it that you told Sabian? I am young and agile?" Pavan glanced away, his cheeks growing quite warm.

Beaumont was not smiling, when Pavan finally looked up.

"You heard me?" he whispered.

Shaking his head, Pavan downed the remainder of his drink, placing the empty glass of the nearest table.

"I am not blind, Monty...you are close to the king of the south. Brendolyn explained the particular history leading up to the war...but it was not the death of the Princess Kryana that began the war...I have learned in my research that there was a breach of purity. One that Jorn holds to the root of its core." Pavan slowly moved to the armchair nearest to the king.

Beaumont was frowning, not able to look up at Pavan.

"You were always the perceptive one." The king finally smirked, glancing up. Downing the remainder of the drink in his own glass, standing to lumber over to the table to pour himself another drink.

"I understand your connection, Your Majesty, but there is a fault in your perception of what should be done in this treaty." Pavan stood, following the king.

Beaumont smirked. "You speak of Barrow's arranged marriage?"

"It is not wise, Your Majesty...he loves Brendolyn. Loved her so much they married in secret."

Beaumont became flushed. "You know of this?"

"She told me."

There is a long moment before the king finally speaks. "Have you spoken to her often?"

"Since I saved her father, that girl has more questions than reserve...but Barrow is in love with her. Being forced to marry another, what would that drive him to do, Beaumont?"

Beaumont shook his head. "Barrow is headstrong, raised to one day be king..."

"If he does not marry Lisetta—"

"The council will never agree to it...the contract has been signed. It is to be fulfilled in a fortnight." Beaumont was shaking his head.

"Because he is in love with a faie?" Pavan asked.

Beaumont smirked. "Brendolyn is a charming girl, but her mother's heritage is a black stain in Corad. Sabian's advisors would not give him leave to allow her to sit upon the throne of Jorn."

"DeFay is not a name in the Corad books, she is of Jorn, is she not?" Pavan asked, remembering the conversation he had with Brendolyn about her mother.

Beaumont's eyes grew wide. Turning on his heel the king hurried into the adjacent room within his apartments. Pavan followed, watching Beaumont as he reached a large leather-bound book, extracting it to lay it open upon the nearest table. Pavan watched as the king shuffled through the pages, scanning with a knowing eye until he let his finger fall upon the page.

A tree made of gilded leaf shimmered across the page, alive in the magick that wrote the pages, to legitimize the line, each leaf that bore a name was wilted, faded to a mute gray.

"Hana DeFay, daughter of Duke Amend DeFay..."

"Who holds the dukedom now?" Pavan asked, leaning over the table beside Beaumont to read the page. All of the tree was marked deceased, but the little leaf after Hana was bright. A name that made Pavan's chest tighten—Brendolyn.

Beaumont shook his head. "This is absurd, the council will never agree to it."

"Are they undecided? If the council is split between the two realms, would the deciding factor be split?" Pavan asked.

"They are all well informed and I believe many of them are deep within Bannon's pocket." Beaumont shook his head.

"Do not change the treaty."

"How would that work, if we should spare Barrow's mind…"

Pavan leaned in again. "Barrow wants to marry Bren. If he has a chance to allow himself to be married to her, change your will. Your last testament of the deed upon your death."

Beaumont sighed, reading over the page again.

Pavan continued, "Restore the namesake of DeFay to the land in Augusta, it has been without for years."

"She would give up her rights of Corad…how could I ask of her to do it?"

"She loves your son, Beaumont."

Beaumont's frustration simmered as he listened to Pavan's unyielding insistence. "Yes, I believe you are right. But I do not believe this would work in our favor."

Pavan's gaze remained steely. "You must retract the marriage treaty. If Barrow holds any form of regret, Beaumont, there is a chance Bannon could exploit it for his own gain. Surely you see this?"

Beaumont's shoulders tensed, and he shook his head slowly, a trace of frustration lining his voice. "Bannon would not be so negligent, Pavan."

"You are blind to his true intent," Pavan retorted, his voice cold and unrelenting.

The king's eyes flared with anger. "You are not king here, boy!" his voice thundered, echoing through the chamber.

The room fell silent, thick with a tense magick that crackled like electricity. Pavan's eyes narrowed as he scrutinized Beaumont, feeling the potent, dark magick swirling within the king. Beaumont's expression betrayed a flicker of regret as he turned away abruptly, leaning heavily against the edge of the table.

Pavan approached cautiously, his own magick pulsing with urgency. The sharp pain of darkness pressed against his temples as he laid a hand on Beaumont's broad shoulder. "Monty," he whispered, his voice trembling with worry.

Beaumont, unable to meet his gaze, shook his head. "I will be alright," he insisted, though the tremor in his voice spoke otherwise.

Pavan shuddered, his voice tight with desperation. "How long has this magick been corrupting you? Monty, please, look at me."

"It is not easy, letting that man walk about my home…walking amongst my people, knowing what he has done to my family." Beaumont's voice was strained, laden with anguish.

Pavan felt a knot of horror tighten in his gut, the dark magick weighing him down. He wanted to retreat, to escape the torment, but he held firm. "*Monty*...please, look at me," he implored, his voice breaking.

Beaumont's blue eyes finally met his, filled with a pained resignation. "I know I am dying, Pavan."

Panic surged through Pavan, his face contorting with fear. "Let me help you."

"You waste your magick, Pavan..." Beaumont's voice was barely a whisper.

"I cannot let you die," Pavan said fiercely, stepping closer, his own magick burning hot within him. He reached out, his hand cupping Beaumont's cheek, trying to soothe the pain.

Beaumont's resistance waned as Pavan's magick worked its way into the cracks of his defenses. "You risk too much," Beaumont murmured, his voice faltering.

Pavan's expression hardened with determination. He gently guided Beaumont's face to his own, their foreheads touching. "Please," Pavan breathed, his voice a raw plea. "I can feel the darkness touching your heart...let me help you."

The king shook his head, his strength ebbing. "You risk too much."

Pavan smirked, sensing the king's resolve softening under the allure of his magick. His own desperation clawed at him, pushing him to take greater risks. With a tender yet fervent touch, Pavan drew Beaumont into a deep kiss. His magick wove through the kiss, seeking out the encroaching darkness, entwining with it.

Beaumont's body tensed, and he gasped against the intensity of Pavan's touch. Pavan pressed closer, his hands moving to Beaumont's throat, fingers curling around the delicate flesh. The dark magick within Beaumont responded, reluctantly relinquishing its grip as Pavan's own power absorbed it.

"I won't stop, Monty..." Pavan growled, his voice thick with determination. "Not until I feel the last pulse of his magick leave your body."

Beaumont's gasps grew more labored, but he yielded, allowing Pavan to draw the corruption from him. The darkness flowed into Pavan, burning hot and consuming. As Beaumont's body began to relax, signaling the absence of pain, Pavan drew back slowly, his own magick spent and the king's breathing easing.

Pavan stumbled, his head spinning, pain sharp behind his eyes.

"Pavan, breathe." Beaumont's voice was far away. Pavan heaved for breath as magick flooded through him, his muscles were tightening and contracting as he resisted.

"I can't...not now." Pavan staggered back, catching himself on the back of a chair. Beaumont grabbed him, his strong hands like fire on his skin.

"This was folly, Pavan. What can I do?" Beaumont's voice swirled in Pavan's mind and the king's strong hands grasped under Pavan's arm, keeping him upright.

Pavan's head was swimming, as he fought the urge to vomit.

"*Don't touch me*," Pavan growled, his body shaking violently.

Beaumont pulled back.

Hunkering down, his body shivered, agitated in the aftermath of taking the sliver of darkness from Beaumont. Each breath came sharper, his mind in agony as his own magick coiled against the intrusive gloom. Each wave further increased the desperation of consuming.

"Pavan, should I get someone...Lahrs? Should I get the elf?"

Pavan gulped, tasting death and decay, blinking to bring the king into focus. The figure swayed, Pavan scrambled away, unable to concentrate on anything but the agony in his heart, and the consuming dread.

Watching the king fade away, leaving Pavan in his state of consuming darkness.

Beaumont's urgency was palpable as he burst into Lahrs's quarters, his face a mask of distress. Lahrs, initially startled by the king's sudden entrance, quickly assessed the situation. Beaumont's pallor, flushed cheeks, and disheveled robe spoke volumes of the turmoil he had endured.

"You must come to my room, at once," Beaumont said breathlessly, his voice trembling with an urgency that was hard to ignore.

Lahrs, recognizing the gravity of the situation, wasted no time. "What happened?" His concern was immediate, as he ushered the king out of the room and into the corridor.

They moved swiftly, their steps muffled by the thick carpets, their breath mingling in the cool night air.

Beaumont's large frame heaved with exertion. "I—It is best to be discreet, Sir Lahrs. This matter is of utmost importance. "

Lahrs halted, his eyes widening in alarm. "Pavan?" His whisper was barely audible, but Beaumont's grim nod confirmed his fears.

Lahrs sprang into action, his mind racing with possibilities as they ascended the stairs to the king's chambers. "How did you leave him, Your Majesty? Was he conscious?" His questions tumbled out in a rush, his concern evident.

"Just so, but I needed to seek your assistance," Beaumont replied, his voice strained.

In the hallway before them, Sir Eero appeared, his eyes widening with concern at the sight of Beaumont and Lahrs together. Ignoring the formalities, Lahrs grabbed Eero's arm. "Please hurry to the kitchens, Eero. Find Thad and bring him to the king's bed-chamber immediately. Quietly and without detection."

Eero nodded, his expression serious as he bowed and hurried off.

Lahrs glanced at Beaumont, his voice low but urgent. "Is he the right man for the charge?"

Beaumont's gaze was troubled. "Eero is one of the few I trust for such a delicate task. And Thad is crucial if my suspicions are correct."

They hurried along the darkened corridor, their footsteps echoing softly as they approached the king's chambers. The heavy scent of blood and dark magick greeted Lahrs as he entered the room. The atmosphere was thick with a foul odor that made his stomach churn.

"Pavan," Lahrs called out, his voice echoing through the dimly lit room. There was no response. His heart raced as he scanned the room, his eyes darting around in search of the source of the overpowering stench.

Beaumont's face was etched with worry. "He was here. Would he have gone out?"

Lahrs moved quickly, checking every corner of the room, his hands running over surfaces and his eyes peering into shadows. "We need to find him," Lahrs said urgently. "He could be in a dangerous state."

The room seemed to hold its breath as they waited, the silence amplifying their anxiety. The flicker of candles cast dancing shadows on the walls, heightening the tension as they waited for Eero and Thad to arrive.

Lahrs turned suddenly, ignoring the king's queries, quickly hastening to the door of the wardrobe against the far wall. Lahrs grasped the handles, yanking it open. There, hunched beneath the hanging jackets and tunics, was Pavan.

Lahrs checked Pavan's pulse, a fluttering beat beneath his fingers. Relief mingled with concern as he sighed. "Pavan..." he called gently, but Pavan's eyes remained glazed and vacant. "Can you hear me?"

Pavan's only response was a low, defiant curl further into himself. The room's tension was palpable, and Lahrs' worry deepened.

The door creaked open again, and Sir Eero entered with Thad at his heels. Lahrs's gaze shifted to the faie, whose presence brought a glimmer of hope. Thad's face darkened as he took in Pavan's state, and Lahrs knew he would need to manage both the faie's emotions and the situation.

"Pavan, it's Thad...he's here," Lahrs said urgently.

Thad approached the wardrobe, his eyes assessing Pavan with a mixture of concern and determination. The faie leaned in, checking Pavan's eyes and pulse with practiced precision.

"What happened?" Thad's voice was sharp, his gaze darting back to Beaumont with barely contained frustration.

"We were talking..." Beaumont began, his voice faltering as he looked away from the intense scrutiny of the faie. The king's discomfort was evident; his face was flushed crimson.

Irritation crackled in the air, a tangible sign of the magick at play. Lahrs placed a calming hand on Thad's arm. "Thad, focus on Pavan...let the king explain. You need to concentrate on your task."

Reluctantly, Thad returned to the wardrobe, though his anger was still palpable. Lahrs turned back to Beaumont, his eyes serious. "Please, Your Majesty, explain."

Beaumont swallowed hard, his face marked by deep unease. "There was dark magick...it had infected me. As we spoke, I became overwhelmed by anger. Pavan was drawn to the dark magick. He insisted on removing it...I couldn't refuse." The king's blush deepened, a mix of shame and embarrassment coloring his features. "He...he took the darkness from me..." Beaumont's voice trailed off, leaving him visibly distressed.

"How could he do that?" Eero asked, his voice filled with a mix of awe and apprehension.

"He is Ehlfern," Lahrs explained with a sigh. "He has great power, but it's dangerous."

"Don't touch me!" Pavan's voice rang out, deep and charged with magick, startling everyone. The man's aura shifted, his power palpable as he moved within the wardrobe, his anguish reverberating through the room.

Thad stepped forward, hands raised. "It's me, Pavan...let me help you."

Lahrs moved to give them space, watching intently as Thad spoke soothingly. "I am here with Lahrs. We can stop the pain, Pavan. Just let us help you."

The response was a tortured cry. "*It won't stop...it won't stop...*"

The broken words pierced the room, the agony almost tangible and Lahrs felt a shiver of dread. "He needs to go to sleep, Thad..." he warned, sensing the room growing colder. Ice formed on the surfaces, a clear sign of the escalating magick.

Thad nodded, his focus unwavering as he inched closer to the wardrobe. "Pavan, I need you to remain calm."

A heavy silence followed, but then a loud crack reverberated through the room. Thad was hurled backward, colliding with the table and sending it skidding a few inches. He groaned, struggling to his feet, his chest heaving from the impact.

Lahrs moved swiftly, positioning himself between the wardrobe and Beaumont. "Stay back, Your Majesty," he instructed, while Eero took a guarded stance nearby.

"What's happening?" Beaumont asked, his voice tinged with panic.

Lahrs observed Pavan emerging from the wardrobe, blood streaking his pale face. His eyes had turned a stark white, a clear sign of his power spiraling out of control. "He is losing himself to his power..." Lahrs said, his voice steady as he cast a protective shield around them. He watched as Thad approached Pavan with renewed urgency, ready to confront the escalating crisis.

One swipe, then another—Pavan's large form moved with surprising agility as he dodged the faie's relentless strikes. Despite his impressive speed, Thad remained unyielding, his determination evident as he circled back after Pavan's powerful arm had sent him sprawling.

Lahrs maintained a shimmering barrier of magick between the violent clash and the king, whose wide eyes betrayed a mix of fear and fascination. Thad, relentless and focused, launched himself at Pavan with a precision that spoke to his extensive training. A well-aimed strike hit Pavan's jaw, yet the faie remained standing, his strength unshaken.

Thad narrowly avoided a retaliatory blow, sidestepping with practiced grace before swiftly moving to get behind Pavan.

In a decisive move, Thad leaped onto Pavan's back, his grip tightening into a headlock. "Go. To. Sleep," Thad gritted out, his voice a low growl filled with intense concentration.

Pavan's growl of resistance reverberated through the room, his immense strength evident as he struggled against Thad's hold. But Thad's grip was unrelenting, every muscle in his body straining to maintain control. With a surge of effort, Thad managed to force Pavan to his knees, his arms and legs secured in a vice-like lock. The room seemed to pulse with the strain of their struggle, magick crackling in the air.

Finally, with a last, shuddering gasp, the dark runes marking Pavan's skin began to fade. His eyes, once fierce and wild, grew vacant before fluttering shut. Thad held him for a moment longer before releasing him, letting Pavan's limp form fall heavily to the floor with a dull thud. The sudden stillness in the room was profound.

Lahrs let out a breath he hadn't realized he'd been holding, the protective shield dissipating as he surveyed the now tranquil scene. He glanced back at Beaumont, whose shock was palpable, his mouth hanging open in disbelief.

"Beaumont," Thad spoke, breaking the silence with a voice laden with exhaustion, "we should place him on the bed."

Beaumont shook himself from his stupor, nodding with a nod that spoke of his struggle to regain composure. He was silent, his gaze fixed on the unconscious man.

Thad, his energy visibly depleted but his resolve unshaken, bent down with practiced efficiency. He grasped Pavan's arm with careful precision and hoisted the large man effortlessly onto his shoulders. His movements were smooth and fluid, showcasing his adeptness at handling such burdens. With a weary but determined gait, Thad carried Pavan towards the king's waiting bed, the weight of his unconscious frame a reminder of the intensity of the recent struggle.

"Thad, the other side," Lahrs instructed sharply, his eyes fixed on Pavan as he neared the bedside.

Without a word, Thad complied, moving to the opposite side of the bed with practiced precision. Both men positioned themselves strategically, their focus unwavering. As they began to chant in unison, the air around them shimmered with ancient magick, a complex web of runes and sigils forming above the bed. The enchantment wove itself into the fabric of the room, a protective cocoon of magick enveloping Pavan's unconscious form. The glow of the spell illuminated the room with a soft, ethereal light, casting intricate patterns across the walls.

Beaumont, still pale and visibly shaken, finally found his voice. "What enchantment is that?"

Lahrs, breathless from the exertion, glanced over with a mixture of relief and fatigue. "We're placing him in a deep slumber...with wards around the bed to keep him in place. He mustn't be moved just yet. It's crucial for his recovery."

Beaumont nodded, his face a mix of worry and resignation. "Of course," he said, his voice soft, barely above a whisper. The weight of the situation was heavy on his shoulders as he watched the enchantment take hold.

CHAPTER

37

Beaumont sat at his desk, his pen scratching furiously across a letter. The quiet of the morning was punctuated only by the faint rustle of parchment and the distant chirping of birds as the sun began to crest the horizon, painting the sky in soft hues of pink and gold. As he finished, he sealed the letter and handed it to Sir Eero, who stood by, ready for his task.

"I need this delivered to Lord Andreas without delay. Discretion is paramount," Beaumont instructed.

Sir Eero nodded and departed with the letter.

Beaumont rose from his desk and moved to the window, letting his gaze wander over the serene royal gardens. The tranquility of the scene did little to quell the heaviness that settled over him. The sight of Thad, seated near the bed where Pavan lay motionless, drew his attention. His brain hurt, residual of the remnants of the magick that Pavan had taken. Now he saw things with his own eyes, clarity overwhelming him.

"Thaddeus," Beaumont said softly.

The faie looked up, his orange eyes flickering with a mixture of exhaustion and guarded emotion. "King Beaumont."

"Your strength is commendable, as is your duty to protect those dearest to your companionship. Pavan must mean a great deal to stand at his side."

Thad's expression hardened. "I am not his servant."

"Of course." Beaumont nodded, his heart hammering in his chest. "But you cannot hide from me now, Thaddeus."

"Your Majesty is mistaken." Thad held himself firm, glaring hard at the king.

"You have been hidden from my sight," Beaumont continued, his voice tinged with thoughts of regret. "I thought it was just a fleeting dream, clouded by Simeon's magick. But now, with clarity restored your magick is unmistakable. I remember everything, Thaddeus."

"You are mistaken." Thad scowled, standing to his feet and making for the door.

Beaumont stood in his way. "I thought you were dead."

"I died the moment the axe dropped on Orin Gaur's neck." Thad's voice dripped with bitterness.

"Orin Gaur was renowned in Jorn, there were those who mourn his loss."

The faie's anger surged, tears of rage welling in his eyes. "That man deserved a hundred deaths, and I would not mourn him for a thousand moons. His corpse could rot in the ground, and I would not shed a tear. I care little about your opinions of that man. Nor any man thereafter. You *ruined* me..."

Lahrs stepped in, his voice firm but calm. "Thad, control yourself. This is not the place for this."

"Not the place for this," Thad hissed, glaring hard at the elf, angry tears glittering down his pale freckled skin. "He welcomed the man who murdered his father into his home, Lahrs. Beaumont has let the snake slither into his kingdom, to allow the man his pedestal of power to consume the blood of my people. Do not tell me I have no right to condemn what he has done."

Lahrs attempted to defuse the situation. "Beaumont is aware of Maison's transgressions. He understands the risk in letting him remain at his station. But now, with Pavan, there is more than what any of us can see."

Thad's disdain was palpable. "You and Meilyr and your secrets, both conspire to use Pavan as a weapon to stop this great evil..."

Beaumont's stomach churned with discomfort.

Lahrs sighed. "Thaddeus."

"I understand the pain of seeing Charles Maison at my side," Beaumont finally said. "Orin bought you from Hilvaer, from Eske, those men given the freedom to exploit and murder at will. If it were within my power, I would have put an end to that torment. The torment with which I understood you suffered…"

Thad's fury exploded. He pushed Lahrs away, his eyes blazing with a fierce intensity. "You understand *nothing*!"

The room was suffused with a charged silence, broken only by the harsh breaths of those present. Tears streaked down Thad's freckled face, his orange eyes burning with a deep, unrelenting fury as they locked onto Beaumont. The king felt an overwhelming guilt twist his stomach, suffocating him.

"You promised you'd come for me," Thad's voice choked with emotion, trembling with every word. "You fucked me, leaving with your empty words of freedom, and then abandoned me to endure my master's cruelty alone. I was broken, reshaped to his cruel will. I have betrayed my own people…" Thad's words hung heavily in the air, the room's silence amplifying the pain in Beaumont's chest. The look of anguish on Thad's face was mirrored in Lahrs' shocked expression.

Beaumont could not deny the painful truth of Thad's accusations.

In a swift, fluid movement, Thad pulled a blade from Lahrs' belt now pressed threateningly against Beaumont's throat. "But I no longer fit your vision of happiness, after you chose your new wife over me."

Lahrs tensed, preparing to intervene, but Beaumont raised a hand to halt him. He met Thad's blazing gaze, feeling the raw intensity of the faie's anger and heartbreak. The blade's cold edge against his skin was a stark reminder of the pain he had inflicted.

"You're right," Beaumont admitted, his voice quivering. "I chose her above everything else. But it wasn't just about her, Thaddeus. You knew her name, you saw her in my thoughts."

Beaumont, trembling but resolute, reached out and gently touched Thad's tear-streaked cheek. He tried to steady his own fear, breathing in the familiar scent that once consumed him.

"Isaac…" Thad's voice cracked, a mix of sadness and simmering hatred. His grip on the dagger tightened, his resolve hardening. "You didn't protect him. You didn't stop them from hurting him."

"I couldn't save him, Thaddeus. Just like I couldn't save her, or Henry, and like I couldn't save you," Beaumont said, lowering himself until he was kneeling before Thad, his exposed neck positioned dangerously close to the blade.

"Your Majesty," Lahrs warned, his voice strained with concern.

Beaumont's gaze remained fixed on Thad. "He's right. You've always been right, and I never listened, did I, Thaddeus?"

"I wanted to kill him," Thad confessed, his voice heavy with despair. "I wanted to drive my blade into Simeon, just as I did with those assassins. It was his hand that orchestrated everything from the start. His men were the ones who tried to kill you that night, years ago."

"You saved me then, Thaddeus," Beaumont responded, his voice a whisper of gratitude.

Fresh tears fell from Thad's eyes, his rage warring with his sorrow. The hand holding the dagger trembled, and finally, it fell to his side, the blade clattering softly against the floor.

"I cannot kill Simeon," Thad admitted, his voice breaking. "He is too powerful."

Beaumont's heart ached as he looked up at the faie. The intensity of their shared history, the unresolved pain, and the burdens they both carried seemed to converge in that moment of raw vulnerability.

Lahrs stepped in. "Right now there is only one person alive who can kill Bannon. There is only one who can remove the source of your anger and shame. Only one..."

Beaumont breathed easier, standing to his full height, but saw the restraint of passion in the faie, the pain and anguish. Those eyes looked forlorn upon the bed, where Pavan lay motionless. Reaching out a hand to Lahrs, returning the dagger to its rightful owner, he looked up at Beaumont, tears spilling onto his cheeks.

Then Thad's gaze shifted to Lahrs, bitterness written as his lip curled back.

"I've had enough of your will in his life. Pavan has suffered enough because of your prophesying, witch." he spat, taking one last lingering look at Pavan. "He doesn't deserve to be sent as a pawn in your scheme to conquer the darkness of this world."

Lahrs tightened his expression. "It has to be his own choice, Thad...whether he goes to Sanna or not, the choice will always be his."

Thad sneered, shaking his head. "You know him well enough that he would sacrifice himself if he knew it would save those he loved. He would give everything up if it meant keeping them from harm..."

"He would not be so heedless."

Thad rounded on the elf, shouting, "You don't understand him as I do, Lahrs!"

Beaumont took a hesitant step back, his voice trembling as it broke the suffocating silence of the room. His gaze was fixed on Thad, whose attention was entirely absorbed by the elf. Lahrs, too stunned to intervene, could only watch as the scene unfolded.

As the light from the rising sun began to filter into the room, Beaumont noticed a flicker of reflection from Thad. His eyes were drawn to a pendant hanging around the faie's neck, catching the early morning light and casting shimmering patterns on the walls.

The sight hit Beaumont like a jolt. There, hanging from Thad's neck, was a pendant—one that Beaumont had once given Eleanore. It was the very token he had believed would protect her from any harm. The realization struck Beaumont with a heavy ache in his chest. In this moment of clarity, he saw the situation in a new light.

"Thaddeus, you must leave Jorn."

Thad scowled. "I will not leave—"

Beaumont stood taller. "You are banished from Jorn, Thaddeus. Return to Entheas, by my last breath you may not return to this realm upon punishment of death."

"You cannot possibly be serious." Thad narrowed his eyes.

Lahrs even turned into bafflement, but Beaumont remained firm, unable to back down.

"I do not jest." He crossed his arms over his broad chest, locking eyes with Thad. "You will be escorted to Denorn. There you shall be placed under guardianship of Arienne of the Blessed Light. Whereupon a ship will be made ready for your deliverance over the waters to Entheas."

Looking at Lahrs sternly, Beaumont continued, "Take him to Eero. Do I make myself clear?"

At once the elf bowed and escorted Thad from the room.

Morning called to the world from beyond the shut windows, Beaumont sat his large frame upon the dark green couch in his sitting area, body aching as the night's events caught up to him. His eyelids drooped as he fought sleep.

A knock roused him and Beaumont shot up, looking briefly to the opened door to the bed chamber, where Pavan lay sleeping, then to the shut door leading to the corridor, when a knock came again.

He went to it, opening it to see a maid standing with a tray of tea. Jenne was shocked, her eyes looking him over.

"Your morning tea…" She fought to keep her eyes on Beaumont's face. He looked down, remembering the ripped tunic, at once he closed his dressing gown. Smiling down at the maid.

"Thank you." He nodded, reaching to take the tray.

"Shall I tend your fire? It is a chill morning."

Beaumont panicked. "No."

Startling her with his sudden frankness, Beaumont immediately regretted it.

"Sorry, not this morning, Jenne…I am warm enough, thank you…and do not bring up my lunch tray. I shall be dining away from my rooms…" He began to retreat into his room, when he thought of another predicament.

"And send word to Locklan that there shall be no one who enters my chambers, they can take my linens another day…is that understood?" He could see the maid's cheeks grow red, as her gaze quickly flitted to the room behind him.

"Yes, sir, should you need a second cup? For your guest?" She was quiet as she spoke, and Beaumont smirked.

"That won't be necessary…he does not take tea."

Beaumont watched the maid curtsy as Beaumont balanced the tray on one hand, slowly nudging the door shut with the other. Sighing heavily, his stomach churned.

The tray clattered as he set it hard on the table. Gripping the back of the chair for balance and breathing against the pangs of a headache behind his eyes.

CHAPTER
38

Denorn. Realm of Jorn.

Eero stepped down from the carriage, the midday sun casting a warm glow on his armored form. Fatigue weighed heavily on him from the lack of sleep, and the events of the previous night were still vivid in his mind. The sight of Pavan of Eir in such a dire state had shaken him deeply. Shaking off his disquiet, Eero looked up at the imposing spire of the chapel, where the sunlight danced upon the stained-glass windows. The grandeur of the building, a symbol of the Blessed Light, brought him a semblance of calm.

"Sir Eero," a voice called out, pulling him from his reverie. Eero turned to see one of his guards standing by the locked door of the iron bars. The young knight, Henrik, awaited instructions.

"Thank you, Henrik. Tend to the horses while I handle the prisoner," Eero instructed, taking the keys from Henrik's outstretched hand. With a nod, he approached the massive iron gate.

The keys turned in the lock with a series of clicks, and the heavy bar slid away with a loud scrape, revealing the interior of the carriage. Eero peered inside, where the prisoner slumped against the back, his feet casually propped on the bench.

"What trouble have you stirred up this time, Thaddeus?" Eero's voice carried a note of exasperation as he scrutinized the faie.

Thaddeus, with his unnatural orange eyes glinting with disdain, glanced up. A sneer twisted his lips as he shifted on the bench, squinting into the sunlight filtering through the open grate.

"Your king is infatuated with keeping his court unsullied with blood..." Thad spat.

Eero gripped Thad's arm hard, yanking him towards the chapel. Where the gates remained open, he could smell the fresh scent of orange, and the hint of lavender fresh in the air.

"He does what he believes necessary," Eero muttered as they walk along the gravel path, through the quiet gardens leading up to the open doors.

Thad scoffed. "Necessary. I hear more talk of what is necessary, only when the solution is far too messy—"

Eero yanked the faie back, glaring at him. "You should understand as much as many what is at stake here."

"I understand, but I know the king is wrong." Thad lowered his tone, as two sisters of the light meandered up the path, their lowered gaze did not lift up towards them. Eero guided them onward, nearing the front door.

"You have become blind in your lust for revenge."

Thad dug his heels in, refusing to move. "I have no lust for bloodshed, Eero. I have a hand upon justice."

Eero glanced about, his grip tightening on Thad's arm, leaning closer to the faie's ear. "From where I stand, Thaddeus...your path is riddled in bloodshed."

"What are you talking about?"

Eero shoved Thad further, keeping his position close, so no one could chance to overhear him. "I have heard whisperings, Thad. They do not credit your time in Denorn...Do you believe none of your former *acquaintances* would not recognize you? I have heard rumors."

They slowed their steps on the stairs leading into the door.

Thad was stunned. "Don't be absurd."

Eero guided Thad through the front doors, silencing them both in the customary silence of the sisterhood. Walking through the open foyer, down the steps that lead into the lower chambers. Coming to the first door, Eero opened it, pushing Thad inside.

"You are walking on thin ice, Thaddeus," Eero spat under his breath before shutting the door behind him.

They were alone in an unused chamber, with one small light casting in through a small window. Shedding light onto the stirred dust that fluttered about from the empty shelf, a chamber pot in the corner, and a small bed pushed into the corner.

Thad squared up, glaring at the knight.

Eero rolled his eyes. "Lord Hoban was found with his throat slit, Thad...Leuthere already has men on the hunt for the man responsible."

The faie's eyes widened, lowering his arms.

"I didn't kill him," he stated, defensively.

"Yes, I am well aware. But his damned servant remembered a faie with orange eyes and a haughty constitution threatening his master..." Eero hissed through his teeth, eyeing Thad with a knowing look.

"I went searching for answers, but that was some time ago..."

Eero shook his head. "Simeon Bannon does not need evidence to have you put to death, Thad. You are faie. For this city...that is enough."

There was a long silence, while the faie's face drained of color. Eero ran a hand over his head, raking his fingertips through the short hair upon his head.

"It is for the best, that you leave for Entheas..." he began, finding it difficult to say the words.

Thad stepped up, his features shifting, scowling. "They want me gone. Lahrs only agreed with the king for the purpose of what my presence would do to their plans."

Eero shuttered, caught under the faie's gaze.

"They plan to use Pavan. It has always been their great plan...once Lahrs discovered the truth about Pavan's birth. Once he was discovered to hold a great power...Lahrs has been scheming with his witch to sacrifice Pavan to the darkness."

Eero staggered back, but the faie was still pressed on him, his orange eyes shimmering in the low light, glaring at Eero.

"If you love Pavan, you will let him go, Thad..." Eero shook. Trembling, a hand instinctively fell to the hilt of his blade.

Thad sneered. "Love...what do you know of my love for Pavan? Have you felt the beating heart of a fatebonded mate, Eero?" The faie was so close, Eero tasted the citron magick fizzle beneath the surface, tickling the back of his throat.

Eero shook his head.

"I thought not...it is a burning desire that never quells. Not even my long nights of unfinished desire could compare for the longing I have for Pavan...he is everything to me. My beating heart, my reason for living...Would I leave him, willingly? Could I abandon my love for the very beating of his heart?"

Eero was shrouded in heat, the desire crashing in waves through his body, emanating from the faie where he burned with angered passion. Hatred lingered on the tongue, tasting the bite of magick.

He grasped the handle of the door, keeping himself grounded, unable to let himself be lured into the stifling heat.

"You should step away," Eero growled, his gaze sliding to meet the faie and those orange eyes flickered in agitation.

"I shall not relent," Thad hissed, a quirk of a smile played on the impish man's lips. "Unless you make me."

Eero hated that it had resorted to this. Removing his hand from the hilt of his sword to the metal chain that was thrumming at his hip, he was swift. With a flick of his wrist the metal chain was wrapped loosely around Thad's slender neck. At once, the faie stumbled back, cursing loudly, his fingers clawed at the enchanted chain that slowly began to tighten around his neck.

"Get this fucking thing off!" Thad shouted, yanking hard at the metal but Eero stood taller.

"It will not harm you, it only suppresses your magick. I will remove it, if you sit on the bed..." Eero stated, calmly.

Thad was frantic, clawing at the skin on his neck, the chain tightened, drawing his breath in gasps. Eero knew he would resist, raising his hand and letting his own magick radiate through the room.

"I said, *be calm*," Eero spoke clearer, seeing the faie not resist, not struggling. His eyes glanced up, widening as he took Eero in, as if seeing him for the first time.

"You..." Thad couldn't form his words, his skin flush.

Eero stood tall, calming his own mind, slowing his own heart rate. "Sit, Thaddeus."

It was a long moment, but Thad stepped back, stepping again until his legs hit the bed, the faie collapsed upon the rickety bed, eyes widened and bewildered as he took Eero in full.

Eero stood before Thad, touching the chain, feeling the metal give under his fingers, releasing the faie from its hold but Thad remained seated, eyeing Eero with wonder.

"All these years, you have hidden your magick," he breathed.

Eero said nothing for a long moment, looping the chain again at the latch upon his belt before finally, meeting the orange gaze.

"My heritage is none of your concern."

"You are not a man, Eero...you are something far more dangerous. Tell me, does your king know of your true worth? Does your prince?" Thad smiled, gleaming up at him.

Eero frowned. "Do not speak to me of my prince, Thad. I have not forgotten your disgrace. I have not forgotten your seduction."

Thad sat back. "I was desperate."

"He is changed, Thaddeus. Your words, whatever they might have been, have changed him. He grows paranoid, far beyond another man I have seen afflicted in this court. Have you not realized your meddling has caused nothing but harm? You are the destruction of their hearts."

Barrow found Brendolyn standing alone in the garden, her presence as captivating as ever. She looked up, surprise mingled with a soft, melodic tone in her voice.

"Forgive me, I was not expecting you," she said, a delicate blush painting her cheeks.

"You are waiting for someone?" Barrow asked, struggling to mask the pang of jealousy that gnawed at him. He forced a smile, hoping it would hide his true feelings.

Brendolyn hesitated for a moment, then smiled warmly. "Only a friend. I haven't seen them since yesterday. I hoped to chance upon them again here." She stepped closer to him, her gaze full of concern. "Are you alright?"

Barrow inhaled deeply, catching the scent of the floral oils that made her dark curls gleam in the sunlight. He reached out, placing his hand gently on the small of her back.

"I was worried about you," he said softly, lifting her chin to gaze at her delicate features. His eyes traced the soft curve of her lips.

Her lashes fluttered against her flushed cheeks, her breath catching as he drew closer. "We cannot meet like this," she whispered, her voice trembling.

Barrow's resolve hardened. Ignoring her protest, he leaned down and captured her lips with his. He felt her gasp against his mouth as he held her tightly to his chest. For a moment, all his doubts and fears melted away, consumed by the depth of his longing.

"I love you, Bren...more than life itself," he murmured against her lips, his hands tangling in her curls at the nape of her neck. He searched her eyes, the soft yellow gold shimmering with emotion.

"Don't..." she pleaded, shaking her head gently. He could sense her attempt to pull away, but he tightened his embrace.

"I care not for the courtiers," he declared fiercely. "They can hang themselves. I love you, and I want only you." He bent down for another kiss, his passion unyielding.

Brendolyn stepped back, her gaze filled with sorrow. "You shall be married to Lisetta. I cannot take that away from her."

"Be with me..." Barrow whispered into the curve of her temple, his hands grasping her waist. The barrier of fabric between them seemed unbearable.

"We shouldn't," she said, placing her hands flat against his chest.

"We can," he insisted, his voice soft but determined. "There is only you. Always." He caressed her cheek tenderly.

"It would not be right," she said, her voice trembling. "To be a mistress, to be second to another. Perhaps I am selfish, but I want your heart entirely. Not to share it." Tears glistened in her eyes, and he brushed them away with his thumb.

"You will be my only love, Brendolyn," he vowed. "The marriage to Lisetta is only for appearances, to appease the council and the people. But my heart will belong only to you. There will be no one else."

Brendolyn's smile faltered, turning into a frown. She traced his jawline with a touch that was tender yet tinged with sadness. "I cannot compromise my heart, Barrow. It is me alone, or not at all." Her words cut through him like a dagger.

He pressed a kiss to her open palm, leaning into her as he sighed deeply. "Give me a chance to change the council's mind," he implored.

Her eyes met his, a flicker of hope and resignation in her gaze. "Very well," she agreed softly. "If they do not relent, we must end it."

Brendolyn approached the hot house, her steps soft on the gravel path. Through the window, she could see Lahrs working among the plants, his focus absorbed in trimming away dead branches. The sun cast dappled shadows on the floor, creating a serene atmosphere around him.

As she drew closer, Lahrs continued his task with practiced ease, his movements precise and deliberate. He didn't look up, but Brendolyn could tell he was aware of her approach. His concentration remained steadfast, as if the work before him held all his attention.

Finally, Brendolyn reached the door of the hot house and gently pushed it open, stepping inside with a quiet grace. "Lahrs," she called softly, her voice a gentle intrusion into the tranquility of the space.

Lahrs paused, his hands stilling mid-motion. Slowly, he looked up, his eyes meeting hers with a calm but guarded expression. The brief pause seemed to stretch, the air filled with the soft rustling of leaves and the distant hum of the greenhouse's quiet life.

"You should not be wondering about, Bren."

She sighed. "I was hoping to have a moment to talk...I know you have been busy, being the liaison between Entheas and Jorn...your importance in this treaty has kept you from me."

A snip, and a dead branch was placed in the basket beside him.

"You carry your dagger on you?" He did not look up at her, but she felt the urgency in his voice.

"Always." Brendolyn touched his arm. "Is everything alright?"

Lahrs turned to her then, looking down at her. "It is my duty to keep you safe and protected."

Brendolyn's stomach dropped and her lips went dry.

"Oh," she breathed. Instinctively, her hand pressed to her side, feeling the concealed dagger beneath the pleats of her skirts.

"I do not mean to frighten you..." He placed his gloved hands over her shoulders. "Now, what is your business with me?"

She smirked. "Have you seen Pavan?"

"I have not...he will most likely have returned to Eir."

Brendolyn frowned. "The festivities have not concluded...why would he leave so soon?"

"Beaumont thought it wise to send the performers home, they left early this morning, Bren."

She felt as if her chest was going to burst.

"It is for the best," Lahrs reassured her but there was something strange in Lahrs' manner. He looked pained, his words did not quite match the pangs of his heart.

"Is there a change to the treaty?" she wondered, but the elf still remained distracted.

"Not that I am aware, Bren." He tried to smile but Brendolyn knew something was off, she could feel the distraction in his glances, the stiffness of his stance.

"Is Beaumont ill?"

He softened his gaze. "I don't believe so. I had a conference with Beaumont this morning, he seemed only worried about the treaty."

"Are you alright, Lahrs? You are acting strange."

Lahrs smiled, taking Brendolyn's hands in his. "I am very well. But tired from the long boring hours in a room full of old men."

She chuckled. "You should fit right in then. You are after all a hundred."

He knocked her chin playfully with his fist, laughing at her joke with her but his gaze looked beyond her to the door.

"I shall not keep you from the flowers..." Brendolyn turned away, gesturing to the roses. She waved briefly before turning on her heel and charging from the hot house.

It was abnormally warm as the sun was high overhead and Brendolyn returned to the castle, a headache formed behind her eyes.

As the courtiers twirled and the chandeliers cast their golden light across the great hall, Brendolyn felt a pang of longing. From her elevated seat on the dais, she watched the prince and Lisetta, their effortless grace and shared smiles a stark reminder of the love she yearned for but could not claim.

The music flowed like a river through the hall, its melody mingling with the rustling of gowns and the soft laughter of the guests. Yet, beneath the surface of the celebration, Brendolyn felt an overwhelming sense of loneliness. The opulence around her did little to mask the ache in her heart.

Her eyes swept the room, hoping to catch a glimpse of the dark-haired man who had been absent from the festivities. The tall silhouette she sought was nowhere to be found; Pavan had returned to Eir, leaving her with an emptiness that was both physical and emotional.

Brendolyn sighed deeply, the weight of her solitude pressing heavily upon her. The joy and vibrancy of the evening contrasted sharply with her internal despair, making her feel even more isolated. She clutched the edges of her seat, trying to steady her emotions, but the sight of the prince and Lisetta, dancing so effortlessly, only deepened her sense of loss.

"Good evening, Brendolyn," Beaumont greeted as he approached, his regal presence evident even in the simple act of standing beside her. His tall frame cast a protective shadow, and a warm smile illuminated his face.

Brendolyn forced a smile in return, though a sharp pang throbbed behind her eyes. Beaumont settled into the chair beside her, his gaze sweeping across the grand hall, taking in the swirling colors and the exuberant crowd.

"Are you well?" she asked, her voice laced with concern. Beaumont's gaze shifted back to her and though he maintained a facade of calm, Brendolyn could sense an undercurrent of sadness beneath the surface.

Beaumont sighed deeply. "I tire of these endless celebrations. The thought of spending another coin on extravagant feasts for courtiers I scarcely know does not sit well with me."

Brendolyn's gaze settled on the dance floor where the prince moved gracefully with Lisetta. Barrow, with his captivating presence, had not glanced her way since her arrival, fueling a pang of jealousy. "Barrow is most celebrated tonight," she remarked. "This, after all, is to impress the vanity of my sister."

Her words, tinged with bitterness, elicited a compassionate look from Beaumont. "Forgive me," Brendolyn said, her gaze falling to her trembling hands. "I am not in the best of spirits, Your Majesty."

"Would a dance lift your spirits, princess?" Beaumont's smile was genuine, a comforting warmth that reached her despite her turmoil.

"It is not that..." she said, her voice barely above a whisper. "Perhaps it is foolish, but a friend has left...without saying goodbye."

"You speak of Pavan?"

"I do." She nodded, her voice heavy with resignation. "But it is for the best, after all, if the danger is true."

Beaumont's gaze roamed the hall once more, then returned to Brendolyn with a weight of unspoken words. "You shall be leaving as well, Bren?" His tone held an edge of anticipation.

She flushed, looking down at her hands. "Lahrs has a ship ready to depart before the week is out."

"Your father does not object to your traveling to Entheas?"

Brendolyn hesitated. "He is preoccupied with documents and advisors. I do not believe he would notice if I remained. It must, after all, be a kindness to not remain where I feel only heartbreak."

Suddenly, Beaumont stood, causing Brendolyn to startle.

"Come, Brendolyn. It has been years since I've had a proper walk. So many days spent hiding away in my libraries, lost in books and letters. How many years it has been since I have felt the freedom of the air upon my cheek. I wish to walk my gardens with a beautiful woman upon my arm." He lowered his hand further.

She took his hand, rising gracefully, and together they moved away from the vibrant hubbub of the great hall. The cool evening air met them as they reached the balcony leading to the gardens. Footsteps echoed behind them, and Brendolyn glanced back to see Sir Eero, clad in padded tunic and armor, his expression solemn. He nodded in acknowledgment, his presence a silent testament to the gravity of the situation.

Beaumont's voice broke the silence. "Sir Eero is an old friend."

"He is very kind."

"I trust him with my life." Beaumont patted her hand that rested upon his arm. "He has been by my side for so many years. There are not many that I can say that about, Brendolyn. He is someone you can rely upon should you find yourself without my company."

"It is a calm night; the stars are out," Brendolyn remarked, looking up at the sky. The vastness of it, adorned with countless stars, brought a touch of serenity to her troubled heart. Her eyes misted as she turned her gaze back to Beaumont.

"This realm has not been kind. We both have lost so much in the wake of this damned kingdom. Ehnarea guides us in these treacherous times. I hope our paths cross again, Brendolyn. Whether in this realm or the Veil. " Beaumont's words held a melancholy weight.

"You're frightening me," Brendolyn admitted, her voice quivering.

They arrived at a bubbling fountain, its gentle sounds a soothing backdrop to their conversation. Beaumont's shoulders sagged, revealing a weariness Brendolyn had not seen before. He sighed heavily, looking into the cold dark trickling waters.

"I am a poor king," he began, resting his weight against the stone of the fountain's edge. "In my foolishness I have allowed a dark magick to enter my kingdom. He is dangerous, far more than I had originally anticipated."

"Who is it?" Brendolyn took his hand, her fingers felt so small.

Beaumont trembled, his aching heart pounding out the lurking danger that shadowed over his mind. "It is too soon to speak of him, Bren, but you must not think ill of me, whatever shall pass you must not think ill of me."

"Is that why you sent him away?"

"You are intelligent," Beaumont chuckled, wiping away a sudden tear that began to trail from his eye. "That is Lahrs' doing, I am certain. He would not have raised you in this world to sit idle and let others dictate your thoughts."

Brendolyn nodded, her features soft. "He is more my father than tutor. I would be grieved without him. As I would be grieved without you, Beaumont. In your kindness you have shown me strength in facing an unjust realm."

"I am flattered, but your goodness has not seen the faults of rule."

"You are a great king," she squeezed his hand. "At the fall of the great war you have done what you believe is right for your people, for your son...how could you be less of a king for defending those you love and hold dear?"

"Your heart is pure, Brendolyn...I cannot argue with your keen sight." Beaumont offered a reassuring smile, though it was tinged with sadness. "Come, let us not linger in sorrow. There is still beauty in this night, and a future yet to be faced."

Brendolyn nodded, following Beaumont as they continued their walk, the path illuminated by the soft glow of lanterns. The fountain's gentle bubbling provided a soothing background, blending with the distant sounds of the festivities that continued inside the castle. As they reached a secluded alcove in the garden, Beaumont stopped and turned to face her. A moment of silence stretched between them, Beaumont reached into his pocket and pulled out a small, intricately carved wooden box. He opened it to reveal a delicate golden locket, its surface engraved with intricate patterns and laden with a small stone that reflected in the moonlight.

"This is a gift of parting," Beaumont explained, his voice soft. "It was made in the great city of Taastra, by the wisest craftsman. It carries a piece of dragon glass, an enchanted stone that blesses the wearer in safety. I had two made, one of silver that I had given to Fiona upon her name day, and this one..." He carefully placed the locket in Brendolyn's hand, closing her fingers around it. "Is engraved for you, Brendolyn. That even as you part from these shores, you take with you my protection and my love."

She looked up, her eyes wide with emotion. "I don't know what to say..."

"Say nothing," Beaumont said with a gentle smile. "Just take it with you. When you feel lost or uncertain, remember that you are never truly alone."

Overcome with emotion, Brendolyn wrapped her arms around him, clinging tightly. She held on until her arms ached, finding solace in the embrace of the king who had been both a guardian and a source of her deepest affections. Beaumont returned the embrace, his arms enveloping Brendolyn with a tenderness that belied his royal stature. For a moment, the weight of his crown and the burdens of his kingdom seemed to lift, replaced by the simple, heartfelt connection he shared with the girl before him.

As Brendolyn finally pulled away, her eyes were red-rimmed but resolute. Beaumont gently wiped a tear from her cheek with the back of his hand, his touch soft and paternal.

"Shall we?" As they prepared to leave the gardens and return to the grand hall, Beaumont's demeanor shifted slightly. He stood a little straighter, his regal bearing reasserting itself.

They walked back through the gardens, the air filled with a new sense of purpose. The vibrant lights of the grand hall beckoned them forward, but the connection they shared in the quiet of the night remained with them, a cherished memory and a source of strength for the uncertain days to come.

When they finally reentered the hall, Beaumont gave Brendolyn a reassuring nod before returning to his duties, his regal presence commanding attention as he resumed his role among the courtiers.

CHAPTER 39

Brendolyn was exhausted, sitting amongst her pillows as she fought sleep. Elsa sat beside her, reading aloud from the small book she held. Brendolyn listened but felt herself dozing when a sudden knock upon the door broke their solitude.

They looked to one another, then back to the door.

It was really late, but there was a knock again. Brendolyn stood and walked to the door, opening it slightly to peek through to see who it was. Glancing across the hall, but the door where Lahrs slept was closed. Brendolyn looked down at the maid, extending a note sealed with gold wax.

"A note, miss," came the voice from a small maid.

Receiving the note, Brendolyn shut the door. Opening it as Elsa came to her side. "He wants me to meet him." She looked to Elsa.

"Now? He wants to meet now?"

Brendolyn read out loud, "I shall be waiting for you in the third room on the fourth floor of the east stairwell. Every moment apart from you is agony. I have news to share with you that cannot wait until morning." Her cheeks flushed, looking at Elsa before folding up the letter and tucking it into the pocket of her gown.

"You're not going to go?" Elsa asked.

"Elsa, I cannot be seen about the castle so late in the night. I promised so faithfully to remain in my rooms." But Elsa was already fixing Brendolyn's gown about her, tightening the strings in place once more.

"Perhaps he has convinced the council to rewrite the treaty."

"When I saw him before he was keen on keeping Lisetta happy. It is difficult to decipher if he has spoken to them or not. Do you think he will stand up and break the treaty?" Brendolyn asked then, sitting at her vanity as Elsa began to smooth her curls around her fingers.

"It would show he has a true heart and loyalty," Elsa stated absently twirling a few errant curls.

"I should go," Brendolyn said after a long moment. "It would be rude not to call when he has requested so earnestly...do you think he will kiss me?"

Elsa laughed. "I wouldn't be surprised if he tried more than to kiss you, Bren."

She turned on her friend, with a serious look. "I could never," Brendolyn gasped but laughed. Then she thought for a moment. "He is romantic." Her sorrow began to fill her again, her fingers touching the locket that hung from her neck. From behind her, Elsa hugged her and she gladly welcomed it.

"Keep Lahrs busy should he come to call..." Brendolyn asked her friend. "I won't be long in his company, and then I shall return within the hour."

Elsa nodded.

It was easy to sneak through the castle, now without shoes to hinder her, she walked with the barest of necessity of gown, her long hair flowing behind her. Climbing the stairway, all the way to the fourth floor. She stopped. There was a change in the air and her heart fluttered, looking at the long stretch of hall. The door at the end of it, held a sense of magick.

She blinked, turning back to the door that held the prince.

Breathing in deeply, stealing her nerves as she lifted a hand, knocking.

The door opened, standing before her, his tunic untucked from his trousers, his sandy blonde hair spilling over his shoulders—he was gorgeous. Losing her breath at the sight of him, his smile dazzling her. She smiled as he took her hand, leading her into the chamber. Looking around as he closed the door behind them, she blushed realizing this was his private bed chambers.

"Do you have news from the council?" she asked, her face flush.

Barrow sighed. "Forgive me, my darling…" he breathed, a hand caressing her cheek, the other touching the edge of her pointed ear. "They would not break the engagement."

He leaned in towards her, pressing them close together, his lips touching the curve of her neck, sending a wave of heat through her.

"We cannot, it is wrong…" but her words were stilled by the press of his lips to hers.

"I will not guide you to be the company of my bed after I am married, but now…as I stand before you, as yours alone, let me share this one last night with you. One last night before they take me for the kingdom."

She could feel the pound of his heart beneath the press of her palm to the contours of his chest. His body was hot, pressed to hers. "Barrow, it is wrong…"

"Wrong to love you, to take you while we are still united under the eyes of Ehnarea?" Barrow touched her lips. "I cannot endure without the feel of your touch to make the world bearable without you."

Surging forward, she kissed his mouth and he moaned. Leaning into her as she kissed his neck, tasting the salt of his skin. Brendolyn smiled, the fabric of his tunic grasped easily in her hands. "You are wearing far too much clothing."

Lifting his arms, Barrow smiled as she removed the tunic in one swift movement, leaving his chest bare before her. Admiring the toned chest and stomach under her touch, his skin glowing golden against the candlelight and the light from the fire in the hearth. Her hands touched his skin and Barrow smiled.

Then his eyes smoldered, watching Brendolyn as she stepped back, untying her gowns to let them fall before her in a heap leaving her to stand in her sheer cotton chemise.

"I shall remember you as you are now, to keep with me in my dreams." He approached her slowly.

Brendolyn shivered, with less garments the draft touched her skin. His hands slowly moved her hair behind her, touching the curves of her shoulders. His hot hands grazing over the thin fabric of her chemise down the contours of her arm, to her wrist, bringing her hands to his lips to kiss. She sighed, as his lips brushed her arm, leaning in at an angle to kiss the curve of her neck. Barrow's strong hands roaming the dip of her back, his hot mouth finding a sensitive place below her ear, causing Brendolyn to gasp, her hands holding on where they could. One at his shoulder, the other on his arm. Barrow did it again and as she arched into him as he grasped her harder, moving his body against her, with a hand lowering, while the other remained at her back.

His hand that roamed lower squeezed the place at her hip.

"It can be dangerous, doing this," Barrow mumbled, their faces close to touching.

Brendolyn smiled, her body beginning to cool.

"What is life without a little danger?" She snuggled closer and Barrow smiled, bringing her to his chest.

But he became serious. "It would ruin your future if I did something." He sighed, his hand resting on the flat of her belly.

Brendolyn placed a hand onto his, caressing his cheek. "We are out of danger there, Barrow. There is nothing we have done wrong."

He sighed, his hand now leaning to caress her. His sweet face smiling, his blue eyes shining. "This is how things are meant to be, you lying beside me. Sharing our pleasures..." His sweet, delighted face turned sad.

Brendolyn grasped his neck, making him look at her. "Do not dwell on the fact of the future, Barrow. Please, just know that here and now, I love you. I shall always love you."

Barrow softened, his hand grasping her hip as he looked into her eyes.

"I love you," he whispered, taking her lips once more and leaning into her with the force of his weight. Brendolyn smiled, gasping into his mouth.

Beaumont stood by the window, his gaze fixed on Pavan, who lay restless on the bed. The faie prince's breathing was steady but shallow, a stark reminder of the delicate state he was in. Lahrs had examined Pavan's condition earlier, battling against the turbulent magick that clung to him. The elf had urged Beaumont to stay close, advising that the situation was too precarious to leave unattended.

A sudden knock on the door jolted Beaumont from his thoughts. His heart raced, the unexpected visitor adding to the mounting anxiety he felt. He crossed the room quickly, his steps echoing with urgency.

"Monty," came the voice from the other side, familiar and unexpected.

Without hesitation, Beaumont flung open the door, revealing Rhys standing there with a look of concern. With a swift, practiced motion, Beaumont pulled the elf inside and closed the door behind him, the soft click of the latch resonating in the tense silence.

"I know it's late," Rhys began, glancing around the room. His eyes fell upon the bed, where Pavan lay, and his expression shifted to one of surprise and embarrassment. "Oh."

Beaumont's voice was steady, but his eyes betrayed his worry. "He is my son," he declared firmly, an edge of protectiveness in his tone.

Rhys's gaze lingered on Pavan, his curiosity piqued. "Is that the man from Eir?" he asked, his voice tinged with a mix of intrigue and concern.

Beaumont nodded, his head aching behind his eyes. "Pavan, his name is Pavan. Rhys, I know how this looks, but he is in danger..." Beaumont went to his side table, pouring himself a drink.

"You said he is your son. He is your son."

Relief washed over Beaumont as he took a deep draught from his goblet. His eyes drifted to Pavan, shifting restlessly on the bed, his groans betraying the inner turmoil even in sleep. Beaumont's jaw tightened, frustration and worry gnawing at him. He knew he needed a moment away from the oppressive atmosphere of his chambers.

"Walk with me, Rhys," Beaumont said, his voice strained but determined.

Rhys, who had been quietly observing, nodded and followed as Beaumont led the way out of the chamber. The door clicked shut behind them, and they moved into the dimly lit corridors of the castle, away from the oppressive confines of the room.

"I know you cannot say," Rhys began softly, his voice barely more than a whisper, "but you seem troubled."

Beaumont halted abruptly, turning to face Rhys with an intensity that made the elf pause. In a moment of raw vulnerability, Beaumont pulled Rhys into a tight embrace. They had only ever shared such intimacy in the privacy of his chambers, but tonight, Beaumont was desperate for the comfort of the elf's presence.

"I'm afraid," Beaumont confessed, his voice trembling as tears pricked at the corners of his eyes. Rhys wrapped his arms around Beaumont, holding him tightly as if to anchor him.

"Tell me, Monty...anything," Rhys murmured, pressing a gentle kiss to Beaumont's cheek. The king, feeling the warmth and solace in the elf's embrace, pulled back just enough to look into Rhys's soft, understanding eyes.

"Rhys," Beaumont whispered, leaning in to press a tender kiss to Rhys's lips. "A king should never show fear, but here I am, trembling. He poses a danger...to everyone."

"You're frightening me, Monty," Rhys admitted, his voice a mix of concern and affection.

Beaumont ran his fingers through Rhys's long hair, brushing it back from his face. He pressed his forehead against Rhys's, seeking solace in the elf's presence.

"Forgive me, Rhys...forgive me. I am weary," Beaumont said, his voice heavy with exhaustion. The sleepless nights and relentless worry had taken their toll, and the warmth of Rhys was a balm to his frayed nerves. He kissed the elf again, savoring the moment as a way to calm his inner turmoil.

Their moment was interrupted by the echo of heavy footsteps approaching the corridor. Rhys instinctively drew back, his expression a mix of fear and concern. Beaumont's heart raced as he quickly opened his chamber door, pushing Rhys inside to keep him hidden.

"Your Majesty?" Simeon's voice, cold and unsettling, cut through the quiet.

Beaumont turned to face the lord, forcing a thin smile despite the churning dread in his stomach. "Lord Bannon, what brings you to this part of the castle at this hour?"

A sinister grin crept across Simeon's lips, his dark eyes gleaming with an unsettling light. Beaumont felt a wave of nausea as he recognized the telltale signs of dark magick emanating from the lord. His thoughts raced to the hidden elf and the vulnerable figure lying in his bed.

"There is news I have from my estates," Simeon said, his grin widening. "Is it a convenient time?"

Resolute, Beaumont straightened, stealing his mind as he always did. Motioning to Simeon, they walked on, removing themselves from the corridor.

"Tell me what is on your mind."

The castle was shrouded in darkness as Brendolyn made her way back to her quarters, her steps unsteady and her cheeks flushed from the stolen pleasures shared with Barrow. A contented smile played on her lips as she descended the first flight of stairs, her mind still reeling from the intimacy she had experienced. As she reached the landing, she was startled by the faint sound of voices approaching from below.

Panic surged through her, and she instinctively backed away from the staircase, her heart pounding. She raced silently down the corridor, glancing at each door she passed, but everyone was firmly shut.

Desperation clawed at her as she heard the voices drawing nearer. Spying an open doorway further down the hallway, Brendolyn darted inside, slipping into a room that had once served as a tearoom. Shelves lined with books and rich tapestries hung from the walls. She quickly wedged herself between the wall and a tapestry, trying to stifle her labored breaths.

Her hope that the voices would pass was dashed when they grew louder, now unmistakably inside the room. As she strained to listen, she recognized one of the voices—Beaumont.

"This matter is not open to debate," Beaumont's voice was low and firm, addressing his companion with an air of finality. "Guards stationed in Denorn. I've heard disturbing reports about your men's conduct. The people are frightened. They can't even go about their business..."

Brendolyn's breath caught in her throat as she pressed herself deeper into the shadowy recess. The tension in the room was palpable, and she could only hope her hidden presence remained undetected.

Beaumont's face tightened with frustration. "This situation is only temporary, Simeon. Your men have been unchecked, engaging in the illicit trade of slaves and transporting goods beyond our borders."

Lord Bannon's cheeks reddened. "A lucrative venture, Your Majesty."

Beaumont's eyes narrowed. "*Slaves*, Simeon. You're involved in the trafficking of faie into the northern lands. What other transgressions have you committed under the guise of the crown?"

"They are not of your people, Your Majesty. They are filth that has long needed to be eradicated."

Beaumont's anger surged, distorting his normally composed features. "Children, Simeon—innocent children. Perhaps I have granted you too much power."

The king loomed over the lord, who visibly recoiled under the weight of Beaumont's ire. From her hiding place, Brendolyn could see the men's faces, the way they circled each other in their confrontation.

"You cannot stop what has already been set in motion, Your Majesty. What is done cannot be undone."

Beaumont's hand shot out, gripping Lord Bannon with startling force. Brendolyn pressed herself further into the shadows, her heart racing. Grasping the locket around her neck, desperately wishing to disappear.

"No more slavery," Beaumont declared, his voice a harsh whisper. His gaze was fixed on Lord Bannon with a mixture of fury and resolve.

Lord Bannon's lips curled into a sneer. "It's unwise to challenge me."

Beaumont shifted, his posture radiating a dangerous resolve. Brendolyn fought to stay still, her legs trembling from the strain. She dared a glance and met Beaumont's eyes, wide with shock and anger. His expression, once fierce, now turned to something darker and more dangerous.

Brendolyn's hand flew to her mouth, stifling a gasp as Beaumont's eyes flashed with a cold, penetrating loathing.

"A threat?" Beaumont's voice cut through the air with icy precision, his gaze locked onto Bannon and the tension between them crackled like static, thick and electric.

Bannon's sneer deepened into a cruel smirk. "A warning. Have you forgotten the Rule of Council?" His dark aura churned Brendolyn's stomach, filling the corridor with a sense of foreboding.

"I'm acutely aware of your manipulations within the council," Beaumont growled, his voice a low rumble. "Did you think I wouldn't notice how my father's old advisors have been replaced by your Denorn puppets?"

Beaumont's fury was a tangible force, practically igniting the air around them. Brendolyn's eyes brimmed with tears as she watched, her heart pounding with the intensity of Beaumont's rage.

Desperate to stay silent, Brendolyn pressed herself harder against the wall, her breaths coming in shallow, ragged gasps. The confrontation seemed to close in on her, a weight pressing down with suffocating intensity.

"How else do you think it was so easy to manipulate the king of the south?" Bannon sneered, his voice dripping with malice. "All it took was bringing your precious king here to serve my interests while I secured the alliance. It's unbreakable, Your Majesty. Barrow shall make that Felourian his queen..."

Beaumont's eyes narrowed to slits, his anger boiling over. "You tread a very fine line, Simeon. I suggest you watch your next steps carefully." His grip tightened, his knuckles white with the strain.

With a violent shove, Beaumont thrust Lord Bannon away, the lord gasping for breath and clutching his bruised throat. Yet, a dark, mocking laugh escaped Lord Bannon, sending a shiver down Brendolyn's spine.

"Forgive me, Your Highness, but there is no turning back now. The wedding will proceed as planned, but your son will remain as he wishes. His little puterelle will be his plaything."

Beaumont's fist connected with Lord Bannon's cheek in a brutal strike, leaving a red mark. "You will never sway him to your darkness, Simeon. He will resist your corruption."

Lord Bannon's laughter rang out, rich and dark. "So confident, Your Highness. But I have witnessed the shadows within him, felt the seeds of doubt you've nurtured in his heart."

Beaumont yanked Lord Bannon closer, his rage palpable. Brendolyn's chest ached with the king's anguish, her heart racing as she felt the king's tremors.

"I know who you truly are, Simeon. You thought your deeds were hidden, but I know them all...*Charles Maison*," Beaumont hissed, his voice laden with pain. "I know it was by your hand that my father was murdered."

Lord Bannon's eyes widened in shock, but Beaumont's grip remained unyielding, showcasing the king's strength despite the lord's attempts to wriggle free.

"I know you murdered Eleanore." Beaumont's face twisted in agony, tears brimming in his eyes. "You were the one who violated her after she gave me my daughter…It was you who strangled the life from her. I saw the marks of your hands myself—"

Shlick!

All the breath left Brendolyn as she watched in horror. Trembling uncontrollably, she could only look on as Beaumont staggered back, gasping in pain. Tears she had been holding back finally spilled down her cheeks.

A dark, shadowy blade, seemingly born from Lord Bannon's hand, had plunged deep into the king's chest, just below his sternum. Beaumont's gaze shifted from the shadowy appendage embedded within him to the cold, unfeeling face of Lord Bannon.

Lord Bannon remained eerily calm, his eyes coldly assessing in a sheen of white as Beaumont pulled away. The blade slipped from the wound, leaving behind not a gaping wound but a deepening patch of blistering shadow. The area around the wound smoldered like burned embers, eating away at Beaumont's tunic and jacket. The enchanted wound was a cruel testament to the dark magick's insidious power, the shadowy burn spreading with a relentless, malevolent hunger.

"That name shall die with you, as that name died the night she bled out in my arms." Lord Bannon's smile was sickening. "Eleanore's death was my rebirth. Now, you shall be spared the misery of watching me unravel Barrow's mind. You will die knowing I am his ruin."

Turning on his heel, Bannon strode from the room.

Brendolyn's breath caught in a strangled sob as the horrific scene settled into her mind. Tears streamed down her face, the weight of what she had witnessed threatening to overwhelm her. The sound of Beaumont's deep, agonized groan snapped her out of her shock and she turned to see the king's slumped form, struggling towards the door.

Desperate, she rushed from her hiding place and reached out to steady him. She grasped his arm and guided him gently to the floor, easing him into a kneeling position. Beaumont's chest heaved with labored breaths, his eyes clouded with pain and tears. He clutched at her arm weakly, his heavy frame trembling under her touch.

"*Bren…*" he murmured, his voice a painful rasp.

Brendolyn's heart shattered as she cradled Beaumont, easing him to rest on her lap despite the weight of his large body. She fought to keep her weeping in check, focusing instead on soothing the king as best she could.

"What do I do?" she cried softly, her voice trembling as she tried to avoid the enchanted wound. She gently patted at the slow-burning patches on his tunic and jacket, desperate to offer any relief she could. Her hands shook with fear and helplessness, her heart aching as she tried to comfort the man she had come to care for deeply.

Beaumont struggled to breathe again, wheezing, "Stay...with me."

"You cannot die," Brendolyn whimpered, her chin quivering. Brendolyn touched his cheek, tears falling freely down her face.

Beaumont reached up with trembling fingers, his hand caressing Brendolyn's cheek with a final, tender touch. His breath came in ragged, painful gasps, each one faltering as the dark enchantment in his chest spread its relentless grip.

"Sweet...Bren..." he whispered, his voice choked with agony. The pain seemed to consume him, the enchantment's shadow growing darker with each passing moment. His breaths turned into a gurgle, his strength waning rapidly. "Tell...Barrow..."

Beaumont struggled to force out his last command, tears streaming down his face. The effort of speaking brought another wave of pain, and his eyes welled up. The sight of his suffering was unbearable.

"He knows," Brendolyn shushed him softly. "Don't speak."

She held him closer, her arms cradling him as she wiped away his tears. Brendolyn's voice, sweet and ethereal, began to sing. Her faie melody wove a gentle embrace around them, a soothing caress that filled the room with a comforting glow. The song, a blend of elven magick and heartfelt sorrow, painted visions of golden fields and Ehnarea's warm embrace. Her voice, mingled with her faie magick, created a haven of calm.

As she sang, Beaumont's chest heaved less violently, his breathing slowing as her magick shimmered between them, a tangible relief that eased his suffering. Beaumont's expression softened, the agony in his features melting away as the thump of his heart beneath her palm slowed, becoming more distant and faint. His hand, still resting against her cheek, moved to wipe away her tears.

"Rest, Beaumont. *Favor find you, until we meet again.*"

Looking down into Beaumont's stormy blue eyes, now calm and serene as the storm passed, Brendolyn saw the pain had ebbed away. Her tears fell more freely now, mingling with the gentle light of her magick, as Beaumont's final breath escaped him peacefully, his hand fell heavily to his chest.

She brought his limp hand to her cheek, but his arm slipped from her grasp, too heavy for her to hold. Silent tears gave way to deep, wrenching sobs as she clung to the king, her heart shattering with every breath. Kissing his forehead, she rocked his head gently, her grief pouring out in anguished cries. The world around her seemed to blur and collapse into the dark void of loss.

Brendolyn wept louder, a raw, mournful sound in the stillness of the room.

Beaumont was dead.

After

T had emerged from ice cold water.

The anguished cries of the faie girls echoed as they struggled towards the shore, their forms silhouetted against the chaotic night. Thad, concealed in the cloak of darkness, paddled furiously towards the rocky beach, pursuing the three faie who had clawed their way onto the shore. Dahlia, Chloe, and the third faie were helping each other, but Thad's attention was diverted by the sight above.

He scrambled up the jagged embankment, his heart heavy as he looked up at the sky, fractured by the blazing fire that illuminated the heavens. The once hopeful Chapel of Light stood in ruin, its spire engulfed in flames that sent torrents of anguish through Thad. The beacon of hope and life for Jorn was now a towering inferno.

The feeling in his chest was a dark knot of regret and fury. He had begged Arienne to leave with him, using every faie charm and pleading with desperation, but she had refused. Her duty, divinely decreed, bound her to stay. Her stubbornness had driven him to leave in haste with the three faie girls from the Velvet Crown, whom he was supposed to escort to Entheas.

"Thad," came a soft voice from behind him.

Turning, Thad saw Dahlia descending the rocky incline, her concern evident as she approached the trembling girls. Chloe, wide-eyed and fearful, clung to her arm. Thad rushed to them, his hands steadying despite the turmoil within. His own hands shook as he worked to heal the burn on Chloe's arm, the blistered skin beginning to mend under his touch.

"It's alright, Chloe," he murmured, his voice quivering with emotion. The girl whimpered, closing her eyes as the third faie wrapped her in a comforting embrace. Thad's heart ached, each stitch of healing magic a bittersweet reminder of the hope that was slipping away.

"Thad, why is the chapel on fire...there were men..." Dahlia knelt beside him, her damp hair hanging limp around her shivering shoulders.

"I don't know." Thad shook his head.

Behind them, Thad heard the sounds of a horse approach. He shifted, pushing the girls behind him, watching with anticipation as the large black stallion appeared at the top of the embankment. He sighed, seeing Lahrs approach.

"Thad." Lahrs was breathless, clutching a note in his hand as his boots sunk into the sand as he hastened towards him. "I was unsure if this source was correct."

Embracing him, Lahrs held tightly to Thad, his disregard for the drenched faie when Lahrs would have never done so before. Thad felt the flare of anxiety, the trembling in the elf. There was something wrong.

Thad pushed away. "What happened?"

"It is uncertain..." Lahrs began, his voice trembling. "Thad you must make haste to the docks before the soldiers flood the seaside."

Fear trickled in, like a cold that grasped at his heart.

"What happened, Lahrs?" Thad whispered, swallowing back the lump in his throat.

"Beaumont is dead."

All the air in Thad's lungs was punched from him, unable to move as Lahrs' words crashed around him. It was quiet, except for the waves that crashed against the shoreline.

"Thad, they are searching for the man responsible."

Looking sharply at Lahrs, he knew what that meant, he understood the declaration that the elf made. His chest ached and tears sprung to his eyes, as he shook his head.

"It can't be," he hissed.

"He was seen leaving the room where Beaumont was found." Lahrs shook his head.

Thad was angry, his sorrow for the king becoming rage as he glared at the elf, hearing the accusation against a man they both knew so well.

"Pavan is not a killer!"

"I cannot dispute the facts, Thaddeus. I cannot prove against the eyewitnesses that saw him," Lahrs raised his voice. "But what I can do is send you away, to be certain you have returned to Entheas."

Thad scoffed. "You expect me to leave him now?"

"You cannot remain in Jorn, Thad. There is nothing left of protection that will stop Simeon from taking you."

"I do not fear him, Lahrs."

Lahrs sighed, standing close enough that he could rest his hand upon Thad's shoulder, fighting with the racing thoughts, and the sadness that overwhelmed them. Thad could feel the agony, the pain emanating from the elf.

"It is not of fear, but of what is right. There are those in Entheas who need you now. Do not abandon them in your quest for revenge."

"I cannot let Pavan to his fate, to die by his father's hand."

"Pavan is gone, Thad. He disappeared in the night." Thunder rumbled in the distance, a storm rolling in from the east towards the sea. "You must go now while the tide is clear. Only you can sail them across the seas in this storm."

Thad felt the tears on his cheek.

"Don't ask me to abandon him," Thad whispered.

Lahrs touched Thad's cheek. "He doesn't need you."

"Is my sister safe, Lahrs?" Dahlia's voice cut in through the rush of the waves as the wind began to pick up, sending a chill through Thad's bones.

"Audry is under Eero's care. It was she that received Arienne's message before the soldiers reached the chapel. Audry shall remain in Jorn." Lahrs nodded, retrieving a second letter from his jacket pocket and extending it to the girl.

Thad saw the young faie touched girl nod, clutching to the letter as a tear fell from her eyes, unable to utter another word but Thad could feel her silent agony.

"Come with us, Lahrs," Thad pleaded, his desperation evident as he willed the elf to abandon the castle. "I will only go if you are with us."

"I cannot," Lahrs replied, shaking his head. "My duty is to the princess."

Thad stepped closer, his voice dropping to a hiss. "Your duty to that girl has caused nothing but trouble. What compels you to stay by her side? It can't be the lure of titles—there are better namesakes waiting for you in Tauf."

A long silence fell between them, punctuated only by the crash of waves and the rumble of distant thunder. Thad searched Lahrs' gray eyes, the eyes of the brother he had fought alongside for so long. But now, they were filled with unspoken secrets.

"I made a promise," Lahrs finally said.

"Your oaths to the king mean nothing—you didn't swear a blood oath to Sabian."

"No, it was not to Sabian that I promised to keep her safe," Lahrs admitted, his voice steady. "I must remain, Thad. You can't ask me to leave her, not now...not ever."

Thad recoiled, astonished. "I thought I imagined it when I felt the magick before. When I touched her hand, I sensed the faie magick, but there was something deeper—ancient, like the bloodline of the high elves."

Lahrs shot him a warning look, raising his hand. "Do not speak your visions here."

Tears of betrayal burned in Thad's eyes. "Sabian is not her father, is he, Lahrs? Tell me the truth. After all these years, you've kept this secret, even from her."

Lahrs stood as solid as stone, rain dripping down his fair skin.

"You are her father," Thad whispered.

"I loved Hana with my soul, Thad. Nothing could have prepared me for the heartbreak of watching her devote herself to those who despised her ancestors. They spurned her name, cursed her heritage." Lahrs' voice trembled with anger, an emotion rarely shown. "I delivered Brendolyn alone. I watched as the heart of my soul bled out before me...I held Brendolyn in my arms as they tossed Hana's body into the sea without ceremony."

Thad trembled, quivering in the cold rain that pelted against their faces.

"Don't think me void of sacrifice, Thaddeus," Lahrs continued, his voice heavy with emotion. "I sacrificed everything to raise my own flesh under the roof of a man so unloving and cruel. I knew that if I spoke the truth, her life would be forfeit for my own transgressions—for loving a faie girl when it was forbidden."

"Lahrs," Thad choked out, tears streaming down his face, mingling with the salty spray of the sea.

"Leave these shores, Thad," Lahrs urged, drawing closer. "Take these girls to our father, so he may nurture them as only he can. Take refuge in Tauf, knowing there is nothing but pain and death for you here."

"I cannot." Thad shook his head stubbornly.

"Pavan must follow his path," Lahrs said, gripping Thad's arm to steady his shaking. "He must not be prevented from reaching Rhun. It is your duty to let his destiny unfold. But there is another who needs you more."

Thad's gaze hardened. "There is no one in Tauf who could entice me to leave Pavan here," he growled.

Lahrs' touch was tender as he cupped Thad's cheeks. "Lilja broke her bond with Pavan. You know the magick, better than most."

Realization dawned in Thad's eyes as Lahrs' words sank in. "He has a child?"

Lahrs nodded, his voice gentle. "He's only four years old, headstrong and stubborn like his father. Meilyr dotes upon him, as does Kristjana. But there is only one who can raise Pavan's son, Thad. Only one whom Lilja would trust to keep the child safe in this dangerous world."

Thad's grip tightened on Lahrs' arm, his chin trembling. "His son."

"Go now, Thad. Take these girls and sail far from these shores. I cannot lose my family to this darkness," Lahrs whispered, his eyes filled with sorrow.

Thad wrapped his arms around Lahrs, bringing them close in an unbearable rough hug, forgetting the cold of the storm, as his heart ached for those lost. But his hope shimmered, gleaming in his chest as he saw the faie that stood waiting for him to fulfill his promise. A new resolve in Thad shut out the pain.

"Favor find you, brother." Thad drew back to arms length. "We shall meet again on the shores of Tauf, when the white sails have brought you safely into our arms again. Do not fear, I shall care for them in your stead."

"Favor find you, Thad. Until we meet again."

FAMILY OF MAISON

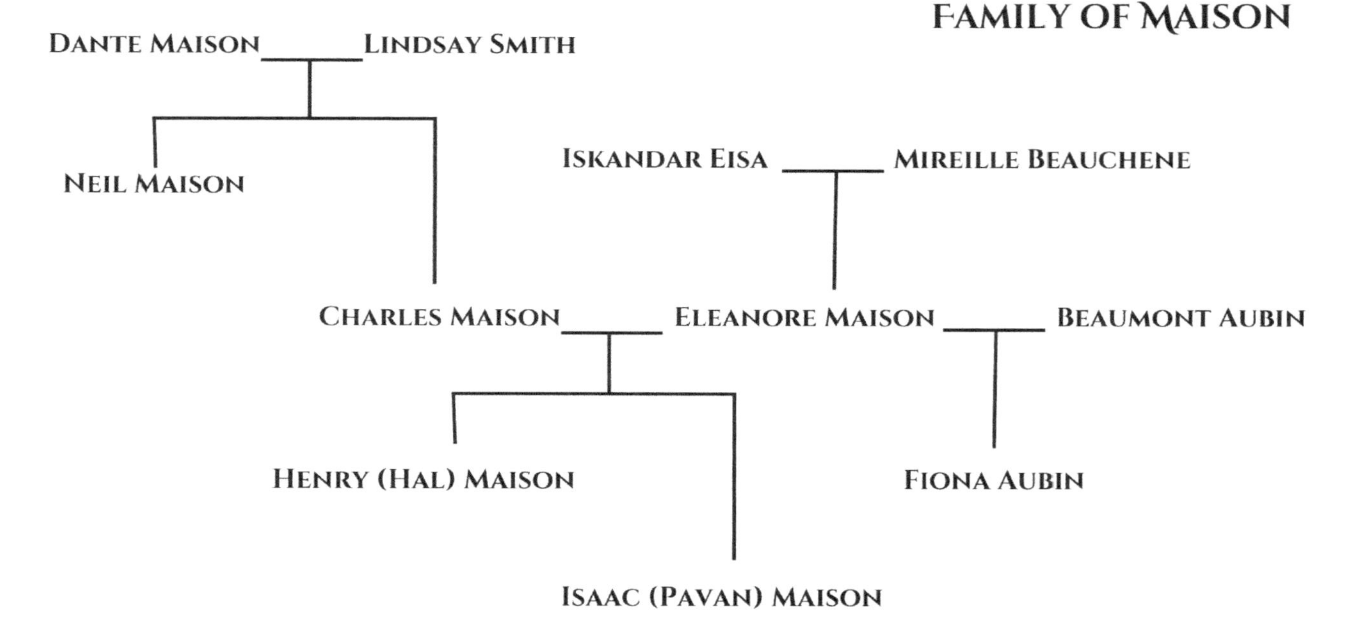

FAMILY OF AUBIN

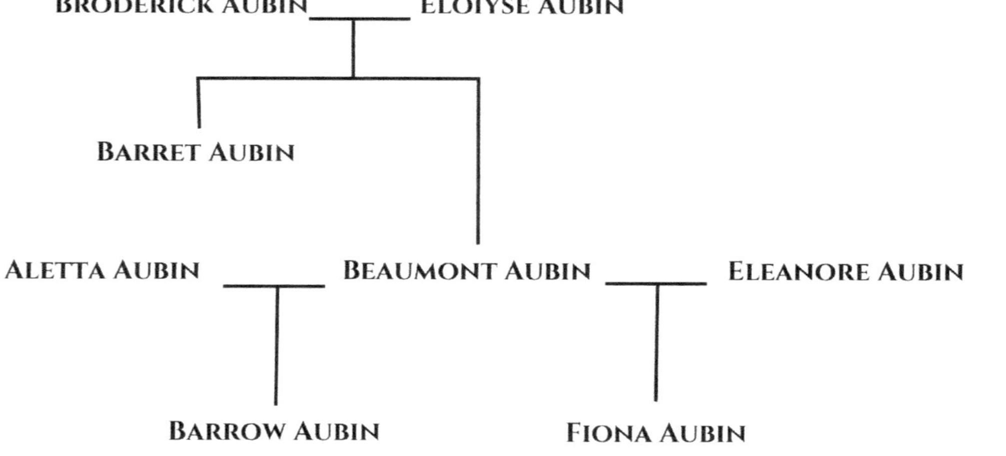

Family of Moreau

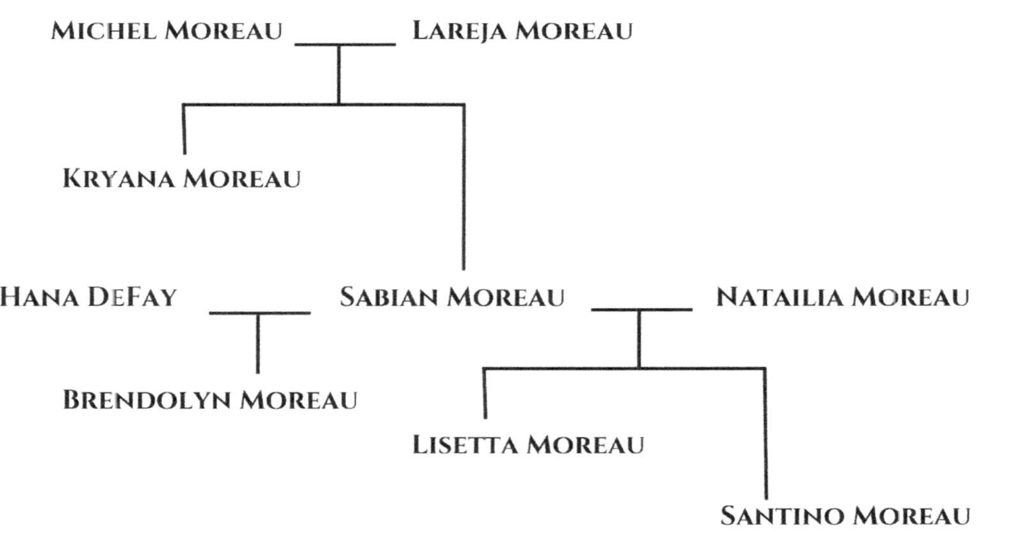

COMING SOON....

FATES OF VEILORE BOOK THREE

FATE
OF
LORDS

IRELAND LYDON

AN IMPRINT OF VEILORE PRESS

Fate of Lords

An unedited sample chapter. . .

Beneath the Field of Thourns. West Rhun.

Sunlight flickered like whispers over the waves of lavender that lined the river's edge, planted long ago by hands now forgotten. Concealed within a veil of ancient magick stood the cathedral, its spire piercing the clouds, unseen by the war-torn lands that sprawled beyond the hills. The cathedral, lost to the memories of those old enough to recall its presence, remained a sanctuary for one who could peer into the fabric of magick, discerning the hidden truths that lay between certainty and the unseen.

Centuries passed in solitude, unnoticed and unremembered by the western realms, where the name Sanna held no meaning. Beneath the protective shield of magick, she wandered through her garden, a place where the warmth never waned, and blooms flourished in perpetual sunlight. Her hands, delicate and purposeful, tended to plants and herbs, harvesting what she needed for the potions she had her familiars deliver at the gates of R'hun. These offerings, marked for the Blessed Lady of Light, Blaihr, sustained the city behind its stone walls, curing ailments and concocting powerful balms, though the true source of this aid remained a mystery to those who sought the goddess of light, Ehnarea.

Sanna's movements were fluid, her basket resting in the crook of her elbow as she walked along the hedge at the garden's edge. Her gown, once a garment of fine craftsmanship, had faded and softened with the centuries, hanging loosely from her thin willowy frame. She reached out to a bush of roses, her fingers brushing over each velvety petal with practiced care. Though blind, a sacrifice made to the goddess long ago, Sanna's world was vivid in her mind's eye, shaped by magick and a deep connection to the life around her. Each snip of the shears was deliberate, her touch guiding her to the perfect bloom before it joined the others in her basket.

But as she reached for the last rose, something shifted—a ripple of unease coursed through the magick that bound her world. The sky beyond the shroud darkened, clouds twisted ominously, and a chill wind, foreign to her garden, threaded through the air. Sanna's smile faded, replaced by a rare tremor of uncertainty, her fingers hesitating as the familiar gave way to the unknown.

Sanna gasped, her head falling back as a vision came, grasping her body in a force that paralyzed her.

Brendolyn wept openly, her hands grasping the curve of the dead king's hand. Unable to perceive the man with dark hair crouched beside her. He was soothing her, whispering to her, Sanna could just hear the eager words of Pavan as the Ehlfern helped the princess to stand.

Trembling, the princess was unwilling to leave the king, her agony crippling the room with despair. Her emotions are agonizing and cruel. But Pavan was firm, grasping the princess by the hand, guiding her with hastened steps to the window. Cold blistering in through the room as rain began to mist their faces. Pavan heaved his frame into the window, grasping firmly to the jagged stone and twisty vines that grew along the wall.

"Hold onto me," Pavan spoke calmly, easing his large frame towards the window, reaching in at the princess.

Brendolyn's breathe hitched, but did as he asked. Pavan eased the princess around his neck, magick shifted. Sanna felt the warmth envelope her as her sights flickered, watching the Ehlfern descend into the depths.

Now, deep in the dark shroud of night. Pavan set the princess on a bench under the shelter of the gazebo.

"Brendolyn," his hands gently grasped her shoulders. Her thin frame shook under his touch, looking directly into her golden eyes so wrought with fear it made Pavan tremble.

Pavan clenched his jaw, forcing away the grief that began to claw through him. The princess sighed into his touch.

"Listen to me carefully…you must return to the castle on your own. Can you find your way unnoticed?" He spoke, but Brendolyn could not answer, her chin trembled. She shivered, agony gnashing through her body. He melted, grabbing her cheeks delicately. His heart was beating faster.

"Bren." He spoke, gentler.

Fresh tears fell, it broke Pavan to see her, to feel Brendolyn so terrified. "I can't…he is there…I can't." She shook her head.

"He cannot hurt you, Brendolyn, I promise. You are so brave, you are strong, fearless. Now, return to Lahrs. You must return to him now."

She nodded, her body shaking under his hands. Vulnerable. He was sickened by the pull, being drawn to her then. Keenly aware of the connection between them, Pavan pulled his hands away.

Pavan stood, taking a step back.

"You will not return with me?" She asked, looking up to him desperately. Her eyes wet with fresh tears.

"You must return, I cannot stay here…" he began to say, his magick festering, growing rampant.

"Don't leave me," she begged.

Brendolyn rushed forward, wrapping her arms around his middle, as she had done beneath the alcove of the steps. Pavan felt his heart beat wildly. Holding her for but a moment, then, yanking her arms free of him. Letting her go.

"I am so sorry…" He disappeared into the darkness.

Sanna gasped, her breath catching as the vision tore through her mind, leaving her trembling. Her basket slipped from her arm, roses scattering across the garden path like crimson tears. She reached up, her fingers trembling as she wiped away the blood that traced a thin line down her upper lip, her gaze scanning the once vibrant garden now cloaked in shadow.

Above the shroud of magick, dark clouds churned, casting an ominous gloom that seeped into the very air. Ignoring the scattered petals beneath her feet, Sanna moved as if drawn by an unseen force, her steps unsteady as she approached the edge of her sanctuary. The shimmering boundary of magick pulsed before her, a barrier she had not crossed in centuries. Her hand lifted, trembling as it neared the shroud, but something deep within recoiled.

A surge of pain exploded in her mind, a sharp, searing agony that brought her to her knees. Sanna's body convulsed, her vision blurring as tears of blood welled in her milky-white eyes, the color slowly shifting to a vibrant, unnatural green.

The second vision struck without warning, more violent than the first, leaving her paralyzed by fear. She clutched her head, desperate to quiet the screams that echoed in her mind, to silence the voices that howled in her ears. The taste of blood filled her mouth, and the acrid stench of burning fires and death invaded her senses.

Sanna crumpled, the weight of the visions pressing down on her, her body trembling as she fought to resist the overwhelming terror. The garden around her faded into the background, replaced by the horrors that flickered behind her eyelids, vivid and unrelenting. The vision held her captive, a harbinger of the darkness that loomed just beyond the veil.

"Blessed be," Arienne gasped, her body convulsing, blood spilling from her pale lips.

"Arienne," Pavan soothed her, holding the woman in his arms, even as the chapel burned around him. As the screams of the Blessed Sisters dying echoed in Sanna's mind. *Pavan remained at Arienne's side.*

Arienne was burnt, her once magnificent hair blackened, burned away to one side, the side of her face bubbled with burns, Pavan held her, shielding them with what little magick he could command.

"It is too late," she spoke, Arienne's final words tearing from her smoke heavy lungs. Shaking away the attempts that Pavan wished to heal her. Pushing away with a turn in hand.

"I can save you..." Pavan argued, hoisting the woman further into his arms, but he winced, the woman cried out in agony.

Arienne's hand clenched tightly to her chest, the skin was raw, but extended it out to Pavan, feeling the weighty pendant and chain fall into his open palm.

Pavan grimaced, the weight of the pendant mirroring the grief that now anchored itself deep within him. Sanna's empathetic sorrow echoed in her chest, the connection between them magnifying the pain that surged within Pavan's heart. *As the realization sank deeper, his tears fell freely, unbidden, tracing a path down his cheeks.*

"Thad," Arienne whispered, her voice a faint gasp that seemed to echo in the stillness. Her body convulsed violently, each breath a desperate struggle, her eyes wide with terror until, suddenly, she went still.

Pavan gently laid her down on the cold stone beneath them, his body shivering as the magick around him tightened its grip. The pendant in his hand felt like a burning brand, the weight of it too much to bear. His teeth ground together as he fought to contain the surge of magick rising within him, clawing at his throat, threatening to overwhelm him. The protective barrier he had clung to shattered, leaving him exposed to the searing fire that raged around him, the air thick with the heat of his own grief and power.

Sanna screamed, *her voice a silent echo lost in the chaos as Pavan's agonizing cry filled the air, a sound so powerful it seemed to shake the very foundations. The stone walls around him trembled, cracking under the force of his unleashed magick, which burned with an intensity far greater than the flames that flickered around him. The sheer magnitude of his power engulfed the chapel of Denorn, reducing the sacred space to a scene of utter devastation, the remnants of the Blessed Light of Jorn lying in ruins.*

In that moment, Sanna felt the bond between them snap, a sudden, jarring severance that left her gasping. The connection that had linked their hearts, their pain, was gone, leaving her isolated, her senses reeling from the abrupt void. The silence that followed was deafening, a stark contrast to the raw destruction that still lingered in the air.

Acknowledgements

This book would not exist without the love, support, and encouragement of so many incredible people.

To my husband, Austin—your unwavering belief in me, in this story, and in every dream I chase has been my anchor. Thank you for your patience, your kindness, and for always reminding me why I started this journey in the first place. I love you endlessly.

To my best friend, Kat—since the very beginning, you have been my champion, my sounding board, and the voice that urged me forward when doubt threatened to take hold. Your faith in this world, in these characters, and in me has meant more than I can ever put into words. I am so grateful for you.

To my editor, Stacey—thank you for your keen eye, your thoughtful guidance, and your belief in this story. Your insight and expertise have helped shape these pages into something stronger, and I am so lucky to have you on this journey.

To every reader who picked up my first book, who saw something in this world worth holding onto, and who encouraged me to continue—this is for you. Your excitement, your words, and your support have meant everything. Thank you for giving this story a home in your hearts.

Author Bio

Ireland Lydon lives in Northern Utah, where she balances the beautiful chaos of everyday life with her passion for storytelling. Between the whirlwind of schedules and the ever-growing list of creative ideas, she finds solace in writing, bringing new worlds and characters to life. Fueled by a love for fantasy and an unshakable determination, she continues to weave stories that have been years in the making—one page at a time.